# The Death and Life of Penny Pitstop

by

## Leopold Borstinski

# PART ONE

## APRIL 4, 2010:
## EASTER SUNDAY

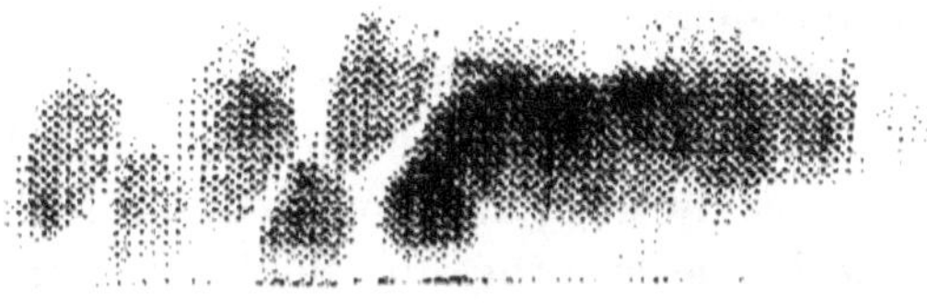

# 1

THE DECKING HAD worked out well for Ray, who wasn't used to manual labour. On any other occasion, he'd have called a local handyman in to build something like a deck, but this was one job he had definitely wanted to do himself. Not all the timbers were parallel but there were no large gaps either. At least, nothing big enough to count as a hole; no hole big enough for anything to fall down below. And the entire structure was reasonably level. Drinks stayed in their glasses, for instance. It had been backbreaking work, but worth it.

There he sat on a newly-purchased sun lounger with a long gin and tonic in his hand, resting the glass on the nearby side table he'd positioned for that purpose. The quiet in the garden was punctuated by the odd noise from next door but Ray felt a tranquillity in his life he had not known for some time.

In a way he missed Penny and felt a certain sadness due to her absence, but another part of him was pleased she was gone. Things had been very difficult between them the past few months and separating themselves from each other was the best solution to their problems.

He had read somewhere that couples who lose a baby are most likely to divorce within twelve months of it happening. They might not have got divorced, but they sure were just another part of that statistic.

A familiar voice floated over the hedge as Ray was thinking his day away.

"Hello? Anyone there?"

Ray stood up and strolled off the deck and into the garden, ambling up the hump in the middle of the lawn with his hands in the pockets of his jeans. By standing a couple of feet higher, he was able to see over the hedge and into the Baldwins' garden. There was Claudia, covering her eyes with her left hand, the other one on her hip. Jacob stood a few feet away on their patio, stoking a barbecue.

"Hi."

"Hi there. How's it going?"

"Just fine under the circumstances."

Claudia looked at him strangely, not understanding quite what he meant.

"Huh? Would you guys like to pop over for a barbie in a little while? Nothing special, just a chilled-out Bank Holiday Sunday."

"I'd love to, thanks. But Penny's not here ..."

"Oh? Shame. Work again?"

"No, not that. I mean, she's gone."

Ray looked at Claudia and Claudia looked back at Ray and eventually she figured out what he meant.

"Gone? You mean, gone... for good?"

Ray nodded and shrugged his shoulders.

"Oh, Jesus Christ!"

"Yep."

"I'm coming round..."

Claudia vanished from view, headed out the garden and back into their house. Five, maybe ten, minutes later, there was a knock on the side return door and Claudia appeared, bottle of red in one hand and house keys in the other.

"I told Jacob this could be a late one. I want you to tell me everything that's happened."

Claudia popped the keys and wine on the side table on the decking and headed for Ray to give him a hug.

"Wow, this is new."

Claudia twice tapped the deck with her right heel. Ray let her put her arms around him and stroke the back of his neck and hair. His arms dangled by his side for half a minute, not quite sure what to do. Then he gave in to the obvious and wrapped his arms around her, breathing in her faint scent of rose water, feeling her body through that cropped T-shirt of hers, noticing the smoothness of her back under her T-shirt, which meant she wasn't wearing a bra. And they held that embrace for an eternity, while Penny's body rested only six feet below them.

# PART TWO
# FEBRUARY 1999

# 2

**PENELOPE**

The weekend was almost halfway through and Penelope had achieved nothing. Her plans were negligible; to empty the laundry basket and buy food for the week, but neither had been accomplished by four on Saturday afternoon.

Instead, she and Mickey had spent the day in bed. She had woken late at about ten and dozed until eleven when Mickey had opened his left eye, looked at her, and rolled over to end up on top of her and then licked his way down her body until he was just about to go down on her.

As ever, he then sped upwards and pushed himself inside her so he could have a quickie. Mickey was a better lover than that, with his equipment and all, but his morning glory was nothing but persistent.

Penelope had got used to his Saturday morning routine and she found if she let him get his way first thing then, an hour later, she could ride him like a banshee until she was a spent force. Such was their routine, both were satisfied by lunchtime.

This Saturday all had gone to plan for both of them, but after she'd got off him and he was still hard, Penelope decided to finish him off by hand. Afterwards, she read while Mickey nipped into the shower.

When he came out of the en suite, he still had a boner. He stood right by Penelope's head trying to hypnotise her with his dick and she kneeled on the edge of the bed so their heads were closer. Mickey leant in and she felt his dick against her body. She took his left hand and placed it on her bush and positioned his fingers to massage inside her.

To encourage him further, she placed her other hand on his balls and rolled and tweaked them in her fingers. He responded until they were both breathing deeply.

Then she squeezed and pulled at his balls, which made him squeal with pain-pleasure. Penelope released him and grabbed his dick instead, massaging his head and stroking his shaft. She liked touching Mickey because his was the largest dick she had ever seen. It was the first one she'd tasted without a foreskin and she was still intrigued by its smooth surface.

Meanwhile, she used her other hand to grasp the back of his neck and pull him closer still. He remained standing, refusing to follow her onto the bed, so she crouched on the edge instead, legs apart, until she felt his dick squeeze inside her. Then she stood up slightly until he'd placed his hands under her thighs and was carrying her around the room. They hadn't tried this before. Her whole weight was bearing down on him so he was deep inside her. Judders of pleasure rippled up her spine to her head and she felt waves of intense pleasure emanate from her groin.

Somehow, they managed to keep this up until Mickey had her pinned to the bedroom wall and he came. Loudly. She had lost count of the number of orgasms she'd lived through and dropped her legs down, leading Mickey back to the bed where they lay down next to each other and kissed and fondled each other until they both crashed out.

Penelope woke up again at four and realised she had accomplished nothing. A strange instinctive impulse compelled her to throw on her underwear—black lace bra and matching thong— before acknowledging to herself she was not going to get up and go do any shopping at this point in her day. She was just fucked.

Instead she looked down at Mickey, dribbling into his pillow, and went to the kitchen to make a cup of tea and prepare some sort of a meal. When she walked into the kitchen, she was thinking brunch, but by the time the kettle had boiled for the tea, the meal had become dinner.

PENELOPE OPENED THE fridge, grabbed some milk and took out some pasta and a pot of tomato sauce. She wasn't feeling creative but wanted feeding and she knew her man would want the same.

Having put a dash of milk in her drink and Mickey's, Penelope replaced the carton in the fridge and refilled the kettle and flicked it on. Then she clattered a medium-sized pan out of its drawer and put it on the hob. When the water had boiled, she poured it into the pan and switched on the gas hob.

Penelope took one of the teas to Mickey to wake him up gently. She always knew she had to be careful waking that big bear of a man because he had the habit of waking up grumpy and that left him sore and bothersome for hours.

She stayed long enough to make sure he was awake and sitting upright, then she returned to the kitchen. The water was bubbling and fizzing around the pan, so she threw in the pasta and a few minutes later, Penelope took two bowels of penne arrabbiata to the dining room and called Mickey out the bedroom to eat.

He had put on a pair of shorts, mainly to protect his privates from any hot sauce splatter and they ate and chatted over dinner. Penelope had cracked open a bottle of Pinot Noir and they chugged a glass or two each.

When there was no more pasta to consume, Mickey took the bowls to the kitchen and Penelope tidied up the dining room table, bringing in the pepper grinder and wine glasses. Mickey was not the most domesticated of men and believed his duty was to eat the food and bring utensils back to the kitchen for a woman to clean them. Penelope had resigned herself to be both cook and cleaner in their relationship, not something she was happy about but Mickey was not for moving on this matter, as she had found to her cost when they first moved in together six months before.

Penelope put the bowls and cutlery into the sink and ran the hot tap. She opened the ergonomically located half dishwasher and, having rinsed knives and forks first, she placed them into the bottom row. Then she swooshed the bowls under the water and propped them in rows to join their brothers and sisters awaiting the coming of the flood. Finally, she cleaned the pan with washing-up liquid and more hot water, placing it upside down on the draining board.

She had noticed Mickey was standing near her all this time— usually he'd have gone to the living room and watched TV—and she had said nothing. He stepped ever so slightly forward and placed his palms on her belly as Penelope was drying her hands on the tea towel. She leaned her head back against his chest and purred at him. Then she slipped her hands back around his waist as far as she could reach until she found her left hand on his bum. She squeezed it coquettishly.

ONE OF MICKEY'S hands went up her body to her left breast and the other hand went down between her thighs. She parted her legs, ever so slightly, to help his right hand with its passage and she felt one of his fingers push past the gusset of her thong and brush against her hairs, and massage her until she was moist. He pushed his finger inside her and massaged her some more.

Meanwhile, his thumb and first finger of his left hand were on her nipple, kneading, squeezing and pulling it. He pushed her bra up to get to her skin. Without turning round, her hands went by his side and pulled down on his shorts until they dangled around his ankles.

"Nice one," he whispered to her as he took his hand out from inside her, grabbed the gusset and pulled down on her knickers until they too were heading towards her ankles. Because her legs were apart, the thong couldn't make the whole journey, so Penelope let her legs go together for an instant until it landed on the floor and she was able to remove one foot from the flimsy garment.

"What now?" she whispered back at him.

Mickey grabbed both her breasts and massaged them in unison and then gently pulled down on them until Penelope was bent in half, holding onto the edge of the kitchen sink to keep her balance, facing downwards. By this point, he had let go of her breasts and one hand was stroking her back, while the other was on her arse, caressing both cheeks with his first finger stretched out, curled around her crack, rubbing her bush, slipping inside and out of her with every hand gesture.

At that moment, Mickey pushed himself forward and entered her deep and long. He stood there not moving, letting Penelope's pelvic thrusts do all the work for both of them. And that was great as far as Penelope was concerned. They stayed like that for a lifetime and then Mickey slowly, slowly moved in and out. For a second, Penelope looked up and thought she saw someone in the opposite apartment's kitchen staring at her, but the place had been empty ever since she moved in.

Her attention was taken back into the kitchen with the incredible pulses of intense heat radiating across her entire body. She gripped the sink and felt the waves get more intense still. Mickey's hand was on her belly as he made sure their bodies didn't separate. They both so wanted this to carry on forever. She felt Mickey's body spasm behind her and she continued with her floor thrusts. Her arms were shaking with the incredible pleasure she was experiencing. There was no way this could last. She leant forward to release Mickey's grip on her body and so that she could breathe normally again.

"Babe..." he started to say with disappointment in his voice, but Penelope twisted round and knelt down so her mouth was around his helmet. A few seconds later and he was coming in her mouth.

After she'd finished swallowing and licking him, she panted, "You are the best fuck ever."

"Straight back at you, babe."

Only one problem; she might be walking like John Wayne tomorrow, but Penelope knew all that was left between them was the sex. Actual conversation had gone from their relationship months ago. It was almost as if the day he moved into the apartment, the door on them as a couple had closed.

Penelope could tell her time with Mickey was coming to an end. Their relationship was like their kitchen sex; great fun but cumbersome and going nowhere whatsoever. She'd have to get rid of Mickey. And soon.

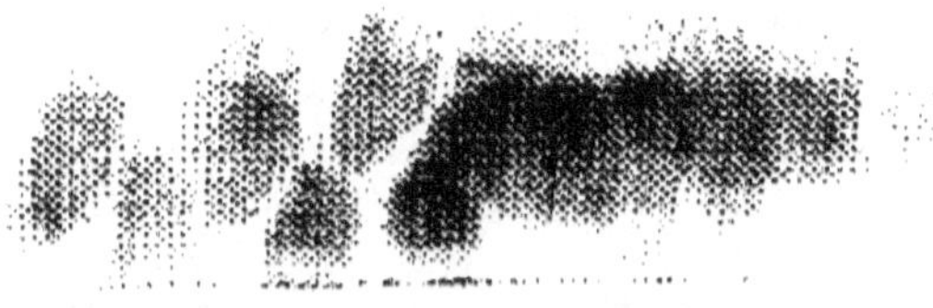

# 3

**RAYMOND**

With the last packing case taken up the service lift and into his apartment, Raymond paid off the moving men with a cash bonus for the foreman to distribute as he saw fit to the guys who'd done the heavy lifting.

He sat down on his sofa and stretched out, creating a star shape with his limbs. He was home, and the silence in the place made him feel all the more comfortable. Raymond had the freedom away from his mother to eat when he wanted, sleep when he wanted, and do whatever he wanted at any time of the day or night.

Moving on a Saturday had been more expensive, but it meant he didn't miss a day's work as a result. Time was money.

The removal guys had put all the boxes into one of the spare rooms so Raymond had space to move about in the flat until he had the time to put everything away—and he didn't have to stare at packing cases every minute either.

Raymond decided the first job should be his bedroom so, if nothing else, he could sleep at night. The bed had been put back together by the movers, which meant all Raymond had to do was to shift the rest of the furniture into the right place and fill the wardrobes with his clothes. An hour's hard graft and the job was done. He went back to the kitchen, made a black coffee and sat at the breakfast bar.

The following hour was spent filling up kitchen cupboards and putting CDs on shelves in the living room. Truth was the man didn't have many possessions he'd wanted to bring with him. Raymond was shedding his past life like a snake sheds its skin.

BY THREE HE was peckish and heated up a ready-made lasagne his mum had given him before he left that morning. Raymond took most pleasure from sitting on his sofa with the plate on his lap and watching the telly, all at the same time.

Then he put his feet up and carried on with a John Wayne movie, The Searchers, which he hadn't seen since he was a kid. When the film ended, he looked at his plate on the floor and knew it was time to do the washing up.

He walked it to the kitchen where he placed it in the sink and opened up the hot tap. Thirty seconds later and there was still only cold coming out. Raymond scratched his head like he thought that might do some good, then he went over to the boiler in a built-in corner cupboard and stared at the switches and dial. Switching the hot water on and flipping little cog wheels to set the heating to come on twice a day, he returned to the sink and opened up the hot water.

Soon steam was coming out of the faucet, so Raymond added some cold to enable him to put his hands in the water without getting scalded. He lathered up his brand-new cleaning sponge and spread the suds around his knife, fork and plate. Then he rinsed them under the tap and placed them on the draining board.

Raymond looked up, just for a second, and saw a couple in the window opposite him, the guy behind the woman. Raymond's jaw dropped as he realised the woman was standing there in only her bra. She bent over and the guy took it off. Raymond could see her tits hanging down. They weren't that big but he saw them come to a point. The guy had tattoos all over his upper body and arms, but

Raymond couldn't make out the images. The bloke appeared to wink at him.

Raymond felt his cheeks redden as he finished off his washing up and went back to the living room, first hovering in the doorway to carry on watching without being seen.

One thought permeated Raymond's head; "I'd kill to have a piece of that." Then he grabbed a box of tissues from the living room and took them to bed.

# Part Three

# March 1999

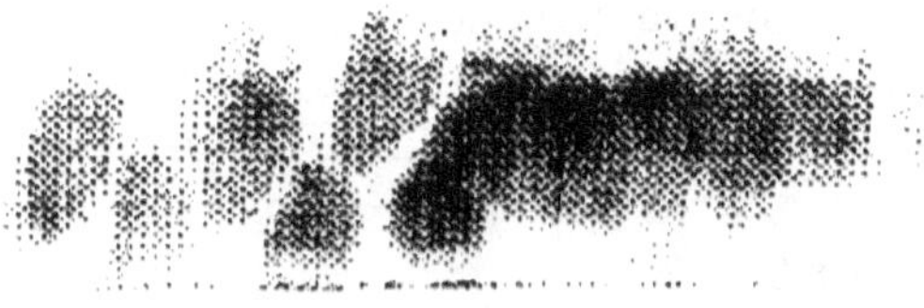

# 4

**RAYMOND**

On the ground floor of Raymond's apartment block was a large atrium containing the concierge and a handful of retail outlets including a no-name drinks concession, which served a sweet but bucket-sized coffee to Raymond when he left for work in the mornings or on a weekend afternoon.

The other side of the atrium had a second set of lifts leading to the other apartments. He'd only been in there once when he was looking to buy, and he'd had a first viewing at an apartment up there. Raymond had chosen the one he bought because he thought the view from the balcony was ever so slightly better. But they had an identical layout inside.

Raymond stood, leaning against the barista bar, waiting for his java-to-go no milk. He was absorbed in his thoughts, unaware of the world around him. Then, something caught the attention of his peripheral vision and made him look up. A tall, quite skinny blonde wearing a black trouser suit was standing right by him. The trousers accentuated her slender stomach and the jacket allowed her round breasts to peep out so he could take in her admirable cleavage hiding beneath her white blouse.

"Large Americano!" called the barista.

Both Raymond and the blonde grabbed for the same black coffee. As their hands nearly touched, they both laughed.

"No, you go on. It's only fair."

"Are you sure? You were in line first."

Thinking about it, Raymond realised, of course, he was ahead of her and it was indeed his coffee. But he wanted to make a good impression.

"Go on, I insist."

"If you don't mind. You're a dear, thanks."

"De nada."

Raymond's auto-response was instigated through old-fashioned British politeness. But as the conversation continued, he found his eyes checking out the sleeve of the blonde and his focus worked its way up her arm, past her neck and to her face, although Raymond allowed himself an extra quarter-second on her neck. It was quite long and hidden behind her shoulder-length hair.

Then his eyes wandered down her body, hovering over her tits, and carried on, lingering a few inches below her belt buckle before heading down to her feet. She wore heels, but they weren't crazy high; she was tall enough, without needing to raise herself above people artificially. Neat.

As she walked away, Raymond took in her black trouser suit, straight blonde hair, and red heels. She held a briefcase in one hand and it appeared to swing forwards and backwards as she strolled out the front door. Cute. He stayed at the barista bar waiting for his Americano, which arrived thirty seconds later. Something made him take a deep breath and he tasted the last vestige of the woman's perfume on his tongue. Vanilla. He sighed and took a sip from his hot brew.

# 5

**PENELOPE**

Penelope left her apartment like most mornings with Mickey still snoring in bed; a personal trainer's life was a long and hard one.

She waited for the lift to arrive, got in and punched the button for the lobby. When the lift bounced and stopped on the ground floor, Penelope and the other occupants stepped out and she headed straight for the coffee concession to the left of the concierge desk.

"Usual?"

"Yes, please."

Dorothea always looked after her. Penelope paid and joined the queue to pick up her drink from the barista bar.

"Large Americano!"

She reached out her hand to get her coffee and some guy pushed in front of her to take it for himself. Douche bag.

"After you."

"No, it's fine. You go ahead." She realised she'd made a mistake because if they'd both ordered the same coffee, he'd be the first to pick up.

"No, I insist. It's fine."

"Thanks. You're very kind."

He had a cute smile and a brightness in his eyes that Penelope found mildly attractive. His accent placed him outside of the Thames Estuary and his suit was pretty sharp. There was something about his voice, its soft timbre mixed with a cocksure element, just the right side of arrogant.

Penelope thought about the Neanderthal upstairs and contrasted Mickey to the slicker with whom she'd just spoken. She took a sip from her Americano and smiled at him again. Before she walked away, Penelope eyed him from his head down to his feet and all points in between. She liked what she saw and headed off out the building with a skip in her step.

# PART FOUR
# APRIL 1999

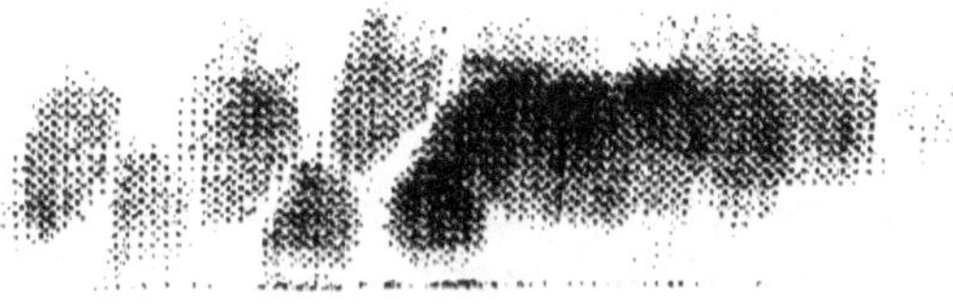

# 6

**RAYMOND**

Another day, another dollar. Raymond was comfortable in his apartment and had organised himself into a settled routine. Weekdays flew by and once a week Raymond went over for dinner at his parents. His mum hadn't yet forgiven him for leaving home, even though she knew she'd had to let him flee the nest.

His day followed a strict routine. Raymond would jump out of bed to switch off his alarm clock and then he'd shower and shave, get dressed, and then grab a slice of toast and jam. A breakfast from his childhood.

Down in the lift and join the queue for a large Americano from the coffee shop in the atrium. The blonde he'd bumped into a few weeks ago was always in the line around the same time as he was, but they hadn't been consecutive customers since the first time they met.

Today, Raymond walked out the lift and headed over and there she was again, but this time she was different. At first, he couldn't put his finger on it, but as he approached the barista bar, he realised. She had already placed her order and was waiting for the coffee to be delivered and was standing two feet away from the bar itself because there was a huddle of people, three or four, waiting for a single order.

And because she was that distance further away, the sunlight, which was streaming across the atrium space, caught her and shone all over her. What was different today? For the first time he realised, she wasn't wearing a trouser suit. Instead, she had on a long black skirt with matching jacket. The skirt went down to her ankles and was held tight against her legs.

Due to the sunshine, Raymond could see the shape of her legs beneath the material of the skirt. Her calves and thighs were clearly visible and he followed the line of her contours until he could see the point where her legs met.

HIS HEART BEAT a little quicker and he caught himself staring at her crotch, trying to see more than was possible on that sunny morning in Canary Wharf.

Raymond joined the queue, ordered his coffee, and waited for the pickup. To his surprise, there was the blonde still waiting.

"Hi. You still here? I saw you when I first arrived downstairs."

"Did you? Yes, Dorothea has let me down today. There was a mix-up and they tried to give me a latte."

"Way too milky for me too."

The blonde pulled a face like she was about to barf and Raymond laughed and touched her arm at the same time, nice and gentle.

The girl looked down to see what he was up to and he withdrew his hand from her sleeve.

"I'm Raymond, by the way."

He reached out to shake her hand.

"Penelope."

"Very pleased to meet you. Do you live round here?"

"Huh? Yes, in the north block."

The girl half-pointed towards the lifts, but she got distracted as more coffees arrived, though none were for her.

"I'm from the south."

Seeing her in the bright light today, Raymond finally made the connection between the girl with the coffee and the blonde he'd seen a couple of times out of his kitchen window. Then he remembered the first time he'd seen her with that guy and he blushed a light red. At least that tattooed lunk wasn't with her.

"We live opposite each other," he added, blurting the information out loud without thinking.

She looked at him, scrunching up her face almost as tightly as her hair was scrunched into a bun—another reason Raymond had had problems recognising her. This was her usual look for work, he guessed, and her home look was very different to say the least.

Then she let go of the scrunched expression and Raymond could see the cogs in her mind whirring and it was her turn to blush—only a darker red.

He noticed the change in her complexion and understood she'd just echoed his own recollections. Although he couldn't explain how, he felt they had made a connection.

"Listen, are you free for a coffee some time? Not now, obviously, but some other time?"

"Um... yes, okay."

"Cool. At the weekend, maybe?"

"Yeah, why don't we have a Sunday afternoon drink?"

"I'll pop round to yours around three?"

"That'd be lovely."

Two large Americanos arrived and they picked up one each.

"See you then. Have a nice day."

"Straight back at you."

They exited the atrium in different directions, but as they walked away from each other, Raymond twisted his head back to get another look at her. The skirt was still revealing all of her legs, but he couldn't spot any visible panty line, even though everything else felt like it was on view.

"Dirty minx," he thought and increased his pace so he could make up the lost four minutes the conversation had stolen from his morning.

# Part Five

# May 1999

# 7

**RAYMOND**

Raymond decided to buy himself a new Italian designer jacket and shirt for his meal with Penelope. He sat at the bar in one of the newly-built chic restaurants in the West End, nursing a vodka martini, waiting for Penelope to show.

He'd booked the table for eight and it was quarter past and still no sign of her. Having arrived early, he'd been glued to the same bar stool for the best part of half an hour. While Raymond wasn't worried, he was still concerned. They had met up for a couple of weekend coffees and had warmed to each other, but he wanted her to be more than a Sunday brunch buddy. Much more.

Raymond figured this was crunch time. Assuming she showed up, if all that happened was two friends had dinner, that'd be fine, because he liked her and enjoyed her company. But he was also aware that he fancied her. If they spent too much time being friends then he'd never be able to convert her into anything else. And he sure did want to convert her. Those legs, her lips. That beautiful smell of vanilla haunted him even when he wasn't with her. Filled up his thoughts and warmed his loins during his lonely nights.

In the middle of this reverie, a hand alighted on his shoulder and a light peck arrived on his cheek.

"So sorry I'm late. I got held up at the office."

"Don't worry about it."

Raymond smiled because he was so pleased Penelope had arrived, but also because she had kept her hand on his shoulder and not let go. That was definitely not what friends did. He figured this might be a sign.

"What can I get you?"

Penelope eyed his martini suspiciously.

"Mmm. A cosmo would be lovely. Been one of those days."

"It's all over now. Chill."

Raymond took a gamble and, because Penelope's hand was still on his shoulder, he placed his arm around her waist hoping she wouldn't move away and he could benefit from real human contact.

Over the course of his twelve-month dry period, he hadn't touched a woman since his rebound sex with Natalie. And that didn't count in his head because it had been rebound sex and he had no emotional investment in anything which happened that night.

The cosmo arrived and Penelope moved onto the adjacent bar stool. She was wearing a knee-length red skirt and blouse, as well as a pair of drop-dead gorgeous heels. For a girl who'd come straight from work, she wasn't wearing the same clothes she'd had on this morning when he saw her at the barista bar. She used his knee to leverage herself up onto the stool and kept her hand resting on him as they talked.

They drank a toast to "Less work, more pay" and carried on chatting and laughing until the waiter came over to tell them their table was ready.

PENELOPE GOT DOWN first, again using Raymond's knee as a leaning post and he followed her to the table. Her skirt was tight around her arse and he thought he made out the faint outline of her pants. If he was right, they were bikini knickers, not thongs, because he reckoned he could see the curve of the edge as it arched over her cheeks. He'd have seen nothing if it was a thong.

They shared a bruschetta to start, which tasted divine, and Raymond had sole meunière with new potatoes. Penelope had a salmon dish and they shared mange tout and broccoli.

Raymond thought the evening was going well. He remembered to keep his body language open and did his best to keep his hands on the table when they were talking instead of any defensive posture which might end up with his arms crossed. Open arms, amid the hope Penelope might put her hand down close enough for him to touch it, but the opportunity never arose.

That said, everything appeared to be going fine. By the time they had ordered dessert, Raymond had managed to create a conversational segue around whether that tattooed guy was a permanent fixture in her life. Even though they'd sunk a couple of coffees together, Raymond had been nervous about being too forward or appearing too interested, in case he scared Penelope off.

Penelope had said there wasn't anyone special in her life and that gave Raymond hope.

# 8

**PENELOPE**

Between leaving her office promptly to get back home to change and the ridiculous crush on the tube and the infinite wait for the DLR to fix itself for the umpteenth time, Penelope was feeling very stressed by the time she arrived back at her apartment.

She only had time for a very fast shower; she had defoliated at the weekend. Penelope had had the smarts to lay out her clothes on the bed that morning so there was no decision making to go through. She popped on her clothes—bra then knickers, blouse then skirt—and rooted around for her favourite pair of fuck-me heels.

Penelope vowed to wear more skirts as she checked herself out in the mirror before starting on her make-up. Not too much slap, but enough to show she'd made an effort. Grabbing a small clutch bag, she popped her keys, phone and money into it and then added a tissue. Another look in the full-length mirror and off she went to grab a cab from outside the apartment block.

By the time she got to the restaurant, she knew she was running late and totally understood if he'd given up and gone home. It was nearly half eight. She overtipped the cabbie and went inside.

Penelope wanted tonight to go well. By agreeing to go for dinner with Raymond, she knew her time with Mickey was over, so she'd asked for the key back and sent him packing to his sister who was renting a place in Limehouse.

The way Penelope figured it, if she was prepared to think about going on a date with a guy then she shouldn't be living with another one. Wasn't fair on Mickey and wasn't fair on Raymond if anything did happen. Either way, it sure as fuck wasn't fair on her. Then she spotted Raymond and these thoughts of decluttering men from her life vanished and she felt that same skip in her step as when she'd first met him.

PENELOPE WALKED UP to him and was so pleased he was still there, waiting patiently for her, she gave him a kiss and sat down.

"I'd die for a cosmo," she said when she noticed there was a nearly empty martini glass by Raymond's elbow with only a dribble of liquid and a twist of lemon remaining.

When it was time for them to go to their table, Raymond had been the gentleman and let her go first, following the waiter to a table for two in the middle of the floor. The place was packed, which explained why they'd had to wait to be seated.

"Friday must be the new Saturday."

The food was scrumptious. Penelope had chosen the salmon en croute, which sounded dangerously old-fashioned but she'd caught a glimpse of someone else's plate and she knew it wouldn't end up being that stodgy '80s cliché—and she wasn't disappointed.

Penelope liked the sound of the fruit salad for dessert, all kiwi and guava. Juicy through and through. They'd shared their desserts too, something which was normal for Penelope, but she sensed Raymond tense slightly when her fork first plunged into his baked cheesecake.

Most important of all, Penelope found the conversation flowed as easily as when they were in the coffee shop the previous Sunday. When she'd agreed to dinner, no one had said anything, but she knew this was a date. And she knew that Raymond knew.

Yes, she had probably spent too much time talking about work, but Raymond seemed genuinely interested and, besides, it's not like he hadn't spent any time talking about stockbroking.

The plates were cleared away and they finished off their second bottle of Pinot Noir. Penelope had chosen it because Raymond said he knew nothing about wine, but she reckoned he was being modest.

"Would you care for a coffee?"

They both looked at the waiter and then at each other with a small glimpse of sadness, because this meant the dinner was coming to a close.

"No thanks," said Penelope. "Do you fancy coming back to mine for a coffee instead?"

SHE HADN'T EXPECTED herself to say it, but she was having a great time and his expression looked as disappointed as she felt.

"Sure. That'd be really nice." He looked at the waiter. "Can we have the bill when you're ready?"

When the waiter returned, Penelope had made a grab for the bill on its little silver plate, but Raymond had been quicker. She offered to go halves but he'd have none of it. Sweet man.

Once the credit card machine had come and gone, they carried on chatting until the waiter informed them their cab was outside. They stood up and headed for the door, walking next to each other, real close. Penelope felt his hand touch hers and she responded by clasping it and meshing her fingers in between his. Penelope and Raymond remained like that until they reached the cab.

Penelope got in first and shimmied over to the right-hand side of the taxi and then Raymond followed and sat down on the left. He leaned forward to give the driver their address and then sat back as the black cab lurched forward on its journey into the night.

She noticed he had stretched his arm around the back of her. Smooth. So she slid towards him and placed her hand on his upper thigh. Then Raymond placed his free hand over hers and they sat in silence, soaking in the feeling of each other's bodies.

Penelope turned her head at the same time as Raymond and their lips were only a few inches apart. They got closer together until she thought "Fuck it" and she leaned fully in and kissed him.

The first kiss was gentle, lips touching lips, and she stroked his leg a little by the time the third kiss had occurred. Twenty minutes later, the cab pulled in and stopped outside the north apartment block. Penelope had her hand on his crotch and Raymond had been kneading her right breast for quite some time. She felt alive like she hadn't felt for so very long.

PENELOPE LET GO of Raymond's hand to give herself enough time to find her key in her handbag and open the apartment door. She put her hand back into his and led him in.

He closed the door behind himself and Penelope popped the keys and handbag down on the nearby radiator shelf. She turned back and put both arms around Raymond's neck and they carried on kissing for a while. She felt his hands running up and down her back, sometimes one hand would halt at her bum and give it a gentle squeeze or two, which felt lovely, and other times, a hand would stop at her neck and stroke it. That felt more than lovely and started the odd tingle to run down her spine.

Penelope allowed their bodies to part to give herself the opportunity to unbutton Raymond's shirt and he responded in kind, undoing her blouse. For the first time, she could feel his skin and she noticed how hairy he was. His touch was soft and gentle, but there was a self-assured note to his massaging.

As he stopped kissing her and started to lick her neck, Penelope stepped out of her heels and placed one hand on his crotch and squeezed a couple of times. Then she unzipped his trousers and put her first and second finger inside, stroking his dick which was already quite hard.

"Follow me," she whispered and nibbled his earlobe. They walked into the bedroom, hand in hand. Penelope took off her blouse and slipped off her skirt when they were stood right by the bed. She could see he was plain staring at her, soaking in the sights and smell of her body.

"LIKE WHAT YOU see?" she asked, cocking her head to one side and leaning on one leg to force the other one to push forward, like a thousand models had done before in a million photo shoots.

"Like you wouldn't believe."

Raymond took off his shoes and trousers and Penelope helped him remove his shirt. They stood there for a second, each looking at the other in their nakedness. Then Penelope reached out a hand and placed a finger on Raymond's chest, twirling hairs around her fingertip. Raymond mirrored her, gently running a finger around her cleavage. More tingles down her spine. She turned to face the bed.

"Help me take this off," Penelope twanged her bra strap round her back. Without too much bother, Raymond undid it and she felt the material ease off the pressure from under her breasts. Immediately, Raymond had put his arms under hers and grabbed a breast in each hand and squeezed. She leaned back into his body and stood there, doing nothing more than soak in the pleasure of the sensations he was creating for her. Then she placed one hand behind her back until she found his stomach and she worked her way down until she was gently playing with his dick.

Again, they weren't rushing and stayed like that for one, maybe two, minutes before Penelope let go of his dick, slipped under the duvet and shuffled over to the other side so that Raymond could follow her in.

LYING NEXT TO each other, they renewed their kissing and caressing as Raymond licked her neck and then carried on down her body until his lips were wrapped around her right nipple. His tongue felt so good.

"Don't stop... that's great."

He carried on for minute after minute and Penelope reached and found his balls and tweaked them all the while. Every time she gave him a little extra squeeze, she felt the increase in sucking on her breast. But eventually, Raymond moved further down, kissing and licking her stomach and shoving his tongue into her belly button.

She lay there, eyes closed, knowing her hands could hardly reach any part of him and Penelope wondered what he would do next. Go further or come back up for air; his head was under the duvet by now. She figured the trick was not to suffocate the guy, so she flung the duvet off them both. The cool air engulfed them and Penelope became aware of every pore on her skin, every fibre of her being.

Raymond's tongue went below her belly button and he placed his hands on her hips. Penelope's breathing increased in anticipation of his next step. His mouth had reached the top of the thong and he flicked it with his tongue a couple of times. Then he pulled down the front of her knickers with both hands so that his mouth could carry on licking and sucking her. The tingles were increasing as she felt the material of the thong dig into her crack.

Penelope raised her buttocks off the bed ever so briefly to give Raymond enough time to pull her knickers completely down. She felt his tongue inside her and the waves of tingles ran around her spine, starting at the point where his tongue licked her and up to the base of her neck.

She remained with Raymond between her thighs for what must have been a lifetime. Her breathing went into overdrive. All the time Penelope'd been with Mickey, he had never once gone down on her and she'd forgotten how incredibly great it felt.

Then his tongue stopped and he took his hands off her breasts. Relatively quickly, he kissed his way back up her tummy and tits until he was lying on top of her and their mouths were together again.

Penelope put her hands on his arse and pulled down his pants. She could feel his dick in between their bodies so she knew she didn't have to do too much more. He raised himself off her for an instant so she could get his pants completely off his bum, reflecting what she'd done for him earlier.

SHE REACHED ROUND his back and put her hands in between his legs until she could tease his balls again. His tongue went crazy in her mouth so she knew he was enjoying it. Penelope let go and encouraged him to move until she was lying on top of him.

Now it was her turn to lick and kiss her way down his body. She really wanted him inside her but first Penelope wanted to reciprocate the oral he'd done to her.

Raymond put his arms behind his head and she reached his pubes. She decided to suck him off a bit and then come back up and sit astride him.

Penelope's tongue licked the helmet and shaft a couple of times, more as a tease than anything else. Then she popped it in her mouth and let her tongue do the work, while her hands kept the shaft steady near her face.

She'd managed to find some saliva left in her mouth—after all that deep breathing—to lubricate his head and she passed her tongue over the tip of his dick three or four times. Then she tasted salty spunk in her mouth and the dick shrivelled away to nothing.

Penelope had come several times when Raymond went down on her, but she really wanted to fuck him, more so now than when they'd first got back into the flat. She moved back up to lie beside him and he turned to face her again.

"Sorry, you're just too sexy for me, Penny Pitstop." With that, he licked a forefinger and massaged her until she came again. Penelope was disappointed but most guys would have rolled over and gone to sleep; at least Raymond was concerned to pleasure her some more.

They curled up and spooned together, Raymond's body engulfing hers, making Penelope feel safe and secure.

"You're my Ray of sunshine," she mumbled as she lapsed into unconsciousness, exhausted and content in the hairy arms of her barista buddy.

47

# Part Six
# June 1999

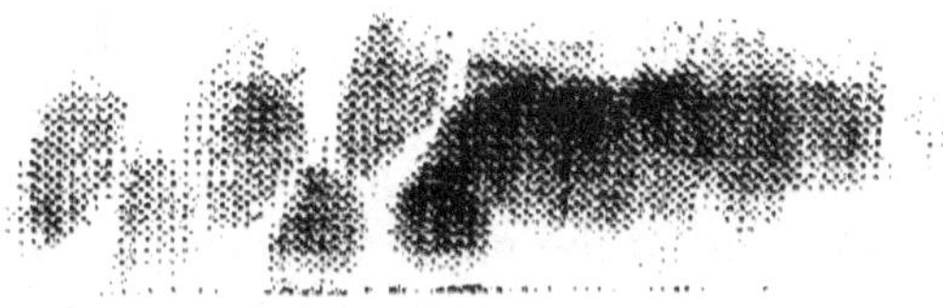

# 9

**RAY**

Despite the hiccup of their first night together, things were going well with Penny. They went out a couple of times a week to a restaurant or the movies, but because their doors were only a minute's walk apart, they spent at least another couple of nights in each other's bed; just because.

Within two months, Ray had seen Penny far more than if they had been living on the other side of London from each other for a year. The good news was he was feeling very comfortable with her. Penny was a wonderful girl and he enjoyed talking with her, hanging with her and fucking with her. Not only that, but they shared stuff in common. They found the same things funny and worked on different sides of the same business. She was a lawyer and he was a trader, but their City aspirations bound them like glue. He respected her commitment to her work and he was pretty sure she reciprocated.

And he loved the taste of her nipples. The breasts were far more pointy than the roundness of her underwire bra ever implied and over the first week he'd felt a bit cheated, but the areolae were so much larger than Natalie's and he only had to touch Penny almost anywhere and her nipples stood up. That was a massive turn on.

RAY'S THOUGHTS WERE jostled out of him as the DLR ground to a halt in Bank station. The sea of people swept him onto the platform and carried him down the corridor and up the escalator. He waited for the lift to take him to the ground level. The first day at the job he'd tried the hundred and fifty-nine stairs to the surface but realised he wasn't fit enough to do it daily.

Out of the station and turn right onto Prince's Street and over the road into Moorgate. Then left through an alleyway and at the far end on the right was Killog Spreckley Soames, just before Camomile Street and the Guildhall beyond.

The brokerage firm had survived into the end of the twentieth century through shrewd management, who then took the easy money when US institutions were allowed to buy British stockbrokers in the late '80s. Killog Spreckley was one of the first to have the Stars and Stripes waving above its front door. Two weeks before, an in-house memo had been sent round letting everyone know that from June 1 the firm would be known as Freiberg Penham Securities. The last truly British name in the Square Mile was about to bite the dust.

Ray wasn't too bothered. To him, this was progress and an opportunity to work for a large US powerhouse. His network could only get bigger and his chances of promotion into the holding company were greater than as an external candidate. So he shrugged off the email as yet more PR bilge ripe for deletion.

There were more important matters to worry about than the name on the door as you walked in. Ray was a European equities trader, working on the proprietary, or prop, trading desk. Some of the guys traded on behalf of their institutional clients, fund managers and the like. Other guys bought and sold shares with Killog Spreckley money; their bonuses were bigger but the risk of getting fired for losing your own company's money was also very much higher too. Ray was one of those guys.

He focused on opportunities on the continent and had made some smart assumptions at the end of last year, building up positions in sectors which would benefit from the introduction of the euro, and had made a killing in January. Now his attention had turned to the troubles in Yugoslavia, where NATO had been bombing the crap out of Kosovo since April.

His contacts in the Ministry of Defence told him things would quieten down fairly soon and Ray knew once the violence stopped, there would be great opportunities for companies to exploit; damage repair to utilities and other beneficiaries of Western aggression. He'd ride the back of that monster.

Until then, he sat in the middle of the three-hundred-strong trading floor, surrounded by guys barking trades and deals around the room. Like most of those around him, Ray had four screens on the go at once, pumping information about markets of interest. His eye would be drawn to any position he had where the value went red; the price was tanking. A green block around a number meant the stock was on the rise and he was in the money.

RAY SPENT THE start and end of each trading session on the phone. The best way to know how markets were doing was to speak with people. He understood the theory behind quantitative trading techniques, but Ray had found understanding market sentiment was as big a part of the battle as figuring which stock to invest in.

The most important technique of all on the prop desk? Don't lose money and don't double up if you do. That made you a poor gambler who didn't understand how probability worked. Ray knew if he made a loss in any one day of more than half a million across all his positions, he would need to report to his boss, Bill Carson, who ran all the prop desks.

Although he didn't know the guy from Adam, there was a rumour that Aidan Judd had broken the limit without telling Bill. Aidan worked the French desk and made a tidy sum, focused on the French stock exchange index, the CAC40.

"How'd anyone make a loss on the CAC?"

This question had been uttered by almost everyone on the prop desks in the previous twenty-four hours. It was an open secret that Aidan was in deep shit. The old guys, the ones over thirty, were saying nothing and the traders Ray's age were speculating wildly about what was going to happen.

The answer came at ten thirty-two when Bill took Aidan's chair, gliding it on its casters until he decided to pick it up and carry the damn thing over his head. Bill took the chair towards the lift and threw it into the lobby area next to the floor.

Right on cue, two of the front desk security appeared with a cardboard box.

"Get the fuck off my floor!"

Bill was a short man, but incredibly scary, despite his sweat, baldness and ruddy features. He always looked as though he was about to have a heart attack. His bellow was, therefore, all the more surprising.

Aidan stood there, shoulders sagging, and filled up his box with all his things and proceeded down his walk of shame out the floor, flanked by the two goons. A chant of "Fuck off, failure!" commenced from somewhere in the room. Ray couldn't tell where. Soon, everyone, who wasn't on the phone, had taken up the refrain and people banged on their desks in time to the chanting. Sounded like a football stadium in the City.

Once Aidan had left the room, all the traders went back to staring at their screens and the usual low-level hum of phone calls and chat returned the floor to normality. Just as though Aidan had never existed, the beast, which was the floor, carried on purring like nothing had happened.

Ray focused on the news in Yugoslavia and phoned three friends in other brokerages to see if they had heard anything interesting about any Eastern European stock which had passed him by.

Then he read a bunch of analysts' reports in case there was a pearly gem hidden in the mass of shit that landed on his desk every day. Nothing inspired him.

Knowing he couldn't sit on cash all day, he went long on the French and German banking sector, because they were both safe bets in the absence of any smart moves from himself. You can't make a profit by holding cash on an equities deck. His worst-case scenario would be neutral on the day, but at least he could show he'd tried to do some good.

# 10

ON THURSDAY, THERE was a buzz in the room shortly after opening hours. A new guy had been found to replace Aidan and was in a meeting room with Bill. There were a string of two-seat and three-seat rooms lining one of the walls which were used for internal and client meetings. The blinds were closed in only one of the rooms, so that was the interesting one.

Along with everyone else, Ray craned to see inside somehow, but to no avail. Twenty minutes later, HR had walked in and walked out. Then the door opened again and Bill appeared with the new bloke. Ray had no idea who the guy was, but two people had already gone up to him and shaken him by the hand, so he had some level of renown.

The man sat down in the chair previously used by Aidan and logged into the Killogg Spreckley system for the first time. When the launch screen was visible, everyone let out a cheer and party music was played through the PA. Then everyone left him alone to focus on their own affairs and to let him get his feet under the desk. Also they knew what was going to happen later in the day.

Sure enough, bang on noon a woman appeared on the trading floor and made her way straight to the new guy's desk. As she zigzagged between the various sections of the equity trading floor, a hush fell upon those she was passing. Every man recognised her because they had all seen her at least once before; on their first day on the job.

By the time she got to Andy, a crowd had gathered around the two of them. He was busy typing who-knows-what and hadn't noticed her—nor had he spotted that he was the centre of attention. She tapped him on the shoulder and once he got to the end of his sentence, he looked up.

"Hi, babe. What's cookin'?"

HIS CONFUSED EXPRESSION said it all, so she shrugged, looking round the assembled throng, and winked at her audience. Then she slipped out of her skirt and tore at her blouse, which parted with elegant ease—the way that strippers' clothes are designed to do.

Andy swung his chair toward her and she undid her red bra and placed it like a scarf around his neck. She had big, drooping boobs that hung near Andy's head for a while. She waggled them at him and pushed his head so that it was wedged in between them.

The crowd cheered and she carried on, releasing his head and giving him a lap dance with music supplied by a ghetto blaster she'd brought into the room for this purpose. Having shoved her arse cheeks at his loins for several minutes, Ray could see Andy was getting embarrassed. His eyes were darting left and right. He wanted to be seen as a fun guy, but the dance was making him feel uncomfortable.

Then the woman stopped her dancing and stood facing Andy, legs slightly apart. With a flourish, she whipped off her knickers and stood there with her bush a few inches away from Andy's face.

"Suck or fuck, babe? Suck or fuck?"

Andy looked at her with even more confusion on his face as the mantra was repeated by the assembled masses. They picked up the beat and banged it out on desks, armrests and with their hands.

"Suck?"

With the instruction issued, she bent down and undid his trousers, despite his attempts to ward off her hands. But she was too fast for him.

She put her hand in his pants and started working her magic. Amid the whoops and the jeers, she knelt in front of him and sucked him off in front of them all.

Once she was done, she stood up, licked her lips, waved her hands above her head, which made her boobs jangle about again and caused a roar to erupt from the onlookers. Then she put her clothes back on, waved goodbye to everyone, planted a massive kiss on Andy's lips and walked off the floor.

Ray applauded along with everybody else and sat back down to carry on trading before lunchtime. Everyone met Lola on their first day and, like him, everyone he'd seen had chosen suck, not fuck. Another day, another dollar.

He popped up for air at around two o'clock and left the building for a sandwich a couple of doors down. Usually, he stayed at his desk and ate something from the sandwich trolley lady, but today was different.

Ollie was already sat there when he arrived.

"SORRY I'M LATE. Got caught up in some shit I needed to sort out."

"Don't worry about it. Shit happens, we all know that. It's what you do about it that separates the lions..."

"...from the tigers."

They smiled at each other. Finishing each other's sentences was only one of the joys of knowing someone as well as Ray knew Ollie.

Ray got his food and sat down opposite Ollie.

"What's up?"

"I'm thinking of moving."

"Job, home, what?"

"Job, you arsehole."

Ollie was working for a brokerage house, much like Ray's.

"Where to?"

"I want to get into investment banking. Trading's a mug's game. By the time I'm thirty I'll have burnt out and that's no good. And the money you make? You could take a dump on the Queen's lap and still have some left over after you'd paid for all the damages."

"Have you applied anywhere?"

"Better than that, I've been headhunted..."

Yet again, Ollie was showing Ray how he would always be number two in their relationship. Ollie was a man who was always faster, bigger, better. His get-up-and-go was in permanent overdrive. Ray loved clinging to his coat tails but being near Ollie could be pretty exhausting.

So to hear Ollie wanted to move into advising companies how to structure corporate deals made perfect sense; there was more money in it for Ollie.

WALKING BACK TO Killogg, Ray thought about how it was he'd become a trader; because Ollie had already got a job doing it and recommended the same recruitment consultant to Ray. The truth? Ray didn't want to work in a brokerage at all. If he was going to do anything in financial services, he wanted to be an asset manager—someone who makes investments for clients. Long term investments like in pension funds. Somewhere he could make some decent money but at least some other people would benefit too.

When he got behind his desk, he caught a glimpse of one of the TV screens; NATO had officially stopped its bombing of Kosovo. Shit, shitty shit.

Ray grabbed the two phones on his desk and made simultaneous calls to an oil desk and to some institutional investor who'd expressed an interest in buying esoteric stock at the right price. Cash from chaos? No, cash from certainty after chaos. That was worth investing in, thought Ray.

By the time he'd squeezed the last drop of life out of the opportunity, he'd made over five million for Killogg and earned himself a cool half a mil in the process. A good day's work even if it was after nine before he walked out of the building and made his way back to Bank station.

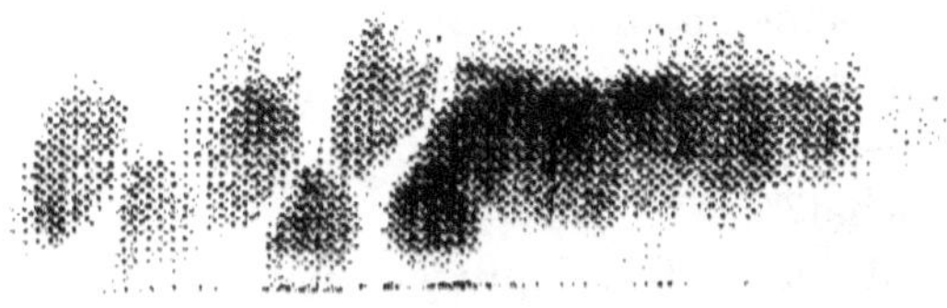

# 11

**PENNY**

Penny had arranged to hook up with Karen for lunch and they popped out to a nearby coffee shop for a bite to eat and a chat.

They were assisting their lead partners on an M&A deal, which meant they were on the meter and could take as long as they liked over their food.

"I don't know how long I can stay at Craigley Mitchum."

Karen twirled her finger in her hair as she listened. She'd heard the same speech from Penny every week for months now and while she liked her friend dearly, she wished there was something else they could talk about than Penny's dissatisfaction.

"Why, what's happened?"

"Yet another junior has got promoted over me. I'm better than Sheila. You know I am, right?"

"Sure thing, darling."

"So why don't the partners take me more seriously?"

It was a good question and one Karen had not considered before. She had been on a fast-track trajectory ever since she left Cambridge and joined Craigley Mitchum as an articled clerk.

"Have you thought about what makes you different from the others?"

Now it was Penny's turn to ponder. She knew she enjoyed her work and got on well with everyone, but the last few weeks she'd noticed she was the one more likely to be asked to pour the coffee in client meetings than take notes or offer advice.

"I'm surprised you've not noticed."

"Noticed what?"

Karen leant forward and put her hand in Penny's hair, whose blonde straightness went down past her shoulders.

"You're kidding me."

"How many women partners have your hair colour?"

"None, but..."

"No buts, darling. Whether you like it or not, they see the hair and treat you accordingly."

Penny contemplated this observation and realised that every female partner had black or brown hair and wore sensible knee-length skirts or trouser suits. She glanced down at her clothes and saw that today's skirt was riding sufficiently high to be indecent; the tops of her stockings were visible. Her skirts had got shorter, the longer she'd been with Ray. Her mother was right; it was nothing more than a wide belt.

"That's shit."

"Sure is, darling. But right now get yourself a makeover or figure out how you're going to sleep with Mackenzie without throwing up."

"Sucking that cock is not on the cards."

"Then learn to change. It's not your natural colour anyway, darling... Don't look at me like that, you told me so yourself."

Penny smiled and nodded, knowing Karen was right.

EVEN THOUGH THE time was long past nine, Penny was the first to get back home. She had tried knocking on Ray's door but no one was home, so she slipped a note under the door and scooted back to her place.

Penny unlocked her apartment and stepped in. The door swung open to the right and on the left-hand side of the door jamb were two light switches. One controlled the hallway and the other flipped the living room light on, but Penny just used the hall light to see her way into the flat. She popped the keys on the shelf and felt the radiator beneath to check the heating had come on; her fingers felt a little chilly.

The radiator was hot to touch so she stayed there a while, letting her fingertips soak in the heat until the feeling returned. Damn train was too cold by far. She must remember to take her gloves tomorrow.

She breezed into the bedroom and had two things on her mind; eating and getting out of her work clothes and into something a lot more comfy. Penny hoped Ray would get back soon so she could cuddle up with him. To that end, she undressed and put on a black baby-doll negligée and matching French knickers. If he didn't show, then after she'd eaten, she'd throw on a vest and an old pair of pyjama bottoms, but right now she was feeling hornier than ever.

PENNY POPPED INTO the en suite to have a quick pee and then out of the main bedroom, back into the hallway, through the living room and into the kitchen.

This was a rectangular space with a window over the sink, like so many apartments before it. There was a small silver half-dishwasher, a washer/dryer whose door matched the rest of the fitted kitchen; pale wood with straight silver handles, and a wooden work surface the same colour as the doors. Penny had bought a huge American style fridge so it could accommodate providing iced water on tap and as much as ice cream as one human being could consume.

She made some toast and created a ham, cheddar, lettuce and tomato sandwich. Penny looked at the breakfast table and pondered whether to eat here or in the dining room. Her tummy rumbled so she sat down immediately and chewed through her construction.

Three minutes later, it was gone and the plate was already stacked in the dishwasher.

Penny ambled back to the living room and flipped on a table lamp near the deep blue leather sofa. She sat down with her legs under her bum, curled next to three orange cushions, surrounding herself with soft furnishings. She grabbed a fashion magazine from the side table and flicked through the pages, looking out for any interesting ideas.

By the time she'd finished with the mag, she was losing faith Ray would show. She stretched her legs out along the sofa and thought about her pyjama trousers. They were pale blue and white striped and made of soft, brushed cotton.

She considered flipping on the TV and watching the news but, as that thought flickered in her head, the doorbell rang. Penny smiled and skipped to the front door. First she took the precaution of using the fish-eye to check who it was and then she opened the door to Ray, grabbed him by the trouser waist and yanked him inside.

THEY KISSED THERE and then and she felt his hands all over her. Maybe she was coming on a bit too strong for a Thursday evening. Fuck it.

"You are looking hot."

"Why thank you, kind sir."

Penny did a twirl so that Ray could see the full effect of her underwear and they walked into the living room and flopped down on the sofa. She noticed he was still in his work togs and must have seen her note and shot straight over. Sweet.

"You should've changed before you came round."

"I know, but I wanted to see you. Been one of those day."

"Yeah? Me too."

They leaned into each other and sat there in a hug for five minutes, soaking in the comfort from each other's bodies. Then Ray let go of the hug and pulled off his shoes and untucked his shirt, chucking his jacket onto the nearby armchair, which Penny had positioned so she could read there but not watch TV too well.

Ray sat back and relaxed into the sofa, turning his body so he was twisted in Penny's direction. She gently pushed his leg down so he was lying flat on his back and undid his trousers, putting her left hand inside them and massaging the outside of his boxers.

After a minute or two, she stopped and sat astride him, her knees close to his hips. They were a tight ball of humanity, kissing and caressing each other in the process of removing his shirt completely. Penny rode his dick slowly through the material of his underwear and she could feel he was getting hard. Meanwhile, her right breast had Ray's hand squeezing and massaging it, while the left one was being licked and teased with his tongue and teeth through the lace of her baby-doll. The tingles in her crotch had begun.

She raised herself on her knees and Ray carried on licking and kissing whatever body part was near his mouth, so she got him to work his way down from her breasts to her tummy and then, because she made sure she was kneeling as upright as she could, his mouth engulfed her fanny and she felt the material of her undies push against it, forced by the pressure of his tongue.

Penny's breathing started to get heavy and she wondered if Ray had any idea how he made her feel when he was tonguing her like that. Trying to maintain some kind of focus, she reached out to see if she could get his trousers off without moving the position of her hips, but it was no good. Her arms weren't quite long enough.

But Ray took the hint—or had the same idea himself—and raised his hips ever so slightly to push his trousers below his knees without losing physical contact of her body with his mouth. Dirty bastard.

BOTH HIS HANDS were clasping her arse, one cheek in each hand and they squeezed as he tongued her, having got past her now-damp French knickers. Occasionally, one hand would move and Penny would feel a finger stroking between her arsehole and her fanny. Once or twice, she felt the frisson of extra excitement as the finger was inside her along with his tongue.

Just as he'd removed his trousers, Ray's boxers went down to his knees and he kept on licking her all the while. Then he pulled down on her knickers, only removing his mouth from her pubes long enough to get the knickers past her hips.

Penny grabbed him by the hair and pulled his head back and lowered her upper torso so she could kiss him fully on the mouth. At the same time, she lowered her hips so she could sit on him. The great thing about Ray is that he was truly turned on by going down on her. Fucking dirty bastard.

She sat still, letting her muscles squeeze him slowly and, over the course of the next few minutes, she increased the frequency of her squeezes and rose up so that his helmet was touching her lips and dropped down so he felt deep, deep inside her.

Without warning, Ray rolled Penny on her side and they carried on for a couple of thrusts and then he rolled them over some more until she was underneath him. He was getting more vigorous with his motions and Penny knew he would be coming shortly. She felt as though her head was about to explode with the agony of the ecstasy of the moment. It was all... so... intense. Almost felt like she could feel every blood cell pulsing through her head.

Then he got more leverage with the floor and pushed until he managed to get her to the point where her knees were right by her elbows. His thighs had pushed her so far, her legs were up in the air. And still they continued with Ray thrusting and Penny squeezing. She could feel his ball sacks thwacking against her arse every time he thrust forwards. Until he came thirty, forty seconds later. They collapsed with Penny slumped, nearly horizontal, on the sofa and Ray kneeling in between her still-parted legs with his head on her Brazilian and his hands resting playfully on her breasts.

Neither moved for half a minute and then, without saying a word, Penny sat up and took Ray by the hand and they went to the bedroom and lay under the sheets, Ray curled around Penny like their first night together.

"I really love the sex we have together."

"Me too, Penny Pitstop."

"And I don't want to have sex with anyone else but you."

"Me too."

Penny turned round and faced Ray, looking deep into his eyes to make a connection with his soul. Her hand moved onto his cheek, so she knew she had his undivided attention.

"Seriously?"

"Yes. Seriously."

She gulped and almost couldn't believe she heard herself say the next sentence.

"So shall we agree to go exclusive?"

He stroked her right cheek with the back of his hand.

"Yes, Penny. I'd like that a lot, not that I've slept with anyone since we've been going out."

They leaned in for a long, lingering kiss and Penny thought to herself, "I'll ditch Mickey now that I've made more of a commitment to Ray."

The lingering kiss became wandering hands and soon Penny was lying face down and Ray was inside her from behind. "Now that was deep," she thought.

# Part Seven

# December 1999

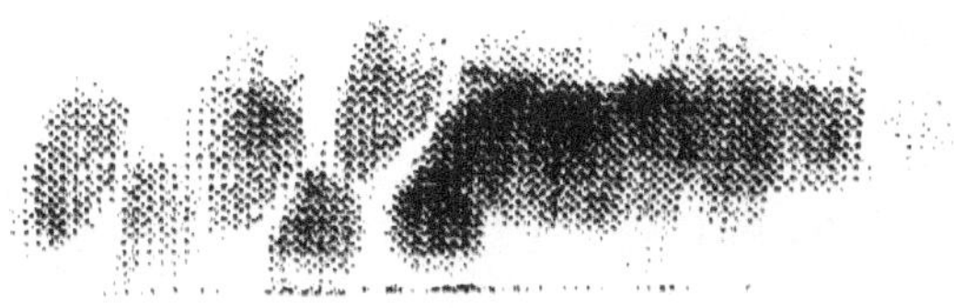

# 12

**RAY**

They had flown out the day after Boxing Day, landed at JFK, grabbed a hire car and headed north to reach Karen's place before sunset. Ray didn't mind doing the driving but he didn't fancy his first time behind the wheel of a US auto at night time.

Penny had the directions Karen had printed out for them and she navigated while Ray's hands clasped the steering wheel like grim death. The worst moments were the first five when Ray got them out of the car park and onto the freeway. Then he hugged the slow lane and let everyone else deal instead with his tourist driving and the snow lightly fluttering onto their windscreens.

Two hours later and they pulled up to the gate of Karen's parents' house. When she'd said the place was big, she wasn't kidding. For starters, the front gate opened on to a drive so long you couldn't see the house from the road. Ray got out the Chevy to speak to the squawk box to get let in. Everyone else would have wound down their window but he'd stopped way too far away for that to be an option.

He leapt back inside when the gate opened and they trundled along, past the immaculately kept lawns, pruned bushes and hedges, until the house revealed itself behind the third bend. It was a mansion and a half.

"Holy mother of fuck."

"You said it."

No sooner had they stopped, Karen appeared out the front door. Penny got out first and they hugged while Ray wrestled the keys out the lock and fought the boot open. He turned towards the two women who were already linked, arm in arm, and heading into the house.

"I'll get the bags then," he muttered. Ray didn't mind that much but he was tired and had been behind the wheel for ages and wanted some attention. 'Karen trumps Ray' was the rule and he knew it deep down.

HE CAUGHT UP with the pair easily because they had stopped in the hallway.

"Let me help."

Karen and Ray brought the bags up the stairs while the two girls chatted like they hadn't seen each other in months rather than forty-eight hours. Left at the top of the stairs and along the corridor to their room.

"I've given you guys a corner room. Hope you like it."

They walked inside and stood there while Karen opened the windows and pointed at the door to the en suite. The room was enormous. Bigger than both their living rooms combined and there was an old-fashioned four poster bed commanding the room.

"I know it looks twee, but I'm sure it'll be okay, darlings."

"We'll survive." Penny gave Karen another hug and Ray responded with a peck on the cheek. Karen left and closed the door behind her.

"Quite some place, huh?"

They both hung up their clothes in the oak wardrobes, one each, and sorted out their toiletries and shoved their undies in a chest of drawers. Karen had told them they were the first to arrive and everyone else would show tomorrow in time for the Millennium celebrations.

An hour later and they both had showered and changed, letting the grime of the journey wash down the shower plughole. Karen had made some pasta, nothing special, and they chatted a short while before both Penny and Ray were hit by a wall of tiredness. By nine thirty, they were walking up the wooden hill for bed.

Ray got in first and watched Penny undress, throwing her jeans and woolly jumper onto a Regency chair. She stood by the chest of drawers ferreting for something in her knickers and bras. Ray had no idea what.

"Come to bed."

"Will in a minute. Give me a chance."

He loved watching the contours of her body, the shape of her thighs and the point where they met. Her breasts were rounder than when he first licked them, he was pretty sure of that. They were more of a handful, but those nipples still tasted divine.

PENNY HAD A bundle of something in her hand when she spun round and scurried into bed. First she sat up and undid her bra, then she lay down and the thong pursued an arc onto the floor.

Ray turned to face her, leaning his head on his left hand under his pillows. He traced the outline of her right nipple with the nail of his finger until Penny took his finger and placed it in her mouth and wrapped her tongue around it briefly. Then she popped it out and revealed what she'd brought to bed with her.

"We have a four poster. Shame to waste it; tie me up and do whatever you want with me."

She wriggled into the centre and Ray smiled inside. She was a fucking angel. He tied up both her arms, one on each upper corner and then proceeded to secure her ankles too. Penny was splayed out like a sexy starfish. He got out of bed and pulled off his shorts. Now all he had to do was anything he liked. In an Austrian accent, he said, "I'll be back."

Off to the bathroom where he'd spotted some glasses and then back into the bedroom with its coffee table and ice bucket. Dropped four cubes into the glass and went back to bed. He held one of the cubes between the first and second fingers of one hand and gently melted it on Penny's left nipple. She giggled and juddered with pleasure.

THEN RAY DID the only thing he could think of which was to go down on her, tied or untied. She moaned and groaned, but because he'd tied the scarves quite tight, she couldn't squeeze his head with her thighs like she usually did. Much better. He withdrew his tongue and popped an ice cube in his mouth and returned to her hairy triangle and pushed the cube out of his mouth and inside her. He could almost experience her feeling of pleasure. Then he rode up her body and they started to fuck. His dick was so cold when he first went inside her. It felt like an icy ocean.

Ray could feel himself start to come and pulled out of her.

"I can do anything, yes?"

"Jesus fucking Christ! Yes."

He sat astride Penny with his legs near her hips, so his dick was near her stomach, although it sure was pointing up at this stage. He leant forwards, putting one hand on the bed near Penny's armpit. He placed his other hand on his dick and finished himself off, coming all over her stomach and her tits.

Once he'd finished, he sat upright with his weight on his knees, so he could still face her but gave himself enough room to finger her one last time before he undid the scarves to free her while still sitting on top of her.

Penny lay there and put both hands on his dick and squeezed it repeatedly over the next minute or two until he was hard again.

"Come with me."

She led him into the bathroom and she switched on the shower. Twenty seconds later she stepped in, followed by Ray. The water gushed over both of them and washed away the spunk she had rubbed into herself, while he was loosening the scarves around her ankles. Then he cupped her breasts in his hands and they fucked again like they were naked in Niagara, only this time with Penny in charge.

As soon as their heads hit the pillow, they were out like a light. Apart from both waking up at around two for a spell, they stayed asleep until six in the morning, fucked once more and crashed again until eight. Then they got up.

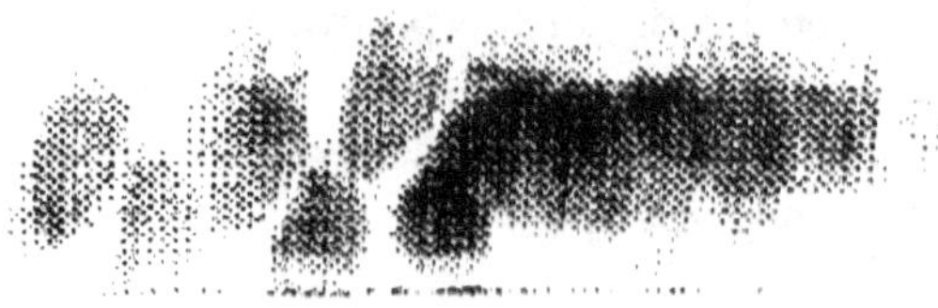

# 13

FRIDAY WAS NEW Years' Eve and the houseguests, along with some local friends, had filled out the mansion. Karen had invited a ripped guy she'd known at school. She'd told Ray and Penny about Reynaldo during their first breakfast together. Also, there were four other couples for the dinner party and celebrations; all had flown in for the event from various parts of the world. Nina and Paul, Frankie and Andy, Elaine and Phil—and another couple whose names Ray failed to catch when first introduced and hadn't figured out since. They looked Chinese or Japanese or something.

They'd been living in a continual house party since the Wednesday when the eight descended on the house. An endless supply of booze and an assortment of drugs to boot; grass, coke, Es and other chemicals. People were getting high, coming down, then getting high again. Repeating the cycle and crashing out wherever they found themselves. Wild times.

RAY AND PENNY had spent most of Wednesday together, clowning around in various rooms and bumping into the other couples and sharing stories with them. On Thursday, Ray had found himself hanging with Reynaldo and Phil, smoking their way through a large bag of grass in a room with an enormous TV playing back-to-back cartoons. They'd talk and giggle at the characters in equal measure. By the end of the evening they knew as much about each other as when they first met, but it had been a great journey getting there.

By the time Ray got back to their room, Penny was already in bed, eyes half-closed, bedside light still on.

"Hey you. Good day?"

"Sure thing. You?"

"Very stoned right now, but yeah. Good times."

Thursday morning, they said they would hang near each other more, but Ray enjoyed spending time with the other people in the place. He liked hanging with Americans. He loved the way they spoke and their perspective on the world. And he loved how direct they were. Ray wished he could be more like an American.

Penny was drawn to the women in the group and, despite their stated intentions, the reality was they both wanted to be with different people, which was fine. So by Friday night, Ray and Penny hadn't seen each other daytime for quite a while.

KAREN HAD SAT the couples opposite each other at the immense dining room table. The dinner was remarkably civilised given the past three days' activity. Everyone had dressed up for the occasion, dinner jackets and posh frocks, and the four-course meal was consumed with an amazing amount of decorum and liqueurs were served by ten. After that, Karen dismissed the staff, who'd been waiting on them hand and foot since their arrival, and the party kicked off properly.

In the basement was a heated swimming pool and they headed off there as soon as Karen suggested it. Ray reckoned it was full size, although given the rest of the estate, he wasn't too sure why he was surprised. He hadn't left the building since they got here but others had mentioned guest cottages in the grounds and all sorts.

Mainly because they'd spent so much time together off their skulls the last few days, no one was feeling particularly inhibited at this point in the night; the mix of alcohol and narcotics coursing through all their bloodstreams had a clear impact.

Each and every one of them took off their clothes and either jumped into the pool or sat on the side, dipping their feet into the water before eventually slithering in.

Ray had never been skinny-dipping before and he splashed and swam around until he found Penny again and they floated opposite each other. They made their way to the side and Penny wound her legs around him and they kissed. He felt the tip of his dick touching the hairs of her bush and they kissed some more.

As he glanced around, he saw Nina and Andy making out on a lounger and Paul and Frankie lying on the lower diving board. They were more open-minded than he could be.

Shortly before midnight, Karen called them out of the pool and they dried themselves in towels, popped back into their party attire and hopped back upstairs, out onto the veranda through the French windows in the living room.

There were heaters aplenty to keep them warm and champagne freshly served, as though there was still the odd butler or maid behind the scenes to look after them.

Although hard to see in the dark, they all knew there was a four-hundred-foot garden beyond the veranda, lined with trees to enable the two guest cottages to have their own privacy.

AS THE CLOCK struck midnight, fireworks erupted from the far end of the garden and they all whooped at the pretty splashes of colour and cheered at the fizzes and bangs launching into the night's sky.

Then they hugged and kissed each other, wishing a Happy New Year. By the time everyone had got out of the way, Ray reached

Penny at the far side of the veranda, who was just giving Paul a light peck on the lips while his hand was firmly grasped on her bum.

As he veered around Nina, kissing her on the cheek as he did so, Penny looked at him and took Paul's hand firmly and placed it by his side. Then she was able to get out of his clutches and rushed towards Ray.

"Happy New Year, my Ray of sunshine."

"Happy New Year, Penny Pitstop."

She kissed him deeply and wrapped her arms around his back, stroking and caressing him as she did. Ray felt safe and secure and banishing Paul from his thoughts, he gave himself to their moment together. He pulled at the rear of her little black sparkly dress but it only raised an inch or two. So he gave up on that idea and put his hand at the front of the dress instead and pushed his finger into her until her felt her flesh.

She leant into him and cupped his balls in a hand.

"Follow me."

They walked off the veranda and scrunched their way along a stone path to the left which led past the row of trees and onto a patio. There were garden candles staked into the grass to show the way and Ray saw a hot tub bubbling away, sunk into the ground on the right, and a bungalow to the left.

"Help me," she said, tapping at the top of her back and Ray unzipped the dress. He stared at her back, which was only interrupted by the black bra, and kissed her neck, solely touching her with his lips.

He undid the zip completely and could see the top of her pants peeping out. Ray put his hand inside the thong and groped Penny from behind.

"Wait."

She let her dress fall to the floor and took off her undies and skipped out of her heels. Meanwhile, Ray had removed his shirt and trousers and was fighting the socks off his feet. By this time, Penny was standing in front of him naked, so she helped him take off his boxers and they stepped into the hot tub and sat next to each other.

THE JETS OF water felt warm and arousing around his body, although that was more due to Penny than the effects of the hot tub. He'd no idea where she'd hidden it, but Penny passed him a joint. He took three deep tokes and passed it back to her and she did more or less the same.

They held hands in silence for a while, soaking in the joyous atmosphere of the party. The other side of the trees, they could hear dance music pumping out and hollers of fun from the others, but Ray was content just where he was.

Penny stood up and waded until she was in front of him and kissed him wordlessly. He drew her near so the whole of their bodies touched; breast to chest, stomachs, groins and thighs. His hands moved from her hips to her bum.

A few minutes later and he had her pinned to the side of the hot tub and they fucked hard until he came. Knowing he'd finished far too early for her, Ray lifted Penny out the hot tub so her legs dangled in and he went down on her until the tensing of her legs was so great, he couldn't breathe any more.

Penny splashed back into the water and they stood hugging each other for another long time. A perfect moment.

Of course, perfect moments don't last forever and eventually Penny broke the silence between them.

"Let's get back to the others, eh?"

"Really? Can't we stay here or go back to the room?"

"Nah. I need to schmooze some more. Tomorrow we're off and I want to speak to Nina again."

"Nina? I thought you were after Paul."

"What? Don't be silly. Paul's no good to me unless I need a gynaecologist."

Penny pulled herself out the hot tub and rubbed herself down. Ray got out and helped.

"Shame. I thought we could have some more fun tonight."

"Don't worry. The fun's not over yet, but I've got work to do before we leave. That's all."

Penny had put her thong back on and was helping Ray to dry himself, paying special attention to ensure his dick was dry. So much so that he got hard and she jerked him off standing there.

"See. The fun's not over yet." She bent down to grab her bra and dress, which were still lying on the other side of the patio. Looking at the sight of that fabulous arse and her hairs visible between her legs in the candlelight, Ray thought he might love her but he said nothing because he wasn't feeling American enough.

They helped each other back into their clothes and returned to the main house.

# 14

**PENNY**

On the veranda, Penny had been chatting away with most of the couples over the last few days and she'd got to the point where she felt comfortable around them. The randomness of being connected only by knowing Karen had worn off and she was beginning to forge an independent existence with each of them, especially the women. But that was no surprise.

All of Karen's friends were lawyers and their partners were all professionals; two doctors and two tax accountants apiece. Nina and Hua were both corporate lawyers, specialising in M&A and criminal respectively. One day Hua wanted to be a DA and Nina hoped to run her own practice. Either way, they'd need to cut down on their coke intake. Man, could they snort their way through that stuff.

So when the new millennium arrived in a shower of fireworks, Penny hugged and kissed her way around the newly-found American friends she'd made. Of course, Paul had to grope her when she wished him Happy New Year, but Nina had told her he was like an octopus. In fact, Penny relished knowing he'd be dumped by the end of the week; Nina didn't want to sleep alone over the holidays otherwise he'd have been chucked ages ago. Schmuck.

After dealing with Paul's roving fingers on her bum—the fresh bastard—Penny was pleased to fling herself into Ray's arms. Now he was hugging her and nibbling her ear, she realised she had missed him.

Their time in the pool had been too short and he'd really turned her on when they were naked next to each other. She'd wanted to fuck him then and there, but he didn't seem interested. His eyes were darting every which way but at her. Perhaps he was getting bored of her?

PENNY HADN'T GOT bored of him though. No one could say Ray would light up a room, but he was a stayer with prospects. More than she could say about Mickey Boone—he was just gratification sex thousands of miles away.

Penny figured she should show some interest and then she had an idea.

"Come with me. I've got something to show you."

She put an arm around Ray's waist and they sauntered off together, off the veranda and along one of the paths. She'd been to the bungalow earlier that day with Nina and Hua for a chat, champagne and a line or three of the white stuff. Even so, Penny was pleased to see the candles flickering. It was practical, but quite romantic, and so typically Karen.

When they arrived at the patio, Penny turned to Ray and kissed him with both hands on his cheeks. They stood and kissed for three, maybe five, minutes and she let herself experience his tongue and nothing more.

Then Penny undid his shirt buttons, while Ray sorted out his cuffs, and undid his belt and unzipped his trousers. Once he'd whipped off his shoes, he stood up in only his shorts, a bulge in the black material indicating he was hoping they weren't finished just yet.

"Help me out of this."

Penny turned her back to Ray so he could undo the dress. She'd trawled through countless boutiques off New Bond Street to find this little designer number with tiny diamonds sewn into the black satin. It literally cost a week's salary. Now it was lying on a dirty patio in the middle of winter.

No sooner had the dress dropped to the ground, Penny felt Ray's hands on her breasts and she looked down, placing her own hands on top of his.

"Mmm. Every time you touch me, you turn me on."

She took his left hand and carried it down under her pants until the tingles began to flow. Despite her own desires, she stepped forward, took off her bra and pulled down her knickers and hopped into the hot tub.

THE WARM WATER was intoxicating and the bubbles around her crotch were unexpectedly sensual. Ray arrived a few seconds after Penny and they sat next to each other holding hands for a while. She soaked in the sounds from the house and the sensations running all over her skin. And she honed in on the feel of his fingers against hers. This surely must count as a perfect moment.

Then she let go of his hand and put her left arm around his shoulders and leaned in to kiss him. Her right hand ventured under the water and found his leg, so she worked her way up his thigh until she made contact with his groin.

Once Penny had got him hard, and he'd made her tingles zoom up and down her spine, she sat on him and he helped manoeuvre their bodies until he was inside her. She was hit with a bolt of intense sexual energy, rattling through her entire being. Must have been the mix of drink and drugs, but she'd not known such intensity before.

Exhausted, she got off him before he came because she was certain she was about to pass out. Ray was still hard and looking quite disappointed.

"I literally thought I was going to die. Your dick is dangerous... Sit on the side for a minute."

Ray hauled himself out and propped himself up with his legs still dangling into the water. Penny flopped her hair round the back of her neck and sucked him off real slow. As soon as his breathing got heavy, she'd stop for a short while and kiss him instead, so by the time he was done, he looked as though he was about to die too.

"WHY DON'T WE spend the night in the bungalow?"

"Don't know about that. I need to get back to Nina."

"Nina? Not Paul?"

"Why'd I be interested in Paul? He's a doctor. Nina might be looking to hire. She's the one I want and I need to speak to her some more before we all leave tomorrow."

Penny could tell Ray wanted to spend his time fucking their way to dawn and, on any other night, she'd have agreed. But not tonight. There was business to transact. Besides, if he had been more amorous at home, she wouldn't have needed to see Mickey so much. There was something in the air that had woken up his dick.

They got out of the hot tub, dried themselves on two nearby towels, put their clothes back on and walked, arm in arm, back to the veranda, legs in perfect synchrony.

The veranda was empty, save for a couple of unopened bottles of champagne. They found two glasses and Ray opened one of the bottles. Penny and Ray walked into the vast expanse of a living room to see Nina and Xun chatting on a sofa on the left side with Frankie and Elaine stood next to them deep in their own conversation. Paul, Andy, Phil and Hua were huddled on the other side of the room, chuckling and playing pool. Karen and Reynaldo were nowhere to be seen. Penny went down to the swimming pool to check Karen was all right, leaving Ray to head off to join the boys.

PENNY POPPED HER head around the door to the pool for just enough time to see Karen on all fours and Reynaldo fucking her in the arse. Literally, a private moment, she thought, smiling to herself as she went back upstairs to seek out Nina and erase the memory of Reynaldo's shaft bobbing in and out of Karen's bum cheeks.

Back in the room, she noticed Ray was engrossed in a game of pool with Andy. Penny wound her way around until she was leaning on the sofa from behind so she could join in the conversation with Nina and Xun without breaking everyone and everything up. She wanted a more relaxed vibe before she hijacked the evening.

"So I said, Bitch, either you take your hand off my man's dick or I'm gonna have to slap you to next century!"

The two women laughed and Penny realised this wasn't personal revelation, but the punchline to a joke. She smiled at both of them and waited for Xun to take another swig of champagne.

"Nina, did you mention you were looking for a European angle for your department?"

"Sure, hon'. Do you know someone?"

"Reckon I do."

"Do tell, hon'."

Nina's German-Swiss accent was quite thick now the champagne had been flowing in her bloodstream for so many days, but Penny wasn't stupid enough to assume she wasn't firing on all cylinders.

"I've given what you've said some thought. How you want someone in the UK, who can help finesse the US cross-border deals?"

"Uh-huh."

"And how you needed someone you can trust and is self-sufficient?"

"Uh-huh."

"And who already has direct experience in acquisitions and handling American clients?"

"Uh-huh."

"Nina, I'd like the role. It's me down to a T."

Nina smiled.

"About fucking time, Penny. I've been dropping hints all week."

"What?"

"Karen told me you weren't happy at Shithead and Cock Wrangler."

"I see."

Penny's eyes lit up. This was a match made in heaven; the chance to work directly on big ticket deals with huge US names and still remain living in the UK and not have to give up her roots. A dream opportunity.

"We can sort out the details later this week. If you don't hold out for too high a basic, you can start as soon as you've handed in your notice."

"Let's cover that in the cool light of day, okay?"

"For sure, hon'.

They hugged and then shook hands and Nina grabbed a very drunk and tottering Xun toward her and told them both another dirty joke, involving a nun, a midget and a bar of soap.

PENNY LOST TRACK of the time, basking in the light of a new job and friendly faces all round. Karen appeared around three and Penny hugged her too and thanked her.

"Your talent got you the job, darling. Nothing to do with me."

"I owe you big time anyway. Cock Wrangler's been doing my head in all year. It's a great place for you—you've already made partner for fuck's sake—but it was slow death for me."

"I know, darling, I know. I couldn't stand to see you pining away. I had to do something."

More chat, one glass of champagne and three lines of coke later, Penny found herself with a taste for Ray coming over her.

Her eyes sped round the room until she spotted him, slumped in an armchair, one leg flopped on the armrest, holding a stogie of a joint and toking occasionally on it. He was trying to blow smoke rings but had only succeeded in making smoke balls.

Penny shot over to him, grabbed the spliff from his hands and inhaled deeply, again and then a third time. She stubbed it out in a nearby ashtray and yanked him into a standing position.

"Let's get you to bed."

Ray looked happy to go and Penny worried he hadn't had a good time, but business was business.

When they were in bed, they fooled around a bit. Licking, kissing, teasing each other. She got a bit tingly but nothing intense. Penny opened her bedside table drawer and took out a pillbox which contained a small spoon and some white powder. She pulled back the covers on Ray and dipped the spoon into the coke and snorted a line she'd made for herself with a blade from the drawer and the glass top of the table. Then she popped the spoon back into the powder and traced it along the edge of Ray's helmet.

Penny licked it until his dick had absorbed the coke. His massive inhalation meant the fun was about to start, just like she'd promised...

# Part Eight
# April 2001

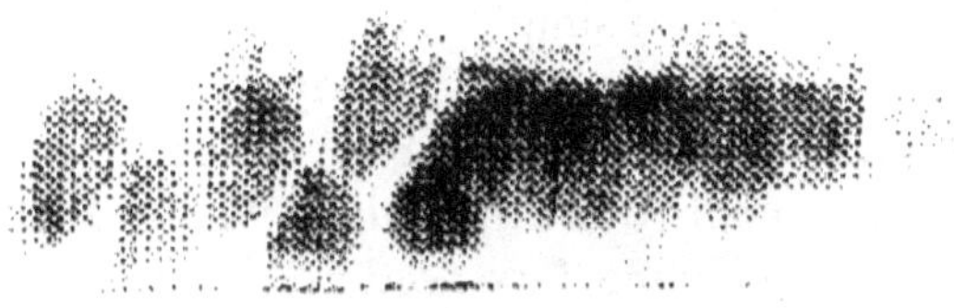

# 15

**RAY**

Memories of the millennium party were fuzzy by the time Easter approached but it had given a focal point to the first half of the year. Ray and Penny worked out they were spending whole weekends together and almost every night. The question was obvious, but Ray had waited for Penny to ask it;

"How'd you feel if we moved in together?"

He was lying on her lap, stretched out on his sofa while she read a book and he daydreamed. More specifically, Ray stared up at her breasts and focused his attention on whether he could discern one or both of her nipples through the material of her jumper. He had concluded that the answer was both, but he stared some more in case he was wrong—and because it was a beautiful view.

With his head so close, he could smell her groin and he liked the smell of stale sex mixed with vanilla entering his nostrils.

"Yeah, makes sense, doesn't it? And I'd like to, anyway. I mean, we get on real well and it's the next grown up step, isn't it?"

He watched her looking at him, her chin accentuated because of the angle her neck was forced to make. Penny smiled and stroked his forehead.

"Yep. We shouldn't get ahead of ourselves, but it does feel the right thing to do, don't you think?"

"For sure. So... which one of us should move in with the other—or are you thinking of us getting a new place together instead?"

"Jeez, no. Let's keep it simple for now. Let's rent out one of these apartments. If we turn out to be Woody Allen and Mia Farrow, we can reverse back without it being a big problem.

"Don't worry. I really don't think there will be but having a second apartment will be a lifeline if we need it."

"I understand; it's cool. And it makes sense to me too. No decision is irreversible."

Ray raised a hand up to her left nipple and gave it a tweak.

"Not now, darling, I'm reading. Besides, we need to agree who moves in and who stays where they are."

RAY AND PENNY were silent, thinking through what was the best solution. Ray wanted Penny in with him, mainly because it would be less hassle and he guessed Penny was of a similar, but opposite, mind.

"Ultimately, it doesn't matter really, but my place is bigger than yours," he said eventually.

"That's what I was thinking. I mean I love my balcony but how often have I been out on it this year? And we'll find the extra room of more use to us."

"You sure you're okay with that?"

"Sure I'm sure."

Ray was happy. There'd be no more of the bullshit of tripping between the two places and he'd stay in his man nest. Nicely handled. Logic can trump emotion.

That conversation had been about a month ago and now Easter weekend was upon them. Most of Penny's furniture was staying put so it could be included as part of the rental. All her clothes were in boxes and her dressing table, a stool and a chest of drawers were being lugged down one lift, along the atrium past their coffee shop and up the other lift.

Ray had borrowed a gurney for the boxes from Ricky, the concierge.

"If you prefer, sir, I could help you on the day."

Ray spent about half a second weighing up the pros and cons and immediately agreed. Let Ricky do the work and for the sake of fifty or a hundred quid, the job'd be done and Ray wouldn't have broken into a sweat. Great plan.

When he told Penny, she was equally delighted because she'd be sure her furniture would still be in one piece by the time it arrived at Ray's.

BEFORE LUNCH, ALL Penny's belongings had been relocated and Ricky had received his payment plus one hundred per cent bonus. Always keep your concierge happy, thought Ray. Ricky walked down the corridor with a glorious grin on his face.

Ray had only used a fraction of the storage space in his flat and they had agreed to turn the second bedroom into a dressing room, at least for now. This gave Penny the opportunity to fill the entire room with her wardrobes. She decided to keep ordinary work things in the master bedroom, as well as some day-to-day casuals. The rest would be in the second bedroom and they'd even bought a standalone mirror made of wood and silver.

The dressing table was in the master bedroom too because she'd have felt strange taking herself off just to put on make-up.

By three, everything was as put away as it was going to be and they both sank into the living room furniture, Penny grabbed her book and Ray thumbed through a film magazine.

In a week's time, Penny's tenants would move in so Ray had agreed to pay his cleaner for an extra two hours' work to quickly run round Penny's place with a vacuum, duster and some bleach. Penny's woman was on holiday, back in Belgium for an extremely long weekend, lasting eight days.

Ray hadn't bothered much about the tenants as Penny had said she knew of a brother and sister, Michael and Theresa Boone, who were looking for a place in the area. So why should he care who they were? They were splitting the rent, after all. He sank further into the sofa, almost entirely horizontal.

"Shall we go out to eat tonight? You know, to celebrate?"

"Celebrate?"

"Yeah, moving in together. That's what's happened today in case you'd forgotten."

Penny giggled.

"You're right, we've moved in together."

She laughed again and stretched herself out, spreading arms and legs into the four corners of the armchair—and just hung there, doing nothing more than relishing the moment. A cute bundle of cushions surrounding a torso. And what a torso.

WITH THIS THOUGHT ringing in his ears, Ray stood up, padded over to her and knelt down between her outstretched legs. He let his arms dangle over the armrests, hanging over her thighs, and dropped his head into her lap.

Penny was wearing a pair of blue-and-white striped leggings, which showed off the shape of all of her body. Ray had heard her call them her glad-rags, but they were more than that to him. For Ray, he imagined he could see every pore under that material and he was certain there was a discernible bulge from her bush.

He nudged it with his nose.

"What you up to?"

And then Ray did it again, but this time, he kept rubbing his bridge over and over the point where the stripes from Penny's left leg met the stripes from the right leg.

"You turning into Pinocchio?"

He looked up at her with a big, toothy grin. Then, more dramatically perhaps than he originally intended, he let his head drop back, opened his mouth and engulfed her crotch with his lips.

Penny giggled some more, but in a very different way than before. This laugh came from deep within her.

He let his tongue do some work until her leggings were damp from his saliva. Then he stopped for a second.

"Take them off. I can't get close enough to you."

Penny first removed her shirt then tugged at her leggings until Ray could pull them off both legs. He bent down again and carried on with his mouth around her lips, only this time his tongue was inside her—Ray used one of his hands to hold the gusset of the blue thong out of the way.

With his spare hand, Ray unbuttoned his own shirt and undid his belt. He even managed to unzip his jeans and wriggle them off his hips without stopping from his slobbery task.

"I'm going to get some ice cubes," and Penny pulled Ray's head back and skipped out of the chair before he could do a thing to stop her.

HE CHASED HER into the kitchen and caught up with her as she reached the fridge then took her in his arms and kissed her, massaging his hands over her body, popping fingers inside her one minute and tweaking her nipples the next.

Ray had her pinned against the kitchen drawers—or at least he thought he had—when Penny jumped up and sat on the counter. Ray moved forward so his torso was still touching hers and Penny wrapped her legs around his thighs.

"Gotcha."

She pressed her heels into him and pulled down on his boxers so he was standing there, butt naked. He didn't care because all he was thinking of was the wondrously sexy spectacle that was sitting right in front of him.

Penny squeezed his dick some and all the while they kissed and licked. When she leaned back on the counter, they were perfectly poised for Ray to suck on her nipples. His second favourite pastime.

As he was doing this, he realised he could feel her hairs against his dick. He was just the right height. He pulled her knickers out the way and she helped him get inside her.

The rush was amazing and soon Ray was pumping hard and finished soon after. They stayed exactly as they were for what felt like forever but was only a minute at best. Then Penny slithered off the counter and leant into Ray, kissing him with both hands around the back of his neck.

He could feel every point where their bodies touched and it was so good. Ray had never known such contentment as he felt in that kitchen.

"I'm gonna change. I think you made my leggings wet." And that fabulous arse and pointy tits slunk out the kitchen, away from Ray's touch.

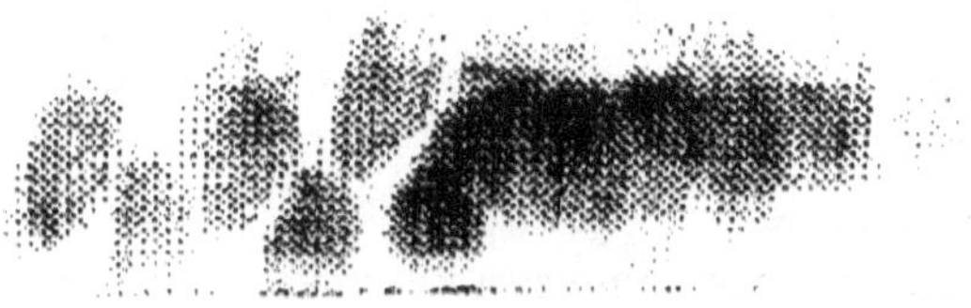

# 16

RAY HADN'T SEEN Ollie for nearly two weeks. Ignoring holidays, this was probably the longest they'd been apart. He missed the conniving, arrogant fucker.

Two sausage sandwiches arrived at their table, along with two waters and two coffees. The waitress plonked the items down and returned behind the counter.

"Nice arse."

"Yeah? Didn't notice."

"Not surprised to hear that; you're a married man now."

"Fuck off. We've shacked up, not got married."

"Keep telling yourself that, my friend. She might have you on a long leash, but it's still a leash all the same."

"Talking out your arse."

Ray didn't mind the regular ribbing he received from Ollie. They'd known each other long enough for it to be without genuine malice. But on this occasion, Ollie had a point. There wasn't much difference between sharing payments on a mortgage and being hitched. Even more so because Penny had got him to sign an agreement which gave her rights to half the equity moving forwards as she was contributing to the mortgage payments. The luck of having a lawyer for a girlfriend.

"Changing subjects subtly, how's the world of investment banking? Missing the floor?"

"It's great and not at all—in that order. I've supported a number of structured deals and I got the nod yesterday I can go out and find my own ones now."

"Wow, well done."

"I'm going to make some serious money. You eat what you kill in investment banking and I've got myself a hunger."

With that, Ollie tucked into his sandwich, and melted butter and sausage juice, mixed with ketchup, dribbled out the corner of his mouth.

"YOU SHOULD COME over to the dark side. You've always been smarter than me—can see moves way ahead of me. And you'd have more money in the bank to keep your young toots happy, dear boy."

"No question about the cash. And that young toots is the same age as us and twice as clever as both of us put together."

"Damn right, otherwise how else has she got you believing you're only living together when she got you to sign your soul away in a compact with the devil?"

"Fuck you. Look, if you need a referral to a lawyer you can trust, who'll be on your side, let me know. Penny's firm is all over that."

Ollie'd had an easy ride from the moment he arrived at uni, before even. His parents had funded his time there; not just fees but living expenses too. Then his dad's connections had got him the job at Killogg Spreckley and, of course, he was in the same firm as his dad now. An easy ride.

Investment banking was a harsh world. Filled with men putting together financing deals so smaller companies can be bought by bigger companies and the bankers took a commission irrespective of whether the deal was good for either company. Ray knew it was a beautiful business to be in and had no problem earning commission out of his own efforts.

Still, there must be better ways to make money in the City that help people too. Ray remembered his mum saying there was nothing wrong with making a profit, provided someone benefitted along the way. To Ray, investment banking didn't fit the bill, but he did hanker for a change. Trading was fine but he was definitely feeling unfulfilled. He needed something with a little bit more, but he wasn't sure what that was yet. Insurance, investment management, advisory? Who knew?

Besides, Penny had only been gone a couple of days and he was missing her. When he got home that evening, the flat seemed empty without her. Crazy, because only last week, she didn't even live there, but a Penny-sized absence filled the living room.

MAYBE OLLIE WAS right. Maybe Penny was trying to tie him down, moving in and everything, but he'd agreed to her suggestion almost immediately. Okay, she had suggested the idea first, but it wasn't like the thought hadn't crossed his mind too. The best thing about this experiment was that it was reversible. Her apartment was there, being lived in by strangers, but it was a lifeline. If things didn't work out, they could go back to the way they were and carry on regardless. No sweat.

The annoying thing was Penny'd gone to the States on Easter Monday so they'd lost a day of their long weekend. But work was work and he knew it was an important trip for her.

Ray went into the kitchen and pulled out one of the ready meals for one with which Penny had stocked the fridge before her departure. Tonight it was cannelloni. The microwave went ping and he let the pasta slither onto his plate. He grated some cheddar cheese to give it some flavour and sat down at the breakfast table.

Five minutes later and the plate was empty, apart from the smearing of sauce around the edge. Ray stood up and went to put the things in the dishwasher. As he bent down to pop the plate and cutlery in, at the periphery of his vision, he thought he saw the tattooed guy from the first day he moved in.

Ray looked up properly and stared at the window opposite his own, but nothing. All he saw was an inky blackness and, in the distance, a woman walking past the kitchen to another room. Must be losing his mind.

He was missing Penny. So much so he didn't know what to do with himself for the rest of the evening. He tried flicking through magazines, but he only had the film mag he'd already read. The rest in the pile on their coffee table were beauty tips and articles about how to nab yourself a fella. Ray wasn't right for either demographic. The telly offered the usual mix of crap and shit. When they said satellite TV would mean more choice, they didn't mention the options would be all the same.

Flipping through the million channels on offer, Ray found a movie and dipped into a story about a maverick cop in New York trying to free a girl, who'd been buried alive, before she ran out of air. Before the end, Ray had dozed off while he lay flat out on the sofa.

He eventually hauled arse and slunk off to bed. When he was under the covers, he missed Penny again. Only now did he realise how much he enjoyed having the warmth of her body next to him as he fell asleep. He rolled over and inhaled her pillow so he could rekindle his memory of her vanilla scent. Then he fell asleep.

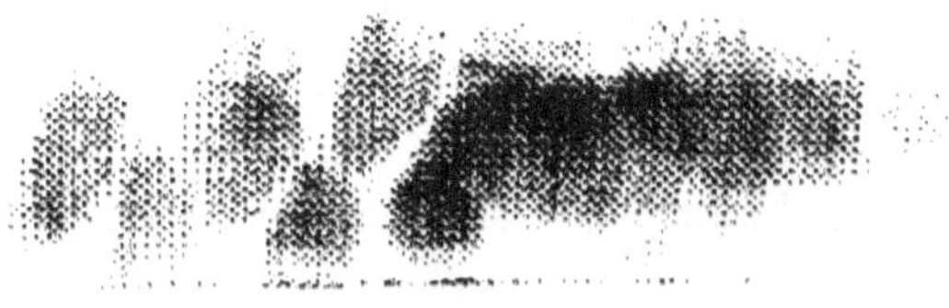

# 17

**PENNY**

Even though Nina's was a small firm, they still expected their people to travel in comfort, if not in style. Penny relished turning left when she boarded the plane and was happily ensconced in her flat-bed cubicle, sipping a glass of champagne from one hand while reading her book held in the other.

She'd decided to dress relatively casual as no one was going to see her until the following day. Black designer jeans, floppy white shirt and black heels. Blue chi-chi jacket and brown cashmere coat.

An hour into the flight, she put down the book and opened up a manila folder with the main papers she'd need for the trip. The client was a US software giant seeking to make a UK acquisition and they'd found a bunch of guys working out of their garage—the cliché was real—and the code they'd written was in direct competition with their client. So the aim was to strike a deal with a ceiling on the price. But a deal needed to be struck to take them out of the market and grab their customer base. Bottom line; it boiled down to a wrangle over intellectual property rights and how long before their options would vest.

Having reread all the detail so it was fresher in her mind, Penny put the file away, placed the complementary headphones over her ears and tried to watch a movie. Ray would have been happy here, she thought, but her mind couldn't concentrate on the wafer-thin plot offered by the rom com she'd found. Apart from the film she'd picked, there was an old one from the 1970s and some male bonding action shite, which she had no desire to even flick to, not even for a second. Penny sighed and took out her book again.

This was going to be a long flight, even though she was incredibly excited about being given the responsibility to be the lead attorney on the deal. First time Nina had entrusted her with anything this large—and she really didn't want to screw this up. She put her hand between her thighs, curled slightly on the flat bed and stared at the pages until she fell asleep. Luckily the steward kept her three-course meal for when she awoke.

THREE DAYS IN a row, sat in the same meeting room with the same people arguing over the same clauses. Penny was used to dealing with New Yorkers and their abrupt ways, but every so often, the cultural differences reared their head and they would be thrown into disarray.

Bob Huber Jr was President and Chief Executive of KrunchPixel Inc, based in Silicon Valley but registered in Delaware. He had made the company what it was today; a multi-billion-dollar enterprise, which sold productivity tools to consumers and businesses alike. Originally, Bob had cut his own code and created the world's first commercially viable file compression algorithm. But that wasn't enough. Bob wanted more money and the only way to get it, at the speed Bob wanted it, was to buy up others so the earnings figures were improved just by acquiring the new company's current year profit.

Earnings would be forecast to rise because the headline rate was upwards, even though the forward projections demanded Bob and his team rationalised the cost base along the way. They never did and so the leadership team put itself under even more pressure to keep shareholders happy by delivering higher earnings and so they needed to acquire ever more companies. Webber Paine loved them because they were the firm's biggest cash cow. There hadn't been a year since the partnership was created that either Nina or Anita hadn't had three or four deals cooking with KrunchPixel.

Like many American self-made men, Bob was brash, arrogant and unpleasant to be near and Penny had remembered Nina's advice before she flew over.

"Listen carefully to what Bob wants and work out precisely how to give it to him without any compromises. And whatever you do, don't sit next to him in any meeting because his breath stinks to high heaven, hon'."

Bob set out his position for the third time today. His people weren't listening to him and he was pissed off.

"NOW, PEOPLE. THIS is not a complex transaction. What I want is this; the deal must close this quarter or there will be no deal. All IPR must end up in KrunchPixel and I don't care what those numbnuts at Spank the Monkey think."

Penny knew he meant Span Gorilla and this was his little joke and she also knew every time he said it, he would look at her and wink. Clearly, he thought the way into her knickers was to tell wank jokes. Interesting ploy.

"And finally, I don't want to spend more than fifty mil, but our tax position means there's no way on this green earth we can afford to pay less than twenty-five. So can we please cut the bullshit and wrestle this to the ground."

Penny had been fine with all these items on Bob's wish list. The IPR—intellectual property rights—was why she was in the room. As the target company was domiciled in the UK, English law was key to unlocking that hot chestnut. The rest was mere papering an agreement, from her perspective, but the tax accountant refused to be pinned down on any detail. Penny thought she could smell his fear and guessed he hadn't prepared properly and was winging it. Bad mistake.

By Friday night, Penny was spent. Bob Huber Jr would get what he wanted, just as he had in every other deal in the past. Whatever was left to negotiate, the head of terms was clear in their minds, even if the target hadn't agreed yet. The rest was pure execution and Penny was comfortable she could deliver on her end.

NINA WAS IN town, working on a second deal and they took the opportunity of being in the same city on the same day to hook up. They spent the first ninety minutes having a coffee in the hotel's brasserie to take care of business. All was fine.

Then they went back up to their rooms to put their paperwork away and met up in the Vodka Bar on the first floor, as the Americans called it, to let down their hair and party.

"What goes on in New York stays in New York, hon'."

Several cosmos later and the women were nicely lubricated. They decided to head to Alphabet City to take in a club but realised they were at least four hours too early. So they ordered some food, a salad each and a selection of vegetables, and ordered more cosmos.

By ten, there was a horde of guys surrounding them, buying drinks, talking to each other and to Nina and Penny. And by eleven, their number had thinned out to only two, Chad and Mark. Both wore chiselled faces in a classic square-jawed manner. They'd been jocks at school and now they were part of the bridge-and-tunnel crew; in the city for some fun on a Friday night.

The four took the advice of the concierge and went to Avenue B, but no further—Avenue C was too dangerous to deal with—and waited in line at the Quadro, an Old Skool '80s club until it was their turn to go in. By offering the bouncer a small stipend, they were able to enter the VIP area and settled down at a table, ordering a bottle of French champagne.

Mark was sat next to Penny and Chad had homed in on Nina. Penny didn't care too much who she was chatting with. Both guys were equally interesting to her, although she did prefer Mark's hair; slightly longer and a darker brown. Their buff physiques were almost identical too, like they were carbon copies of each other.

She talked with Mark for about five minutes and realised that, while she liked the look of him in his chinos and T-shirt, they had nothing left to say to each other. Not enough going on in between his ears.

"LET'S DANCE," SHE suggested and they went onto the floor to the electro pulse of a New Order remix. A couple of tracks later and Nina joined them, followed by Chad, as Soft Cell kicked off on the turntable.

Two hours later and they had finished another bottle of champagne and spent three quarters of the time on the dance floor.

"Shall we hit another club?"

"Nah, hon'. I think we should go back to the hotel, don't you?"

"With or without them?"

"I'm taking mine back. What you do is up to you."

Penny thought for a minute and decided to give Mark a go. Outside the club, the men took the task of grabbing a cab and all four squished into the back of the yellow vehicle.

The Hotel Bristol was a relatively small boutique affair, full of weirdly-shaped designer furniture in the lobby and chi-chi little details in the rooms. Penny made sure she visited the women's bathrooms off the lobby so she could buy a rubber from a dispenser.

Then she took Mark up to the fifteenth floor and fucked his brains out, chucking him out before she went to sleep; the last thing she needed was to have to deal with that lunk in the morning. Nina did the same to Chad in a room on the tenth.

Nina and Penny shopped until they dropped on the Saturday and then took the red-eye back to London in the evening.

Penny arrived back at the apartment around eleven in the morning and Ray had already got up and was sitting on the sofa. He met her at the door and they hugged a while until Penny caught wind of her armpits and realised she needed a shower.

She kissed Ray once more and left him to wheel her bag into the bedroom as she scuttled straight to the shower and washed the New York grime off her white flesh. All the while, Ray stood in the doorway, staring at her, not wanting to leave. Hanging around like some sort of puppy.

Mark might have been an empty human being, but he had some life, some sort of get-up-and-go, which was lacking in Ray. This was a man who had no energy about him. The world happened around him, in spite of him. She felt comfortable with him, for sure, but his personality didn't light her on fire.

She had enjoyed her time in Manhattan and yearned to return almost before she'd landed at Heathrow. Bob Jr was on his way to being made a richer man and Penny had enjoyed feeling a different dick inside her.

Ray opened the door to the shower and Penny realised he'd taken his clothes off while she'd been daydreaming about the US. She splatted some suds onto his chest and proceeded to rub the soapy froth all over him. Without a single word said between them, they reacquainted themselves with every inch, every crevice, of each other's bodies.

# PART NINE

# NOVEMBER 2001

# 18

**PENNY**

Yet another transatlantic flight, yet another flat bed, yet another few chapters read from her book. Penny was spending her whole time in the States—or at least that's how it felt. You've spent too much time in the air when you know the menu before you get on the plane and when the stewarding staff know your name. Your first name, that is.

Her vodka tonic was ready for her almost before she'd settled in and Penny stretched her legs out and pointed her toes away from her head. She was tired; she and Ray had been out late the previous night; Ollie had held one of his infamous parties. This time he'd hired out an entire country manor for twenty-four hours, which meant they had been partying almost all that time, apart from the odd hour or two when she'd crashed out under the billiard table and the half hour she and Ray had spent shagging in the library, surrounded by the Chippendale furniture. The rest of the time, Penny had maintained her levels of spritely consciousness through the use of a vast array of chemicals. Now she was wrecked.

She awoke with a start and hoped the plane was descending but her eyes had been closed for no more than three-quarters of an hour. Damn.

With adrenaline pumping through her bloodstream, Penny couldn't get back to sleep, so despite feeling like the bottom of a cockatoo's cage, she pulled out the case file to prep for the coming week. Her assistant, Kelly, had done a good job of providing a series of notes on the current state of negotiations—Penny had taken two days off the preceding week in the run-up to Ollie's party.

One day in the spa, including a mani-pedi and some deforestation; she felt like she'd grown a hedge in her privates and had restored herself to a neat triangle. Ray hadn't gone down on her for weeks and she was concerned she had let herself go. He'd certainly appeared more enthused yesterday but they'd been interrupted in the library by a couple who were seeking their own trysting place and Ray had gone soft halfway through.

The rest of the time was spent having some deep massage and in the sauna with a half hour swim to round the day off.

ON FRIDAY, SHE'D hung at the apartment, reading and chilling, knowing she'd need to pack for the trip and for the party—when they got back home, she'd showered, changed, kissed Ray goodbye and, vroom, off she went to Heathrow in a black cab organised by Ricky, the concierge.

Penny realised her mind was wandering because, for a second, her arm slumped down and her papers fell onto the floor. She picked them all up, placed them back into the correct order and put them away. There was no point skimming the content; full focus or none at all.

With both hands now under her blanket, Penny snuggled into the flat bed. Her left hand was lying on a leg and her right hand was on her tummy. Idly, she popped it beneath her shirt and absentmindedly circled round her belly button. Then without giving much thought to anything, she breathed in and let her hand slip under her jeans and then under her pants...

When she woke up again, this time the jolt was caused by the undercarriage hitting the Newark tarmac. She took her hand from out of her knickers and folded the blanket out of the way. Penny might not have felt refreshed, but those five hours sleep was more than she'd had in the previous day and a half.

Next morning, she awoke in the Hotel Bristol, the same boutique place she always stayed in, just off Times Square, a decent midtown location, forty-five minutes from Wall Street if necessary, but close enough to Fifth Avenue if she was able to pop out of a meeting and grab an interesting item of jewellery or some such trinket. Every trip she promised herself she'd buy something for Ray, but she never did.

One of the things she loved about the Bristol was that the room designer used oil paintings for headboards, so each room was unique. There was always some kind of found art lying around you'd never expect or whose incongruity would make you laugh.

PENNY OPENED HER eyes the following morning to see a plastic penguin on her bedside table and she smiled. Crazy, totally crazy. And she loved it. She hopped out of bed, bleary eyes still hanging out the front of her skull and bumbled into the shower. After brushing her teeth, she thought her period was a little late this month —she was usually regular as clockwork—and gave it no more brain time, as she had been partying hard the last couple of weeks and her body's natural rhythms could easily have been thrown sideways.

Out of the room and the usual interminable wait for the lift. Why do hotels not invest in more lifts, she pondered. Three minutes later and she was down in the lobby. She sensed a strange atmosphere and couldn't put her finger on what was wrong.

There was a tension in the air—not with the hotel guests but with everyone else. People were talking in hushed tones and there was concern, genuine worry, on their faces.

"What's going on?"

"Haven't you heard?"

"No. What?"

"There's been a plane crash."

"Crash? Again?"

The concierge nodded and Penny instantly understood. Six weeks after the World Trade Center and now this. Fuck. The whole of Penny's world caved into one single shot of experience. She was scared and the narrow scope in which her vision resided could only see herself, opposed to the rest of the hostile universe. Fuck.

"Do they know..."

"No, ma'am. Bridges and tunnels have been shut down, so no one's going off Manhattan today, but that's all I know."

The blood drained out of Penny's cheeks as she nodded and walked away. She sat down in a nearby chair to take stock of her world. She hadn't minded flying into New York so soon after the attack because, for one thing, the hijacked flights had all been domestic. But now she was only a few miles from a crash, Penny felt incredibly vulnerable.

SHE TOOK OUT her mobile and regained control. She rang Ray but got no reply. Not that surprising because international calls on mobile phones were rubbish at the best of times. Then she sent him a text and hoped he'd receive it before he saw the news, but she was all too aware he would be trading off the newswire. Chaos was opportunity, or some such bullshit.

Penny stood up and headed out for the day to see if she could get a taxi, but no joy. She walked the three blocks down and two blocks across until she reached the offices of United Petroleum, her illustrious, acquisitive client.

The marble atrium demonstrated their top dollar fees were well targeted; United Petroleum was swimming with cash and wanted to spend rather than pay tax, hence the burning desire to close three deals this fiscal year. They were six months in and nothing was signed or sealed, let alone delivered.

She was ushered into their client meeting level, right at the top, with a view of the Hudson and the Empire State, although it did look an awful long way away. Penny sat down with her back to the vista so that when they sun shone in, others could be blinded.

Today's session was an initial briefing and advisory before the games began later in the week. Penny waited five minutes and the door opened and they all walked in, talking to each other as they entered. First in was Frank Delaney, President and Chief Executive of the holding company with a whole host of senior management in tow, desperately trying to justify their existences.

Frank was a classic New York wasp with light brown hair and fairly large paunch. He wore a dark blue suit, blue shirt with white collar and cuffs, and a red tie. The uniform of the Manhattan leader.

Handshakes and introductions ensued and Frank sat at the opposite end of the table to Penny, clearly a power move as everyone else held back to give him a chance to make his seating choice, and they all fell in line from there. Typical corporate bullshit.

Coffees and water were offered and they all settled down.

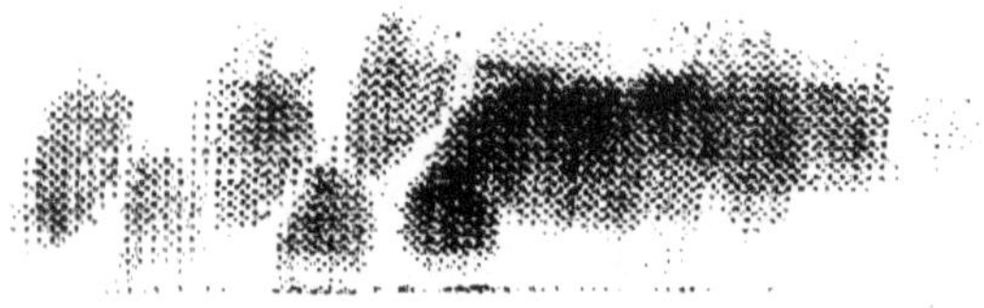

# 19

"THANKS FOR COMING over, appreciate it."

"We're always here to help, you know that."

"For sure. Let's get to it."

Penny picked up her fountain pen, ready for legal action.

"We have held an exploratory meeting with the board at British Oil and we have a headline agreement to acquire one hundred per cent of their stock."

"Congratulations."

"Thank you, but there's a long way to go before we uncork the champagne.

"First, the offer price was far from firm. All I could say was that the ceiling was at ten billion but the floor was eight billion at best."

"Why the spread? Where are the uncertainties you are concerned about?"

"Good question. I'll come on to that, don't worry. The primary objective is to close the deal before fiscal year end, which doesn't sound too problematic. But we need to conclude at least three deals in the same time frame.

"We need to purchase some losses to offset our fantastic current year, otherwise our taxation costs will inhibit our ability to announce an increase in earnings per share."

"And your EPS will buoy your share price," interjected Penny.

"Exactly. I'm glad we have an adult in the room."

Frank eyed some of the others sat in front of him and Penny realised there was office politics tension in the room. She had assumed it was due to the downed plane.

"The biggest challenge to wrestling this bear to the ground will be the jurisdictional aspects."

"How so?"

"For historic reasons, British Oil has interests in Saudi Arabia and Iraq, as well as Kuwait and Kazakhstan."

"To what extent are those subsidiaries essential to the deal?"

"Until we kick off the due diligence, I've got no fucking clue, pardon my French."

Penny nodded and thought how half-cocked the deal sounded before it had even left the starting blocks. She also knew it was her job to get to the finishing line in one piece. Somehow.

SHE FIRED OFF a volley of questions to ensure Kelly's notes were current. The Iraq angle was a surprise and the deal value was soft, so soft she almost wondered about the real purpose of the transaction. Burying profit made some sense, but unless the deal closed almost immediately, she couldn't see how the profits would get recognised in this year's accounts. Penny made a note to get that assumption checked out back at base.

Then she moved on to ask about the Middle Eastern subsidiaries and the political ramifications of purchasing an Iraqi company. Bottom line; she knew they'd need to put in place some back-to-back divestments with a consequent price adjustment or British Oil would need to sell up prior to deal closure, which would slow the process to a halt once everyone got wind there was a fire sale with an April 5 deadline. This was the third deal Penny had been involved in where her membership of the New York Bar would be of value.

As she carried on controlling the meeting, her questions became more intense and she strafed the room, trying to get a clear picture of the terrain she'd be focusing on until well after Christmas. The Group Finance Director sent his people scurrying back to their desks for numerous pieces of detail and pretty soon, Penny looked at her watch and saw it was nearly lunchtime.

"Are we going to brown bag or step outside for lunch?"

Frank smiled.

"We've ordered in—should be next door."

That counted as an announcement for everyone to rise and head to the adjacent room. Frank asked Penny if she'd like to join him for a cigarette and she agreed.

Although Penny didn't smoke, she knew this would be the best time to catch Frank on his own and he wanted to speak with her otherwise he'd have just walked out and left her.

They took the elevator down to the lobby and Penny retrieved her passport from the building reception. Since September 11, the US had witnessed a huge increase in security around publicly accessible buildings. If you were a visitor, you handed in photo ID before you got past the lobby area and you only got it back on your departure. This meant a foreign visitor risked their passport with a total stranger; locals always carried driving licences.

Frank and Penny left the building and stopped outside the main entrance. Frank sauntered a little further on so that they wouldn't be surrounded by lunchtime puffers.

"Want one?"

"No thanks."

Another Frank smile.

"Sensible. Wish I didn't smoke too."

"We all have our vices."

"True."

"Listen, there's something you need to know that no one else in our organisation knows."

Penny stood there, her head tilted slightly to one side in a classic listening pose.

"Go on."

"Ray is out. In three weeks' time, he's gone."

"Ray?"

Penny was confused.

"Yes, Ray."

Now it was Frank's turn to look perplexed. Penny stared blankly at him, not understanding his problem with her. Why would Ray be gone in three weeks? And why the hell would Frank have an opinion on the matter?

Then the penny dropped.

"The CFO, you mean?"

"Uh huh. Who else was there?"

Penny chuckled.

"My fiancé's name is Ray."

Frank laughed.

"Don't worry, we're not chucking him onto the fire—unless you want us to."

"We're good, thanks."

"Anyway, Ray is out, so ignore his negativity for now. He won't be a permanent blocker. It just means we'll be relying on his people to provide any numbers you need for the foreseeable."

"Duly noted. And thanks for telling me. I had noticed something in the air."

"The smell of his fear, I'd guess."

Frank took two long, hard inhalations on his cigarette and snubbed the butt onto the sidewalk. Then they went back upstairs after Penny had deposited her passport back in the rack.

WITHOUT FRANK IN the room, everyone had been politely sipping the OJ, but no one had wanted to start digging into the filled bagels, salad and fruit which were there for the taking. Penny continued to be amazed at how hierarchically United Petroleum behaved, even though it was already the twenty-first century.

There was less tension on the street this lunchtime or at least that's how it had felt just now, she thought. Then Penny's mind wandered back to September 11 and the events of that day.

She'd been in an offsite meeting the whole of the afternoon, disconnected from the world outside, so she only found out about the towers' collapse in the late afternoon when she'd gone straight home.

Her offsite had been a strenuous one and when Penny arrived home, the first thing she did was to take a shower. How could she have broken into a sweat in a meeting? Simple; the offsite took place in her old flat because she was still seeing Mickey. With his sister, Theresa off on holiday, clubbing like a crazy bitch in Ibiza, Mickey had the place to himself, so she'd popped round to collect the rent.

Penny still had a key so she let herself in and called out when she was stood in the hallway with the door firmly shut behind her. She thought she'd seen Ricky spot her from the far side of the atrium. Penny made a mental note to give him a fat tip next time she saw him.

Mickey mumbled something from the bedroom so Penny walked towards the door while unzipping her skirt and slipping it off. Before she'd pushed on the handle, Penny had thrown her blouse down onto the carpet too.

MICKEY LAY ON the bed wearing only a pair of blue Y-fronts and a grin, head resting on both his arms. His pants were small and he filled them completely. His bulge left nothing to the imagination, which was fine by Penny because she wanted a damn sight more out of him than a bulge.

Mickey grunted his approval of her underwear, leapt off the bed and kissed her on the mouth, while taking off her bra and pants within a matter of seconds. He was hungry. And so was Penny.

Within a minute or two, he was inside her and she was barely able to breathe. The man was a Neanderthal, but he fucked like he was king of the beasts.

Once they'd both recovered, they fucked again and then Penny went home and straight into the shower. Into her pyjamas and then onto the sofa and flipped the TV onto the rolling news. Before she'd moved in with Ray, she'd always read a newspaper, but she'd got out of the habit since sharing a sofa with him.

Then the news hit her and she stared at the images of the collapsing buildings over and over again. Transfixed. Unable to believe what she was seeing and then, when she had to acknowledge this was no hoax, still finding it hard to process the information or any of its implications.

Talking heads desperately tried to fill the aching void of silence surrounding this broadcast. Looking back, the only thing she remembered from all the words spoken that day on the TV was how quickly they were saying it was Al Qaeda. Penny thought it strange no one had claimed responsibility but someone was already there to be blamed. The numbers of the dead were the other thing she found weird. The estimated dead dropped from fifty thousand at the start of the broadcast down to five thousand in the space of a couple of hours. Over the next three or four weeks, the number fell still further to somewhere between a quarter and a half of that figure.

Ray was at work, trading off the news of the catastrophe.

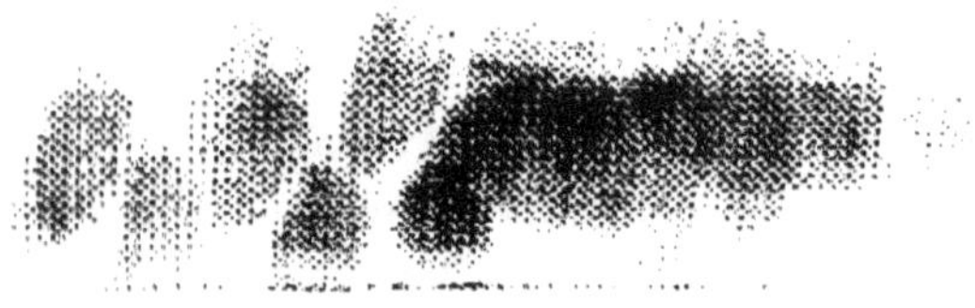

# 20

"THE AFTERNOON COMPRISED a series of arguments between Frank and Ray, thinly disguised as a series of clarifications and recalibrations. Penny kept her head down and let the client decide on what course she should take. Needless to say, that meant listening to Frank and ignoring Ray's protestations.

His main objection to Frank's deal was the negative consequential damage to the United Petroleum brand once the deal closed, due to the nature of some of the subsidiaries of British Oil. This is where matters got sticky by the end of the afternoon.

"Calcutta is an accident waiting to happen and we should not be investing in it. No good will come of it."

The blood vessel on the right of Frank's temple was pulsing away. The man was angry and doing his best to remain calm, despite himself.

"The fact there is a chemicals factory in some turd city in India is no reason to call off the entire deal. Makes no sense, Ray."

"Have you forgotten Bhopal? Look what it did to the share price. And the amount of money pissed down the drain defending the indefensible and then paying out to the victims."

"May I remind you, we need that subsidiary inside the tent because there are unrealised profits we need to bolster on our balance sheet. Or have you forgotten the situation we are facing, right now?"

"Of course, I haven't forgotten, Frank. But I've already shown you how we can get the same corporation tax benefits without taking on the potential liabilities of a chemical spill. It is 'when' not 'if'."

Frank sighed. They were getting nowhere. Ray refused to let go of the bone and Frank didn't want to hear from him anymore. Penny sat there and watched the spat wind down to its inevitable non-conclusion. By Christmas, Ray would be gone and the subsidiary would remain on the purchase list.

PENNY'S THOUGHTS WERE more about how realistic would the demand for indemnities for the next decade be to cover the spill which Ray was sure was coming down the tracks. She figured they could ask but would be unlikely to get. In which case, a fire sale a few weeks later might be the easiest solution. Frank would get the tax credits he so clearly wanted and after April they could flog the subsidiary to anyone who had a pulse. Price wouldn't matter. They could propose a management buyout if there were no commercial takers.

At least the destruction of a chunk of India wouldn't be on their conscience, assuming the place lasted until April. Perhaps the trick would be to demand an April 3 date for closure to mitigate the risk of a spill between ownership and divestment.

By the time they packed up for the night, the pulse of Frank's temple had increased a couple of notches. It was just gone eight.

"Would you like a drink?"

Penny agreed and Frank took her back to the Bristol and they hit the Vodka Bar.

Frank ordered two vodka martinis, straight up with a twist. They carried on chatting; him about his wife and family. The wife didn't understand him and his family didn't respect him. The usual midlife crisis car crash of a marriage. And in between his breaths, Penny managed to give him a hint of her life back home—with her Ray.

A second martini was consumed by both and then Penny explained she was tired and needed to go back to her room. Frank made a rather clumsy attempt to go up with her, but Penny was able to fend off that client/attorney moment without causing him embarrassment or creating a problem between them. His fees were too important to put at risk for a fling in a foreign town, even though the martinis had certainly put her in the mood.

When she got to her room, she called her Ray to tell him about the downed plane and to reassure him all was okay. The story hadn't even made the news yet, so Ray wasn't even worried. Then they played phone sex before she fell asleep.

THE NEXT DAY, a different set of meeting rooms, but the same cast of thousands with only two leads in the assembled throng. Frank and Ray appeared to have cooled down from last night's heated discussion so Penny was hoping Tuesday would go more smoothly. As ever, Frank kicked off and set the scene;

"It will come as no surprise that the biggest market for British Oil is the UK, but we already have a significant presence there."

Penny smiled and nodded. Another reason she was sat in the room was due to United Petroleum's UK interests. The fact she was a member of the US Bar meant they could extract more value from her —and her day rates were higher to reflect that situation. A bunch of evenings studying and a $750 fee was well worth the effort.

"This means we will need to take advantage of some operational synergies as soon as possible, post-deal closure."

"What would they be?"

"We have a refinery in Cardiff and so do they. We'll close one of them down in the same financial year as the deal. The longer we leave it, the more it'll cost us."

"Are you going to want us to assist in the search for potential acquirers?"

"Not this time, thank you."

Bad news for Penny as running a suitor parade was easy meat. A legal secretary does the work but a partner signs it off. Money for old rope.

"Oh."

"We already have a target locked and loaded."

"So we will just need to paper that deal—and manage any regulatory hurdles."

"REGULATORY HURDLES?"

"HM Government may not be too pleased if you shut down an oil plant in Wales. Also, given the market share you hold in the UK, somewhere between twenty-five and thirty-five per cent I believe, there could be an issue with competition rules. I'd need to understand British Oil's corporate structure before I can give more specific advice on that."

"Are you seriously telling me we can't buy the company and fire five thousand people without Tony Blair shoving his nose into my affairs?"

"Not the Prime Minister himself, but certainly those whose job it is to keep the playing field level."

"Level, my arse, pardon my French."

"Before we worry about this problem, let me review the actual circumstances and reach a recommendation. I mentioned it to stop it being a surprise if it does become an issue later."

"Understood. I appreciate that. It's why we pay you the big bucks."

And so the day progressed into a litany of potential lawsuits, difficulties and unplanned for liabilities with little chance of obtaining any indemnities or warranties. In other words; the usual large value M&A transaction.

In the evening, Penny declined the offer of a cocktail from Frank because she knew refusing him entry to her hotel room twice in two days would lead him to take things personally. And this was business—or rather she didn't want to fuck him. Not in the mood and, since she'd got engaged to Ray, Penny was trying to keep on the straight and sexual narrow.

They'd agreed to take things to the next level over the summer. In fact, it was when they were on holiday, they'd had a chance to talk about how life was going between them and of their hopes for the future. Penny talked and Ray listened, although he didn't seem to disagree too strongly.

THAT EVENING THEY had carried on the conversation in a hot tub in the grounds of their Jamaican cottage. Penny remembered looking at Ray's willy as it bobbed around under the water and realising she'd be prepared to live with him for the rest of her life. And that didn't sound alien or scary at all, which showed it was the right thing to do.

And Ray had knelt before her in the bubbling water, resting his arms on her knees, and proposed to her, all formal. Then he'd got nearer to her by parting her legs and nuzzling forward so she could feel his body against her crotch. She remembered him rubbing himself up and down which really turned on the tingles in her back. That was quite a night. Luckily all she had to do the following day was lie on a sun lounger. Since then the sex was drying up between them. Maybe they were both just too busy and were passing each other in the apartment like cars in a contraflow system.

The next day, Wednesday, Penny returned for the final round of this first bout of United Petroleum versus British Oil.

On this occasion, Frank covered the outer reaches of the British Oil empire; Afghanistan was home to a small company, set up decades before to act as a centre of influence into Iran and Iraq and other oil interests. Only the day before, the US and its allies had invaded the country as part of George Bush's war on terror.

Frank described his problem with classic understatement. "Today, we will need a carve out for British Oil (Kabul), because that is toxic to us. Alternatively, depending what happens over the next week, this could be the most valuable asset in the entire group."

"Have you any concerns about what your shareholders will think of United acquiring a company based in a terrorist state?"

"Not at this point, but I am very aware the situation is altering on an hour-by-hour basis."

"We are living in interesting times."

Penny thought about the whirlwind energy that had erupted out of that genuine sense of dread, which emanated from the World Trade Center attacks. From that night, watching rolling news show the destruction on a loop, through to today, the news bulletins were filled with stories of Bush getting support for his invasion of Afghanistan and then the invasion itself. Two months ago, no one had heard of Al Qaeda and now no one could avoid talk of them unless they lived in a cave.

"IS THERE ANYTHING you'd like me to address right now or do you think it advisable to operate on a wait-and-see basis, at least for the next week or two?"

"Wait-and-see. If the US takes Kabul then oil will be one of the primary raw materials needed in the country and we might need to change our negotiating strategy. But if Uncle Sam gets bogged down in endless desert skirmishes then we should carve out the subsidiary and leave the damn thing alone. The highest priority is to execute the deal so we can gain the tax advantages on offer from the holding company. The rest counts as a bonus."

"Understood. I'll wait on your instructions."

Timing being everything, this was the moment when Frank's cell phone rang. He looked at the screen and took the call. Less than a minute later and he'd hung up.

"News just in, people. We've taken Kabul."

This meant there was an invaluable asset in the outer reaches of the British Oil group, which promised great riches provided they didn't appear too interested in it—otherwise the asking price would shoot north of anything reasonable.

And at the same time, due to the tremendous political risks associated with doing business in that shitty opium-infested part of the world, Penny knew they'd have to carry out some incredibly painstaking due diligence before the deal could be closed. She was going to be kept busy for the next few months, on this case alone. She made a note to herself to ask Nina if the rest of her desk could be cleared until Christmas at the earliest.

# Part Ten

# June 2002

# 21

**RAY**

Ray had hired a cute red sports car for the weekend. He revved the engine impatiently as he and Penny sat in the curved lines of the vehicle as the gates slowly opened and Ray followed the driveway round the meandering lane until the wooded area ended and they were left with the view of Tickhurst Manor.

The estate was beautiful, no two ways about it. True, the first time they'd visited about a year ago and still true now. There was a small amount of creeping ivy reaching up from the ground on the left-hand side of the building and the most amazing roses growing to the right. In the middle were immaculate lawns, fit for playing croquet. Ground floor, first floor and the occasional attic room, but the whole pile oozed charm. Old-fashioned charm.

Ollie had liked the sound of the place so much, he'd hired the manor house out the previous winter for one of his parties. He should have had the decency not to hire their wedding venue but Ray remembered they'd had a brilliant time. The library had made a real impression on him as he recalled Penny and himself spending some time in there.

As before, by the time they arrived outside the front door, a butler was waiting and helped Penny out the car and took the keys off Ray. Without a flurry, or a word being spoken, two footmen in full tails, brought their cases out of the boot and their car was driven off for them. Ray knew the next time he saw it would be when they left and the thing would have been cleaned and polished to within an inch of its life. Shame it was only a hire car, really.

The butler, Colin, introduced them to the other staff in the hallway and then he showed them the way to their room. This was in one of the corners of the building and had a stunning view of the lake on one side and the front of the manor on the other. Ray glanced at his watch: noon. In four hours they'd be hitched.

ONCE COLIN HAD left, Penny opened up all the wardrobes and drawers, just to see what was in them, spun round in the middle of the room, then launched herself onto the four-poster bed. She lay face up like a starfish.

Ray threw his jacket onto one of the chairs and joined her on the bed.

"This is it, Penny Pitstop."

"I know, my little Ray of sunshine."

They hugged and kissed each other a couple of times, but nothing more. Despite trying to play it cool, Ray was feeling nervous and the more he thought about what was due to happen this afternoon, the more anxious he became—even though he was happy to be marrying this sexy and smart bundle of fun. Sure loved the taste of her nipples.

Penny changed into her ankle-length blue dress made of chiffon with silk darts. Unlike almost all her formalwear, this was not tight fitting at all, but flowed in a wonderfully majestic way. Ray, on the other hand, wore a handmade charcoal grey suit from Milan with a white shirt from Jermaine Street and a cream designer silk tie. Ray checked himself out in the full-length mirror and reckoned he looked okay. Then he glanced at Penny, who had put the finishing touches to her hair and make-up. She looked a million dollars.

Ten minutes later, once they'd taken the opportunity to sit down and chill for a while, the pair walked downstairs to greet their guests.

They glided down the curved staircase and out onto the front terrace. As soon as they opened the doors and their feet crunched into the gravel, all the guests burst into applause. A warm spontaneous welcome from their closest friends and family.

Even though they were holding hands as they walked out, within seconds Penny had separated away from Ray, off talking to Karen, Nina, her parents and her friends and he had done the same making a beeline for his best man, Ollie, and his side of the guest list.

"Looking good, dear boy."

"Thank you. Are you sure?"

"Of course, you big lummox."

Ray put his hands in his trouser pockets and refused the option of a glass of champagne. He and Penny had left strict instructions it'd be no more than one glass per person before the ceremony itself. They wanted people to be merry, not smashed. Afterwards, the opposite was true.

"AND WHO'S THAT fine filly with Penny then?"

Ray looked round to discover who Ollie was talking about.

"That's Karen. I've told you about her before, remember?"

"Not a fucking word, dear boy. Tell me again."

"They met at Penny's last law firm. Karen was the youngest partner since the Second World War. Mighty smart American; she went to Cambridge and her parents are filthy rich New York Jewish Democrat types. Most of the money was earned, not inherited."

"Let's not judge, dear boy, let's not judge."

"Ollie, you are the product of inbreeding that dates back generations. I've told you before it's a fucking miracle you have ten fingers in total and not just on one hand."

They both laughed and gave each other a manly hug. Ray had made the same statement more times than either could remember.

"And did that pair of tits and arse come with a plus one. Or are they alone?"

"Quite alone. And there's no one at home either apparently."

"Interesting. Very interesting."

"She's the maid of honour, so at least wait until you've both done your marriage ceremony duties before you make a move on her."

"Never fear, dear boy. I'm here for you one hundred per cent."

Then Ray moved over to his parents.

"Hey, how are you?"

"Marvellous, darling. Just marvellous. And don't you look marvellous too."

His mother had run out of words to say and the afternoon had only just begun. Ray remembered why he'd stopped visiting them every week shortly after he left home. His mum had sipped the one glass of champagne into non-existence and now she was in bad need of a long glass of cool water.

His dad said nothing, as was his wont, but shook Ray's hand and slapped him on the back. The closest thing he'd had to an honest conversation with the man in fifteen years. Ray felt proud.

Then Penny grabbed him and yanked him away; it was time. Colin announced guests were invited to make their way to the library where the wedding ceremony would commence in a few minutes.

RAY AND PENNY had already gone inside before Colin started speaking so they would have some time alone before the wedding began. All the details had been organised with the registrar and Colin had been briefed before the day.

The couple stood in the billiard room, adjacent to the library. They'd selected the introductory music for before the ceremony itself months ago and could hear it playing now.

Penny looked at him and they smiled at each other, not saying a word. Ray felt his heart beating like it was about to burst out of his chest and his throat was dry. Real dry. Despite how he felt about the idea of marriage to Penny, he was beyond nervous—almost like a terrible performance anxiety.

Then he heard the opening strain of the intermezzo from Cavalleria Rusticana, straight from the movie and one of the most beautiful pieces of music either had ever heard. They knew they were no more than two minutes away from walking out of the room and into the beginning of their marriage.

Ray put his hand out to Penny and they stood next to each other, listening to the music as everyone's voices died down and their friends and family came to order. As the last notes from the strings faded to nothing, Ray squeezed Penny's hand and they walked out into the start of their life together. Or rather their married life together.

For a second, Ray thought how unnecessary all of this was. They ate together, they laughed together, they slept together. Why did they need a piece of paper to say the state was giving them permission to do all that? Penny wanted it so that was the reason.

Then he snapped his mind back into reality as he saw all eyes stare at them as they made their way up the central aisle between the chairs and stopped by the registrar, who gave them a brief smile and the ceremony commenced.

PHOTOS, CHAMPAGNE, HUGS and kisses. The previous hour had been a blur. Ray knew he was now married because he could feel the unusual sensation of a ring on his left hand's third finger but he had no clear recollection of any individual moment which had made that a reality. More photos, champagne and hugs—from his parents, her parents, Ollie, Karen and everybody else. And yet more champagne.

By the time they were sat at the wedding reception, Ray's head was spinning and he was using all his available energy to concentrate on eating his food and giving his speech. Between him and Ollie, Penny had said a few words too; there was no way she could have spent the whole day and not spoken. This was the twenty-first century after all.

Once coffee was served, he and Penny officially left the room first and everyone dispersed into all the building's nooks and crannies on the ground floor; the bedrooms were on the first and second floors.

Having gone round to do his duty mingling, mainly with Karen and her lawyer cronies, Ray was able to check in with Penny and go off into the billiard room to hang with Ollie and the assembled men.

The drinking games started about three minutes later. For some reason Ray couldn't fathom, he kept losing and was knocking back vodka shots like they were going out of fashion.

Unfortunately for Ray, too much vodka turned him into quite a belligerent son-of-a-bitch so he cooled off away from everybody else.

Ray lay under the billiard table with a smile on his face and his eyes firmly shut as the guys played above him. He thought about his time with Penny and their future life together. Of how they'd decided, once they'd started to share a mortgage, to take out life policies to the tune of a million quid each. If one of them popped their clogs, the other wouldn't be saddled with two mortgages and only one salary to service them.

Despite the risks he took in his day job, Ray was glad Penny had suggested de-risking their financial relationship. And then Ray thought about the other aspects. How he trusted Penny and the vows they'd made to each other just a few hours earlier. And the smile remained fixed on his expression.

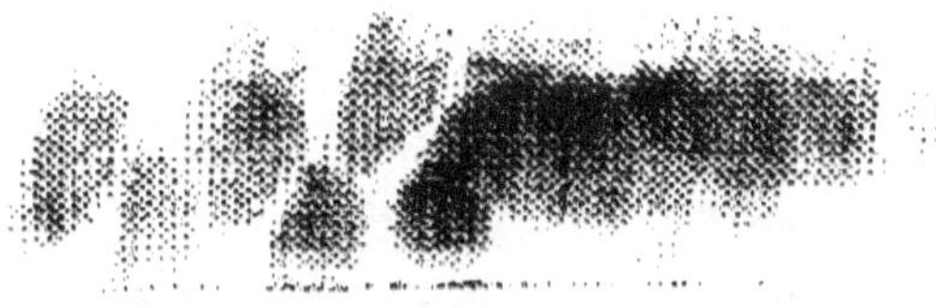

# 22

**PENNY**

Ray had been an arsehole in the billiard room, refusing to come out from under the table, but had been the charming gentleman to her parents. Now they were alone together as wife and husband in their marital bedroom. The whole idea made Penny laugh inside.

She glanced at Ray as he teetered on his feet, trying to maintain his balance and take off his clothes at the same time. With little success. He made her smile as he gave up the pretence and sat on the bed to wrestle off his trousers and socks.

Penny had already taken off her make-up and unbraided her hair. She looked at herself in the dressing table mirror, staring hard at her imperfections. Her nose wasn't straight and it was too pointy and she had never liked her smile. Her lips were long and thin; she'd always wanted round ones like a little button. Her wedding dress was draped over a chair. There was a small tear on the hem but it had survived the day intact, more or less.

Penny stared at her breasts and wondered how long they would last before they headed south and bumped into her knees. She pushed them together and up, contemplating what shape her body would take in five, even ten, years' time. Absolutely unimaginable.

In the periphery of her vision, Penny could sense Ray had stopped fighting his clothes. There was no more rustling and the bumping sounds had ceased. In the mirror, Penny saw Ray was lying in bed, staring at her.

THE DAY HAD been lovely and everyone had seemed to enjoy themselves. The two sides of the family got on as well as could be expected. That was always going to be the hardest part because the only thing they had in common was Penny and Ray—and most of them didn't know Ray either.

A lovely day and a fun evening; it was kind of Karen to front a couple of lines as a wedding present. Better than a set of steak knives, for sure. And although she couldn't say quite what or why, Penny felt as though there was something missing with Ray. Then she closed and opened her eyes and asked herself why she tried to find the negative in everything. Be thankful for what you've got, she told herself again.

Ray was still staring at her.

"Like what you see?"

"You bet, Penny Pitstop."

Penny took off her bra and let it drop on the floor. Then she stood up, shimmied out of her knickers and scurried under the covers to nestle next to Ray, her husband.

"You're all warm."

Ray ran a hand over her shoulders.

"You cold thing. Poor you."

He rubbed her upper arms to get the blood flowing again. Then he made sure her nipples weren't cold by rubbing them until Penny felt the bolts of electricity firing up and down her spine.

"You're warm enough there."

Then he moved his hand down onto her thighs and did and said the same thing. Finally, he put his hand between her thighs and massaged until she felt his finger nudge inside her. Penny gave in to the pure sensation of pleasure emanating from her crotch, created by Ray's first finger.

"You're definitely hot down there," he giggled and carried on.

PENNY OPENED HER eyes for a second, her back arched and both hands kneading her breasts. Ray was lying next to her with his head held by one hand and his other was under the covers. She could feel exactly where those fingers were every second.

Despite the growing intensity she was experiencing, Penny resented Ray's idle manner. Didn't look as though he was putting any real effort into this. Tonight of all nights. They might have fucked a thousand times before, but this should have been special somehow, she thought.

Penny closed her eyes and gave into the moment. Feeling around inside the bed, she was able to find Ray's stomach and then she followed the hairs down to his balls, which she played with until she got bored and moved onto his dick, which was already hard.

She removed his hand from inside her and rolled on top of him before he had a minute to think about what was going on. She edged forward so she could sit on his dick. His body juddered as she squeezed his shaft and slowly, slowly lowered herself on top of him. He fit so well inside her, like he was made for her.

Perhaps due to too much booze, perhaps not, but within ten or twenty seconds, Ray had stiffened his body and then Penny felt his dick recede and pop out from inside her. He hadn't held back or anything; just thought only about himself, the bastard.

Penny rolled off him to her side of the bed and turned her back to him. A few seconds later and she heard his deep breathing; he'd fucked her and flaked out, the fucker. She put a hand between her legs and finished herself off. Then fell asleep too, only she didn't snore.

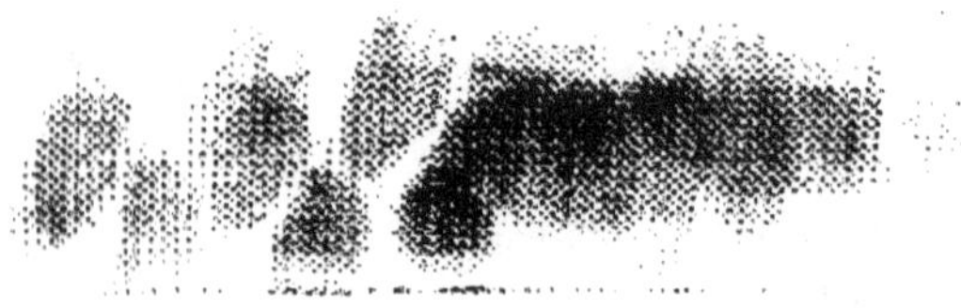

# 23

**OLLIE**

This day was the first time Ollie had a real chance to check out Karen. Up until now, she'd been one of the many people fluttering around Penny but hadn't turned Ollie's head. Somehow today was different.

Maybe, he thought to himself, it was the figure-hugging dress. Previously she'd always come for drinks straight from work and looked quite drab. Today's dress was red and came in close around her tits and carried on clinging to her body until it ended at a throbbingly indecent length way above her knee. If this was the '60s, it would have been called a minidress, he reckoned.

If it wasn't the dress then perhaps Karen's hair had caught his eye, tied up in a bunch to give clear sight of her throat and neck, offering a glimpse of cleavage before the dress stole that image away. And she had great legs, even though they were hidden beneath flesh-coloured stockings. Ollie knew they were stockings and not tights because every so often, he'd spot the clasp of the garter peeping into view because the dress was so short.

Man, she was hot.

Ollie went up to a butler and grabbed two glasses of champagne. Then he walked up to her as she was talking to Penny's parents.

"Excuse me, but I thought you might be thirsty."

"How very gallant, hon'."

"You're more than welcome. Sorry to interrupt."

The last phrase was spoken directly to Penny's mother and father, a fine, upstanding couple who appeared out of their depth at the moment. They did the decent thing and walked away to find Ray's parents; the only other people of their age on the guest list.

Ollie switched on the charm and asked Karen about her job and how she was doing. By the time they had emptied their glasses, Ollie had his arm around Karen's waist as they went on a search for a quiet place to do a line or two.

By the time they emerged from an unused room near the back of the house, adjacent to the billiard room, Ray was under the table and two others were playing on regardless.

Ollie and Karen were too wired to be able to suffer the pace of the billiard table, so they went into a front room to dance. Half an hour later, the buzz from the coke had faded and they realised they'd been dancing in perfect sync all that time.

As if planned by Ollie, a slow track kicked in and most people fled the floor. But Ollie and Karen stayed on. He put his hands on her back and Karen leaned in and placed her fingers on his neck. His lips were right by her ear and he whispered to her while his hands travelled up and down the seam of her dress, gently in time with the music.

Karen leaned in some more and planted a kiss on his cheek. He turned to face her and they kissed on the lips.

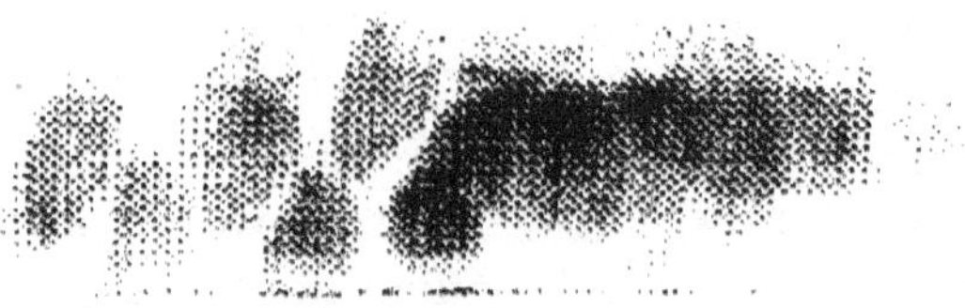

# 24

**KAREN**

After they had danced and kissed for quite some time, Karen suggested they go somewhere more private to carry on the party and Ollie agreed immediately with a squeeze on her arse for good measure. She knew his reputation—from the stories Penny had told her over the years. But she was enjoying herself with him and was feeling horny.

They walked out of the dance room, arms around each other's waists, went back to the hallway and up the main staircase.

"Your place or mine?"

"Whichever, I don't mind. They put us in opposite corners. I think mine is nearer."

"Decision made."

So they shuffled off to Karen's room. She unlocked the door and they walked in. Once she'd closed it behind them, Ollie grabbed her and kissed her again on the lips, while his hands busied themselves undoing her dress. Karen liked his directness; too many Brits spent too much time not getting to the point.

AS SHE THOUGHT those words, Ollie's hands pulled her zip down and one squeezed her arse, while the other one went round the front of her body and headed straight for her crotch. Two fingers massaged between her legs until one of them entered her. Karen gave a sharp intake of breath, even though Ollie's actions were inevitable, there was still that amazing frisson of excitement and pulse of heat she felt wrap around her spine.

Karen started to unbutton Ollie's shirt, but before she could get the job done, he'd pulled his finger out of her with a jerk, causing a pain-pleasure pulse to rip through her crotch. He pulled the dress off her so she was standing in front of him with nothing but her underwear; he was still fully clothed apart from a couple of shirt buttons.

Ollie grabbed her arm by the wrist and took her over to her bed, pushing her over so she ended up lying on the edge of the bed, Ollie standing between her knees. He bent down and placed a hand on her crotch and pushed his first finger back inside her and withdrew again a few seconds later.

"Warm yourself up while I get undressed. You're going to need to be wetter than that if we're going to fuck."

Karen had never been spoken to like that before. So cold, so dismissive of her, so controlling and so assertive. Despite herself and all her upbringing, she found she was aroused by Ollie.

She did as she was ordered, shut her eyes and fingered herself until she was moist. Ollie stood by her again and she felt his leg directly against hers so she knew he'd taken off some clothes. She carried on because she really was enjoying the pulses of pleasure running around her body.

Karen opened her eyes and saw Ollie, naked, just standing and staring at her. He grabbed his dick and moved his hand back and forth along its shaft. Watching him do this made Karen more aroused than before.

OLLIE BENT DOWN and put his hand over hers as she masturbated. Then he held onto her arm with one hand, pulled her fingers out from inside her and swapped his fingers for hers—just for a minute.

"Get your head on the pillows otherwise I'll fall off the bed."

She scurried up the bed until her head reached its target. Ollie got on the bed, kneeling with his hard-on.

"Turn over," he instructed and Karen did as she was bid, face squished against the pillow.

Ollie lay on top of her and poked his dick around her arse until he found her fanny and pushed himself inside. She squealed with the pain of his entry and then moaned as he moved in-and-out, deep inside her one second then hovering near her lips the next. He carried this on for a lifetime and eventually, Karen was breathing so hard, she thought she'd faint. The intensity of the pleasure was getting too much.

"Fucking stop, for fuck's sake!"

At that moment, Ollie went rigid for a spell and Karen could feel him coming, then his dick shrank away.

Ollie got off her and sat astride her, forcing her knees together to accommodate his frame on her thighs. He slapped her hard on the arse and then she felt his torso, warm against her back again. Only this time, she found his hands were burying themselves by her breasts. She pushed herself up like she was doing a sit up so his palms could wrap themselves around her nipples. He squeezed each one real hard making Karen feel pain and pleasure at the same time.

OLLIE PULLED ONE nipple until it hurt but then let go just before Karen complained it was too much. Then he'd start on the other nipple, doing the same thing. Meantime, he'd got a hand back on the first nipple and was readying it for its next assault. They spent minutes like that, Karen alternately experiencing shooting pain one second and intense pleasure the next. By the end, Karen realised she could feel Ollie's dick was hard again.

"Roll over."

Karen dutifully followed Ollie's order and he then grabbed both her arms and pinned her down so she could hardly move. He shifted his hips and then pushed his hard-on into her. Again, Karen hurt when he went inside her. He was rough but there was real pleasure too.

This time they fucked hard and fast. Karen barely had any time to think about how they were doing before Ollie's breathing went loud and deep. His thrusting went into overdrive and she felt him pounding into her body. Then he came and it was all over.

"Move over. I want to sleep."

Although she couldn't believe she complied so readily, Karen watched herself do precisely that. Her body was tingling still with the waves of pleasure but was also tender from the way he'd treated her body with such contempt. Her nipples were sore and her crotch was aching. She had no idea if he'd ripped her, he'd been so callous when they'd fucked the second time. She touched herself and looked at her fingers but there was no blood.

Karen also knew how much she'd enjoyed giving up control; the same control she spent her entire life trying to maintain over everyone else.

Ollie had started snoring. Karen wrapped the covers around herself and waited for most of the tingling sensation to abate before she was able to get to sleep.

# PART ELEVEN

## JUNE 2003

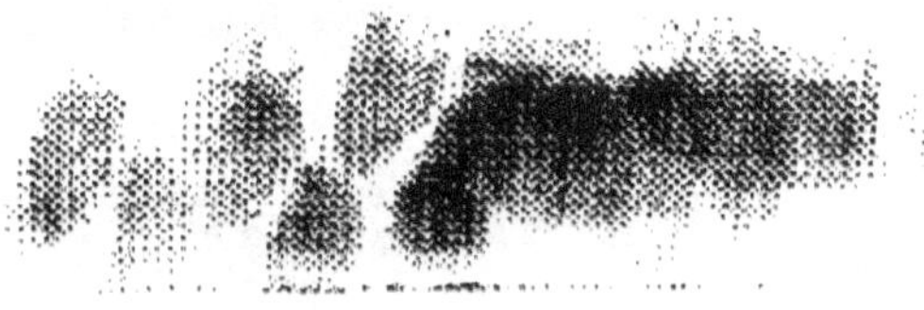

# 25

**RAY**

Ray had spent far too long at Freiberg and was empty. The only pleasure available to him was outside work and he tried to throw himself into the vacuum that was his private life.

Time with Penny had flowed like a constantly dripping tap since they'd got married a year ago. They both threw themselves back into work once the glow of their honeymoon had ebbed from their memories and the intimacy they'd shared a couple of years ago had faded. Sexual and emotional.

Ray decided he'd spent far too long on the European desk at Freiberg and wanted to spread his wings. If he wasn't going to leave —and he'd been headhunted three times in the last eighteen months —then he should figure out a way to rise up the hierarchy.

So he'd tried selling UK equities, but that was just flogging the index to pension funds, which was very dull and then he moved over to the prop desk to take some real risks with the bank's money. This was much more interesting as he found himself dealing in some of the newer instruments like derivatives. At this point, they weren't much more than futures and options. In themselves, these instruments were designed to give companies a way of spreading their risks into the future—like umbrella companies who needed to spend money on making products now in the hope it rains heavily next winter. But Ray and the rest of the desk figured out they could trade them without having to connect the product with the instrument they were derived from, as was traditional.

WHEN HIS HUNCHES proved right, Ray made a killing, especially as he only had to put up the margin at the time of purchase; an amount of money less than the full purchase price of the derivative. The rest got paid later so Ray had more cash in his book to trade further. Naturally, if his predictions went south then the bank lost much more than the original margin; sometimes the loss was bigger than the potential profit offered by the derivative. That was the lottery game being played out by Ray and the rest of the desk.

The good news was that Ray was a fine seer into the future. He was called the Prophet by the other traders on the prop desk and he was called the Profit by his boss. Both were right.

While this success was piling up around Ray's feet, he knew Penny was forging ahead with her US clients and expected to be made partner very soon. One more big-ticket deal under her belt and she reckoned that would be enough to swing it at the end of year partners' meeting. He knew she'd do it. Penny worked like a dog; she spent weeks at a time on the East Coast and when she was in the country, she stayed in the office even later than he did. No one could accuse her of not putting the time in.

All the years they'd been living together, they'd been financially prudent; squirrelling away bonuses and a percentage of their basic into savings to build up a sizeable deposit for their next place. The original plan had been to buy somewhere together and to still hang on to both apartments. Ever the trader, Ray believed real estate values in the Wharf had plateaued so they should cash in at least one of the flats and use the substantial equity to seed a house in the suburbs.

RAY AND PENNY had talked about leaving Canary Wharf for months. Penny, more than Ray, missed the sense of community of her home town and wanted to rekindle that vibe. Ray didn't see the point because she spent more time in New York and Boston than she did in the Wharf, but he did have a nostalgic glow for the kind of area he'd lived in as a child. The irony was Ray had vowed never to return to Hertfordshire the day he moved into his apartment.

"Never go back. Never."

This had been his mantra and, now they were thinking of areas to move to, the idea of finding himself in Stanmore or Edgware didn't sound that appalling. Not today, at any rate.

Penny wasn't too pleased to be heading so close to her in-laws, but Ray knew they wouldn't be rushing round the corner every weekend for Sunday lunch. He wasn't nearly close enough to any member of his family for that to happen anymore. This wasn't a function of physical proximity, but emotional closeness. He'd seen his parents twice since he and Penny had got married—and Penny understood deep down that being near her in-laws wasn't a problem. She would never be good enough for their darling little boy.

Ray agreed with Penny they should keep the other apartment because it was a decent income stream even though its days of significant capital growth were over; 9/11 had seen to that. Also, they had enough equity tied up in his flat to not need to cash in the other one to get an excellent loan-to-value ratio for the mortgage on the house. In fact, it was down to only about thirty per cent. They were laughing; even if they found something ridiculously out of their intended budget, they could still afford it with money to spare.

After Easter, they'd agreed to start the search and, two months later, they were about to exchange on a three-bed house in Edgware. They kept telling each other nothing is agreed until it's agreed, but secretly Penny and Ray were excited. They'd got the place at a bottom dollar rate, mainly because the old woman living there had been booted into a nursing home by her children and they needed to sell the place to pay the nursing fees. And that was the story they came up with even before they started negotiating. Schmucks.

IN THE END, they were able to offer to pay cash for the entire pile and had enough money left over from the proceeds of the apartment to refurb the house into the twenty-first century. The interiors were shabby at best and every room had been decked out in the 1970s and left to rot ever since.

Once the house sale had completed, Ray sent in their builders to gut the place back to the plaster and to start again. They punched into the loft space to make a master bedroom the width and length of the house, albeit with a square cut out for a small en suite. They replaced the kitchen and all its units, then they went to work on reshaping the bedrooms and separating the first-floor bathroom from the toilet. The rest was cosmetic only, apart from ripping out the fireplace to make some smooth lines in the living room. Neither Ray nor Penny liked the old-world charm of open fires with hearths and 1930s tiles. Instead, new double radiators were fitted throughout with underfloor heating in the living and dining rooms because there was a crawl space below the house. Ray was offered the chance to go into it but he declined the opportunity to wedge himself in the three-foot area beneath the floor.

In a highly predictable manner, the work overran by several weeks, but the builders were on a flat fee, so Ray reckoned trade was sparse and they were killing time before their next job.

Eventually, all the works were complete and Ray and Penny were able to stand in the living room on the freshly constructed wooden floors, with light beaming in from both the front and back gardens. The only other major job left was to remove the Anderson shelter from the middle of the back garden, but they didn't see why they should wait until that task was done. They were itching to get in and if they didn't shift by the end of July, they'd have to rent somewhere anyway because Ray's flat was going to complete then. The Anderson shelter could wait.

THEY SAT ON the floor in the living room, leaning against the newly-painted walls. Ray faced the kitchen and Penny faced Ray.

"Can you believe we've finally got this sorted out?"

"Never thought it would happen."

"Really?"

"No, but you know what I mean. It has taken a fuck of a long time."

"Sure has, Ray."

They were silent for a spell, comfortable in the quiet.

"Imagine what this will be like when there are little 'uns scampering about."

"Imagine as much as you want."

"Huh?"

"Unless you're planning on getting a cat, there won't be any pitter-patter of tiny feet. Not for a long time. A very long time."

"I thought... I thought you... you've always talked like you wanted kids."

"Want them? Sure. But not now. I'm not ready. Not ready by a long mile."

Penny shrugged and smiled at him, then she stood up, opened the French doors and went into the garden, leaving Ray sat there like a stuffed gorilla. He wasn't feeling broody, but he had images of him playing with a little boy and a little girl. But those pictures weren't in Penny's head.

He felt cheated by her and a strange feeling appeared at the pit of his stomach, somewhere between dread and foreboding. Ray remained exactly where he was until he could focus more than a few inches in front of his face. He felt as though he'd been slapped by a cold piece of stainless steel and didn't know how to process the information he'd heard.

Out in the garden, Penny was sitting on the massive hump that was the Anderson, left behind from the Second World War. Her face held upwards as she caught the British sun beaming down.

"I'm shocked."

"Shocked?"

"Yes."

"I've never said to you I wanted kids. I'm just saying, right now, I certainly don't want any. Who knows what the future may bring, but at this point in my life, at this point in my career, they'd be a noose around my neck. Around our necks. Who knows what tomorrow may bring?"

PENNY GOT UP and draped her arms around Ray's neck.

"I love you, my little Ray of sunshine."

"And I love you too, Penny Pitstop."

Ray said the words but didn't know if he meant them. They rang hollow in his ears almost before the sound had gone past his lips, leaving him a shell inside. That feeling in the pit of his stomach remained until he fell asleep and he even woke up with it the next day too. By Tuesday it had faded sufficiently for him not to notice it, but the sensation was still there for two or three more weeks.

The sinking feeling finally departed from Ray's mind by the time he hooked up with Ollie again. They met up in the evening and grabbed a bite to eat in the West End at a fine dining establishment on the edge of Mayfair. Penny was off in Boston.

Ray and Ollie jaw-jawed until food was served and then Ollie became quite serious very quickly.

"What desk are you on?"

"Derivatives prop. Why?"

"I have an opportunity I want to share with you, but only if it'll fit within your normal line of work. It's not the sort of deal where we'd want any eyebrows to be raised."

"I see."

Ray's mind raced, attempting to figure out what Ollie was really talking about.

"THERE'S A CLIENT we are working with who's about to issue an initial public offering, an IPO."

"And you want me to buy a tranche?"

"Yeah, would be handy to leverage however much has been pre-sold."

"Not much presumably otherwise we wouldn't be sat so near to Park Lane."

"Don't be like that. We were hooking up anyway."

"I'm messing with you. Get over yourself. Which sector?"

"Consumer. A hotel chain."

"That actually is interesting. How much are you hoping I'll take?"

"This is the thing. If I can pre-sell over fifty per cent of the stock then we get a stonking kicker to our commission. But no one wants the bastard thing."

"Why?"

"Wish I knew, dear boy."

"No skeletons, then?"

"There are always skeletons in the closet, dear boy. It's whether they plan to come out and haunt that concerns me."

"And what are its prospects?"

"This is the sweet part of the tale. You see, within the next month to six weeks they are going to win an enormous contract relating to a new event that's running in Birmingham. The price will rise—and I mean rise.

"You'd just need to buy-and-hold for no more than two months. Hold your nerve for two months tops and then you can make a killing for Freiberg and look like a hero."

"Genuinely sounds too good to be true."

"Well, if you don't believe me, you can always hedge your position."

"True."

"And there'd be personal appreciation from me."

"I don't need your thanks, honestly."

"If you're in, you can have that anyway; it's free and in bountiful supply. No, I meant a more tangible sign of appreciation, dear boy."

"How lovely."

"Half a mil wired to a bank account of your choice."

"Jesus H Christ. That's quite some commission you're earning!"

"You have no idea. Buy-and-hold for a couple of months. Three at the most. Personal bonus mid-year and a tidy profit for your firm. So are you in?"

Ray thought about the money and the opportunity it represented.

"How much is the stake—in dollar terms?"

"About fifty-five million, but I could close on fifty-four if it made a significant difference to your end."

"Well remembered. I have a fifty-five limit on direct equity investments."

"And I can assure you, we don't want too many people looking at this deal."

Ray then thought about the commission he'd make off the profit generated by the deal—even if there was only a fifty per cent hike in the value, he'd be able to hit his third quarter target easy.

"I'm in."

"Good news. I'll text you a chat room we can use on the Caldwell terminal. It'll stay nice and private that way."

"Capiche."

Caldwell was a network of terminals used by the trading community. Their screens looked much the same as all the other screens on Ray's desk but they contained unique pricing information you couldn't get anywhere else. Also, they had a private, secure email system no one could hack into—the perfect place for private chats between guys in different firms.

Ray tucked into his sole and relished the rosemary on his new potatoes. The thought of that money coming in made his heart race a little faster. And he was helping out a mate too. What were friends for, right?

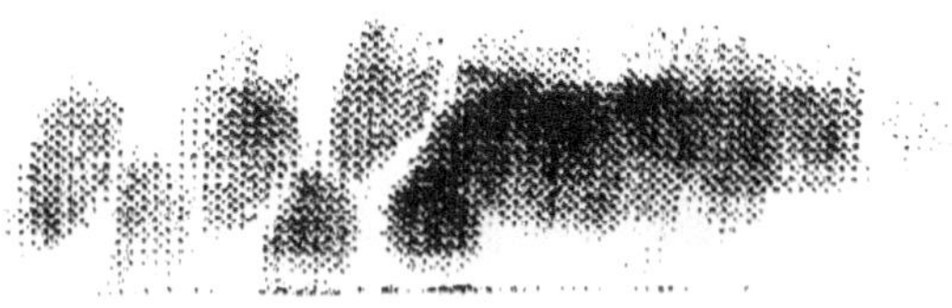

# 26

**PENNY**

The only time Penny seemed to have to think was on a plane heading for the US. Then she had six long hours to kill when nothing but thoughts would play across her mind. This time she was on her way to Logan International to advise a Harvard faculty on its intellectual property rights.

The marriage had only just got off the blocks but she knew it was stagnating. The fact she spent so much time away from home didn't help. But it takes two to tango; Ray owned half of the responsibility too. He had given up trying, not just since the wedding. Ray'd grown complacent almost since they moved in together. Like he didn't believe he needed to try now that he had her.

In Penny's head this was why she was still seeing Mickey. Although there was nothing to him apart from good looks and a big dong, he did offer a level of comfort. Sexual comfort in the main, but there was an implicit emotional connection with the man, so she thought.

Mickey and his sister, Theresa, had been renting out her apartment for two years. For Penny she knew she could trust them to look after the place and they were also good for the rent. And it gave Penny an opportunity to stay in touch with Mickey.

Now she and Ray had moved out to Edgware, there were fewer chances to see him, but Mickey was still part of her life—to some extent anyway.

A FEW DAYS before they left the Wharf, Penny had arranged to see Mickey. She had let herself in and scooted round to make sure Theresa was not around. They'd never got on. Oil and water.

The only sign of Theresa were her smalls hanging in the guest bathroom, draped over a wire extending from one wall to its opposite number. Large black knickers and bras. Functional, not sexy, thought Penny.

Mickey was in bed waiting for her when Penny finally walked into the room. She smiled at him, took off her clothes and slid in beside him. Just as she had done every other time she'd been round these two years.

Penny thought about the half dozen words they shared when she was over there. The man took taciturn to a whole new level.

"You okay?"

"Sure thing. Rub my back"

"Okay."

They'd fool around some and, eventually, Penny would feel his dick poking into her and know it needed to be serviced, one way or another. She'd sit on it, take it from behind, take it up the arse, but take it for sure. And although any individual bit of fucking was no more interesting or exciting than any other, all in all it did add up to something.

What's more, she only ever visited Mickey day time on a 'client visit' on a weekday so Ray had no idea what was going on. A healthy tip for concierge Ricky prevented any loose talk costing anyone's lifestyle. Only, Penny knew, now she was living twenty miles away, her time with Mickey was coming to an end. The worst thing was she couldn't decide if she was happy it would be over or sad he was receding from her life. Was there ever anything more to him than a big dick and some pretty pictures emblazoned across his chest?

THE FUNNY THING was he did represent some comfort to her—and continuity. Penny had met him shortly after she came down to London from far away Manchester. He was her personal trainer at the gym near her work. Mickey asked her out for a drink two sessions into the programme and they'd never looked back.

In a way, he was London to her. Wild, aggressive and temperamental, but with a well-intentioned heart and a zest for life. The more she thought about him, the more she realised she would miss him and their afternoon sessions. Penny couldn't think of a single part of her body where that man hadn't either come all over or come inside. More seed than Gardeners' Question Time. Penny smiled inwardly and sipped her champagne.

She compared the excitement of visiting Mickey with the constant monotonous grind of living with Ray, not that he was a bad man or anything. It was just... it was just they had got into a rut and neither seemed interested in doing anything about it.

Penny knew the bit which annoyed her most about Ray was that he wouldn't confront anything head on. He might plot and scheme—and that appeared to be his professional raisin d'être—but Ray would never come out and just say what he was thinking. And that pissed her off.

Of course, the other way Ray had disappointed her, over the last year, was that their sex had dried up and had reduced itself to once a week on a Saturday night. Their coitus had been reduced to a chore and Penny hated that fact and resented Ray for it. Where was the spark to go with the tingles?

Another sip of champagne and Penny settled into her flat bed and headed off to sleep for a power nap.

PENNY AND RAY were surrounded by boxes and furniture, most of which was in the right room. They had closed the door on the removal men about half an hour ago and had spent the intervening time walking around the vast expanse of their empire. The apartment felt so pokey compared to all the rooms here, even though they'd been perfectly happy for all those years.

Despite the need to at least get the bedroom organised before tonight, Penny found the key to the French windows and opened up the back door instead.

The freshness of a gust of wind slapped her in the face, but she had no idea where it came from because the afternoon was quite warm and almost balmy. She felt the presence of Ray standing behind her.

Penny stepped onto the grass, hands in the pockets of her jeans, and climbed up the slope to see what she was going to see. Their house was at the end of the row, so on one side was their hedge with the road the other side. The left side, looking from the house, were their new neighbours. Even though she was standing on top of the Anderson shelter, Penny could only just see over the hedge to try to spy on them. She thought that was a good thing as it meant they would have even more difficulty seeing her and Ray—unless they also had an Anderson slap in the middle of their garden.

"Hello there!"

A DISEMBODIED VOICE called out at Penny. Her vantage point offered no hint from where in the next-door garden the voice emanated.

"Hi there! Shall we both pop round to the front?"

"Sure thing!"

Penny scuttled down from the hillock and Ray followed her along the side return, through the gate and out to the front drive. A couple was standing there.

There was a guy stood with his arm dangling around the neck of a woman, presumably the person who'd been shouting over the hedge.

"Hi, I'm Claudia and this is Jacob."

"Hi, we're Penny and Ray."

Everyone smiled at each other. Penny reckoned the couple were in their twenties, around their own age. He was probably a year or two older, but no more. Jacob appeared around six foot with short black hair, not fat but chunky for sure. He had on a pair of baggy jeans and an Oasis T-shirt. Claudia was five foot five at best with long black hair and blue eyes, and wore a pair of dungarees and a plain white T-shirt underneath.

"How are you doing?"

"Just fine thanks."

"Are you settling in okay?"

"We only arrived this morning."

"Yeah, we saw the removal van."

"How long have you guys been here?"

"Oh, we moved in only a year or two ago. After we got married, right, babe?"

Jacob nodded. He'd contributed about as much as Ray to the conversation so far. The men sidled off towards the garage, leaving Penny alone with Claudia.

"DO YOU KNOW any of the others round here?"

"Not really. Most people keep themselves to themselves. For some it's their age, you know."

"Yeah, I guess that'll make a difference."

"But don't worry, we're not one of those couples."

Penny looked askance at Claudia, standing there in her denim dungarees and cropped T-shirt. What kind of couple did she think we were, Penny wondered.

"The sort who won't leave you alone!" Claudia laughed nervously, but not as nervously as Penny, who was becoming less convinced as the seconds passed.

She glanced over and saw Ray and Jacob were hitting it off, laughing together over their man talk. Penny wished her conversation was going as well as his. This was painful and it wasn't because the woman was unpleasant or tedious. Penny was picking up some kind of negative vibe, she couldn't put her finger on. Then it hit her. There was something not right about Claudia; she dressed like a girl, not like a woman. That was off-putting. Deeply off-putting.

Having found what was missing, Penny was able to relax herself into the conversation more easily and she picked up tips about the local shops and how parking on the street worked out and the days for the bin collection. The sort of useful information which was dull but vital.

After five more minutes, Penny remembered what she'd known all along; there were ten tons of crap to deal with inside the house and they were back to work on Monday.

"Well, nice to meet you. Once we're settled in, you must come round for drinks."

"That'd be lovely. Just let me know when, okay?"

"Sure will... Ray!"

He turned his head and nodded, the tone of Penny's voice had been sufficient for Ray to understand the meaning in her call to him.

They said their goodbyes and Penny and Ray returned to their back garden, closing the side gate behind them.

"They seemed nice."

"Yeah, but..." and Penny leaned into Ray so she wouldn't need to raise her voice above a whisper. "...she's a bit young, don't you think?"

"Young? Nah. They were at uni together. They are no more than two years apart."

"Really? I thought it was more."

"No way. Definitely."

Penny and Ray sloped back inside, went to the bedroom and unpacked all its boxes and those for their en suite bathroom. Then in the second half of the afternoon, they blitzed the kitchen and the living room. They'd be able to function for a week until they got a chance to do more unpacking. Penny knew she'd be leaving most of the rest of the work to Ray, because she was off to the East Coast again on Wednesday and had a wraparound weekend stay because she was in New York this week and in Boston the first half of the week after. Busy times.

# Part Twelve
# April 2004

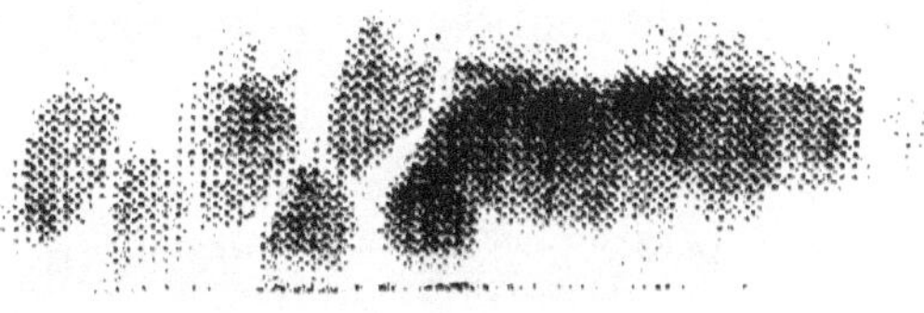

# 27

**RAY**

Time on the prop desk had been good to Ray, but he was beginning to feel like an old man and he was only in his mid-twenties. Truth was Ray had seen many people rise up the ranks, who had started after him.

Ray understood why some of the old Killogg Spreckley crew were overlooked because they were from the wrong side of the tracks, so to speak. But Ray had his North London heritage to fall back on, and even that was doing him precisely no good whatsoever.

When the new management arrived shortly after the name change, Ray would have put money down that old Bill Carson would have been for the chop, but somehow, he had evaded all the bloodletting on the floor. He remained head of trading even though there was an American poised to take over from him. Bill must have some amazingly damaging photos, thought Ray.

The reality was Bill had a long history of delivering revenue and had been given a simple ultimatum the day the new gang arrived in town; deliver the numbers or pack up your things and go. The first time quarterly profit lowers is the first quarter you'll be walking the street. No secret photos, merely the appropriate motivation for a guy who was in his early thirties and was earning off the backs of those around him. The job of head of sales involves getting a team to sell hard while grabbing a share of their commission.

Ray began to wonder what he'd need to do to take over from Bill. The man was getting old and Ray had a sense Bill's time was about to come to an end.

SALES HAD BEEN down last quarter and that meant knives were being sharpened and a cardboard box was going to be allocated for his personal effects. And if Bill did make the walk of shame across the floor, what chance would Ray have of taking over from him?

In the natural order of things, an American would come in, probably someone from head office. One of those New Yorkers who wore blue shirts with white collars and cuffs. And a red tie. Ray had seen them a thousand times on the streets, pouring out of the other US firms in the City. Drones, the lot of them. Teetotal, fun hating, desiccated shells.

The only area Ray hadn't covered yet was the bond desk. Those guys were a law unto themselves. Bond trading was still all done by voice; a deal was struck through a series of discreet phone conversations. There was no electronic ticker firing out the current value of the assets being discussed, which meant for corporate bonds not traded often—the illiquids—you could charge the institution whatever the hell you wanted. They had no idea what it was worth or the risk of the asset.

Ray understood the biggest issue with bonds was the lack of transparency around price and how institutional investors—the pension funds in the main—got screwed every day. He decided this was where he needed to plant his feet. Either he positioned himself well for head of trading by demonstrating all round success or he would at least increase the size of his network by hooking up with the credit desks where the bond traders lived.

THE DAY HE moved onto the credit desk, he got a call from Ollie with another IPO opportunity, which as ever he grabbed with both hands. They were a lucrative sideline which had netted him a cool two million gross since they'd started their little arrangement.

Another advantage of moving over to the credit desk was that the Caldwell was standard fare for bond trading and was the primary source of bond data, whereas Ray's involvement with futures and options had been his only justification of demanding one when he was trading equities.

To celebrate another successful public offering, Ollie and Ray had picked an appropriate restaurant to their taste. This time it was Ray's turn to pay and he'd selected a gourmet French number in the heart of the West End, round the back of Bond Street.

After cocktails at the bar—a couple of vodka martinis, straight up with a slice—they sat down to eat and talk. Old friends catching up on the latest gossip with each other.

"Still unhappy at Freiberg?"

"Yes, 'fraid so."

"If you're that out of sorts with the place, I don't understand why you don't up sticks and go, dear boy."

"It's complicated. I've told you before."

"You tell me it's complicated, but you hand in a letter of resignation at five to nine and you'll be out the door before nine. You know that and I know that. What's so complicated about it?"

"It's not the leaving. It's where I go after that."

"Do you need to go anywhere?"

"Huh?"

"You've been squirrelling away a pile of cash these last few years. Haven't you got enough stashed to not work?"

"That'd be even worse. What the fuck would I do with my days?"

"High class hookers and an unfeasibly large pile of the white stuff would be where I'd start in your position, old fellow."

"Seriously."

"I am being serious. That Penny is never around. You deserve to have some fun and a whore-and-coke combo would do you the world of good."

"Nothing against the coke and nothing against a hooker. But I don't think both are for me."

"Shame. I was hoping to persuade you to join me after our meal at a little place I know that offers both in a very discreet environment."

"Not for me, thanks. I'm a married man. Unlike you."

"Karen and I will tie the knot soon enough. You can be sure of that, but we've an understanding and I for one believe in taking advantage of it as much as I am able.

"Don't get me wrong. Karen is a lovely girl, lovely. She is sexy, funny and has a brain on her. But keeping to one food type makes for a bad diet. My appetites require a varied selection of pussy."

"Nicely put, you douche."

THEY LAUGHED BECAUSE Ollie was sufficiently self-aware to understand what he said made him the unacceptable face of misogyny. Only, he didn't give a fuck; with the amount of money he earned, he could have anyone or anything he wanted. And he frequently did.

Ray wished he had half the chutzpah of his closest friend—and half his connections too. Ollie might have made a mint in the City, but he had got his start in life thanks to Daddy Warbucks.

And Ray's parents were a barber and a secretary. They had worked their knuckles to the bone to put food on the table and to enable Ray to get to university, but they had none of the advantages Ollie had received. Ray always wondered whether his friend had any real idea what life was like for ordinary people living away from the City or the shires. He doubted Ollie had a clue, but the man had an energy about him that had seen them both through college and onto their early years in the City. Ollie in his dad's investment bank and Ray in the brokerage house.

What Ray really wanted to do was to feel less guilty, because he had earned more money in his first years of work than both his parents had made in their lifetimes. He knew whatever desk he sat in at Freiberg, he'd still feel the same way. The problem wasn't with Freiberg Securities but within himself. He needed to leave brokerage and do something to help people like his mum and dad.

From Ray's perspective that meant working in or near a pension fund and, given his contact book, it probably meant investment management. Those guys looked after billions of pension fund holders' money, aiming to increase the size of their portfolios.

Ollie and Ray finished off their meal with a cognac for Ray and a single malt for Ollie. Conversation veered into much safer territory and when they were getting ready to leave, Ollie double-checked whether Ray was going to join him at his Soho club.

"As it's that kind of club, I'll give it a miss, thanks all the same."

"Your loss, dear boy. Within half an hour, I'll have my dick dipped in finely cut cocaine and a pussy on the end of it."

"There's an image that'll haunt me no matter how hard I try to vanquish it from my mind. Thanks for that."

"You're welcome, dear boy."

OLLIE GRABBED THE first cab and hightailed it to his upmarket whorehouse, leaving Ray to wait for another one to arrive and take him back to the comforts of Edgware.

As the vehicle sliced its way through the night-time traffic, Ray stopped taking in the blur of lights passing him by and focused instead on finding something concrete to do to change his world.

Of course, displacement activity was at the front of his mind so he vowed to himself he'd attack the mound in the garden; the Anderson shelter.

Ray decided to prise the door open and clear as much of the interior as he could in one weekend. With Penny still away, he knew he'd either do something constructive or veg in front of the telly until it was time to go back into the Freiberg building.

He woke up early Saturday morning, put on his glad rags and found a pair of heavy-duty gloves in the shed at the bottom of the garden. He also spotted a jemmy on the floor under some makeshift wooden shelving and knew he'd be needing that along with an oil can.

Ray traipsed over to the small sloping path which led to the entrance to the shelter. Grass, ivy and moss had taken over the frontage, but a couple of minutes slashing with the jemmy freed up enough door for Ray to be able to attack its hinges with oil in the hope this would loosen them up a bit. When they'd bought the house, they were told there was no key to the shelter door, so Ray didn't bother looking for one. Grabbing the jemmy in both hands, he plunged the sharp, curved end into the crack between the door and the jamb, just above the lock.

HE HEAVED AT the metal lever with all his body weight, pushing and pulling until he felt some movement in the jemmy. And again with the pushing and the pulling and he saw the door shift ever so slightly.

Ray pushed on the jemmy and the door flung towards him, the jemmy lost its hold and he lost his balance as the lever flew out of his hands.

"Holy fuck!"

He sat on the slope to regain his breath and to take stock of what had been achieved. Then he tried to peer inside without actually getting up from his rest position.

"Torch."

He got up, went inside and grabbed a torch from the understairs cupboard. Back outside, he switched it on and stood at the entrance to have a proper look inside.

An Anderson shelter was fundamentally a small metal cage designed to fit a family during German air raids. It was never going to be a panic room from the movies or a basement dwelling. There were a host of insects scuttling around the floor—it was buried under soil in a garden after all—and some plant life had eked itself an existence near the entrance.

Ray walked round to the nearest shop and bought some bleach, a scrubbing brush and some bin bags. By lunchtime, he'd managed to remove the stench of damp foliage and had disinfected the interior walls and metal girders so he felt he could bring himself to hang out inside it.

Off to a DIY store to buy a lounge chair and some hanging battery-powered torches. Ray also grabbed a small flat pack bookshelf and a lock to put on the door. While he had no idea what he would use his man cave for, he knew it was ready and waiting for him when he did find a purpose for it. Job done.

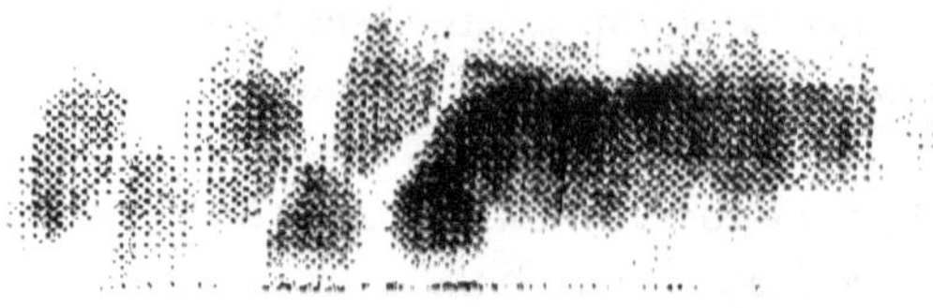

# 28

**KAREN AND OLLIE**

That Sunday, Karen and Ollie were sprawled on their bed, naked, reading the papers with breakfast crumbs on their duvet and plates and cups lying on the bedside cabinets.

Their time since Ray and Penny's wedding night had been spent in a carefully choreographed coitus. Neither of them had been prepared to commit to anything other than casual sex for the first six months. An occasional text would be enough to get one to pop round to the other for some carnal fun; almost always Karen would be submissive and Ollie would be dom. They both preferred it that way and neither was offended if the other was busy and didn't reply. Friends with benefits was the phrase doing the rounds, which described their situation to a T.

Later on, they found themselves spending whole nights together and, within a few weeks, Karen would pop round to Ollie's City crash pad and see him for a week at a time. Then their time together encroached into the weekends and, for the last two or three months, she had moved in, more or less, although she had kept her apartment in Notting Hill as a defence mechanism because she knew from speaking with Penny that Ollie had a wandering dick. He was a party animal and would go anywhere or fuck anyone if he sniffed a thrill along the way. Karen accepted that part of him, which abhorred her so, because she recognised her own behaviour in his. They both liked to party hard, for sure. Ollie was more overt and unashamed about it than Karen.

However, Karen had noticed they were acting more as a couple since she was full-time in his company. He would invite her to join him in his escapades around London and the Home Counties—and she enjoyed being there with him as they hung out with the extreme characters, who Ollie described as friends but she knew were mere acquaintances.

KAREN DROPPED HER newspaper on the floor and turned towards him to stroke his chest. He grunted and carried on reading his tabloid; a guilty Sunday pleasure in which Ollie would find the most pornographic red top a couple of quid could buy and have it delivered with the rest of the papers. Karen noticed he'd only started getting it once she'd been a regular fixture in his Sunday bedroom, so she understood it was one of his childish provocations.

She went under the covers and sidled down until his dick was in her mouth and there was spunk pulsing into the back of her throat. As she moved up his body, she made sure she ended with her legs around his and eventually she was sat on his groin and had thrown his paper on the floor too.

"I've had an idea."

"What's that then, dear girl?"

Ollie leaned forward and licked her nipples.

"Wait a minute. Let me tell you my idea first."

"Okay. Hit me."

"We both know we have issues of commitment, right? Trust is a problem for the two of us."

Ollie nodded and let his hands rest on her thighs, slowly stroking her inner legs. Karen put her hands on his so he could focus.

"And despite that, we've had some real good times together these last few weeks."

Another nod, pensive, waiting for a punchline.

"So why don't we cut the crap and go to the logical conclusion of all this without the bullshit that normally goes with it."

"Uh-huh?"

"Why don't we get married? We'll both get security from the other but we don't have to do anything more than we do right now. And, besides, it'll get my parents off my back and your parents off yours, you know?"

"And what about..."

"Ask no questions and tell no lies. That's all I ask of you and expect back from you."

"Are you sure about that?"

"What goes on in Vegas stays in Vegas."

"I'd hate to stop fucking you."

"Straight back at ya, buddy. So will you marry me?"

Karen jiggled her arse so she could feel Ollie's dick rubbing against her pubes.

"Yes I will."

She carried on her jiggling until Ollie was hard again and then they fucked the rest of the morning away.

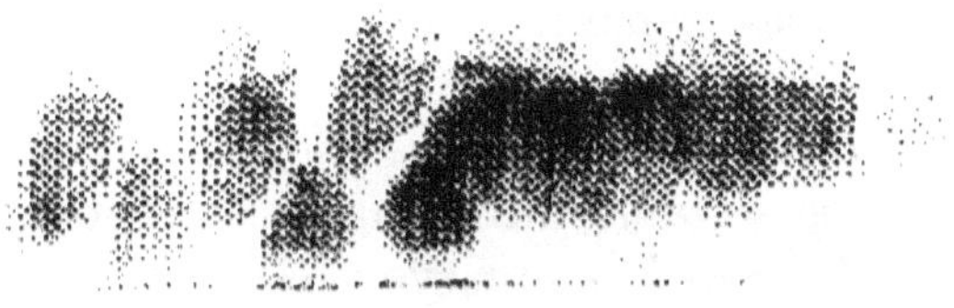

# 29

PENNY

They sat in the meeting room and Penny poured two cups of coffee, one for herself and one for Nina. Having put both on the table, along with the milk jug, Penny sat down opposite Nina and the performance review began, but only after Nina had poured a dash of half-and-half into her cup.

"How's the year been for you?"

"Excellent. My billable hours are up on last year, I've added three hefty clients to the roster and my new client pipeline has over a million in forecast new revenue."

Nina smiled and Penny sat back in her chair. The opening to their negotiations—or discussions as Nina preferred to call them—went well. She'd put her positive cards on the table and not carped about the ridiculously long hours and zero support from her boss as she'd hammered together a number of acquisitions, running point on both sides of the Atlantic. Today was the day for payback.

"You certainly have done very well and the partners are pleased with your progress. Of course, in the post 9/11 environment..."

Penny stopped listening. The bullshit was about to begin and she didn't really have the patience to listen to it. While the country had suffered an economic downturn in the wake of the World Trade Center attacks, Penny knew multinational corporates had bounced back early, fast and securely. Given that was their target market, she knew the rest of Nina's speech was wallpaper with no content.

"...but that doesn't mean your contribution isn't going to be rewarded."

"Sorry, Nina. Let me get this straight. I've delivered year-on-year new revenue rises, while increasing billable hours from existing clients. When I joined this firm, you told me you operated on the basis of a meritocracy and not on the basis of tenure. From what I see, I have outperformed every associate partner in the firm and it sounds like you're about to give me another kiss off about not being ready to make me a partner."

Nina smiled a much warmer smile than before; this time she meant it.

"Darling, hold onto your hat. I haven't finished yet."

Penny stared at her with a fierce expression. She was tired of all these excuses and tired of Nina treating her like a second-class citizen, even though she had so much time for her as a person.

"I was going to say there is no space at the half-year to increase the number of partners, but there will be a vacancy arising at the end of the year. My intention is to recommend you join us as an equity partner."

PENNY'S EYES WIDENED with the implications of Nina's words. A partner was a construct to allow people to rise up the hierarchy of a law firm and separate them from the associates, but Penny knew it was really just a job title. An equity partner went way beyond that; she'd have a stake in the business and would share the profits of their enterprise along with Nina and the other equity partners.

"Thank you. Thank you very much."

"Darling, you deserve it. Now onto far more weighty matters."

"Go on. What's up?"

"Here I am in the UK for three weeks and I have no one to play with in the evenings. A girl's going to get bored all by herself and, as much as I love spending time with you, you're not what I'm seeking as a bedtime companion. No offence, darling."

"Absolutely none taken."

"So, do you know of someone you could connect me with who could plug my lonely gap at night?"

Penny thought for about half a second and then Mickey popped into her head. She hadn't had him inside her for months so there was, as lawyers are prone to say, no conflict of interest.

"Bear with me one minute."

Penny took her mobile off the table, turned it face up and dialled Mickey and hoped he'd take her call. They hadn't parted on bad terms but, on the other hand, she had made no attempt to speak with him from the day they fucked last to today.

"Mickey, how's you?... No, I'm afraid I can't, but I've got a friend over from the States for a couple of weeks who'd love to meet you. I've told her all about you and she's desperate to hook up for a drink and God knows what else..."

That night, Penny arrived home and sprang up the stairs into their bedroom. She unravelled her bun and brushed through her hair. It was real long by now. Dead straight and when she let it dangle at the front, the ends of the strands went below the base of her breasts. She flicked it all back and half-turned in front of the mirror to see it nearly reach the waist of her skirt.

She changed out of her suit and bustled downstairs. Only then did she realise Ray had yet to come home. She grabbed a ready meal and shoved it in the microwave. With the steam rising, she gave it a stir and gulped the rice and curry down in a matter of minutes. By the time her fork was scraping the bottom of the bowl, Penny heard the key in the lock and Ray arrived in.

RAY DIDN'T SAY a word, went upstairs and came down again wearing jeans and a shirt. He too grabbed a microwave meal and heated it up. Then he sat down opposite Penny.

"Hi."

"Hi. How was your day?"

"Same old, same old. You?"

"I'm going to be made an equity partner at the end of the year."

"Nice. Well done."

"Is that all you have to say to me; nice?"

"Huh?"

"Equity fucking partner. I'll be earning at least the same amount as you, if not more."

"Look. I've had a long day. I'm tired. I don't have the energy for a long conversation. I didn't know you had such good news. I'm pleased for you, of course I am, but don't give me shit for saying the wrong word."

"You're tired. I'm tired. That's not the point. Are you happy with how things are between us?"

Ray looked at her, gazing blankly back at her question as if it was rhetorical, even though they both knew it was not.

"Don't stare at me like a smacked fish. Say something!"

"Look I care."

"But you don't show it. You don't act like you think anything is wrong. You go to work, you come home and you go to sleep. Occasionally we fuck, but only if I instigate it."

"I do instigate..."

"When? When was the last time you took me upstairs and we fucked? I can't remember when. Last week? Week before then? Last month? When do you think this happened because I damn well know I wasn't in the fucking room."

Silence. Mouth agape, Ray slowly shook his head but had nothing to say.

"Even now when I'm asking you straight questions. You're not talking to me. Fucking say something, Ray!"

Penny's voice was at full shout and she could feel she was getting hoarse.

"Fuck this."

She stormed upstairs and got into bed. A few minutes later, she heard Ray walk up the stairs and enter the bedroom. Penny rolled over to turn her back on him. She felt him get into bed but he did not touch her. She shut her eyes and tried to control her breathing. She was so mad with him. Eventually, he switched off his light and the bedroom was plunged into darkness.

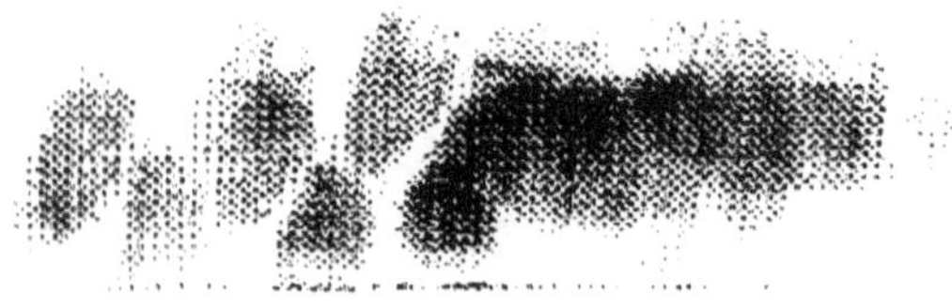

# 30

WHEN KAREN AND Ollie announced they were getting married, both Penny and Ray were surprised. Penny knew they were more or less living together in Ollie's cavernous house in Hampstead. But she felt they had only just started to share living space and now they were going to get hitched.

To celebrate the engagement, Ollie hosted one of his infamous parties—this time at his parent's pile in Buckinghamshire. They would have complete privacy and Karen had given Penny a taste of the kind of party they were planning. It would be like none of Ollie's previous escapades, where the aim was to have as many people as he could physically fit inside the venue consume as much booze and drugs as possible. Instead, Karen and Ollie had handpicked a select few of their closest friends and no one else.

Penny and Ray arrived on Saturday afternoon, went into their room and hung out on a side patio until the others arrived. Yes, there was champagne and the odd line but they both knew this was not the aim of the game.

The first couple to arrive were Elaine and Phil, Karen's friends they hadn't seen since the Millennium. Then Toby and Helena. He was someone Ollie had known since childhood, whereas Penny knew Ray and Ollie had met at uni at some point.

Finally, Hugo and Katarine appeared about an hour later than everyone else. Katarine had been at Manchester with Ollie and Ray and, according to Ray, she and Ollie had had a thing going but only for a few weeks and it never got serious. But then, until this engagement, Penny didn't think anything was serious for Ollie. He was a man who lolloped through life, bumping into people along the way and paying for the damage he caused with a roll of fifty-pound notes.

ANOTHER CONTRAST WITH previous parties was that they had all been told to dress casual rather than formally so no ball gowns and dinner jackets. Ray was wearing a smart pair of chinos, matching shirt and a designer jacket in a contrasting colour. Penny had chosen a black halter-neck knitted top and a pair of black slacks. She planned on changing for dinner.

Once they'd eaten—and having spoken to the other women, they'd all decided to don skirts rather than trousers for the evening—Karen and Ollie ushered them into his parents' library. The room had been emptied of chairs and the only table was parked against one of the walls. Instead, there were bean bags, blankets and cushions festooned across the floor.

Penny rued her choice of skirt but was thankful at least it was pleated so she could sit sideways and still be comfortable. Katarine and Elaine were in pencil skirts, which meant they needed help just to sit down.

Karen closed the doors of the library and explained their first game, while Ollie fussed around the rest of the house.

"We are going to play hide and seek."

Much muttering and smiles all round.

"But there are a few twists to the rules. First, Ollie is blacking out the entire house. The only light is going to be on in this room. Second, the girls will go and hide and the boys must come and find us. Once you are found, you should make your way back here to the library. And, finally, when you come back, the boys must be carrying one item of clothing they've taken off the girls."

After general chatting and drunk giggling, Penny and the other women took themselves off to hide in the house.

THE PLACE WAS really dark with no lights and curtains and blinds covering all the windows. Ollie had done a good job of forcing everyone to find their way by touch.

Penny stayed on the ground floor and made her way down one of the corridors until she found a door handle, opened it and saw shelving with towels lined up in neat rows. An airing cupboard. She popped inside but left the door ajar because she didn't want to get locked in and she also wanted to give Ray half a chance of finding her. Penny reckoned the fun in this game wasn't being found but what happened afterwards.

Time slowed to a crawl and then she heard a muffled shout from all of the men in unison.

"Ready or not, here we come."

She must have been hiding for no more than a minute or two, but it had felt like forever. Penny leaned against the shelving for a while and once, maybe twice, thought she heard someone rustle past but no one opened the door. She began to wonder if she'd hidden herself too well when the hinges creaked and a silhouette appeared and joined her with the towels and other laundry. But Penny couldn't see who it was and he hadn't said a word.

The guy came towards her, bent down and kissed her on the neck. At the same time, she felt a hand on her skirt and the fingers grabbed at her crotch roughly. Penny knew immediately who it was and grabbed Ollie's hand off her and pushed him away.

"Don't get fresh with me, Ollie."

"Apologies, dear girl. It is so very dark, isn't it?"

He leaned in for another kiss but hit his head on one of the shelves.

"Bugger."

Rubbing his head to diminish the pain, Ollie stumbled out of the cupboard and bounced his way down the corridor and away.

WHAT FELT LIKE five or ten minutes later and there was another visitor to Penny's cupboard. This time, she recognised the cologne; she knew it was Ray, who whispered;

"Hey, Penny Pitstop."

They groped and kissed each other. Ray's hand up the back of her halter-neck until she felt the snap of her bra relaxing around her breasts. At the same time, Ray's other hand was round her bum over her skirt. Then it was under the skirt over her knickers. Next, he was squeezing her cheeks without any material getting in the way.

Finally, Ray stopped for a minute and pulled off her top, licking her nipples through her bra, which he then removed so she felt his tongue circling her areola. The tingles along her spine kicked in and became more intense when his hand came back under her knickers and his fingers went inside her.

They carried on like this for an unbelievably long time, but eventually Penny had to stop Ray and get him to remove his fingers; she couldn't be sure she'd be able to breathe if he kept going.

"Jesus, Ray. You nearly fucked me to death."

She took his hand by the wrist and manoeuvred his fingers into her mouth so she could taste herself through him. Ray helped her put her top back on and they strolled back to the library, her arm around his waist and his arm over her shoulder.

All they had to do was to follow the light and, when they arrived, Penny saw the only couple missing was Karen and Ollie. In the middle of the floor were three pairs of knickers, on top of which Ray threw her bra sheepishly.

Penny looked at Ray, not understanding why he'd not wanted to grab her thong given how intimate he'd just been with her. Ray returned her glance and his cheeks reddened slightly. Just then, Ollie and Karen entered and Ollie twirled a garment around his finger making it impossible to tell what it was he'd taken off Karen. Then, with an inevitable flourish, the item flew off his finger and landed on the pile on the floor. Karen's red bikini briefs had entered the room.

"Fuck it!" said Penny and she stood up and hitched up her skirt and pulled down her pants, knowing full well that everyone had seen her fanny in all its manicured glory. She chucked the blue lace onto the pile, turned to face Ray and lifted her skirt so his head was captured underneath it. She parted her legs slightly and he obliged by licking her gently, sending bolts of tingles all over her body.

THE FOLLOWING MORNING Penny and Ray lay in bed completely exhausted. Even by Penny's standards, they had fucked a huge amount last night. The sheets were on the floor and she was sitting in between his legs using him as an easy chair, while his hands rested on her thighs—a finger or two occasionally stroking near her crotch more out of habit than with intent.

Penny thought back over the previous night and one thing niggled her; that bra.

"Last night, why didn't you take my knickers like everyone else?"

"Dunno," Ray said after a while. "Just didn't feel right. I was a bit embarrassed and I didn't want you to be the only one..."

"Prick," she retorted.

# Part Thirteen
# November 2004

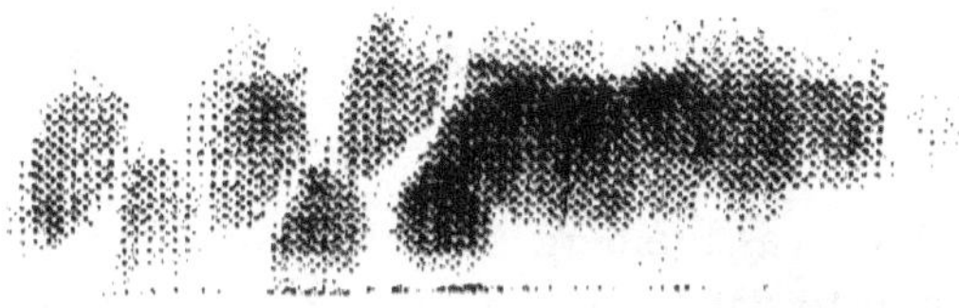

# 31

**RAY**

On the first of the month, Ray walked into his new place of work having spent the last twelve weeks on gardening leave. Of course, he had done no gardening the whole time, but he had sat inside his Anderson man cave a couple of times to relax in the cold, dark empty silence.

Most of the time, he'd been waking up late and watching TV. After a couple of weeks, he joined a local gym, as much to get himself out of the house as any interest in keeping fit. Ray had enjoyed doing nothing but was sure ready to get back on the conveyor belt and run along with all the other hamsters.

The one thing he had spent time doing, while propped up on a sofa, was thinking about Penny and what she'd been saying to him over the last six months, ever since the engagement party. He hadn't been pulling his weight and he had been getting lazy. Too focused on his work and not enough on the woman he loved.

His time on the trading floor had left him tunnel-visioned and he didn't want that to happen again. While Penny had been spending a huge amount of time in the US, he had allowed his anger at her to displace into complacency. That wasn't good enough and he hoped by changing his work environment, he would reawaken his inner Ray, the guy he was when he'd first seen Penny clinging to the taps in her apartment.

HIS NEW NEST was Freiberg Asset Management, which used to be Rieterman Investment Management, a name in the City until it fell prey to the US securities houses who had picked up what was left of the old guard after 9/11. Then it was gobbled up by the Freiberg behemoth and had its identity stripped until it was left a shell of an organisation with a balance sheet containing assets under management and fund managers who earned their money making short-term bets to achieve long-term investments.

So, while Ray was technically working at a different company with Chinese walls between them, he had kept his employee number because payroll was one of the many facilities operated at arms' length by a service company. By now, nobody seemed to care who owned what, just as long as there were no ugly scenes of old aged pensioners losing their savings. The days of Robert Maxwell were officially over, even if most in the City believed he hadn't drowned but was living a pleasant life somewhere on a beach in the Caribbean.

Freiberg AM was in another part of the City near St Paul's. There had been a redevelopment of several ancient buildings a couple of years earlier and after the London Stock Exchange had signalled it was moving from its Threadneedle location, suddenly the area filled up with brokerages, asset management and investment banking businesses.

These were relatively low buildings, no more than five or ten stories, as the architects had all been forced to preserve the skyline around the cathedral itself.

Now he was an investment manager, Ray had his own office and his own PA in the form of a girl called Erin Briggs. He'd never had either before and wasn't too sure what to do with them, but he knew he'd figure things out pretty quickly. This wasn't rocket science.

THE BIGGEST DIFFERENCE between the last job and this one was who owned the money Ray would be playing with—and the scale of the assets. On the trading floor, he would invest a few million at any one time, but here, he would be responsible for billions.

At the get-go, Ray would only get a fraction of one billion but as he grew his client base then his assets under management would end up as big bucks. And there was one other very important difference; now he wasn't playing with his company's money. This was cash earned by people and invested with him and his job was to increase its value over time so they could retire and live off the proceeds.

The weight of this responsibility bore down on him as he walked into the building, but the thought dissolved as he was introduced to people and the locations of important things like the toilets and the kitchenette. Erin would be the person responsible for keeping his coffee mug filled, so Ray paid little attention to many of the details offered him.

The Human Remains girl led Ray to an office with one wall of sheer glass, floor to ceiling. He noticed his name was etched into the glass door. There was a desk, a bunch of screens, a Caldwell terminal and a leather swivel chair, all near the window. There was a filing cabinet against one wall near a modern art painting comprising a red square with a blue dribble pouring itself out of the frame. Nearby was a round metal-and-glass meeting table and four chairs.

Ray sat at his desk and the HR leech left the room, shutting the door behind her. He sat back and switched on his screens and waited for everything to boot up. While this was happening, a short woman with an auburn bob knocked on the door. Ray beckoned her in and Erin introduced herself, wearing a navy skirt suit and a powder blue blouse. She wasn't wafer thin, but she wasn't a fatty either. Ray decided she was well-rounded, but not big boned. Her blue eyes were trained on him as he was checking her out. She wore black high heels in an attempt to counteract her height; she was way shorter than the average woman, heels or no heels.

"Is there anything you need right now?"

"Not really, thanks."

"You've got back-to-back meetings this afternoon starting at two, but before then you're clear. Once you've settled in, you can decide whether you want me to run your diary or if you're going to make appointments yourself."

Ray couldn't see why he wanted to relinquish that much control over his life, but he nodded sanguinely at the prospect of this serious consideration.

"I sure shall. Do you think you could find me a cup of coffee from somewhere?"

"Will do. How do you take it?"

"Black, no sugar."

"That's easy. Back in a min."

Erin strode out of Ray's office allowing him to focus on the undulations of her arse, which he appreciated as her cheeks swayed from side to side under the influence of her high heels. He imagined what she looked like without the skirt on, but all Ray could focus on was the outline of her pants, clearly visible. She didn't go for skimpy; the material seemed to engulf most of that round posterior and almost all of Ray's attention.

HE MET UP with Ollie for lunch a week or so later—a decently sufficient time to get his feet under the desk before he lunched outside. Now he'd moved to the dark side, Ray was much more free to manage his time as he saw fit. While there was still a culture of not being the first out in the evening, the length of your lunch was less a gauge of how close you were to getting fired.

That said, Freiberg was still a US firm with a new world attitude to drink and drugs; not on their premises and not visibly associated with your excesses if you're not in the building. This boiled down to a simple set of rules City folk had grown used to. When you hit a boozy lunch, don't go back to the office and if you're on a corporate jolly then don't get off your tits, especially if you are the host. Apart from that, what goes on in a strip club stays in a strip club.

Ray was sat in the restaurant for ten minutes before Ollie appeared.

"Dear boy!"

"How's it going?"

"Marvellous, just marvellous."

A firm handshake and Ollie sat down opposite Ray and they dispensed with the pleasantries by the time the waiter took their order.

"How are they treating you on Easy Street?"

"The first week's been fine but I know that once all the induction crap is over, they'll make me work for my money."

The starters arrived. They'd both picked out a salad to balance out the impending steaks for their mains.

"Are you still interested in any IPO deals on offer?"

"Sure thing but I won't be able to take the kind of positions I used to. I'm Mr Long-Term now."

"Of course you are, dear boy. Of course."

A wry smile spread across Ollie's face, an expression which refused to leave no matter how much Ray protested and argued.

On the way back to the office, Ray took his time as he fought against the crowd along Cheapside and crossed over New Change to reach the new development past a chunk of the original London Wall.

Every which way he looked, he spotted new buildings replacing old ones long vanished from the skyline. Ray wasn't a Luddite; he was comfortable with glass and concrete and the feel of the new buildings but he still found some comfort in recognising the old ones anyway. Occasionally they contained the memories of a meeting with some joker who made him stuff his pockets with quality catered biscuits.

Of course, the biggest change wasn't in the look of the buildings at all, even though there was constant change in the skyline. As soon as the World Trade Center buildings reduced in height, a pall spread across the financial centres of the West. The relaxed tone dissipated, a change which had been engendered by the American firms, who'd come over to London in the wake of Big Bang and the Thatcher/Reagan liberalisation.

THE US GRIP on the City went much further than pulling back on the amount of drink and drugs taken during the day. Upfront there was an unbridled belief in the supremacy of the American dollar and that wholesale financial markets could generate unbelievable profits. And they did.

Even though there was a crash—a market correction, the locals called it—in 2001, as ever, within eighteen months, equity and bond markets had bounced back. With collective short-term memories shot to hell, the entire City appeared to forget the recession into which it had plunged itself.

When Ray returned to his office, all hell had broken loose. News just in; the Iraqi city of Fallujah was being attacked by US and British forces. As in any industry, uncertainty creates volatility in markets and where there's volatility, there's opportunity. When prices spike up and down, if you can time purchases and sales correctly, there are huge profits to be made in the space of a few minutes. If the uncertainty continues for a day—or even days and weeks—the upside can be astounding. Naturally, the opposite is true; you can lose your shirt several times over.

Now as Ray knew, an investment manager exists to look after his clients' portfolios over the long haul; the vagaries of day-to-day market activity should pass them by as the transient whims of speculators. But Ray also knew he was going to be judged on his quarterly performance and in wholesale financial services, your performance wasn't defined by how nice you were in meetings or whether you were trying your hardest every day for the benefit of the firm. Your performance was the amount of money you made. So when the markets went haywire, Ray knew he needed to take advantage of the volatility, just as he had done when he was trading on the Freiberg equity desk.

You can take the man out of the trading floor but you can't take the trading floor out of the man. As soon as Ray sat at his desk and saw the newswires streaming across his screens, he shouted at Erin for a bucket of coffee and settled in for an afternoon's research, purchase, and sales.

SHORT TERM GAINS were made within an hour when he bought and sold US oil and then he focused his attention on longer term projects for the eventual reconstruction. As in the past, you could bet your house the infrastructure contracts would go to US government approved American companies, so Ray went long on them, knowing that construction and consulting sectors would benefit substantially once the fighting was over. He chose not to delay those purchases because by tomorrow everyone would be buying the stock and as demand rose, so would the price.

Next, he turned his attention to some more canny opportunities, thinking about what he could short. This is the process of selling something you don't own today so you can buy it later at a lower price. What you sell today, you borrow from another firm and you make sure the numbers stack up so you can make a profit out of the whole shenanigans. Sounds crazy, but there are financial contracts, like futures where this is common practice. A fund manager might want to buy certain stock, oil companies say, but would also want to hedge his bets in case the price of oil goes down and not up. In that case, he could short the future price of oil so he'd make some money back out of the opposite of what he actually wanted to have happen. All's fair in love and war.

What Ray was planning was to just short some positions based on an overall belief that some sectors would tank. Air travel was an obvious industry; fewer people travel when there's war going on and profits reduce accordingly.

He carried on picking out all the sectors he could think of which would fall as a result of American and British involvement in the Iraqi war. Erin kept him primed with caffeine and he got her to do some of the background research on sectors and stock; he was lucky to have her as his PA, he discovered. She had a brain on her as well as a fabulous arse and what he thought might be a great pair of tits beneath that dwarfish frame and navy suit.

BEFORE THEY WENT home at ten, Ray offered to buy Erin a drink to say thanks for her effort that day, but she declined. He couldn't tell if she thought he was coming on to her or what, but he did know he was doing it out of politeness and nothing more.

When he arrived at Edgware station, he took a taxi from the tube, because he couldn't be fagged to walk the fifteen minutes to their house. Too tired.

Penny had already gone upstairs so Ray sat downstairs for a couple of minutes to unwind and then headed up himself. He undressed and hopped into bed; Penny was reading, propped up by a couple of pillows, her breasts hiding under the top of the duvet.

"All okay?"

"Yeah, long day. Fallujah meant we had to deal hard."

"I thought you stopped trading so you wouldn't have to make money out of death and destruction?"

"I'm making money for pensioners now..."

"...out of death and destruction."

"Out of any opportunity that arises to help them have a better retirement."

"Do you really believe that?"

"To be honest, right now, I'm too tired to believe anything."

Penny put her book down and cuddled up with Ray. He felt the smoothness of her back with his hand and, having stroked it up and down several times, he let his hand rest on her bum, squeezing it occasionally as she rested her head on his chest.

Ray relaxed for the first time since lunch, calm in the arms of a woman who loved him, even if she didn't approve of how earned his living. As the tension eased from his body, he noticed the sensation of his dick nestling in the hairs of Penny's crotch and he felt his penis twitch.

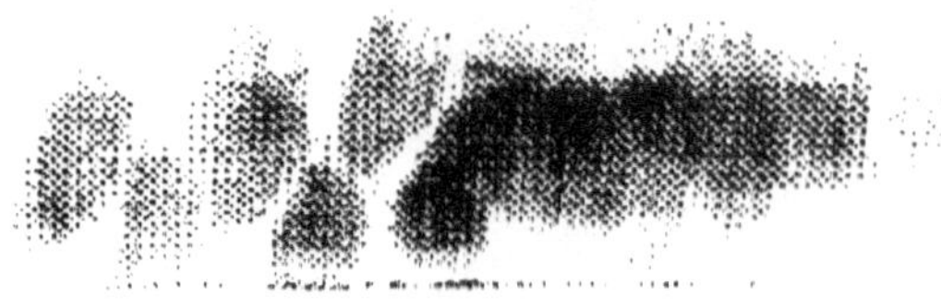

# 32

**PENNY**

The following Saturday, on a rare weekend in London, Penny arranged to hook up with Karen. They hadn't seen each other for absolutely ages, but every week they'd speak and there were innumerable messages a day on their phones. If there had been a chance they'd drift apart, this was terminated as a possibility by the fact Karen was now married to Ollie.

As she sat in their chi-chi café off Bond Street, Penny reminisced over the engagement party and the games they'd played that night. With reddened cheeks, a smile rippled across her face with the recollections of what they had all got up to in Ollie's parents' mansion.

The wedding in the summer had been low-key and incredibly tame in comparison. To spite both their parents, Karen and Ollie had got married at a registry office with just she and Ray as witnesses. They'd gone for a meal afterwards and had arrived home before midnight. Since then, Penny had spent so many weekends in New York, she'd thought she'd never catch sight of Karen again.

No sooner had a glass of red wine been delivered to her table than Karen appeared in the doorway. Penny waved in her direction to get her attention and Karen waved back, heading towards the table. They hugged and Karen sat down to order her own glass of red.

After some small talk and checking out each other's heels, the serious business of chatting began in earnest.

"SO HOW'S MARRIED life treating you?"

"Okay, I guess. I mean, it's only been a couple of months and we've been living together for ages, so it's not like there was this big leap when we jumped the broom."

"But you're happy, aren't you?"

"Sure..."

"But?"

"No but, hon'. It's just we are leading quite separate lives."

"Tell me about it."

"Eh?"

"Never mind. Go on."

"Ollie has all sorts of... passions. And I only satisfy some of them. He goes off some mornings and I don't see him for days."

"Jeez. What does he get up to?"

"Coke binges sometimes and he'll be holed up in some private club of his. Or fetish whoring his way through Mayfair in another club he goes to. And sometimes, he goes to a casino and plays roulette until he runs out of cash."

"I'm stunned."

"He's a wild man, for sure. And I've known that about him from the moment we got together."

"At our wedding."

"Yes, at your wedding."

"From what you were saying, you were fucking before I got a chance to that night."

Karen smiled and chose not to answer. That was her first taste of dominant Ollie and her first realisation she was a submissive Karen. Now they had a room dedicated to that part of their sexual relationship in the house, she explained to Penny.

"You kinky vixen. And I suppose you do threesomes too."

Penny giggled, even more so when she saw Karen's expression. She held her hand to show she was only joking and they agreed Ollie was more than a handful for any one woman to handle.

The question for Karen was whether she could tolerate his behaviour or whether she should jack it in before she found herself the wrong side of forty with a pile of regrets in her rear-view mirror.

KAREN DIDN'T KNOW. She was far from happy with Ollie when he wasn't with her but in ecstasy when he was. Penny could see Karen was conflicted, because the sadomasochism clearly was her thing.

"You might not like this suggestion, but... why don't you tell Ollie you'd like to join him in a club visit. That way, at least you'll find out what goes on instead of leaving it to the darkest reaches of your imagination."

"Hadn't thought of that. He sets these things up so there's not even a choice about my going along."

"Well, you've nothing to lose and you might enjoy it. Never know."

Karen agreed to think that one through and let Penny know what she decided. Then she made sure she turned the conversational spotlight onto Penny and her life, but Penny was having none of it. The last thing she wanted to do was spend a day talking about taciturn Ray and their non-relationship. The last time they'd really fucked was at the engagement party, after all. That was a lifetime ago —or so it felt.

"And how's work?"

Karen winced.

"You know about the glass ceiling?"

"Yeah."

"I've hit it."

"How so?"

"I made junior partner real quick, hon', but that's as far as I've got. No matter how much money I bring in, no matter what new client comes to the firm because of me, someone else gets made partner instead."

"You've asked the question, right?"

"Sure have, hon'."

"And the answer?"

"Others better qualified... not the right time... the usual bullcrap."

Penny was silent, mulling over Karen's situation.

"If you're sure that's what's happening to you, why don't you leave?"

"Honestly? I would, but I don't have the energy to fix my issues with Ollie and to fix my issues with work. Not at the same time, hon'. Just don't have the mental capacity for all that in one go."

Karen's eyes reddened and Penny squeezed her hand. Karen was close to breaking point and Penny hadn't even had a clue. Some friend she'd been these last few months, wrapped up in her own little world.

She allowed the conversation to twist back to her life but made sure she spent most of the time talking about Nina rather than Ray. Listening to Karen sob her way through her life with Ollie, Penny realised her relationship with Ray might not be in all that bad a shape after all. He might not express how he felt about himself or her as much as she'd like him to, but he didn't go around fucking other people, missing in action on coke benders...

PENNY HAD BEEN away from home for what seemed like forever. She couldn't be certain, but she felt as though she was gaining an American accent. She had noticed some mid-Atlantic intonation creeping into her Mancunian vowels, albeit steeped inside a London drawl, she'd been living down south for so long.

On top of that, Penny'd been feeling guilty about the way she had been treating Ray. The guy had finally moved to a different company after years of her encouragement, or nagging, depending on your perspective. No sooner had he jumped ship than she ran off to the US most of the summer to help close another deal, but a deal big enough to clinch her equity partnership.

She complained when he wasn't speaking to her and then she'd turned her back on him when he could have used some support. Now his gardening leave was over and, despite her best intentions, they hadn't been able to take advantage of his free time for a long, summer break or even a short autumn week away somewhere European.

To make amends, Penny had planned a weekend away to Paris; off on Friday night and back on Sunday in time for work on the Monday morning. All Ray knew was to pack a bag for a couple of nights, bring his passport and to meet her at Waterloo. There was a direct train to Gatwick, which Penny banked on Ray assuming was their destination. In fact, they'd be taking a different train straight to the Gare du Nord and hopping into a taxi to go to the Richelin Hotel.

The plan worked perfectly, and before Ray could figure out what was happening, they were waiting in the business lounge for the announcement that their train was ready to depart. A couple of glasses of champagne, and a light meal later, and they were checking in at the hotel reception.

BY THE TIME they got into their room, it was already past ten, mainly because of the hour's time difference with the UK. They quickly changed out of their travel clothes and slipped into something less casual.

Penny had brought a hardy perennial; a little black dress, which she knew Ray would like. It was virtually a minidress, but she wore dark stockings to hide how obscene it could be if she didn't sit properly. Ray wore his classic shirt and chinos with a jacket. He had several designer items in a number of subdued tones from which he always mixed and matched. Ray was not adventurous with his clothing, but he allowed the occasional splash of colour too.

Downstairs, they sat in a lounge and ordered cocktails. Ray had a vodka martini and Penny chose a cosmo. They sat at one of the tables and watched the upper-class nightlife float by on the way to a jazz club—or whatever Parisians were into nowadays.

For the first time in years, perhaps the first time since they started dating, Penny and Ray held hands and relaxed into each other's gaze. She reminded herself how much she loved him and how poorly she'd treated him this past year or two. A sadness filled her. She didn't deserve Ray.

He stroked her hand, casually moving a forefinger along the crevice between her thumb and fingers.

"Thanks for bringing me here."

"You're welcome. You deserve it."

"We deserve it," he responded, emphasising the first word. They chatted away, talking about Karen and Ollie and avoiding the one topic that frequently created the tension between them; work commitments and their unending capability to take on more at the expense of their personal lives. Well, that was true of Penny herself, she thought.

Two more cosmos and Penny was ready for bed. Ray had matched her in martinis so they were both pleasantly smashed.

"Shall we go?"

RAY NODDED AND they stood up and headed for the lift, Ray's hand on Penny's bum. She put her arm around his waist and they waited for the lift doors to open. Perhaps because for Paris the hour was still early, they were the only ones in the lift. After the doors shut, Ray turned to face Penny, his hand still firmly entrenched on her arse. With his hand edging under the hem of her little black dress, they kissed until the bell rang and the lift doors opened onto their floor. The tingles had begun.

In their room with the door shut, they stood and kissed again—this time with both Ray's hands on her bottom, squeezing in rhythm to their kissing. Penny enjoyed the sheer simplicity of their affection and the sensation running along her spine from her crotch to her neck. Ray always did this to her; the lightest of his touches turned her on. They were made for each other.

Penny felt Ray's hands move up her back and her dress felt loose around her body as he unzipped it. She grabbed the shoulders and let the dress slip to the floor. There she stood in just a bra, matching striped pants and stockings with their garter. She unclipped the garter and Ray knelt and rolled down the stockings, one by one.

Then he stood up and took off his shirt and trousers. And they kissed some more, standing so close Penny could feel the individual hairs of his body tickle her tummy and press against her legs.

They slipped into bed, throwing the meticulously laid-out cushions onto the floor and Ray went down on her before they made love once, twice and nearly three times. Penny fell asleep after Ray, bathed in a warm afterglow of love towards her man. They fit so well together, like his dick was made to be inside her.

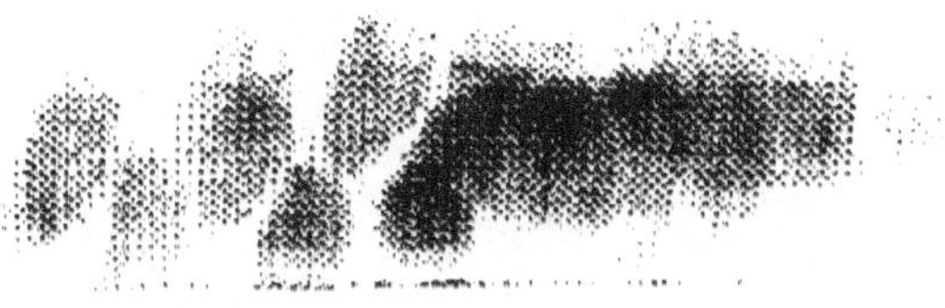

# 33

**RAY**

Ray's abiding memory of the weekend was a moment captured in his mind's eye when they arrived. As he went to lick her out when they got back to their room the first night, he noticed Penny wasn't wearing her usual thongs. Under her dress, she had on a pair of pastel striped bikini briefs.

He looked at the front and saw the shape of her bush causing a bulge to protrude. He was utterly captivated by the sight of that bulge and imagined the hairs beneath—and her flesh peeping out from beneath the trimmed forest. Ray's eyes followed the horizontal stripes down into the gusset as he pushed his tongue through the material until he heard Penny gasp and her legs twitched twice.

Later when Ray was falling asleep, the image of that striped bulge came back into his thoughts.

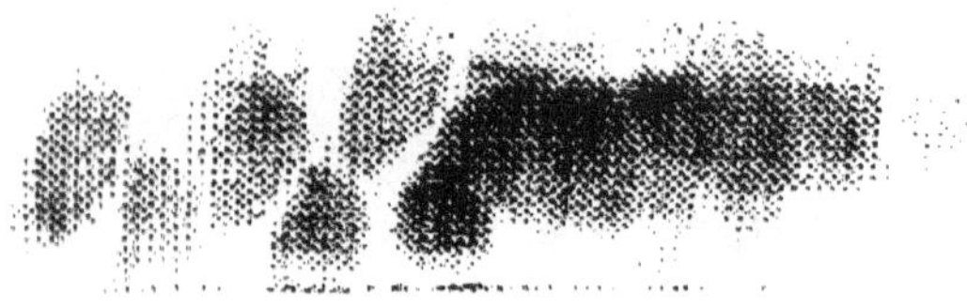

# 34

**PENNY**

For the rest of the weekend, Penny and Ray split their time between people watching in cafés, taking in the odd museum like the tourists they were, and copious amounts of extremely relaxing but incredibly intense sex.

Penny reminded herself before they left on Sunday to bring back to Edgware the same warmth and affection they felt towards each other in Paris. The location wasn't the important thing; it was how they felt about each other that really mattered and she vowed to remember this even when she did have to catch yet another flight to the East Coast.

# Part Fourteen
## July 2005

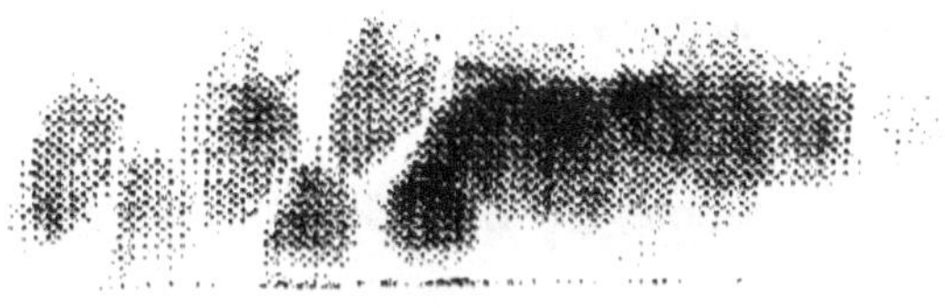

# 35

**RAY**

Most Fridays the fund managers would leave their offices around five, exit the building and reconvene at the King's Lion around the corner. Four years before, it was a sorry spit-and-sawdust affair languishing in the middle of derelict buildings. Since the redevelopment work, all that had changed and the beer company that owned the property knew enough to invest heavily in the place.

After a complete refurb, the King's Lion re-opened with its comfortable chairs and Scandinavian wooden flooring, upon which chrome-and-glass tables stood with pride. The venue had been reinvented as a wine bar with a pub's name and that suited the clientele down to the ground.

A couple of martini glasses apiece in front of them, Ray, Jackson and Freddie sat at a table near the window, talking through their week as the world hustled by, desperately trying to get to the weekend.

"So did anyone make a killing this week or have we all been treading water?"

"Fuck all from me."

"No good news here, either."

"At least I'm not the only one then, but fuck. Doesn't feel good, does it?"

"Fuck's our quarterlies, that's for sure."

"Damn straight."

"We've got time to recover though; we're only six days in."

"I know, I know. But I prefer to come out the stalls sprinting, not limping."

"Some you win, some you lose. Good job we're in it for the long haul."

All three laughed at that joke. Long haul was three months in investment management compared to three hours for equity trading —and three minutes for hedge funds.

"TALKING OF WHICH, do you think Freiberg will spring for our bonuses this year?"

Ray looked at Jackson, who looked back at Freddie.

"They'll have to do something. If they don't, there'll be defections. I mean, how long are you prepared to stay if profits are up, assets under management are up, but packages are flatlining?"

"Good point," she noted, before swinging her head over to Ray to hear his thoughts.

"I'm with Jackson. One year of stasis I can suck in. If it becomes a habit, there are plenty more firms in the sea. I've been damn loyal to the Freiberg family, but if that's not being reciprocated; fuck 'em and the horse they rode in on."

Freddie nodded.

"I'm with you one hundred per cent. No woman, no cry."

Neither of the others knew what she meant, but neither of them had any energy to pick her up on it. They were too engrossed in their own little bubbles to care what gibberish she came out with. Freddie had a habit of quoting lines that sounded like they connected with a conversation, but usually just hung there until someone wrestled the conversation away from her. One more for the road later, the three musketeers left the Lion and headed home.

The following week began much as any other; the one highlight for Ray was an Ollie lunch and Ollie was paying, because Ray was the client. He enjoyed the benefits of his new location within the wholesale financial supply chain. Pensioners gave Freiberg money, who paid Ray to invest it for the long term by paying brokers to go to exchanges and agree deals with other brokers, typically operating indirectly for some other pension fund holders on the other side of the transaction.

The trades were conducted on a daily basis to improve the value of the portfolio over a twenty-year profile. In theory, buy-and-hold was the order of the day—and had been the rule for decades—but now investors were being given greater transparency into what their fund managers were doing with their money. Greater scrutiny meant individual fund managers wanted to appear more active, more like they were doing something other than sitting on their haunches collecting their annual management fees.

THIS DESIRE TO show you were doing something was magnified by the reporting cycles of the investment management firms themselves. US companies report back to their shareholders on a quarterly basis, so every three months senior management wants to tell a positive story. Usually this means saying sales are up, costs are down or, preferably, both states of affairs are true.

In a world where buying a stock and holding it for twenty years is the appropriate action, quarterly results force you to create activity for yourself to appease your line manager who is being watched by the leadership team. Everyone conspires to artificially generate movement, irrespective of whether it is in the best interests of the clients' money.

This was Ray's world and he looked forward to a slap-up lunch paid for by an investment banker who was also his closest friend. Ray working on the west side of the City meant Ollie could take him towards the law courts and Holborn where fine food and excellent wine had been consumed by the learned members of the legal profession for centuries. The venues were painfully old-fashioned but were a refreshing change from the rootless anonymity of the newer City-based establishments. Here you could have a steak or a Dover sole and know there was a tradition to its cooking dating back to William Pitt the Younger. Or someone.

"I've got a US company you might find interesting."

"What is it?"

"VuScreen. It's a website where people upload film footage and share their content."

"And that's a business because...?"

"They sell advertising on the viewing pages."

"Sounds like bollocks to me."

"Dear boy, I'm not asking whether you think it'll fly. I'm asking you to take a tranche upfront and flip it the following quarter. With our usual accommodation to sweeten the process."

Ray knew the six and seven figure backhanders were what kept him interested in Ollie's initial public offerings. Everyone was a winner and, to be fair to Ollie, not one of the companies had actually tanked before or after Ray had sold for a profit.

EVEN IF HE put aside his thoughts about his accommodations with Ollie, Ray wasn't comfortable reconciling the need to place safe bets that'll last the decades against the overwhelming requirement to deliver positive quarterly returns. He had left the trading floor so he wouldn't have to spend his time speculating, playing with his firm's money and earning commission just for delivering short term profits —even if some of the derivative contracts he used to hedge his bets had long term negative cash flow implications; the securities house would lose money in a year's time or twenty years' time, but he hit his target that quarter.

For Ray, these concerns were not his; he was finding the quarterly grind through the performance table annoying and dull in equal measure. Annoying because there was an arbitrary moment in time when he had to book business and it hampered his efforts to do the right thing. If he outperformed the market with a week or two to go before quarter-end, Ray had little incentive to do anything more in case a play turned into a loss for him.

Dull because the conveyor belt world of quarterly results put Ray on a permanent back foot of repetitive corporate bullshit, for which he had zero stomach.

The week before the end of the quarter was usually the time Ray wondered if he should be in another line of business. Trouble was he enjoyed asset management but pension fund work did his head in. It never felt like he had much of an edge. He'd take in the broker research at the start of the day and, if he was tired or feeling lazy, all he needed to do to justify his salary was to buy something on offer from either Freiberg Securities on the other side of the City or from one of the other brokers touting their wares.

No imagination, no thought. Just pick up the phone and buy whatever shit was on offer that day. It was like buying a selection box of vegetables from the greengrocer; all very worthy, but nothing exciting in there at all.

Ray had spent too many years on the trading floor to not want that buzz of making on-the-fly decisions and the pit-of-the-stomach sensation when you place a multi-million-pound bet on some financial instrument. At the same time, Ray knew he should be doing something more than making money for the Freiberg family, because the truth was the Freibergs had no real need for any more greenbacks in their coffers.

This meant Ray thought about asset management with an edge. The derivative markets—like futures and options—had spawned a response within the fund management community. Hedge funds were high risk-reward firms, where people tried to increase the value of their clients' portfolios, but typically had their own skin in the game.

# 36

THE FOLLOWING THURSDAY, July 7, Ray got to work as normal, and was sat behind his desk by eight. Erin delivered his first coffee of the day within a couple of minutes of his arrival. He checked the overnight numbers from Asia, which had been trading while the UK slept, and read up on anything political or corporate worldwide which had occurred since he was last sat at the same desk.

This was how Ray started most of his working mornings and gave him just enough time to get his mental house in order before the bell; the start of trading on the London Stock Exchange, where brokers traded with brokers on behalf of their pension fund customers.

Today, normal routine was broken. Ray was calling up the UK Equities pages on his Caldwell when a newsflash ripped across the screen. Breaking news of a bombing on the London Underground. Then a minute later, there was an update that there had been more than one explosion in more than one tube train.

London was under attack.

Ray ran out of his office and down the corridor.

"Erin, have you heard?"

"Y... yes."

"Are you okay? Sit down and take some deep breaths."

He could see she had all the makings of the start of a panic attack. Ray rushed to the kitchen area and brought her back a glass of water.

"Stay here and wait. Keep an eye on the BBC news."

When Ray and Penny had watched the World Trade Center fall, they had used the rolling twenty-four-hour news at the BBC as their source for all those hours. Now was the time to turn to the Beeb again.

RAY SPED DOWN to the other offices and saw Freddie with her arms tightly folded, staring at the screens in front of her. Jackson was leaning back in his chair, a solitary tear rolling down his cheek.

"Jackson…"

"I think she was on one of the trains."

"How?"

"I dunno. Just feels like…"

"Snap out of it. Until you know for sure, you know shit. Understand?"

Jackson's wife worked in the West End and reports were coming in that trains had been hit in Holborn and Kings Cross, but no one knew anything for sure. They were all preparing for the worst.

Back in 2001, everyone had known tens, even hundreds, of people who had perished in the 9/11 attacks—the nature of international finance meant lots of Brits knew loads of Americans. Somehow these bombings felt different. They were far closer to home. Close enough for Ray to take it personally.

He felt an impending sense of foreboding, caused in part by the atmosphere in Freiberg and partly because London was being bombed.

An hour later, a bomb on a bus went off and everyone on Ray's floor screamed as the news broke and Erin sat back down and breathed even deeper than before. The sense of dread deepened inside Ray's stomach. There was an overarching taste of death in the air. It hung above their heads, unmoving, clouding their judgements and permeating their thoughts.

Ray was the first to snap out of it when he realised this was the moment to trade—assuming he could find somebody to take his instructions. As people around him were discovering, mobile phones were proving useless; either everyone was using them all at the same time and the cell towers couldn't cope or the same towers had been shut down by either the authorities or the terrorists. No one cared at that moment in time.

OLD-FASHIONED LANDLINES were working perfectly and Ray dialled nine for an outside line and called a broker from Freiberg. He went long on consulting firms and he found the supplier and manufacturer of the tube trains and went long on them as well. Then he shorted sterling against the dollar and shorted the price of oil. It was ten thirty and Ray popped his head outside his door to see if Erin was up for making him a bucket of coffee.

She was sat at her desk with the news flickering on her screen.

"How are you holding up?"

"Fine thanks. I just can't believe it, you know?"

"I know. It was like this in 2001."

"Yeah?"

"Yes... Look nothing's actually happened for over an hour now. We're in lockdown and nothing more. So get yourself a sweet tea and rustle me up a coffee while you're there, okay?"

Erin looked at him and nodded. She knew he was right. Everyone around was talking, a few people were getting on with work, but there had been no change in their situation ever since the bus went up. A message from HR, signed by the chief exec, had been sent around half nine telling everyone to stay put inside the building until they were given the go-ahead to do anything else, but there'd been zip since then.

When Erin returned, she had a tea and a coffee in her hands and she passed the coffee over to Ray, who'd been leaning on his doorpost since their conversation; he had wanted a respite from the screens himself.

"Thanks."

"You're welcome."

Ray looked down at Erin and thought he might have been able to catch a glimpse of the roundness of her tits, but that didn't seem very important at this point on this day.

Thirty minutes later, word came to their floor that the police had instructed everyone to leave the building and make their way home.

RAY WAS TORN. He wanted to get the fuck out of the area as soon as he physically could, but he knew he had a duty to ensure Erin got home safely too. The taxi firm used by Freiberg had no vehicles available for the rest of the day; once the drivers heard there were bombs popping off across London, they fled like any other rational human being. To be more accurate, there was one car left which had been caught in town and the guy was leaving now, heading out in Erin's direction. Ray had got Erin to pass him the phone and explained to the fat controller on the other end how the driver was going to stop outside their building and get Erin home safely and without fuss. There was a fifty-pound bonus on top of the fare if everything went to plan.

While Ray didn't approve of bribing people to do their job, he knew this was a time when rules were meant to be broken. Out of the building they went and Ray made sure Erin got in the limo and was off nice and safe.

He looked around and witnessed a bizarre sight; apart from the departing taxi, there were no vehicles to be seen, only people. Some on the pavement, but most on the road. Like the City had become a ghost town. The sounds from the shops were nowhere to be heard, just the clunk of footsteps on pavement and road. Ray stood and sucked in the moment, deep inside.

SINCE THE FIRST blast, no tube trains had been running across London, so how was he going to get home? The answer was simple; Ray would have to walk north until he got sufficiently far away from the centre so that the buses would be running and he could grab one for the rest of the journey. All the footsteps echoing down the streets showed the rest of the City had reached the same conclusion.

Ray undid the top button of his shirt and undid his tie. Then he thought about his mental map and reckoned it was time to head north, cutting through the back of the Barbican and on to Islington. From that point he could decide whether to head towards Kings Cross where there'd be more buses but more people trying to catch them, or off to Islington and a more direct route home, but with less chance of a bus to shorten his journey. That'd be a while off yet.

He had decided to leave his briefcase in the office because it would just be something to carry and weigh him down. Standing outside the Freiberg entrance, Ray had no idea if he was going to be walking the full fifteen or twenty miles home and, whichever way you added that up, it was a long fucking schlep.

As Mao had said, the longest journey starts with the first step and Ray began the walk by going straight north and heading past the Museum of London and on to the Barbican.

He took advantage of the strangeness of the day by walking in the road. There were people on the pavement walking more slowly and the power-walkers were where the cars should have been. There were trainers on some of the feet, but most of the office workers had not prepared themselves for a multi-hour stroll across London. Ray was one of them.

AFTER AN HOUR and a half, he'd reached the Angel end of Islington and stood waiting for a bus for a second or two. The only ones that had passed him on the way had been completely full and, even when they stopped, no one got off. They were filled to the gunnels with people from the burbs trying to get home—and no one else.

So, for that reason, Ray didn't waste his time standing still. He understood the only way he was going to get home today was by getting himself there and not by waiting for someone else to take him.

Office workers weren't the only ones to be part of the city exodus; all the shops had shut and the retailers were on their way too. A loaf of bread from a supermarket, tourist tat, a bottle of water from a newsagent. None of these things were available for purchase anywhere on Ray's route. His mouth was dry and his stomach was gently rumbling, but there was nothing to service his needs.

To save walking time, he decided to go along the hypotenuse of Liverpool Road instead of following Islington High Street, followed by the Holloway Road at Highbury and Islington overground station. This was a residential street with only one bus route and, naturally, no double-decker showed up while Ray was trudging along it.

By the time he reached the other end and turned left onto the Holloway Road, Ray's feet were hurting. He could feel a blister had formed on the outside of his right big toe, but he had no choice other than to continue.

There were more buses on this main drag, but they were as full as all the previous ones had been. Nothing was picking up just yet.

The relentless grind carried on for another hour or two until Ray arrived at the other end of the Holloway Road and he crossed the junction which took him either on the left fork up to Highgate village or the right fork, which took him along the Archway Road and near Highgate tube. The village might have a cafe still open but the Archway Road was way less steep, so Ray took the easier option.

THERE WERE STILL people walking alongside him but the density had reduced; workers had fanned out from the centre of the City towards all the possible outskirts and suburbs where they lived.

Ninety minutes later and Ray had dragged his sorry arse up the slope of the Archway Road and had reached Highgate tube station, which had a bus stop outside it, for buses heading north and others heading east to Muswell Hill.

Ray stopped to catch his breath and noticed there was a concession window open at a newsagent. There was ice cream on sale.

He dug into his back trouser pocket and found a few coins; enough to buy a small vanilla cone. Ray leant against the wall of the building and focused his entire being on the consumption of that iced confection—until it was all gone. Then, like an Old Testament miracle, a bus pulled up and the front door opened. There was space for one and he was it. Not only was there space, but it was going in the right direction; north to Hendon.

Suddenly, for the first time since he'd left the Freiberg offices, Ray's phone buzzed; it was a text from Penny in Boston: "Tell me you are OK."

He responded in the affirmative and clung to the handrail on the bus, squished next to a large woman with a young child in one hand and a bag in the other.

When Ray arrived at Hendon, he headed to a cash machine and took some money out. Then he sat down in a local taxi firm's office until a driver was ready to take him home. Twenty minutes later and he was on his way to Edgware.

Before he sat down at home, Ray found a bowl, boiled up some water and added cold too. He popped it onto the floor of the living room next to their sofa and flipped the TV on. He pulled off his shirt, undid his trousers and finally pulled off his shoes and socks. Then he dipped his feet into the tepid water and sat on the sofa, like a man whose clothes were trying to unpeel themselves from him until he fell asleep.

When he woke up around eight in the evening, the house was pitch black, the water cold and he wrapped his feet in a towel to dry them off. A slice of toast and a mug of coffee and he was ready for bed. He fired off another text to Penny so she'd know he got home safely and then creaked upstairs and fell asleep as soon as his head hit the pillow.

# The Death and Life of Penny Pitstop

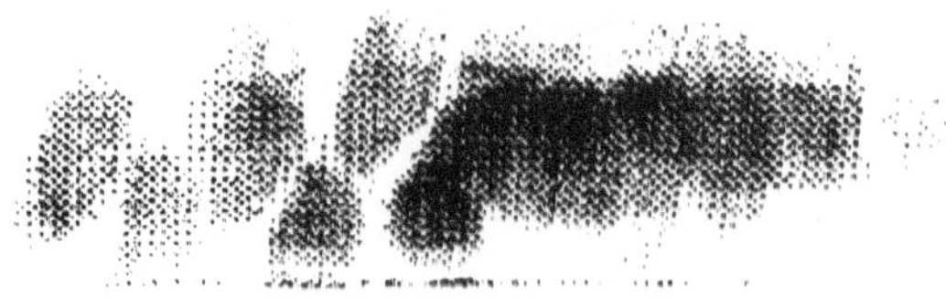

# 37

**PENNY**

She had been back a couple of days, having stayed in the States the weekend after Independence Day. Penny caught up with her UK case file and spent the evenings sat next to Ray on the sofa. They even had a date night when they took the soft top out for a ride into the country to a gastropub in the wilds of Hertfordshire.

Penny noticed the apartment rent hadn't been paid, so she arranged to meet Mickey to get things sorted the following day. She booked out an afternoon's client meeting so she could pop over to the Canary Wharf apartment.

The car deposited her outside the north building and Penny strode inside and nodded at Ricky, whose eagle eyes protected the apartment blocks from riffraff. She must remember to drop him a twenty when she left; always best to look after Ricky, so he could look after you.

Up in the lift and out onto the third floor. Then Penny rummaged around in her bag until she found her key. She turned it in the lock and the door opened—no chain on, like she was expected.

"Hi there!"

A muffled response from either the kitchen or a bathroom. Penny couldn't be sure which. She stood in the hallway for a second or two then strolled into the living room and sat down on a dining room chair. Almost all the furniture in this room is mine, she thought.

There was a flushing sound and Mickey appeared in the living room. He smiled as soon as he saw her.

"Hey, you."

Penny smiled back, aware of the potential awkwardness of the situation, given their history.

"Do you want to check the place over?"

"NOT REALLY, MICKEY. The cleaning company does that, not me."

"I know, but still..."

"How have you and Theresa been keeping?"

"Fine, just fine. Still doing the same old, same old."

Mickey was still a fitness instructor and Theresa, his sister, was a secretary, or PA as she preferred to be called.

"Well, if things are going okay with you both, why didn't you pay your rent last month?"

Mickey smiled a broad grin, sat down, and relaxed his legs so his knees drifted slightly further apart.

"Thing is, I missed you and I couldn't think of any other way to see you."

"You're kidding me."

"No, straight up. I miss our time together."

"That was a while ago, Mickey. Not now, not today. Those days are gone. Long gone."

Mickey leaned in towards her and put his hand round the back of her neck, hoping to draw her head towards his, but Penny was having none of it.

"Get off me!"

Immediately, he let go.

"Sorry, I just thought."

"That was always your problem, Mickey. Thinking; you never did any of it. Always acting through your dick, not your brains."

"I like my dick," he sulked.

"There's nothing wrong with your dick. That's not my point."

"You like my dick, don't you?"

"What? Yes, it is undoubtedly the largest cock I have ever known and you sure as fuck know what to do with it."

Mickey smiled again, happy with the compliment he had received.

"But the days of your dick being waved near me are no more... Do you understand?"

"Yeah, I know."

His disappointment hung in the air for ten, twenty seconds. Penny wasn't too sure how she could swing the conversation away from Mickey's old fella.

SHE LET THE tension dissipate and pretended to check something on her phone, giving Mickey some recovery time in the hope he'd be able to focus once she resumed.

"So what are we going to do about the money, then?"

"I'll send it to you later today."

"And this month's rent?"

"It'll be back on track, Penelope."

"Good news."

Penny relaxed because the worst was over, now Mickey was calm. She knew he was capable of lashing out and there was no way she wanted that to happen again. She stood up, followed by Mickey. There was nothing more she had to say.

"Hug for the road?"

Penny nodded and Mickey wrapped his arms around her body and she let her arms drape over his shoulders. They remained there for thirty seconds, Penny breathing in his masculinity and remembering why she'd shared a bed with him.

She felt his hand stroking the back of her neck and was about to remonstrate when she realised he still felt good to her. Despite knowing a big mistake was about to occur, she let him carry on, enjoying the sensual moment.

His other hand was over her arse and he squeezed one of her buttocks playfully, slowly. Penny noticed a tingle, emanating from her crotch, sprint up her spine. Mickey carried on squeezing and, after a while, she felt he'd moved his hand around her bum enough to be able to get his forefinger between her legs and push towards her crotch. The tightness of her work skirt prevented him from getting any further.

MICKEY'S HAND STOPPED trying and, instead, she felt it rise above the skirt waistline and slip under the material to get to her via another route. She pulled her stomach in to allow the hand to gain entry. He lunged downwards, under her stockings and under her thong to squeeze her bum and then to reach between her legs and up to her crotch. Penny felt his fingers stroking her. A rush zoomed through her body and, almost without thinking, she placed one of her hands over his tracksuit trousers and stroked his dick through the material.

"Hang on a minute," she whispered in his ear. Penny unzipped her skirt and pulled down on Mickey's trousers, kneeling in front of him. He had no pants.

She grabbed his dick with her hand and licked it until it was in her mouth. Then the front door banged open and a voice shouted.

"Surprise! I'm home early."

Penny pushed Mickey's fast-shrinking flesh out of her mouth and grabbed her skirt. Before she had a chance to put it on, Theresa arrived in the room.

"What the living fuck?"

Penny managed to get both legs into the skirt and pulled it up around her waist. Mickey started to grab his tracksuit trousers, still lying around his ankles.

"Theresa. It's not what it looks like."

"Mickey, are you fucking insane? What the fuck do you think it looks like? Because from here, it looks like your old girlfriend has come into our home and was sucking you off."

Penny had zipped up her skirt and was edging away from Mickey, but there was nothing she could think to say at this point which would do any good at all. Theresa was right. They were fucking insane.

"And you, you fucking whore. What have you got to say for yourself? You, only married recently and everything."

"I came over because the rent was late."

"You've got a funny way of collecting it!"

Penny winced.

"This has been one big fucking mistake, for sure, but it's between Mickey and myself."

"In my fucking house, missy."

"Which you are renting from me. Or rather, Mickey rents from me and you sub-let. What happened just now should not have happened in this living room. I agree, but you're high moral tone is unnecessary and uncalled for. Mickey's a big boy. He can look after himself."

Penny grabbed her bag from the dining room table and headed for the door. As she opened it, she heard Theresa shout, "He sure can look after himself except when around your cun..."

She closed the door behind her and hurried to the lifts. Before she pressed the down button, she gave herself a minute to catch her breath and to get her heart rate down towards normal. As she left the building, she approached Ricky and shook his hand to pass him over the twenty she'd promised herself she'd give him.

"Everything all right?"

"All's fine, Ricky. Haven't seen the place for a while."

"We miss you."

# Part Fifteen
## 2006

# 38

**RAY**

The timing was perfect; Ray's new job started on January third, the first working day of the new year, and he felt good. This was the right fit for him.

Pension fund management hadn't agreed with him, but Ray had taken a while to figure out where to go next. He'd had enough of trading and from what he'd heard from Bill Carson, his old boss, there was just a pile of oversight and compliance standing on their shoulders and that didn't sound fun.

Ollie gave him the answer without realising it. At one of their fine dining experiences, he had mentioned to Ray his bank was going to buy a hedge fund and Ray thought long and hard.

Hedge funds were part of the asset management world, but they operated by investing in derivatives or other alternative assets. And then they placed opposite bets to reduce the risk of their investments going wrong, leaving them with egg on their faces. What caught Ray's imagination was the edgier risk profile which still focused on investment instead of naked profit. So when he received a call from a head hunter, he'd agreed to meet and have a conversation about jumping ship to Bespoke Horizon.

"And there you have it in a nutshell," Charlie sat back in his chair looking very smug. He'd given Ray the full pitch and had failed to cover anything that mattered to Ray whatsoever.

"And how financially secure is Bespoke? When I checked it out at Companies House, it had yet to file any accounts. The nominee owner is located in the Bahamas and I couldn't find out anything about him. I'm assuming they are a man and not a woman."

Charlie's smiling expression evaporated and his serious face took over. At times, Ray wasn't sure he could hear what Charlie was saying because the shininess of the designer suit was too loud. Expensive but gaudy.

"I'M GLAD YOU'VE done your homework. Shows me you're a serious applicant."

"Charles. I am not an applicant—you contacted me. And who exactly owns Bespoke? Tell me now or I'm walking out of here."

The boy was flustered but outlined the ownership structure to Ray. There was a tax exile who had backed the original hedge fund manager, Eliezer Romano, and he was using it as an income vehicle now and nothing more. Eliezer managed the business and still ran his own book. There were three other fund managers and they were seeking a fourth because business was growing and they recognised they needed to have a diverse approach to investment.

The rest of the meeting went well and Ray made sure he gave enough information up so Charlie would want to recommend him to Romano. Sure enough, the following day Charlie arranged a second interview, this time with Romano himself and not his gimp. The meeting took place at the Bespoke Horizon office in Mayfair.

Eliezer was dressed suit casual; immaculate two-piece dark blue suit with a white open-necked formal shirt, but no tie. Since 9/11 this had been the uniform of senior management and demonstrated the caring side of wholesale financial services.

The offices were moderately open plan with glass walls in every space so conversations were private but everyone could see everything going on in the company.

There was a receptionist who sat him down in a meeting room and five minutes later, Eliezer appeared.

"Hi."

"Pleased to meet you."

"Sure. Coffee?"

"Yes please."

Eliezer winced because he clearly had no desire to serve Ray any hot drink. He called in the receptionist who did the honours instead.

"So this is the second interview in the process. What do you want to know about us?"

RAY HAD PLANNED a couple of questions like any well-trained interviewee, but he hadn't expected to be given free reign. Clever. He could be judged by his questions rather than his answers.

"You've been with the firm since the outset. How would you say the company has changed?"

"It hasn't. Next?"

This was going to be a cutthroat interview, far worse than any he'd prepared for in the past. He decided to ditch the nicey-nicey stance and stick it to the man.

"You approached me. What have I got that you think will benefit the hedge fund?"

"Good question; much better. We've checked up on you from the various parts of Freiberg you've worked in and people have good things to say about you. And your performance is sound too. Finally, we saw you were hedging your investments early on, so we know you understand the hedge fund business even if you haven't been in it before.

"And we are interested in growing our customer base and you can bring in some long-only clients." Long-only was a phrase used in the hedge fund world to describe pension funds, who technically should never short a trade.

"I'm interested. Keep talking."

"Next question." Eliezer smiled, only slightly, out of the corner of his mouth. They'd get along fine. The man hated bullshit, is all.

"How many new clients do you expect me to bring in my first year and what returns do you expect me to generate?"

"The number doesn't interest us as much as assets under management. First year, half a billion will suffice. We eat what we kill in Bespoke and we expect our managers to invest in their own funds. It's the hedge fund way. So you take out in earnings what you put in as investment ideas. Returns? Thirty per cent would be disappointing; we're not into shaving a few basis points over the index. You'd be working with the big boys now."

A basis point was one hundredth of a per cent and hedge funds were high risk—and high return—vehicles. Ray knew he was ready because it felt so right.

THE THIRD INTERVIEW was a shoo-in, which involved Ray meeting the other managers. Charlie had told him this was a culture fit session and that Eliezer wanted him to join. After that, there was his package to negotiate and everything was ready. As soon as he told Freiberg he was leaving for a hedge fund, a security guard was found and his own personal cardboard box. He was followed around the building as he packed up what was left of his possessions—he'd taken the important stuff like client lists out the previous day—and then he went round to say goodbye to Jackson, Freddie and anyone else he knew and half-cared about. Finally, he went over to Erin.

"It's goodbye for today, but I'll give you a call after the weekend. Would be great if you'd work with me at Bespoke Horizon."

She nodded, stood up and kissed him on the cheek. Ray caught a whiff of her perfume and copped a look at the point where the curves of her tits met. Mighty fine cleavage, he thought.

"I'll see you around, Ray. Let's not lose touch."

"Let's not, Erin."

Then he was out the door and heading home. By moving to a hedge fund, Ray had been able to argue, quite legitimately, that his non-compete clause didn't apply. So he had three months gardening leave instead of six. Of course, Freiberg extracted their pound of flesh for that by listing all his clients in a compromise agreement and asserting he wasn't allowed to approach any of them for business for twelve months after the termination of his contract. Lisa, his employment lawyer, told him to sign it because she didn't think it was enforceable and Ray had been at home since the start of October.

THIS GAVE HIM plenty of time to think. To think about what strategies he would employ at Bespoke. To figure out the best way to get Erin hired so she could continue to look after him. And to think about his life with Penny in Edgware.

He arrived back around eleven—he'd stopped off at his coffee shop first, round the corner from Freiberg, enjoying the freedom of watching the worker bees scurrying past. Then he pinged Penny to let her know the deed was done. She'd get the message in an hour or two when she woke up; she was on yet another trip to New York.

The house was empty and once he'd decanted the contents of his personal property box into a drawer in the spare room upstairs, Ray sat on the sofa and contemplated his navel. With all his mental meanderings around the new job, he'd forgotten how much he missed Penny. He wanted her and she wasn't there. Wouldn't be back until the following morning; she'd be on tonight's red eye. Then she'd flop into bed and be jet lagged for the week until the next trip back over.

This wasn't a life for them. This wasn't proper and was nowhere near what he'd imagined marriage was going to be like. Marriage to anyone, let alone marriage to Penny. He hardly ever saw her and when he did, her head was in the office or in the States. And then she'd vanish for another week or two and he'd be left in Edgware and Freiberg. At least the company name would change; that made his heart feel lighter as a surge of excitement spread across his chest. But he knew it would be short-lived. Ray understood he wouldn't be happy until he sorted things out with Penny.

HER ATTENTION WAS always on the States, that was the trouble. Either she was coming back or she was getting ready for the next trip —and this cycle repeated on a nearly weekly basis. Ray knew her schedule but he couldn't bank on it. Even on the odd week Penny was home, she'd be out in the evenings either working or catching up with friends like Karen or having dinner with Nina.

Penny had no time for him and appeared to have no interest in him either. There was their Saturday night fuck but that was an obligation; there were times he felt she was just going through the motions. Teasing his balls, squeezing his dick. And they had been together so long, he knew exactly what to touch and how to touch her body to almost guarantee her breathing would get heavy and that she'd come while he was inside her. Nothing like when they first hooked up—or even like the wild times they'd had at Ollie's engagement party.

He giggled to himself as he recalled what they'd got up to that night and then a flick of dread hammered his insides as he recalled that bra. Why had he chosen her bra? That decision had haunted their lives for far too long afterwards. Like she wanted to hold something against him; like she was deflecting something away from him.

Ray gulped and gripped the sofa arm. Perhaps there was something she didn't want him to find out about. Perhaps that attack on him was the best form of defence. All those days in the US meant there were all those nights in the US too. The possibility that Penny was sleeping with someone in the States entered Ray's mind for the very first time. And his stomach felt heavy with the realisation she might well be doing just that. She was fucking some American.

The thought echoed and rattled inside his head. Ray noticed his breath was shortening and his fingers had gouged themselves into the sofa arm. His mind tried to flip through his memories to see if he could find something more concrete than a belief he couldn't shake off.

It was the lack of interest in him and the nagging when she was in the same country as him for more than two days at a time. Half an hour later, rolling the same idea around his head, Ray had more. Penny was distant as though she had other things on her mind and she didn't mind showing him how low he was on her priority list.

He couldn't let the thoughts alone and ended up going to bed early and masturbating over the memories of their first sexual encounters.

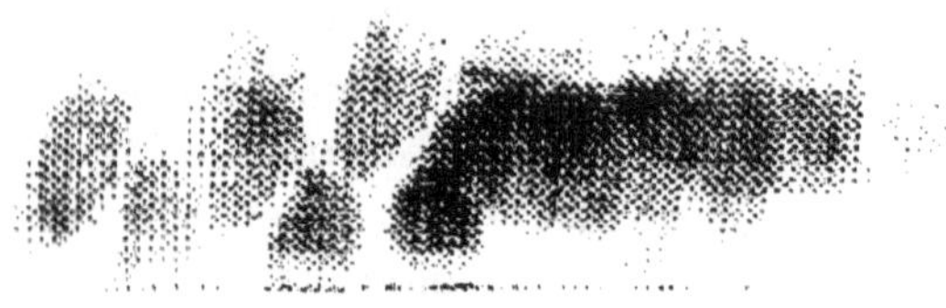

# 39

**PENNY**

A moment's peace in an otherwise troubled world. Penny sat on the armchair with one leg dangling over an armrest, a book held in her hands. She wanted to finish off the last chapter because she'd fallen asleep on the plane before she could get to the end.

Saturday afternoons after the red eye from the East Coast were always a mixed blessing. There was the calm of being home and having Ray around, but there was always the unending fight against jet lagged sleep, which reared its ugly head around three or four in the afternoon. Penny had trained herself to not crash out as soon as she got home, instead delaying the pain until later in the day.

Ray was pottering in the kitchen doing who the hell knew what, but the sounds of domesticity were a pleasant backdrop to her reading. She was ten pages away from the end of the novel when Ray returned to the living room and sat on the sofa with a splat. She furrowed her brow and carried on soaking up the words, trying to ignore his wilful rustling on the leather upholstery.

"How was New York?"

"Fine," she mumbled, attempting to focus on the words on the page and not the noise in her ears.

"Get up to anything interesting in the evenings?"

"No."

"No fun in the Big Apple then?"

"No."

"Who do you hang out with in the evenings?"

"No one."

"Nobody at all?"

"No one. No."

"After all these years, you've met no one."

"No. No one."

"Really?"

"Yep."

Penny was getting irritated; Ray wasn't leaving her alone to finish her book. What was his problem? A few minutes of peace in a turbulent world.

"So you go to a restaurant, eat alone and then back to your hotel?"

"Yep."

"That's remarkable."

"Yep."

"I know it must be a terrible burden to you, but could you give me the common courtesy of putting your book down while we speak. What little time we have together doesn't have to be spent with you reading and ignoring me."

Penny sighed and let the book drop into her lap.

"What do you want to talk about, then?"

"About your evenings in New York."

"What about them?"

"As I said, how do you spend them?"

"Alone, Ray. I spend them alone, reading a book and eating in a nearby restaurant or in the hotel. I've done it so many times, everyone knows my name."

"And you've made no connections with anyone over there?"

"No, Ray. International business travel is not fun; it doesn't involve partying every night and working during the day. It's just work and sleep."

"Right. What about the rule; what goes on in Vegas stays in Vegas?"

"I don't know what you're talking about."

"Come on, Penny. Every time you come back from the States, you're always too tired. Too tired to do anything. Like you're all tired out from your trip. But this is every time, like you're tired from something other than work... Are you seeing someone over there?"

"What?"

"You heard me. Are you?"

PENNY'S MIND RACED. What paranoid fiction had Ray constructed for himself? She got out of her chair and sat next to him on the sofa. Reaching out her hand, she placed it on his.

"No, Ray. I'm not seeing anyone in the US."

"You've been so absent lately."

"I know I have. Just been focusing on earning money. That's all. If at some point I stop working and we have a baby, I want to know we'll be okay financially."

"Yeah?"

"Yes."

Penny wrapped her arms around him and they hugged a while, until Ray leaned over and placed his head on her lap. She stroked his forehead and he sobbed a little, tears rolling out of his eyes and delivering a small salty wet patch on her thigh.

That night, Penny cooked him his favourite pizza and chips. Then she took him to bed and sucked him off. Later, he went down on her for the first time in a year.

THE NEXT TIME Penny was in the UK, three weeks later, she and Ray made their way up to Manchester to visit her parents. She knew they weren't his favourite people and, truth be told, Penny found she was always driven to distraction if she spent more than a day or two with them too. But at least he was doing the dutiful thing and she liked the idea of having a couple of days with him away from London, even if it involved sleeping under her parents' roof.

Penny's original plan had been to stay in a local hotel, partly to ease the burden on her parents and partly to get a break from them. But two passive aggressive phone calls later and they were staying at her mum and dad's instead.

Ray opted to drive up and Penny liked the idea of having the freedom to run away in a vehicle at any time too. Paul and Frannie lived in a detached three-bed house on the edge of the city. They had moved there shortly after Paul was made redundant from the menswear shop. He had been in retail sales all his life. Luckily, he had swiftly been hired by one of the big brand chains and was making a modest but uninspiring living selling men's suits and matching shirts. But it was a job and no mistake.

Frannie had made ends meet by doing cleaning in office blocks in the centre of the city. The pay was lousy but she figured, quite rightly, that every little bit helps. Besides, it kept her busy and got her out of the house, as Paul was always quick to point out.

Penny and Ray arrived near ten, having belted up the motorway with enough time to have grabbed a bite to eat in a service station fast food joint. They'd left the City life in the rear-view mirror before they'd even zoomed past Milton Keynes.

RAY PARKED IN the driveway and then they brought their overnight bags inside. Paul took them upstairs while Frannie made them each a nice cup of tea. Ray made an excuse to go help Paul and Penny was left alone with her mum.

"It's so good to see you again Penelope."

"Lovely to be back too."

"It's been a while, hasn't it?"

"Sure has. I've been busy, real busy."

"Well that's nice, dear. I'm keeping busy too."

The conversation dwindled away to nothing as Penny realised what a huge mistake this trip had become only moments into their arrival. Her mum's idea of busy was to mop a few floors. Penny had left this world far behind her; she knew why it had been so long since she'd visited. It was before they got married.

Frannie sipped her tea while Penny sat at the kitchen table. There were ornaments on every shelf, every nook and cranny. No surface was suffering from a lack of porcelain or ceramics. Penny shuddered inside as each object brought back some childhood memory. Her mum had been collecting these bits of shit since before Penny was a little girl.

Ray came down to the kitchen and politely sipped at his tea. He sat down next to Penny and she placed her hand on his knee and kissed him on the cheek.

"Well it's great to see you guys. What have you been up to?"

"Same old, same old."

"The place looks lovely, doesn't it?"

"Yes, sure does," and Penny squeezed Ray's leg to thank him for making the conversational effort. She knew her mum found it hard to talk to her southern daughter and her dad would always rather watch City play on the telly than have a chat with anyone. Penny had finished her tea.

"It's been a long journey, so I think I'll call it a night."

"Me too," volunteered Ray, not wanting to be left alone with her parents.

UP THE STAIRS and Ray led Penny to the back room where they'd been allocated a bed. It was also Penny's bedroom from when she was a kid, but had been redecorated since she left home. Despite herself, Penny had kept the memory of that room as a snapshot in time before she'd moved out, even though Frannie had told her about the changes they'd made. Penny closed the door behind them.

"Thanks for being here," she whispered.

"Don't worry about it. The weekend will fly by. Your folks are fine."

"I'll remind you of those words once we've left, if you're not careful."

Ray smiled and got ready for bed while Penny disrobed and piled her clothes onto a chair by a dressing table. Ray left his things lying on the floor on his side of the bed.

Under the sheets, they clung to each other to get warm as the heating didn't feel like it had been on today even though they were in the middle of winter. Their arms and legs were wrapped around each other's bodies and now, more than almost any other time, Penny was aware of Ray's body hairs against her flesh.

They were both naked under the covers and to help warm her up, Ray was rubbing and stroking her back. This had the effect of switching her tingles on and before she'd thought about what she was doing, Penny was rocking her hips to rub his dick with her body.

Despite herself, Frannie couldn't stop listening to the squeaking of the kids' wireframe bed and was only able to drop off to sleep after it fell silent.

"It's so lovely to have Penelope back under this roof," she thought to herself as she drifted off into unconsciousness.

THE NEXT DAY Penny woke before Ray, grabbed his shirt and scooted downstairs to give him a lie in—and to give her a chance to try to talk to her mum without distraction. She considered untangling her thong from her jeans but couldn't be bothered.

Frannie was already making a brew by the time Penny arrived and poured her a cuppa as soon as she appeared.

"Hello, love."

"Hi."

"So how are things with you and Ray? You look happy. You sound happy."

Penny's cheeks went red when she realised the implication of Frannie's penultimate word.

"Everything's fine, thank you very much. And you shouldn't be eavesdropping, you dirty peeping tom."

"Dear, it's not my fault your dad hasn't oiled the springs of your bed."

"P-lease. There are some things mothers and daughters don't need to discuss and what happens between Ray and me in bed is most definitely at the top of the list."

"Whatever you say, love. And how's things between you—apart from that?"

"We're okay, thanks. You know, it's hard. I spend a lot of time in America and that makes it difficult, but we're doing fine. Just fine."

"And is 'fine' what you want out of the marriage?"

"Mum. Don't go there."

"Why not? All I want to know really is that you're happy."

"I am, Mum. Ray and I are like any married couple; we have our ups and downs, but we're good together and good for each other."

"Does he keep you on the straight and narrow? You were always so flighty as a girl."

"He's an even keel, yes."

"And his work in the City. Is it okay?"

"What do you mean?"

"Well, you hear stories of the goings on there. Does that kind of stuff happen to him?"

Penny chuckled.

"Oh, Mum, don't believe everything you read in the papers. There's only a handful of City boys who take drugs, dress in Nazi uniforms and have sex with hookers on the boardroom table."

"Well, that's all right then."

Penny made a cup of instant coffee for Ray and took it up to their room. He was stirring as she entered and put the cup down on the bedside table near his head. One of his fingers left the shelter of the sheets and made its way straight to her crotch. Penny stood there as she let him explore her hairs, like it was their first time together. Then she took off Ray's shirt and jumped back into bed.

"Warm me up, love."

Ray put a hand between Penny's legs, stroking her crotch and buried his head under the sheets and licked her right nipple until the tingles overtook her.

BACK IN THE office the following week, Penny spent a while thinking about her time as a law partner. Her mum's questions over the weekend had made her wonder whether her career path was the right one.

As a partner in a boutique firm, Penny had a tremendous amount of responsibility for someone her age, but she also knew she'd reached her limit. Not because of any glass ceiling, but because there was only one other role higher than partner; managing partner, and Nina wasn't going to be quitting her own firm any time soon. This meant Penny could accrue tenure, and money, but the only way to get more would be to go to a larger firm and that would probably mean coming in as junior partner and working upwards again.

Alternatively, she could hold out for increased tenure where she was and then seek promotion as partner into a larger firm in five or so years' time. Trouble with that as a plan was the sheer dullness of waiting for some partner in another law firm to die in order to create a Penny-shaped vacancy. Tedious.

There was a third possibility Penny had toyed with previously; leaving law practices behind her and moving in-house to become general counsel instead. There were pros and cons.

Pros: she would get deeply involved in business decisions, offering advice to the management team and seeing that through and all its consequences. One of the things which annoyed Penny was not seeing what happened after a firm took her advice. They rarely came back to say whether the advice helped make them money—or not.

Cons: the chances of obtaining a comparable package, including a theoretical limitless financial upside was slim to none. None really. And she would be giving up a highly effective job to leap into the unknown.

The great thing about working in a law firm was that she had a number of different projects on the boil at any one time, so there was always a fresh challenge. In industry, she would be stuck inside one business and that organisation would hardly be flitting from one flower to the next; it would be embroiled in same-old, same-old every day of the year and, if it was large enough, the company might indulge itself in an odd piece of M&A every few years. Yawn.

Perhaps it's better to be killed by the devil you know rather than the devil you don't.

# 40

**KAREN**

Time had slipped past Karen's grasp since her conversation with Penny about Ollie's night-time club activities. She had done nothing apart from carry on harbouring resentment and realised enough was enough.

That night, she did something about it; carrying on like a Brit with a stiff upper lip really wasn't her style and Karen berated herself for trying to live as though she was from this country.

Ollie got back from work around nine, his usual time, and Karen heated up his dinner—she'd cooked it when she got home an hour or so earlier. They didn't eat together because neither knew when the other would be finished at work and they were both used to the habit.

With a glass of something red in her hand, Karen sat with Ollie as he ate her lasagne.

"Are you going to your club tonight?"

"Yah, think that I shall."

"Have you ever thought I might want to come too?"

"Dear girl, no. I hadn't considered it."

Karen stared at him, wondering if that was true or whether he was acting surprised to deflect attention away from the fact he'd excluded her from so much of his life.

"Would you like to come along?"

"Why yes, I would."

"Excellent. I'll finish up here and we can get ready together. What sport!"

Karen and Ollie went upstairs together and popped into their dungeon room to get to their wardrobes. He put on his usual attire and Karen chose a traditional black basque, thigh high black leather boots and suspenders with a red lace thong. She figured a long cashmere coat would hide her attire until they got to the club.

Sure enough, Ollie had booked a black cab and half an hour later, they were hurtling their way across town to Mayfair. The frontage looked like any of the other houses on this residential street and, for a second, Karen wondered if Ollie had got the address wrong or was messing with her.

But as soon as the door opened, she knew they were in the right place. The interior had been refashioned to create an enormous open plan space out of the entire ground floor of this Georgian mansion. There was an anteroom so that nothing of substance could be seen from the street, but once you'd walked out of the hallway, all manner of sexual inclination was being indulged in by all and sundry. Karen literally didn't know where to look. A maid took their coats and Karen felt right at home.

"We can stay together at first, if you like, until you get the lay of the land, then I'm quite happy if you want to split off and go on your own adventure, dear girl."

Karen kissed Ollie and hugged him.

"Right now there is just so much to see, I don't know what I want to do—but stay with me. Who knows what we could get up to...?"

Her voice trailed off as she contemplated the sexual depravity they were going to commit before their return to Hampstead at four in the morning.

# Part Sixteen

## July 2007

# 41

**RAY**

Over the previous couple of years, the derivative markets had grown in ways and directions few could have foreseen. In turn, that created opportunities for hedge funds and warped the way in which they operated too.

One of the many financial instruments which had sprung into being, was the credit default obligation, or CDO. This was originally designed to allow insurance companies to hedge their bets against a company they were insuring going bust, but now firms were buying them even if they had no insurable risk to hedge against. And the great thing about these derivative contracts was that firms only needed to put up the margin on purchase; they could use their winnings to pay the balance of the purchase price at the end of the life of the contract—when they'd made their profit.

In the summer, the financial world began to get a sniff that the free lunch was over. Up until the arrival of the mass consumption of derivatives, the stock and bond markets had been zero sum games; for every winner, there was an equal and opposite loser because if the share price went up, the current owner won by making a profit and the seller lost by not holding onto the asset for longer. This was because the value of the asset was directly tied to something happening in the world; the success or failings of a company and its products and services.

When financial institutions started trading derivatives without having any connection with the thing the contract was derived from, people started believing everyone could have the free lunch; if you bought an asset whose value reduced, you could own a derivative whose value increased precisely because the initial asset had lost its value. If you won you won and if you lost then you still won.

This was possible because financial institutions could own a derivative without owning the underlying asset. So you could place a bet on a company going bust—an event known as a credit default —without owning any shares in the company.

IN THE US, there was trading in poor quality contracts for residential real estate, known as the sub-prime mortgage market. These were contracts whose underlying value were bundles of mortgages held by those with terrible credit ratings. They had obtained mortgages during the glory days of the consumer boom. Now interest rates were no longer rock bottom, and the West had experienced a near or actual recession post 9/11, ordinary Joes were having serious problems repaying their mortgages.

What so few people realise is that when you take out a mortgage, your mortgage provider sells the future cash flow of your mortgage payments to a different financial firm as part of a policy to mitigate its risks of holding all these mortgages. And, because these mortgages were bundled together and then sold on, the traders didn't think about the value of the underlying mortgages. They only thought about the value of the derivative contract they were buying and selling.

Ultimately, when enough mortgage holders default on the mortgages they couldn't afford in the first place, the value of holding a sub-prime mortgage contract becomes painfully apparent: worthless.

So when one of Wall Street's best-known names had a good look at the sub-prime assets it was holding after a particularly unpleasant default, the bank realised it was built from a house of cards and the venerable financial institution began to implode.

Bear Stearns had been on Wall Street long before anyone could remember. It was part of the US furniture, but over the course of two or three days, rumours were spreading about the state it was in. Phone calls between traders were recorded for security and monitoring purposes, but senior management and compliance were incapable of monitoring what was said in the bars of an evening and they couldn't see what was being written in the secure chat rooms inside the Caldwells either. Word got out.

Ray was one of the many who had leveraged the sub-prime market and bought exposure to mortgage-backed securities. Unlike the herd, Ray ensured he kept his eyes and ears open and as soon as something smelled wrong in the state of Denmark, he put some calls through to old trader mates of his to see if the rumours rang true.

Word on the street; Bear Stearns was dirty and he should not trade with them. Interestingly, none of the traders told a regulator in the US or the UK of these thoughts. Officially, Bear Stearns was good to go—as viable as any other US house, but traders pulled away from dealing with them.

RAY CHECKED HIS book and noticed he had exposure to sub-primes and had indeed purchased some through Bear Stearns several months ago. Over the course of an afternoon, Ray quietly sold all of that holding and invested in Freiberg options. Why? If anyone was going to profit out of the destruction of the mortgage-backed securities market then it would be his old firm. Sharper than the rest of the market put together.

By the end of the week, senior management at Bear Stearns had informed the relevant authorities they were up shit creek with no idea whether they even owned a paddle and the collapse of the US giant had begun.

Markets went wild as traders exchanged rumour and gossip as though it was fact, whipping themselves up into a frenzy, which then spilled over into the perceived value of all financial institutions. If Bear Stearns was in financial trouble, how could anyone know other banks weren't in similar dire straits? After all, everything had been shiny with the company last weekend?

Then there was the natural domino effect; if your economy is driven by wholesale financial services, like in the US and UK, when the banks are in trouble, the perceived value of real-world companies takes a hit too. And so market volatility creates sufficient uncertainty to generate a mini recession.

All this doom and gloom passed Ray by, because he'd sniffed the acrid aroma of the sewage works before most had realised the fertiliser had hit the air conditioning. In fact, before the end of July, Ray had generated his whole year return target out of some sly derivative contracts predicated on the demise of Bear Stearns. Every day that week, Ray left the office beaming, taking Erin out for a drink or two on Friday night because he was happy, not because he had any plans to try to do anything about those oversized tits or rounded arse. He was just happy.

PENNY WAS IN the US yet again and Ray sat in the garden on Saturday lunchtime, with a sandwich and a beer on a table, lying back in a deck chair, knowing he had the next week off work. He'd spent some of the morning tidying up his Anderson shelter, but mostly he wanted to sit down and enjoy the warmth of the sun on his skin.

He heard some clattering from next door but paid no attention. Then he heard the splintering of glass and some sobbing. Ray sprang up and stood on top of the mound to see what had happened. Claudia knelt on the patio with the remnants of a wine glass stem in one hand with the other held to her face, crying.

"Hey, you! Everything all right?"

Claudia Baldwin took her hand away from her mouth and looked around until she made eye contact with Ray. She rubbed the tears off her face and tried to smile.

"Yes... Yes thanks."

"Need a hand or is... Jacob around?"

"What? No thanks. No, he's not." She sighed.

"Hey, why don't you leave that mess and pop over here."

"I'm not sure..."

"I'm on my own too. I could do with the company. If you don't mind?"

Claudia thought for ten seconds, rubbing away a few more tears.

"What the hell. Okay then. Give me a minute."

"Sure thing. Come round the back and I'll let you in."

Claudia took a good ten minutes to arrive. In the intervening time, she'd changed out of her tracksuit bottoms and into her usual dungarees. Ray had put out another deck chair and finished off his beer waiting.

"Can I get you something to drink?"

"Ooh, yes please. What have you got?"

"Beer, wine, vodka..."

"A glass of something red would be lovely."

Ray smiled and went back inside to open up a bottle of Pinot Noir. Two glasses poured, he returned to the garden. Claudia was sitting on one of the deck chairs, head back catching some rays.

He kept the conversation light because Claudia was obviously not in a good place right now.

"You said Jacob wasn't around?"

"No, he's not. Another weekend and he's off speaking at yet another conference. This week it's in Florida, I think. Florida or Oregon. Whatever."

"It's tough, isn't it?"

"Can be."

Ray refilled both glasses and he noticed Claudia had necked hers almost before he'd had time to fill his own glass. He quietly topped her up and tried to catch up with her.

They talked about being married but living on your own; both their partners had abandoned them for the summer. Jacob had a speaking tour of the southern States and Penny had some takeover deal brewing which would close early September but needed all her attention until then. Claudia and Ray were marooned together in balmy Edgware.

RAY ENSURED THE wine carried on flowing and brought out some nuts and crisps to nibble on as the sun started to leave its zenith. With two empty bottles on the grass and another with only a glass left inside, Ray's head was buzzing slightly and, after a lull in the conversation, he turned to see what Claudia was up to; she'd fallen asleep, head leaning on her shoulder, facing in his direction.

He smiled. Luckily not all women lapsed into unconsciousness in his company. Ray left her alone and lay back to carry on soaking in the sun himself. After what felt like only five or ten minutes, Ray opened his left eye—the one nearest Claudia—and took a long hard look at her.

She wore her blonde hair as a bob, just below her ears. The line of the bob was very sharp, so Ray guessed she'd recently been to the hairdressers. As he looked at her neck, round the back of her head, he could see the contrast between the hairs at the back of her neck and the neck itself. Claudia had mentioned she'd packed off the kids to her parents last night to give herself some Claudia time. She must have had the chop this morning, he figured.

Casting his eyes back to her face, he focused on her stubby nose and thickish lips. She'd chosen a scarlet lipstick, but most of that was now smeared on the rim of her wine glass. In the late afternoon sun, she looked pretty, Ray thought, as his eyes wandered away from her head and towards her dungarees, following the line of the edge of the material as it went down the straps and headed towards her chest and then onto her side.

Her arm was flopped off the chair, her fingers almost touching the grass, and Ray looked at the gap between the dungarees and the side of her body. He could make out a white cropped T-shirt; there was T-shirt material at the front of the dungarees, hiding her breasts, but at the side the T-shirt stopped very shortly below her armpit so he could easily see the colour of her flesh; a pure white. Without noticing himself do it, Ray leaned towards her and took in the faint smell of rose water under the much stronger scent of their wine. Then he caught himself doing this and leaned back in his deck chair. She was attractive, even though she was short. He tried to remember quite the shade of her blue eyes but failed.

Lying there, he cast his eyes up and down her body, soaking up the curves he could see under those dungarees and then imagining the curves he could not.

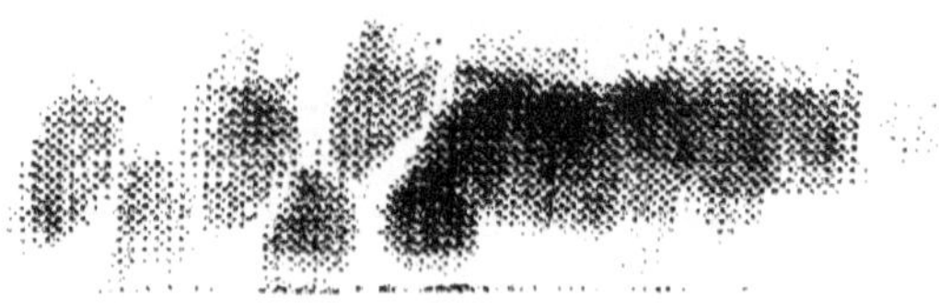

# 42

THE SUN WAS close to setting and the warmth of the day had departed. Claudia awoke with a shiver and flipped her head from side to side like she'd forgotten where she was.

"It's okay. You're in my garden. You fell asleep."

Claudia looked at him and drunk-nodded. Ray stood up and came back out with a glass of water and passed it to her.

"Thanks."

"De nada. When you're ready, shall we go inside?"

Now it was Claudia's turn to nod and a few seconds later she stood up and they wandered into the kitchen then Ray led her into the living room and they sat on the sofa, half facing each other.

"Warmer now?"

"Yes, thanks. Sorry about falling asleep on you."

"Doesn't matter. You needed the rest. Besides most beautiful women fall into a coma near me, so sleep was a refreshing change."

"Oh, don't."

"I'm kidding."

He touched Claudia's knee to reassure her all was fine and Ray followed her eyes as they went from his hand to his face and back to his hand again.

"I was going to fix some food. Fancy some?"

"You don't have to go to any trouble."

"It was only going to be a bowl of pasta, to be honest. So don't get your hopes up too much."

"Pasta would be lovely."

Claudia smiled and Ray saw her dark blue eyes as if for the first time. Intense colour. He went into the kitchen and made them dinner, opening another bottle of wine.

He laid the kitchen table and, fifteen minutes later, they were both sat eating penne with a tomato sauce, peppers and olives. Simple but tasty. The wine went well with the flavours too.

This time, as they drank and ate, Claudia got quite giggly.

"SO, WHAT DOES a man like you do rattling around a place like this when he's on his own?"

"The usual stuff. Catch a bit of telly, read a magazine, watch the odd movie."

"What kind of odd movies do you watch?"

Ray looked blankly at her, not understanding what she was getting at. Claudia giggled and poured herself another glass, then topped up Ray's.

"Do you like adult movies?"

"That's not really my thing."

"Are you sure? Most men like to see naked women. Do you like to see naked women?"

"There's nothing wrong with a naked woman, for sure."

"Would you like to see a naked woman now?"

"Huh?"

"You heard," she giggled, "Would you like to see me naked now?"

Before Ray could answer, Claudia stood up, knocking her chair backwards, grabbed Ray by the hand and led him back into the living room.

"Let's dance. Put on some music for us, Ray-my-man."

Without thinking, Ray did as he was bid and found a compilation CD to play. As soon as the first track buzzed into life, Claudia started tapping one foot and moving her hips, which encouraged Ray to try to do the same. He knew he had no rhythm and was going to massively embarrass himself, but Ray felt he had no choice. He didn't want to upset Claudia and the way she was gyrating her body was beginning to turn him on, despite everything.

SHE HELD HIS hand and danced around him, understanding that his bobbing from one foot onto the next was about as good as it would get. Still Claudia persisted, making moves with her feet and using Ray as a dancing post, enabling her to twist, turn and manoeuvre herself around him. Occasionally she'd get up close, her hands round the back of his neck and he could feel the warmth of her body against his. But then she'd break away and swoosh to the other side of the living room, before reeling herself back in towards him, and repeat the whole process to the beat of an electro-drum.

Then the tempo changed as the last couple of tracks kicked in and the pace slowed right down. Claudia came in close and put her arms around Ray's back and he mimicked her as they moved from side to side, turning around in slow motion. She rested her head on his shoulder and Ray felt her hands sliding up and down his back—or as far up as she could reach because she was only a couple of inches taller than five foot.

Partly in response to her hands, and partly because he wanted to anyway, Ray aped her moves and felt the length of her back with his fingers. The roughness of the denim of the dungarees was uniform and he could sense the point where the cropped T-shirt vanished and there was just her back beneath the denim. He also realised there was no bump where a bra would be, but he figured the sensation was hidden under the thickness of the denim. They carried on like this until one track ended and what Ray knew as the last track commenced.

Claudia took her head off his shoulder and went on tiptoe. Sensing what was happening, at the same time, Ray leaned down and their lips met. They had a chaste kiss and then another. Pretty soon they were kissing repeatedly and Claudia had her hands under his shirt.

Ray used the sides of the dungarees to get to feel her flesh and wriggled his fingers to try to get under the T-shirt. He gave up on that idea almost before he started as it was way too difficult. Instead he let their bodies separate momentarily to give himself the chance to undo the buckles of her dungaree straps. When they first came off, the dungarees took a lurch downwards and he could see the roundness of Claudia's left breast with a nipple pointing outwards. When the second strap fell apart, he pushed it off her shoulder and the whole garment fell to the floor, revealing Claudia in just that cropped T-shirt and a pair of purple knickers.

RAY STARED AT her breasts and at the shape of her thighs and tried to see past the purple material. Driven by instinct, he undid his belt and trousers, letting them fall to the ground. Then Claudia and Ray stood there and kissed again, touching each other's bodies; backs, necks, chest and breasts, buttocks, thighs.

Almost staggering with the sensual overload, Ray put one hand on Claudia's left breast and placed the other hand on her bum. She responded by stroking his dick and squeezing his arse, eventually putting her hand under his boxers to get to his balls. Real gentle. Real caring.

"Come with me," he whispered and took her by the hand and walked her up the two flights of stairs and into the bedroom. They kissed and stroked some more until Claudia sat down and Ray knelt between her legs at the foot of the bed. He licked the inside of her thighs until his tongue was tasting the purple of her briefs. He pulled down at the knickers and she raised herself slightly to help him take them off. Then he licked her triangle-shaped bush until he felt himself get hard. There was something about going down on a woman that really turned him on.

After quite some time, Ray thought his jaw was going to seize up and he had to stop. Claudia sat back up and silently ushered for Ray to stand. She pulled down his boxers and put her lips around his helmet. Now it was his turn to moan.

When his breathing started to get quite heavy, Claudia stopped and edged herself further up the bed. Ray followed immediately and lay on top of her until he felt her bush around his dick.

She wrapped her legs around his as they found each other's rhythm. Eventually, their slow connection built up into a sweaty frenzy. Ray was gasping for breath, trying to hold back, while at the same time desperate to gain release from the intense pleasure-pain exploding in his head. Claudia's breathing was on the edge too and the intensity at the tip of his penis took hold and he ejaculated.

After he felt himself shrink away inside her, Ray rolled off Claudia and they lay next to each other, cuddling and, after a few minutes, sharing intimate thoughts.

"What's going to happen to us?"

"NO FUCKING CLUE. I have no idea at all. But can you stay overnight whatever happens?"

Ray truly wanted to wake up next to that woman the following morning. Penny had been fucking some Yankee for Christ knows how long, so he didn't feel any guilt. But he didn't want to end up alone. Penny wasn't due back for two or three weeks and he knew Jacob wasn't returning until the end of August—and it was July 28 today.

"Yes, I can. But at some point, I'm going to need to get the kids back."

"I know, but not just yet, eh?"

They huddled in together and vanquished thoughts of tomorrow from their minds, happy instead to live for the single perfect moment they'd created for themselves on a sunny Saturday in Edgware.

For the next week, Ray made best use of his holiday, soaking up as much time as he could with Claudia. By day, she'd spend time with her children, but they had playgroup in the afternoons and by six or seven they'd be in bed. Then Ray would pop over to Claudia's or she'd bring the baby monitor over and fuck Ray at his place.

One thing which Ray really enjoyed was the fact she never wore a bra when she was with him. Every time he put his hand on her top, there was a nipple ready to be squeezed. And he'd found those nipples to be the way to Claudia's groin. Even with a light fondle and a small squeeze, she would get on her hands and knees and give him a blow job. Most of the time, Ray found himself wanting to go down on her. He loved her taste in his mouth and the smell of her juices. In the mornings when he was alone, he'd smell his fingers to remind himself of Claudia's body.

ON THE THURSDAY, Claudia told him she'd sent the kids packing back to her parents, who only lived in Hatfield, but it meant they could have another night entirely to themselves.

When she came back from dropping them off, Claudia rang the doorbell and Ray let her in. They had got to the point where he closed the door and by the time he'd turned back round to greet her, she had walked upstairs and into the bedroom. Following her, Ray picked up her baggy jeans and T-shirt, the only things she was wearing.

When he arrived in the bedroom, Claudia was already lying on the bed, naked. Ray ripped off his own clothes and joined her for another night of self-absorbed pleasure.

The strength of their relationship was its inherent weakness; both Ray and Claudia were being ignored by their spouses, but didn't want, or couldn't face, actually doing something about it. Ray was fine sleeping with Claudia for as long as he thought he could get away with it, but he knew he'd lie next to Penny as soon as she returned to the UK. Same for Claudia and her Jacob—and she had the children to think about too.

When Ray went back to Bespoke on Monday, there was talk of Bear Stearns being broken up and some even believed the US government might let it go into Chapter 11 to teach the other banks a lesson. For the first few hours, thoughts of Claudia persisted in his memory, but the sheer reality of hedging against the collapse of the entire US financial services industry helped focus his mind on what he was being paid to do.

That didn't stop him from thinking about her knickers at lunchtime, but only while he ate his sandwich at his desk. By the time Erin appeared with the first of his afternoon coffees, Ray's mind was completely aimed at making a killing or two in the markets.

# Part Seventeen

# August 2007

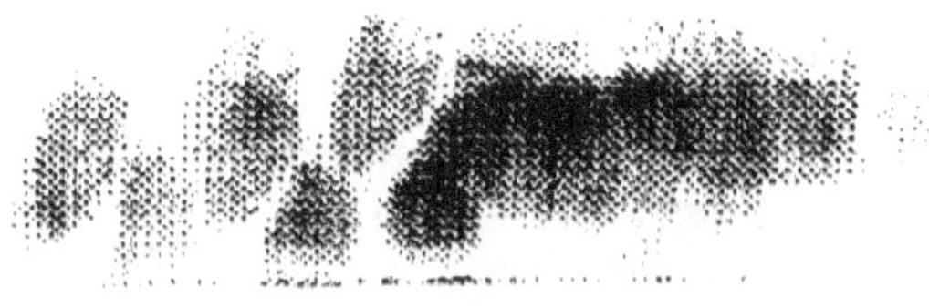

# 43

**PENNY**

New York was at its usual summery ninety-eight per cent humidity, which meant you were swimming in your own sweat between leaving an air-conditioned building and entering a taxi. The city looked beautiful in July and August with jet blue skies and steam coming out of the manhole covers. And it was certainly quieter; any of the locals with money had moved out. So Penny was surrounded by the low paid and the tourists.

She didn't care. Penny was over for one thing and one thing alone; a reverse takeover which would generate hundreds of thousands of fees in the execution and represented millions in forward billable hours as the real work was in the merger and the board appeared serious in its intention to follow through on its pre-sale promises. An unusual position for any board, let alone for a bank.

Penny knew Ray would have wanted to be all over the deal, but this is where her professionalism kicked up a gear. If she'd told him, he'd have traded against them and then the entire market would have known. So she kept the details away from him to earn her money and keep her client confidentiality clauses intact.

The deal was due to close on September first and Penny knew she would be here all summer. There was not much point flying back to the UK at weekends because that would just make her unbelievably tired every weekday she was working, so she used the weekends to tidy up loose ends and to reach out to some of Karen's friends in upstate New York, with whom she'd kept in contact over the years.

One weekend she'd visit Hua and Xun, who slummed it in Jersey, another she'd hang out with Frankie and Andy in White Plains. The guys she liked the best though were Elaine and Phil, who lived in Valhalla, which said it all really. They were a relaxed couple who were totally young at heart. Despite the grown-up jobs, they continued to party at the weekends, which gave them a bit more life than the other couples. They came across as early onset middle-aged. But not Elaine and not Phil.

Penny had been to some freaky parties with those dudes over the years she'd been working in the US, but unlike most of the people at those parties, she had always kept her knickers on—or at least most of the time.

WHEN PENNY THOUGHT about what went on inside her pants there were, after all, only two men in her life. Ray and Mickey. No matter what happened with Ray, she always found herself coming back to Mickey. She'd had weeks and months away from him, but there was something about that man's body to keep Penny returning for more. Even the trouble with Theresa, his sister, didn't and wouldn't stop her.

So when she came home from a trip, instead of going straight home, she'd see if Mickey was free first and see Ray the following day—assuming Theresa wasn't in the flat, because the two of them didn't get on. Not at all.

The trumped-up secretary, who called herself a personal assistant, thought she was better than Penny and believed Penny was holding Mickey back. What Theresa didn't understand was Mickey held himself back by being totally disinterested in anything other than how hot his own body was and finding women to adore him too. The man lived an entirely shallow existence, devoid of hopes and dreams. Theresa had enough for the two of them.

Perhaps that's what Penny liked. No matter what was going on in her life, no matter what state she and Ray were in, Penny could rely on Mickey to flip open his duvet and let her in. And then fuck her like a buck rabbit because that's all he knew how to do well.

Penny understood there was no future for the two of them and that probably added fat to Theresa's fire. She wanted her brother to succeed and that included finding a good woman to make his wife so he could carry on the family name.

When she came home on September 1, Theresa was away for a hen night in Prague, so Penny had Mickey all to herself for the entire day and night.

She shed her travel clothes and had a shower. Then she joined him in bed and they lay there naked for most of the day, occasionally fucking but mainly sleeping, comfortable in each other's company.

By the evening, Penny got bored and took out a book and read for an hour or two, while Mickey watched Chelsea play on the satellite TV. Once the match was over—Penny knew not to interrupt during a game—she hustled round the kitchen to get them something to eat. A couple of microwave meals later and they went back to bed to hump themselves to sleep.

The next morning, Penny put on her travel clothes and walked out the door, down in the lift, and tipped Ricky handsomely as usual. Then into a black cab and back to Edgware.

Monday she started working on a purchase agreement for a chunk of Bear Stearns. So many billable hours, but the bid came to nothing.

# Part Eighteen

# September 2008

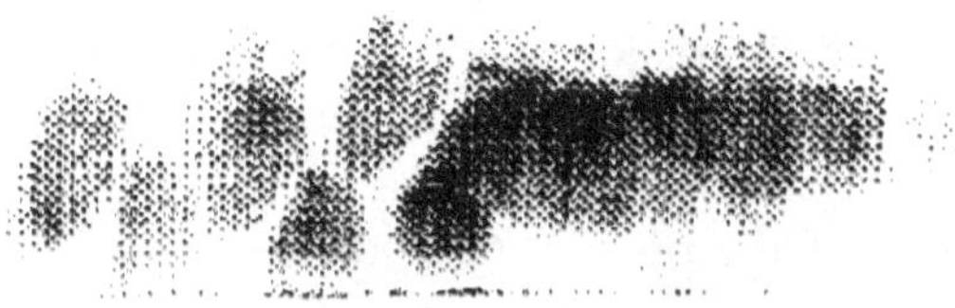

# 44

THE SUB-PRIME crisis had been building for over a year. You could time the moment of its start to the day when Bear Stearns had to give up refinancing its own CDO-based fund.

The point when the crisis spilled over into the real world was the week when Lehman Brothers was stabbed in the heart and left for dead. The main difference between Lehman and Bear Stearns was that the US regulator—and, by extension, the US government—wanted to save Bear Stearns, but no one liked the guys at Lehman enough to want to see the firm carry on.

Just like Bear Stearns, the City knew at least three days before the official end of Lehman that it was not capable of meeting its trading obligations. So brokerage houses and investment banks stopped trading with Lehman. Of course, they didn't officially stop until they were told to do so by the Fed, but before then, lines of credit were withheld, which meant you couldn't trade with someone from Lehman anyway.

The knock-on effect of Lehman's inability to cover its trading losses sent more than just shivers across the system. It was a tsunami in the financial world, from which there was no escape.

FIRST THE SHOCK of such a well-known name vanishing overnight sent people in all the major financial centres scurrying for the hills. Then the implications of what it meant for a bank to fail began to surface in conversation.

Next, the self-same people realised their own banks were just as vulnerable, because every major bank had exposed themselves to poor quality residential mortgages without going to the bother of measuring the extent of the quality of those mortgages.

And if one bank was fit enough to fail then others could fail in a domino effect. By the end of the week, there was talk of every bank in each market self-immolating and there only being a central bank left standing.

Ray was unaware of these Armageddon scenarios. Instead, Ollie had called him on Wednesday, September 10, to let him know the scuttlebutt he'd come across and on Monday September 15, the management made the announcement the bank had met its maker. Naturally, Ray didn't pass the info on to anyone else, but he did place some significant bets based on Lehman not surviving to the end of the month. The irony was that Ray had gone long on CDOs on Lehman, which was precisely the cause of the bank's demise.

Before the end of September, the world stabilised and the death of all banking was off the menu, but the idea of banks being too big to fail became part of the language of wholesale financial services.

The biggest fallout took a couple of years to have its impact felt. Rightly or wrongly, the investments in CDOs and other derivatives were blamed for the recession which was the US and European consequence of the death of Lehman. Certainly, the massive devaluation in the banks' balance sheets was caused by the way they calculated the risk of holding these derivative instruments. Were all derivatives at fault? Of course not. And were all bankers evil? No, but it helped to have a wonky moral compass if you wanted to succeed.

Ray was in a world of his own. There he was sitting in a hedge fund, when the industry was on the edge of catastrophe. The potential for the end of the world was over-predicted and under-delivered, but Ray's mind was split in two directions.

HIS FIRST THOUGHT when he saw what was happening to Lehman was to figure out as many strategies as he could to take advantage of its misfortune. When the TV news showed pictures of Lehman staff walking out with a box of their personal possessions in their hands, Ray considered whether there would be sufficient numbers of them required to cause a cardboard shortage. It was the way his head operated after all those years in the City; he couldn't help himself.

The next thought Ray had was a lot more personal; how safe was his job at Bespoke, if the world was falling apart all around. He reckoned the high net worth individuals who provided most of the assets under management were not going to flee the high reward environment of hedge funds just because a bank had been allowed to go to the wall. Being a smart cookie, Ray validated this theory by calling up most of his investors to see how they were feeling about the events unrolling on the front pages of the newspapers. As he'd suspected, most were relatively calm and those who were from the investment banking world were full of jitters and there was nothing he could say or do to calm them down. Either they'd end up liquidating their positions or not, but it wasn't going to be a decision over which Ray had very much—or any—control.

For no reason and with no explanation, Ray also thought about Claudia Jacobs, his neighbour and erstwhile confidante. They had started sleeping together the previous summer and the affair had gone on until the end of August when Penny returned from the US. Although, if Ray was honest, they had carried on surreptitiously fucking until at least Easter this year, but their conversations in between had become less frequent. By the summer just gone, Ray realised he hadn't tasted Claudia since April and that he didn't have much interest in doing so if the opportunity arose.

This wasn't because his interest in Claudia's body had waned or he felt any remorse; no, he still resented Penny in many respects. But life in Bespoke was keeping him sufficiently busy that he didn't feel he had a gaping hole that needed plugging with someone like Claudia.

THEIR INTEREST IN each other had been an accident of timing; Jacob had been ignoring Claudia at the same time as Penny was ignoring Ray. The fact they were both attracted to each other helped, but the truth was Ray found Claudia's children really annoying. Not the noise or the attention seeking. It was the sheer fact they existed and, when he wanted Claudia the most, the kids would always be there preventing her from satisfying his urges.

Of course, now and again, Ray's mind wandered and he found himself reminiscing about that well-manicured, blonde triangle of hers, but those memories and her taste had faded from his mind. By September, he strained to recall some of the details of her body. By this point she wasn't much more than a pair of nipples to him— unless they saw each other over the garden fence and then she became a whole human being again.

As these thoughts echoed around Ray's brain, he realised how harsh he sounded and he knew he didn't mean to be as cold as his thoughts were making him appear. He liked Claudia; she was cute and had a chi-chi way of dressing—all loose and baggy. She always looked comfortable in her clothes, never stressed or artificial. There was nothing pretentious about Claudia, a dental hygienist from Hemel Hempstead.

Ray's realisation that his interest in Claudia had faded coincided with an announcement he received from Penny one evening.

They were sat in the living room with the TV on, spouting some American criminal procedural show, when Penny put down her book and got Ray to pause the telly. He knew there was something serious about to happen.

"I've been thinking..."

"Oh?"

"...about us, you and I, you know."

"Right."

"We've had some lovely years together, haven't we?"

"Of course, yes."

"Well, as good as it's been—and it has been—I think there's something missing."

"Missing?"

"I know I told you before that the last thing I wanted was a baby."

"Yes."

Ray remembered that conversation only too well and how disappointed and saddened he had become when he heard Penny say those words. She had never even hinted that's what she thought before they'd got married.

"Well, I've changed my mind. Ray; I want us to have a child together."

HE HEARD THE words but nothing sank in at first. His initial instinct was to be happy because it seemed exactly what he'd said he'd wanted, although over the years he had reconciled himself to a life without young 'uns. Then his next thought was about what he was going to lose.

There would be no more lie-ins on the weekend. He would have to stop taking risks because he'd have a family to feed and, perhaps most important of all, there would be someone else in the family to vie for Penny's attention and her affection. And he knew he would inevitably lose; everyone has heard of the bond between a mother and her child. Ray understood he would lose a chunk of Penny's love. This thought settled on top of Ray and didn't leave him for quite some time. Several weeks in fact.

"Wow! That's great."

With those words, Penny got out of her chair and Ray met her halfway and they hugged and kissed, with a warmth and a connection neither had known from the other since the first year they were married. They stood there canoodling for five minutes or so and then, still holding hands, they sat down on the sofa, facing each other.

"So does that mean we're going to need a military campaign to get you all pregnanted up?"

"Military? No, but we are going to need a campaign tied to my cycle, for sure. We're going to be at it like rabbits for a week every month, but sensible rabbits. We need to maximise the chances of your sperm hitting one of my eggs. We don't want them all dribbling out and down my legs."

"I'm not being funny, but how are we going to do that as you spend so much time in the States?"

"Yeah, I've thought about that. My plan will be to let Nina know I want to spend more time in the UK over the next few months. I'll blame my parents, or their health or something. That way, I can be around more when I need to be. And if I do need to make a trip then I'll make sure it's not in the vital week when we need to be banging for Britain."

"Nicely put."

"Sorry about that."

"De nada."

As they were talking, Ray found his hands stroking Penny's legs, even though they were curled under her as she had coiled herself up on the sofa. Even though she was just wearing some jogging bottoms and a sweatshirt, Ray thought Penny was immensely sexy and attractive at that moment. As she breathed in, he could see the impression of her breasts on the grey sweatshirt, which then vanished as she breathed out.

He reached out and placed his palm over her right breast, stroking its side with his thumb. Penny stopped talking and edged a little closer so that her breast was pressed completely in his hand. She placed a hand round the back of his neck and drew him closer so they could kiss. Ray moved his free hand to Penny's thigh and stroked it until the hand was between her legs, despite her coiled posture. She relaxed her position so Ray's hand could start to massage her.

THEN PENNY UNWOUND her legs and knelt on the sofa, enabling Ray to put his hand under the jogging bottoms and under her knickers until he could feel her hairs on his fingers. Penny took off her sweatshirt and he leaned forward to lick her nipples. She raised her arms above her head and let Ray do all the work with his mouth wrapped around her left breast and a finger or two inside her body. Ray was enjoying himself, immersing his mind in the pleasure he was giving her and with the implied pleasure he would experience soon enough.

Penny pulled down her jogging bottoms to her knees and Ray kept his fingers in exactly the same position; moving in and out of her, rubbing his palm against her pubes. He loved the feeling of those hairs and the incredible smoothness of her skin when the hairs vanished. To his surprise, as soon as he'd put his hands under her pants, he'd felt so much smoothness and now, in the periphery of his vision, he understood why; Penny had gone back to having a Brazilian, just like the first time he'd tasted her body.

He pushed Penny over so she fell backwards and lay on top of her so her legs were either side of him. Briefly, he licked her stomach but soon got bored and headed for her knickers, which he took off and he licked her again, letting himself be devoured by the vanilla scent in his nostrils and her taste on his tongue. Ray was in heaven, just as his ears were being crushed by Penny's thighs tightening as her pleasure deepened.

AFTER TEN MINUTES or more, Ray's jaw was weakening and he felt as though his tongue muscle would soon be stretched to breaking point. He stopped and, for an instant, Penny just lay there, soaking in the sensations Ray was conjuring up for her. When he didn't go back down on her, she put one knee up and twisted their bodies so now

Ray was lying on the sofa and she was on top of him. First, she sat on him and moved her pelvis up and down his body, rubbing his dick against her groin until it settled on his helmet and he watched it vanish inside her.

Then he clenched his eyes shut because her pelvic thrusts were engulfing his dick and all his conscious mind. Intense pulses of pleasure slammed inside his head. Suddenly, Penny held her position, not moving with her groin hovering over the end of his dick. She started to make really small movements so that Ray felt his dick peeping in and out of Penny. It was like Penny was constantly touching his helmet but she didn't appear to be doing anything. Nothing at all. And just as suddenly, she stopped completely and his dick popped out of her completely.

Penny slithered down his body until his balls were in her mouth and she sucked and licked them until he thought he was going to burst. By this time, Ray's legs were back on the ground and Penny was kneeling on the floor in between his legs.

Finally, Penny's lips moved off his balls and along the shaft of his dick. No hands, just her mouth, and then his dick was inside her mouth and she was licking and sucking until the inevitable happened and he felt himself ejaculate, pulsing inside her mouth.

Penny sat there, leaning her elbows on his upper thighs. She pulled a pube out from between her teeth and laughed.

"You okay with the baby thing, then?"

"Yeah. It'd be cute to have a little Penny scampering about the house."

"Could be a tiny Ray, you know."

"Either'd be fine by me."

"I love you my little Ray of sunshine."

"I love you, too, Penny Pitstop."

# 45

**PENNY**

Nina Webber, Penny's managing partner was sat opposite her in their offices at Webber Paine, the firm she had formed with Anita Paine once they'd both faced the choice of sitting in for the long haul of being a partner at someone else's firm or to strike out on their own.

Nina met Anita at an international law centre, where they were both studying for master's degrees. Nina went back to Basel and Anita returned to New York. The accident of where they both lived created an opportunity they'd seized on; cross-border companies needing advice from both sides of the Atlantic using lawyers who were qualified in more than one geography. By having an elite workforce they could charge top dollar. And it worked—and had been working well for years.

Karen had originally introduced Penny to Nina and her talent shone through even way back then. Penny had shown she could hold her liquor and still talk turkey, so Nina took a chance on the young junior partner and had hired her eight years ago. She had not disappointed.

Even though Nina had been trying to protect the management board from too many new entrants, she had welcomed Penny as a partner, because she was delivering unbelievable billable hours and had a strong drive to succeed. Nina saw herself in Penny, even though there were nearly twenty years between them.

All these thoughts flashed inside their heads as Nina and Penny settled down in Nina's office to catch up on the latest deal and on Penny's workload in general.

Nina's stature had worked wonders in the male world in which she operated. She was two inches shy of six foot and knew how uncomfortable her height made men feel. Nina only wore fuck-me heels when she wanted to make a point and had learned to accept this would be a rare occasion; if she wanted to get her way or sleep with a guy. That predicament was a major issue fifteen or so years ago, not now. The time for finding a steady had passed as far as Nina was concerned. She was happy to have some fun with any interesting guy who came her way, but the number of interesting, single, middle-aged men could be counted in handfuls. And she spent too much time travelling around the globe to put down any meaningful roots with any one individual.

Penny watched as Nina pushed her auburn hair behind her right ear.

"How's it going?"

Nina always started her meetings with a dangerously open question giving you more than enough rope to hang yourself.

"BILLABLES ARE UP on twelve months to last year and there's still mileage out of Anglo-American Media."

"What're we talking here?"

"The deal won't close until year-end at the earliest. The acquisition itself is facing regulatory approval in four markets including the UK, the US and the EU. Chances are we'll still be talking about this at Easter.

"And, because of that, the bulk of our work has only just begun."

Nina nodded, her silence showing implicit trust in Penny's judgement. This was probably the first time Penny could remember when Nina had done this. It was a diary moment.

"Good. Nice work. Have you spoken to any of the other partners on Anglo?"

"Not yet. I'm comfortable handling it right now as we've farmed out the regulatory advice to locals. To be honest, the biggest problem with the whole deal isn't the deal itself. It's the vendor."

"I know."

What Penny didn't say out loud was the one thing she and Nina knew; the deal was most likely to go south because the owner of Anglo-American was a billionaire who had his fingers in far too many media pies already and the chances were that every government body would line up to prevent Sir Reginald from increasing his reach. And Sir Reginald was paying their wages. This was one of those occasions where Penny was pleased she had chosen to stay in a partnership and not gone in-house.

While Sir Reginald paid his bills on time and was perfectly charming face-to-face to his female counsel, Penny knew he was a git to work for. In fact, the best proof she had was the fact they'd got the gig in the first place. Sir Reginald had an enormous legal department on tap, who were well paid and more than able to handle another Anglo acquisition. But they had decided to outsource this work. Penny figured their general counsel knew this deal was dead in the water and didn't want to tell Sir Reginald this fairly obvious fact.

Indeed, Penny had said pretty much the same thing when she met Sir Reginald for their first briefing, but he had dismissed these suggestions;

"Even if there is only a one per cent chance of success, I want to try. I have a personal interest in the takeover; buried inside a subsidiary is a broadband internet provider. And I want one of those in my group without anyone seeing that's what I'm aiming at."

So Penny was working on a deal with a ninety-nine per cent chance of failure but she could still keep her client happy and generate massive revenue for the firm all at the same time. If she set aside the sheer futility of the work she and her associates were carrying out, there was only upside for them all.

Penny could tell Nina was satisfied with the situation in which Anglo-American had found itself. More importantly, she was satisfied with the position Webber Paine would be in as a result of the deal. Of course, Nina didn't have to deal with Sir Reginald, who was by any measure one of the most obnoxious men ever to set foot on this planet.

IF PENNY HAD to boil down what made the man so repellent, she reckoned there were two main reasons. First, there was the way he undressed you with every look. He never said anything, but his eyes lingered on her chest when they were sat down, his head tilted downwards toward her crotch when they were stood up and Penny had the ever-present sensation he was staring at her arse when she walked in front of him.

That was unpleasant and unsettling. Second, was the condescending way he treated everyone—female or male—and the unashamed disregard for the impact his decisions made on ordinary people's lives. Penny was a lawyer, so she didn't have much high moral ground to stand on, she knew, but even Penny understood Sir Reginald's media interests had a stranglehold on the British, Australian and US markets, which was not healthy and clearly monopolistic.

Finally, there was his appalling body odour, which was stomach churning and indicated he really didn't care what people thought of him. His vast wealth did all the impressing he needed to do and personal hygiene took second place to profit generation. His family-owned business, Haunsley Holdings was created by Sir Reginald's father from monies made out of ransacking Indian tea plantations, but under Sir Reginald, the company had grown and diversified across numerous industry sectors, of which media was the most significant—at least this decade.

Sir Reginald had ditched three previous wives; all much younger than him, all signed a prenup and all paid off handsomely when Sir Reginald tired of their bodies. His fourth wife was marginally older than the previous batch, but Penny thought Sir Reginald was getting older and must be slowing down, so needed a wife he could keep up with.

Bottom line—Sir Reginald had hired a woman-led law firm to wade through the Anglo-American acquisition so he could surreptitiously purchase a broadband provider and, for some reason, he liked Penny enough they'd won the business and she was going to do her damnedest to keep it. Chances of getting any more crumbs from the Haunsley account? Slim to none. Expected return on the current case; the entire year's revenue target in four months. Penny knew she could ask for anything once they'd wrestled this beast to the ground.

"One more thing," Nina said just as Penny was leaving the room, "See if you can find out who's picking at the bones of Lehman Brothers."

# PART NINETEEN
# DECEMBER 2008

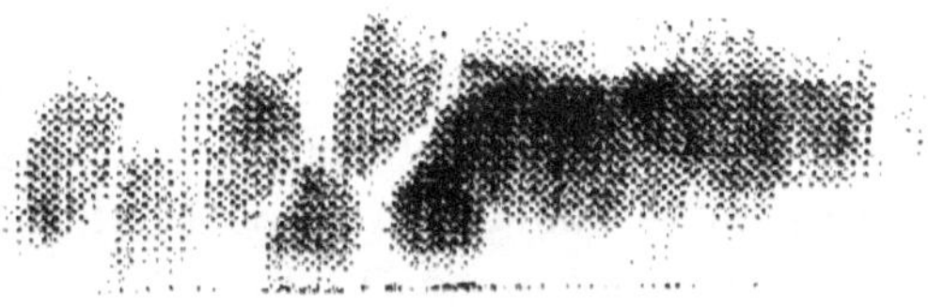

# 46

**PENNY**

A few days before, Penny reaped the rewards of the many phone calls she'd made. Finally, she found a consortium of advisors who were helping a bank pick over the bones of Lehman Brothers and still needed some legals.

She was sat on a conference call with a thousand others talking about the best way to scavenge the carcass formerly known as Lehman. The client, one of the Asian banks seeking to increase exposure to the UK and European marketplace on the cheap, knew exactly what it wanted but the US and European advisors wanted to take more than the pound of flesh the bank intended to extract.

After a spell, Penny noticed she'd started to doodle squares and cubes in her leather-bound notebook. This was never a good sign. Suddenly, there was a lull in the droning conversation.

"Mr Kawamura. With the greatest respect to my colleagues on the line, I'd like to remind us all what we are here to do. As I understand the situation, Kawamura Securities would like to purchase the Japanese warrants and European equities businesses from Lehman at a substantial discount. If that is not achievable, you will walk away from the deal."

"Hai."

"And if by some chance we are able to obtain other parts of the business bundled with those elements, you will consider it but are not wedded to the idea."

"Hai."

"Then instead of spending our time trying to convince you to do the exact opposite of what you want, may I suggest we spend the rest of the time on this call deciding who is going to lead the charge and what strategy we are going to employ to get Kawamura Securities what it has requested."

"Thank you, Ms Kurtz, for summarising the position so well for us."

As Penny was the only lawyer on the call, she knew her bread was buttered whatever conclusions were made about deal runners. After this introductory call, the meter would be running and each of the parties would need to play nicely in the sandpit otherwise the deal would fall away from them.

Penny knew there were many vultures hovering over this particular zebra and, given the amount of media attention, being circumspect was the order of the day. She felt like she was surrounded by a pack of schoolboys and she was right. On days like this, she was glad to be working for some level-headed women and not the kind of kids Ray had to handle. But, if she was honest, he was just as bad as the rest of these so-called men. When it came down to it, he was happy if you gave him a regular supply of pizza and stroked his dick when he was feeling low.

WHAT SHE FOUND much harder to deal with were the games Ray played with Ollie. Penny knew—although didn't explicitly acknowledge to herself—Ray was making nefarious money out of his business dealings with his old uni buddy. And if she didn't think about it then she didn't feel guilty about how he earned his money and who he was robbing blind.

Recently, Ray mentioned how a play he'd set in motion a year ago had come good. He had shorted oil futures based on the fact that one of Ollie's mates decided he wanted to go down in history as the first trader to buy a barrel of oil for one hundred dollars. Ollie and his mate knew the price wasn't sustainable and they also knew the market would follow their lead, at least for a few months.

And they were right. Ollie let Ray in on the trade and they banked on the price of oil subsiding over time. Ray then shorted oil.

"Normally, you have money and you purchase an asset, right?" he had explained to her.

"And that's called taking a long position, but there is an opposite deal you can make, which is to create a short position."

"How's that?"

"I borrow the asset on a repurchase agreement."

"A repo?"

"Yep. So I've agreed to return the asset to the lender at a later date —called covering. Meantime, if the asset decreases in value, I've made a profit; the difference between today's price and the price I end up paying to return the asset to the lender, which will be less if the asset tanks."

"And what if the asset rises in value instead?"

"Then I'm screwed because I make a loss. So the smart thing is never to just short. You include it in a package of deals so you use shorting to hedge your risks."

Finding out how trades were shorted proved useful to Penny as an intellectual exercise when she was working on the Kawamura acquisition, because at least she understood more than the basics of the kinds of assets Lehman had on its books—and the associated risks and liabilities Kawamura was looking to take on.

What Penny didn't like were the backroom deals between Ray and Ollie. The guy had looked after Ray for years and Ray trusted him like he trusted no other man in his life, but Ollie had taken to investment banking like shit to a shovel. If there was a deal to be done, Ollie would strike it and he didn't give any thought to the consequences of his actions to anybody else.

THIS OIL BUSINESS was a case in point. By hiking the price of wholesale crude, Ollie had increased the cost of petrol, for sure, but it had also bumped up the cost of transportation across the globe. And that meant millions of ordinary people had their lives impacted by Ollie's pal who wanted to go down in history as the first man to trade a hundred-dollar barrel of oil, for pity's sake.

While Ollie's wild plans were asinine, Ray had chosen to let himself get involved. He had chosen to make money out of the whole affair and was crowing about it. They had rigged the market and made a mint as a result. That was wrong. That was plain wrong. Sometimes Penny felt she didn't even know Ray at all. She was sure he wasn't like that when they first met all those years ago.

"You're an arsehole sometimes, Ray."

He had looked at her quizzically and put a platinum necklace and ring in front of her as a present to reflect his good fortune.

"Do you want me to take the pieces back?"

She declined and immediately put them on. They were beautiful. Penny sighed and carried on with her day. Ray was a fool, but his saving grace was he had good taste in jewellery. Penny wore both the necklace and the ring on the night of the Bespoke Christmas Dinner and Dance.

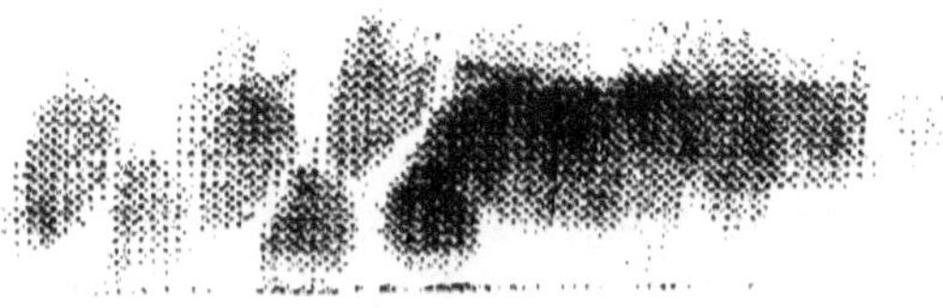

# 47

**RAY**

In the wake of the Lehman crash and the ensuing global financial meltdown, the City knew the world was watching and was not impressed. Under ordinary circumstances, the City would have flipped a finger to the world and told it where to shove its opinions. But this year was different. Headlines were filled with stories of how evil investment banks and their derivative trades had taken the planet to the brink of disaster.

What did this mean? Christmas parties were subdued as financial institutions didn't want to be seen to be frittering money away, even though they had recovered from the worst of the crash. For those in the Square Mile and Canary Wharf, the big blow-outs were off the cards and many firms banned Christmas parties altogether. They didn't want their people to be seen to have fun while governments fed the banks money to stop them going bust.

Of course, the investment banks held the positions and had turned the poor-quality mortgages into something to sell to unthinking and ignorant corporations. The hedge funds, for whom the derivative contracts were originally constructed, were not bailed out because they always made sure their risk position was zero at the end of every day. So Mayfair was a good place to host a party.

Although Bespoke Horizon had no significant reason to worry about how its clients felt about it, there was still a pervading belief held by the senior management not to lord it over the general public. Why was the company not that concerned about its clients? Simple: the clients were more than happy with the returns they had received from Bespoke this year; double digit growth in a portfolio was way beyond the grasp of an ordinary long-only pension fund.

So Ray and his co-workers found themselves in a basement restaurant and bar buried in the middle of the West End to enable them to hide in plain sight because working in the City was no longer the glamour job it had been before Lehman shrank to the size of a nickel.

THE VENUE HAD been selected to deliver for the needs of the older members of staff who would just want to eat a decent meal and carry on chatting over a drink or several. But there was also a club attached to the restaurant at the back so the younger staff could let their hair down.

Ray had been looking forward to the party for a while, not because he was that desperate to party on down, but it would give him a chance to introduce Penny to his fund management crew. It would be a nice night out for the pair of them.

The meal was perfectly adequate and, despite the best efforts to find somewhere with a decent cuisine and a more than decent wine list, the reality of delivering food to over forty people simultaneously meant Ray thought each plate smacked of mass catering. And he wasn't wrong.

After they'd eaten, he and Penny went off to the back and into the club where the rest of his peers had slunk a few minutes earlier.

The club had gone retro for the evening to match the needs of its clientele with the DJ playing tracks dating back to the '90s. Instead of heading into the centre of the dance floor, both Ray and Penny held back and chatted with people who were standing around the edge. Within a minute or two, they had got separated as Penny went off when Ray started to talk to Freddie, who had joined Bespoke only a couple of months after Ray, following him over from Freiberg.

"What's the matter, Freddie?"

"I've just been fired."

"What?"

"By the head of HR."

"Huh?"

"He came over and took me round to the cloakrooms. We stood between the toilets and the kitchen and he took out a letter, signed it by resting it on his knee and handed it to me. They've fired me."

"They can't do that."

"Yes they can and yes they have. They're doing me for low performance over the last three consecutive quarters."

"Are they giving you any kind of pay off? They can't simply terminate your contract."

"With extreme prejudice. Tim said we could negotiate a compromise agreement if I go quietly."

"And will you?"

"Guess so. Depends how much they offer me, doesn't it? Trouble is, now is not the time to be out of a job."

Freddie was right; ever since the TV news showed images of Lehman staff walking out of the building holding their boxes of personal possessions, there had been mass layoffs in almost every financial institution. Hedge funds hadn't been as badly hit but, thought Ray, poor investment performance doesn't win you any friends. And no one likes a loser. She would have been better to have stayed in long-only funds. Freddie was good at that and had been a high flyer.

"And all this happened just now, before the meal?"

"Yes, didn't I say?"

She had but Ray hadn't processed the information.

"What a cunt."

"You said it, Ray. You said it. Love will tear us apart."

Ray gave Freddie a hug because he could see the redness around her eyes where tears had been falling recently. He knew she could do with some human reassurance. With her head near to his, Ray could smell her perfume and he liked it. Oh to be free and single again.

Freddie let go of their hug and wandered off to get herself another drink. Ray made a mental note to keep an eye on her as the evening progressed because she'd either get a skinful and become abusive or sullen and try to do something dumb. Either way, Ray needed to be her Jiminy Cricket.

RAY MADE SURE to wend his way to Eliezer Romano. He remembered the interviews he'd had with Eliezer to get the job in the first place. Since then, he'd been in one or two meetings with the guy but had never found a good enough excuse to pop into his office or to have a quiet word just to get some face-to-face time with his ultimate boss.

Instead, Eliezer worked on the basis that if it wasn't broke, there was absolutely no need to shove your nose in where it wasn't wanted and had left Ray alone because he was exceeding his numbers—in terms of both return on investment and assets under management. What else was there to discuss?

"Hi, Ray."

"Hi, Eliezer. How's it going?"

"Just fine, thanks. Having a good time?"

"Yes, thanks. All good."

"Pleased to hear it."

Ray couldn't see how the conversation could get more stilted if he physically tried. Why wasn't he able to act like a normal person around Eliezer? The man must be giving off some serious vibes.

"Do you think we're over the worst of the recession?"

"As a firm?"

"As a sector, I meant. I know we're doing fine."

"Sure are, Ray. Politicians are more interested in attacking the investment banks and while that's the case, they'll lay off the hedge funds. But if the media gets bored of bashing High Street brands and Americans then we could be in for a rough ride."

Ray pondered these thoughts and could see they had a lot of merit.

"Lehman was killed off by poorly managed sub-prime risks bundled into securitised products, so why would they have a go at hedge funds?"

"Ray, it's not what is true that counts. It's what people believe that matters. The ordinary Joe is unlikely to be able to tell the difference between a poorly managed sub-prime risk and a well-managed derivative risk. Both will count as complicated stuff created by the evil City at the expense of the ordinary man in the street."

"Are they that dumb?"

"Bet your bottom dollar on that."

"So do you really think we'll be in the firing line?"

"Very possibly. I'm just thinking hedge funds have had a free ride for so long, maybe our time has come."

"The end of the hedge fund? Really?"

"Not the end of it, but the Wild West might be over. We've been on the periphery of regulatory oversight for so long, we've forgotten what happens in the rest of the industry. And right now, the rest of the industry has shown itself to be completely shit when it comes to either keeping its own house in order or too damn clever at fending off the regulators."

"So what's going to happen to Bespoke, then?"

"No fucking idea! But we'll roll with the punches. If they regulate hedge funds and we can't make our returns there, we'll move into alternatives instead."

"Wine and property?"

"Why not? Both things are worth owning, aren't they? More use than a CDO squared."

Ray nodded in agreement and cast his eye around the room, in part to see what was happening and in part to see if he could spot Penny.

Eliezer used the lull in the conversation to move onto some other hapless employee. He was always putting his card behind the bar and he had a shrewd eye for intelligent investments, but fundamentally he was a dull man.

PENNY WAS ABOUT twenty feet away, dancing with one of the fund managers, Enrique Rodriguez. As the provenance of his name suggested, he focused on opportunities in Latin Am. At this precise moment, Enrique was focused on opportunities closer to home as he had his hand on Penny's arse and, from what Ray could see, his hand was doing its damnedest to venture under her little black dress and she was letting him.

Earlier, Ray thought he'd seen her laughing and chatting with him out of the corner of his eye, but he had paid no never mind as he was trying to impress Eliezer.

Ray couldn't work out which was making him more angry; Enrique's hand so close to his wife's crotch or Penny for not slapping him and walking away.

It was the former. Ray strode over in the space of a second and gripped his hand on Enrique's shoulder.

"Hey, bud."

Enrique turned to face him but kept his hand where it was. Ray was fuming. He looked at Penny and then back to Enrique.

"Let go, bud."

"I'm not your bud, En-reek-ay. And you've got your hand on my wife."

Enrique traced the line of Ray's staring eyes to his hand which had vanished behind Penny's body. She saw Ray's expression and stepped sideways away from both of them. So now Enrique's hand was in mid-air as Penny moved back. Ray and Enrique squared off at each other and colleagues around them made a space because they could tell something was going down.

"Hey, man."

"Listen, fella. Keep your hands to yourself. This is a staff and partners do. If you want to chase tail do it somewhere else..."

Eliezer appeared and stood between them, alerted to the trouble arriving in the middle of his party.

"Okay, guys. Let's simmer down and call it quits. No harm, no foul."

"Okay by me if it's okay by Ray."

Ray looked at Eliezer then he stole a glance at Penny, whose expression indicated she wanted this whole thing to be over as soon as possible. Then he stared at Enrique and thought for a second.

He held out his hand and Enrique shook it.

"Well done, guys. Good decision."

By the time Eliezer had walked away from the fracas, Penny had mingled back into the crowd and Ray could no longer see her.

LATER THAT NIGHT Ray and Penny undressed in silence, the same quantity of conversation they'd had in the cab on the way home. Ray couldn't get the image out of his head of Enrique's hand on Penny's dress and his fingers so close to her gusset and all that it contained. He was still angry but the initial rage against Enrique had transferred itself entirely into rage against Penny. She had allowed this to happen; she had carried on dancing with him when he first got fresh.

"Are you ever going to talk to me?"

Penny's words lacerated his thoughts. He glared icily at her and threw his clothes in the laundry basket before returning to face her.

"Don't know right now."

Penny sighed, pulled down her knickers and, still naked, followed Ray's example and chucked her underwear into the laundry. Then she slid into bed alongside Ray, his arms folded defensively.

"Why did you do it?"

"Do what?"

"Don't come over all innocent. Why did you do it?"

"Ray, I'm not being funny but I don't know what you think I did. One minute I was dancing with Enrique, the next minute you two were re-enacting a scene from Gorillas in the Mist."

Ray kept his arms folded and carried on glaring.

"Why did you let him touch you up?"

"I beg your pardon?"

"You heard me. He was like an octopus, hands all over you. All over your..."

"Now wait one cotton-picking second. We were dancing. End of."

"Right," Ray cut in with a snort of derision.

"End of story. It was a slowish dance, yes, but that was all that was happening. Nothing else. What do you think you saw?"

"WHAT DO I think? What do I think? I saw his hand all over your arse and you did nothing to stop him. You kept on dancing with him. That's what happened, for fuck's sake!"

The duvet had slipped down and one of Penny's nipples was showing.

"No, he didn't. Yes, he had his hand on my back, but that was okay. It didn't bother me. And yes, he was leaning in a bit too much, but again, that wasn't an issue for me, but he never touched my bum."

Silence as Ray processed her words.

"If he'd done that, he'd have way overstepped the line and I'd have pushed him away for sure, Ray. But it didn't happen."

Ray didn't know what to think. Penny's words seemed very reasonable and he truly, really, wanted to believe her. She had never done anything like that in front of him before and now she described the dance, Ray realised he was sounding crazy.

But he also couldn't forget what he suspected her of doing in America and now she was spending more time in the UK and was desperate to get some sperm up her pipes, Ray was confused and felt a bit dazed. Perhaps he had been wrong after all.

Penny put her hand on his arm and he didn't push her away, despite his thoughts of doing just that. Then she leant towards him so her lips were right by his ear.

"We're going to make babies together, remember. And your babies are what I want, not some deadbeat fund manager's from your firm."

For the first time since the incident occurred, Ray relaxed his body, tension seeping out of his limbs. Penny noticed it too and she carried on whispering to him.

"I want your babies and I want you inside me."

Ray turned slightly to place his hand on her cheek and stroked it.

"I want your dick inside me and I want it now."

She slid a hand under the covers between his legs until her fingers found his balls. They kissed and Ray's worries about Penny dissolved into passion and what sounded like an orgasm for her, with an ejaculation but no orgasm for him.

# Part Twenty
# January 2009

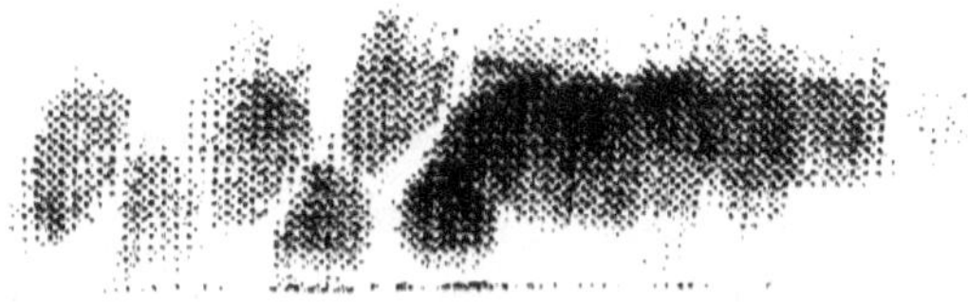

# 48

**RAY**

Sat in a coffee shop with a cappuccino in front of him, Ray eyed Peter Abbott up and down. He'd contacted Ray on a speculative basis and they'd got chatting. Right time and right place.

Naturally, Ray was underwhelmed at the shininess of Peter's suit, but he expected no less. Higher echelon head hunters were not much more than upmarket double-glazing salesmen and Ray knew it. Their suits might be more expensive and their shirts may be tailored from somewhere in Jermyn Street, but a barrow boy was always a barrow boy.

Ray understood the best way to gain access to the most interesting roles was via a head hunter and he also knew how pumped up his ego felt every time he received a call from one of them asking if he knew anyone who was interested in a job going spare.

Peter was more than a boy—probably in his late twenties or even early thirties. He was well known in the City as one of those guys who managed to shift entire teams from one brokerage house to the next, backfilling the departing team with a group of individuals he'd sourced from some other firm along the way. Rumour had it that Peter held the record for the biggest number of moves in a single day; he'd taken a team of twenty and then shifted groups of fifteen from one firm to another until he'd migrated over three hundred bodies around five trading floors. Apocryphal or not, when Ray heard Peter Abbott wanted to speak with him, he took the call.

THE NEXT DAY they sat in a coffee shop, sipping their drinks and talking about the City. Peter began by namedropping various City bigwigs to see who Ray knew and eventually they found there was sufficient commonality for Peter to be prepared to move onto stage two. This involved the part where he asked Ray what he was looking for in whatever his next role would be, without telling him what juicy role he had up his sleeve. This gave Ray the perfect opportunity to shoot himself in the foot before any job interview proper had even begun. Ray talked about how much he enjoyed the policy of "You eat what you kill" that pervaded the hedge fund business—just as it did in investment banking—but he also hankered for something with a bit more meaning to it. And if there wasn't going to be any meaning then a massive bundle of cash would be second best. A very pleasant second best.

"So I've been thinking about investment banking and the opportunities of becoming a rainmaker."

"The Americans are not buying much right now, but I know of at least two European banks who would be interested in speaking with you, if that was something you'd like to do."

"European?"

"One French, a German and possibly an Italian bank—off the top of my head."

"Really?"

"Oh yes, without a doubt. What makes you valuable is your experience across a number of different asset classes and not many people go from a brokerage house into a hedge fund. These are interesting qualities, I think you'll find."

RAY HAD NOT considered his bumbling attempt at a career might constitute something of commercial value to an organisation, but Peter was right. Most people stayed in one silo all their careers and Ray had jumped ship several times, one way or another. But he still wasn't sure what he really wanted. So before he allowed Peter to pull the trigger and contact one of the banks, Ray told him he wanted to think on it for a few days and get back to him by the end of this week or early next week.

Peter was fine with that because he knew, one way or another, he'd place Ray somewhere at some point and that would make today a very profitable two cappuccino investment—Peter would get twenty per cent of Ray's first year base salary. Nice work if you can get it.

When Ray arrived home that Thursday night, Penny was already there, sat on the sofa in a grey hoody and sweatpants. She was beaming from ear to ear and there was no reason Ray was aware of for her happiness. There was a white plastic stick lying on a tissue on the table.

"Hi."

"Hi. What's cooking?"

"I've got some good news."

"I figured. You are smiling on top of your smile."

"Here."

Penny picked up the stick and handed it to Ray, who took it and stared at it blankly. There was a small square display area halfway along the stick with a line running through it. And a symbol. A symbol was showing on the display; two lines intersecting each other in the middle. Ray looked at the two lines and tried to figure out what it was meant to mean. A cross? Some strange religious artefact made of plastic? Made no sense.

Then Ray realised it wasn't a cross; it was a plus sign. Why would a plus sign be showing on a stick? It meant something positive and suddenly Ray twigged exactly what he was holding in his hand and precisely what it all meant. And why Penny was smiling.

"You're pregnant!"

"Yep. I sure am."

Ray didn't know what to think. He was happy. He was scared. He was elated. He was anxious. He was aroused at the sight of Penny. He was fearful of all the things he didn't know about pregnancy, babies and childhood.

"That's. Just. Amazing!"

"Isn't it?"

THEY HUGGED LONG, squeezing each other over again, kissing and hugging some more. Ray's concerns were put to the back of his mind during this time and he lived in the moment, enjoying their shared happiness at this precise instant in time. Penny sure did look sexy in those jogging bottoms.

Those months of monotonous sex, timed to perfection around Penny's menstrual cycle, were over. The daily grind of missionary intercourse for a week and a half had ceased. Penny always lying on her back, his sperm shooting up her vagina desperately seeking an egg eking down her fallopians, in case any of his spunk dribbled down her thighs and the whole exercise was rendered futile.

After he got off her, Penny would stay on her back for five or ten minutes just in case the sperm seeped out. Nothing was less attractive than the sight of her with her knees up, waiting for a sperm to land. The only good news was that she hadn't decided to be one of those women who try to time her ovulation to the second, expecting him to zoom home at the peak minute of her fertility.

Then Ray began to think about their future. What would life be like with another person in their lives, in their family? His relationship with Penny was not great right now. They'd both strayed from the path of true love and they were just about on some kind of an even keel. Of recent months, he could tell Penny was making more of an effort not to ignore or avoid him like she used to do. The quality of their lives had definitely improved now she spent more time at home than in the US. Ray had assumed whatever had been going on there was now over—despite Penny's claim she hadn't had an affair, he knew she had.

BUT THAT WAS now officially in the past and there was something growing inside Penny other than heartburn. That something would become a baby around September or October, Ray reckoned.

Despite the months of rutting, the idea of there being a baby inside Penny seemed unreal, almost beyond his imagination. The concept of a little baby Penny was beyond his comprehension.

Ray tried to picture the three of them in the living room, desperate to give the new being some kind of form, but he found the whole experience too difficult. This third entity was an unknown, a huge question mark in his head. Ray couldn't put any face on it at all, nor any body.

Then the thought struck him; with Penny's attention still not at full pelt on Ray, what would life be like when she divided her time between him and the baby? What would be left of them as a couple?

Ray felt a tear pop out of the corner of his eye and roll down his cheek.

"I'm happy and I'm sad."

"Why? What?"

"I am so happy that we've made a baby. For real. It's great news."

He wiped the tear off his skin with a solitary finger.

"But I'm afraid we'll lose what we have together when the little 'un arrives."

Penny pulled away from their embrace for a second and gripped his shoulders with both hands.

"YOU SILLY BASTARD. We'll be fine. We'll still love each other and there'll be someone else for us both to love. There is going to be so much more love in this house, you wouldn't believe. What's there to be sad about?"

"I feel like you're slipping away from me with the arrival of the baby."

Another tear rolled down his cheek and Penny leant in to hug him again.

"Hey. I'm not going away. I'm here now and I am going to be here forever. You are not losing me."

"I know I'm not losing you. That's not the issue, but there'll be less of you for me. Less of you."

"We'll be fine, don't you worry about that my little Ray of sunshine."

Penny held him tight and he responded in kind, squeezing her to stop her from moving, stop her from slipping away from him on the sofa in their living room. This carried on for enough time for the stress to leave Ray's shoulders and finally, he and Penny relaxed back to just holding each other, stroking a back, touching a neck, embroiled in the warmth and the joy of their news.

Eventually, Ray remembered how sexy Penny was looking in her jogging bottoms—something about their bagginess and the low-slung waistband. It revealed her belly button and half of her hip bones, suggesting more than he could see. Their shape let his imagination run away with itself and he recalled how much he cared for Penny. How much, at times like these, he lusted after Penny in a way he didn't comprehend.

"Do you think it'll affect the baby if we have sex again?"

"Not that I've ever heard of," she smiled.

Ray stood up and grabbed Penny's hand and led her upstairs to the bedroom. He whipped round and planted a kiss on her lips, while grabbing her buttocks with both his hands and squeezing. Penny stopped their kiss briefly to giggle and grabbed his arse too.

His hands slipped under the waistband and he felt her skin under his fingertips. Then he slid his left arm up her back, under the hoodie until he reached the nape of her neck. She wasn't wearing a bra.

They kissed some more and she placed a hand on his groin and then pressed in toward him. He let one finger run along the edge of her thong and then slid it under so all he could do was feel the warmth of her body and not the roughness of the material of her clothes.

His finger continued its journey investigating Penny's body, the curve of her arse, until he felt the place where her arsehole ended and her lips began. Then he stopped his finger's journey and massaged the warm patch of her body he'd found.

Meanwhile, Penny had slipped her hand into the front of his trousers and under his boxers, playing with his balls. Several minutes later—and Ray had no idea of time he was so engulfed in the pleasure of their experience—Penny removed her hand from his trousers and pulled off her hoodie.

"Let's get under the covers and take it nice and slow."

RAY WAS SAT in a different coffee shop with Peter Abbott opposite him again. On this occasion, there was more than a speculative phone call to follow up on. Peter had listened to Ray and rifled through his contacts book until he thought he'd found Ray the perfect role to fulfill his needs; a vibe of trading with some social responsibility to boot. It was not something every City client was after, but that's what made Ray interesting to Peter.

"I've an opportunity for you in a long-only fund management house, which is part of a US international bank. So the good news is it has a balance sheet that's relatively safe in these uncertain times and the other good news is that, provided it hits its numbers, the bank leaves the investment arm alone."

"Okay, but this sounds like a step back to pension fund management."

"Bear with me, Ray. The investment strategy in the diversified portfolio is to take on some hedge fund like risk, but they don't want to run a stand-alone hedge fund. Instead they have a department which operates outside the long-only strategy. This is all above board and all investors, mainly local authorities and other municipal investment shops, know all about it. There is nothing going on under the table whatsoever."

"Right?"

"There's a variety of asset classes covered by this department, as you'd expect, ya-da, ya-da, but there is an opening for someone to trade swaptions."

Ray stared at Peter, who looked back at Ray with a tremendous weight of expectation.

"And you think I should become a swaptions trader?"

"When I say 'trade', I mean you will make specific investments on behalf of the fund in that asset class, but apart from that and the need to generate a positive return, you're your own man. All the freedom of being in a hedge fund with the knowledge that your investments are acting as a return kicker to pension fund holders and other needy types."

RAY'S EYES REFOCUSED as he tried to wrap his head around whether the role had any legs or not. Peter tried his best not to interrupt Ray's train of thought, but the guy was bursting with energy and enthusiasm.

"So what do you think, Ray?"

"I don't know, Peter. I really don't know."

"What don't you know, Ray?"

"Well, first off, swaptions? Isn't that a ridiculously narrow asset class?"

"Yes, it is, which is why I thought you'd like it. You've wide experience across vanilla and derivative instruments, on-exchange and over the counter. Swaptions are obscure, which means when you trade them, you become part of an elite, select group."

Ray wrapped his head around the swaptions market. An option was a contract to buy an asset at a specific point in the future for a price agreed now. If when that date arrived, today's price was lower than the eventual price, you'd take advantage of the option to buy and sell at a profit. If the future price was lower than the pre-agreed price then you don't buy it as you'd make a loss. Simple. A swap was a means for swapping over cash flows between banks. So, for example, with an interest rate swap, one bank might have a bundle of loans delivering revenue via a fixed interest rate and another bank may have a bundle of loans paying them on a variable rate basis. If each bank took an opposite view of whether central bank interest rate values would rise or fall then they'd believe they'd want the other's cash flow. A swap contract would enable them to do just that.

Swaptions, therefore, were a hybrid asset where you'd have the option to buy a swaps contract at some predetermined date in the future. And, because interest swaps were so prevalent, interest rate swaptions were the most common swaption too.

All this flew through Ray's mind as he tried to picture what kind of trading strategies would be needed. Once the initial fear of change had spluttered past his ears, Ray was able to see this was a technical trade rather than the chimpanzee fly-by-wire trading of equities or foreign exchange. Gut feel would be great, but you'd need some proper modelling to get the job done well. This did appeal to him.

"Peter, you might have something."

"I was hoping you'd say that."

They discussed the ins and outs of the role for another half hour until Ray had heard enough.

"Let me sleep on it and get back to you tomorrow."

# 49

**PENNY**

Penny had noticed she wasn't feeling so great and felt as though she was getting plump, but when she looked in the mirror, she saw the same body she'd had since she left school. Of course, when her last period didn't show then she knew almost immediately. To make sure she wasn't imagining anything, she went to the chemists and bought a pregnancy kit. After she'd peed on the stick, she knew for sure.

Penny sat on the toilet in their en suite bathroom for an age, jogging bottoms around her ankles, as the enormity of those two crossed lines hit home to her. There was a baby growing inside her and it would change her life forever. In ways she knew she couldn't even imagine. Or predict. The world had just jolted into a new reality.

Finally, she stood up and sorted herself out, taking off her bra from under her hoodie because, even though it was far too early in the pregnancy to be true, Penny felt as though her nipples were sore and they'd be more comfortable without the material pressing in on them.

Down the stairs and flop onto the sofa, having grabbed a cup of tea from the kitchen. She lay there with a hand absentmindedly on her belly until Ray came in shortly after seven.

"HIYA!"

"Hi, Ray."

"Be down in a min'!"

Penny heard him pound up the stairs, then a few moments silence as Ray got changed, a flush of the toilet and the sound of his footsteps coming down the stairs. She sat up to give Ray some room and he splatted onto the sofa beside her. The pregnancy test stick was still on the table, nestling on a tissue. Ray just sat there, not appearing to notice what Penny thought was glaring at him from the table top. But no response.

"I've got some good news for us."

Penny took one of Ray's hands and placed it in both of hers. He sat up slightly, back straighter than normal, as he anticipated something bad, despite her positive words.

"All the news is contained in this."

She grabbed the stick and waved it at Ray, who took it in his hand and stared at it. Penny couldn't understand how Ray was unable to figure out what was so obvious.

He twirled it around a couple of times and looked at the small display and the telling cross, which meant total positivity.

"We're going to have a baby!"

Penny could contain herself no longer; the truth burst out of her before she could let Ray get to the punchline.

"Pregnant?"

"Yeah! Here!"

She took his hand and placed it over her belly button and over her jogging bottoms.

"That's amazing."

"I know."

THE SMILE REMAINED on her face because, despite any trepidation she might have been feeling, Penny was happy. Real happy to know they'd done it and the whole process had only taken a couple of months.

"My little Ray of sunshine, we're going to be parents."

Ray took his hand off her belly and they hugged for a long time. Penny felt secure in his arms and she was pleased she'd picked this man over Mickey, whose dick was big but whose brain was small.

They remained in their embrace for quite a while and that was fine by Penny. She enjoyed the simple pleasure of human contact with Ray. Then she noticed a salty tear drifting from his cheek onto hers.

"What's the matter?"

"I'm happy and I'm sad."

"How so?"

"It's obviously great there'll be a little baby Penny, but I'm scared you'll slip away from me."

"Huh?"

"You'll be all over the little 'un and you'll have less time and attention for us."

Another tear appeared out of Ray's eye and landed on her cheek. What a selfish bastard. Ray saw her pregnancy as being all about him. Typical self-centred man.

Ray sucked the joy out of their moment together and Penny felt her heart rate rise and her blood pressure soared through the roof. Why had he said that, even if he believed it?

"It'll all be okay, don't worry. There's just going to be a whole lot more loving going on in this house. That's all."

Penny decided not to turn this moment into an argument but she was far from happy now. The pace of her breathing increased as she thought more about what he had said. She couldn't let it go. Not now.

Even though she knew he was merely expressing his own insecurities about having a baby and the changing dynamic of their relationship. To be honest, she thought, he was demonstrating some unusual emotional intelligence despite being a cock.

Penny relaxed a bit as she reminded herself all men are just grown up boys and you need to treat them like that now and again. Today was one of those days.

They carried on with their embrace and Penny regained her composure enough to stroke Ray's back a little and he responded in kind, running his fingers around her neck, occasionally nibbling at her earlobe.

"Let's go upstairs," he whispered and took her by the hand and led her into the bedroom. They stood by the bed as he pulled off her hoodie and gently licked her nipples and they kissed.

Penny put her hand down the front of his trousers and played with his balls. Tingles started flashing from her groin and up her spine. He pulled down her jogging bottoms and she felt a frisson of thrill as she stood in front of him wearing only a thong and Ray was still fully clothed. She took off his shirt and undid his belt, pushing his trousers to the floor.

While on her knees, she put her mouth around Ray's dick, through the material of his boxers and when she could feel it getting hard, Penny stood up.

Ray's hand engulfed her bum and she felt a finger edge its way from behind. The tingles fired up and down her spine, pulsing from her groin.

Penny put her hand in his shorts and rubbed his helmet with her thumb. This caused his finger to massage more intensely until his finger popped inside her and moved in quite deeply. She moaned, which only encouraged him to do it more.

She let go of his dick and pulled down on his boxers and then she did the same with her thong.

"Let's get into bed. We wouldn't want to get cold now, would we?"

He removed his finger from inside her and they lay down on the bed covers. Despite their desire to take things slowly, within a few minutes, Penny was sat astride Ray for the first time in three months and she felt him deep inside.

PENNY WAS STILL thinking about how good she felt on top of Ray and the changes taking place in her body when the call came through from Kawamura. A bidding war had broken out over the Lehman carcass and they weren't going to win because they'd already reached their maximum bid and the auction was continuing to roll along.

As far as Kawamura was concerned, they weren't going to pay over the odds for a failed brand even if one or two business lines were able to turn a profit. Their shareholders wouldn't look kindly on a decision like that. It would be perceived as bad business and Kawamura avoided poor business decisions because they led to negative outcomes and were a drain on the energy of the organisation.

"I understand. Obviously, I'm disappointed but that's life. Some you win and some you... don't."

There was a chuckle at the end of the phone. Everyone had known the venture was speculative at best as the European arm of a US bank would normally end up in Anglo-Saxon hands, but word on the street was that a different Japanese house was looking the most likely contender, especially as Kawamura was pulling out.

Penny didn't care. She had a baby growing inside and this was the most important thing to her right now. Billable hours were still a concern, but she also knew, in a few months, she'd be on maternity leave and all these problems and concerns would pale away into insignificance.

Instead, Penny's mind was full of questions like when she should tell her mum. She was torn between desperately wanting to share the news with her own mother and not wanting to jinx things so early in the first trimester.

She couldn't decide and she knew Ray would be against the idea as he was still adjusting to the situation himself and wanted to keep everything private between the two of them for as long as possible. That Penny's relationship with her mother could be somewhat fraught didn't mean they weren't close and Penny felt she shouldn't hold this secret from her.

THE BEST COURSE of action was for them to visit and take it from there, so two weekends later, after she'd visited the doctor and got everything confirmed, Ray drove them to Manchester on Friday night.

As ever, they arrived well past ten and there was the usual fuss about them having time for a late tea before bedtime. Then there was the normal, but inevitable, conversation whether they'd be warm enough and Paul brought in another blanket in case they were cold in the night. Of course, there was the predictable scuffle over which of the men should carry the cases up the stairs, a fight Ray always won by picking up the cases. He knew possession was nine tenths of the law—he worked in financial services so he knew a thing or two about daylight robbery.

Finally, Penny and Ray lay next to each other in their double bed, with more layers than you could shake a stick at. Ray was in his boxers and rued his forgetfulness for leaving his pyjamas at home. He only had them for their trips to Manchester. By contrast, Penny was covered in checked material—it was January and Manchester and she knew how that added up.

She felt Ray cling to her like a limpet, drawing out her body heat to fend off the worst of the northern chill he could squeeze from her life force. They hugged and kissed but Penny wasn't in the mood for anything else. Her attention was on the big question to which she still had no answer; would she tell her mum about what's growing inside her?

The following morning Penny woke up first, put some socks on and went downstairs to the kitchen, where her mother was already making a cup of tea, of course.

"There you go, dear."

"Thanks."

"Looks like it'll be dry today."

"Yeah, I didn't see any rain in the forecast."

"No. No rain today."

Penny was bursting. So desperate to tell her mum but knowing she and Ray had agreed not to share their knowledge with anyone; it was all too early and who knew what would happen.

"How are you feeling, love?"

"I'm fine, thanks."

"Everything all right, then?"

THERE WAS A smile in the corner of her mother's mouth and Penny could almost discern a twinkle in her eyes.

"Yes. What's up?"

"Penelope, I'm just checking you're okay. If you don't want to tell me then that's fine. I understand, but I'm your mother and I'm entitled to ask."

The woman was talking like she knew something.

"Do you know?"

"Do I know what, love?"

"How can you tell?"

A smile and Frannie leaned back against the counter behind her.

"You are positively glowing, so something had to be up. When you arrived last night, I thought you looked like you might have put on a pound or two—not a lot, you're not even close to showing—but enough for a mother to know."

Penny smiled back and nodded proudly, unconsciously placing a hand on her belly.

"It's true, Mum. But we're not telling anyone yet."

"Of course, when are you due?"

"August twenty-third."

"A summer baby, how cute."

"It's so exciting and so scary."

"You'll be fine. It's perfectly normal to feel that way because it is scary and it is exciting. How does Ray feel about all of this?"

Penny was silent for a second, not knowing quite how to answer. He had certainly improved his mood since she first told him, and he made all the right noises, but Penny still wasn't convinced he was totally up for the adventure two weeks after she'd told him.

"He's a bloke, you know. So he's happy, but he's not skipping through the tulips."

"Your father was the same, but don't worry about it. They come around eventually. To be honest, Dad wasn't really engaged with you until you started speaking. Took him ages. Don't get me wrong; he loved you from the moment you were born, but he had problems relating to you until you started kicking a ball, if you see what I mean."

Penny knew. Men were strange beasts.

# PART TWENTY-ONE
# FEBRUARY 2009

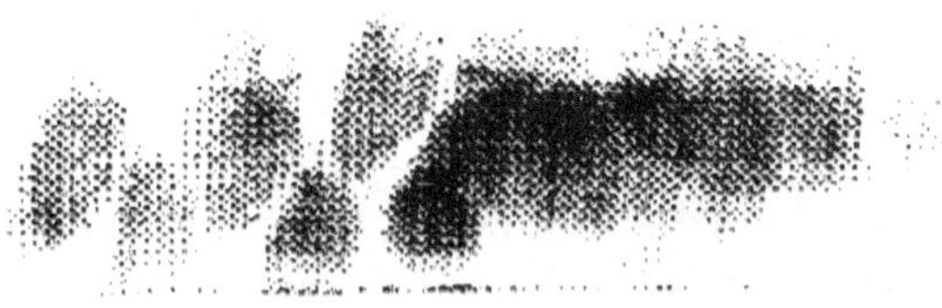

# 50

**RAY**

He had seen lots of strange suits walking around the building in December and had assumed there was a fresh push to acquire new clients, but the email that landed on January 31 showed how wrong he was.

Along with the rest of the staff and middle management not directly involved in the negotiations, Ray was informed that Bespoke had been purchased by Nott Financial, lock, stock and two smoking barrels. He was surprised when he first saw the note because he was hoping that in a firm as small as Bespoke, Eliezer might have given people more of an insight into what was going on.

Then he sat back and realised they were a hedge fund and if anyone had known anything, they'd have traded that information to within an inch of its life. He understood, but he wasn't happy either. Nott was a very large institution from the US with fingers in many pies; a classic universal banking model, with investment and commercial banks, long-only funds and one of the largest hedge fund management arms on the planet. Bespoke would be safe inside its harbour.

"What's going to happen to us all?" Erin asked.

"I think it'll be okay. Since the crash, there's been more and more talk about regulating hedge funds."

"I know, Ray."

"And that's meant big investors have wanted to put their money into larger companies who are more likely to have full oversight from regulators."

"Yep."

"And Bespoke's just too small to survive in that environment. If we weren't part of a large firm, we'd end up losing investors who would need to be seen to only invest with fully regulated entities. It's the way of the world now."

"I know all that, Ray. But what'll happen to us. You, me, the others on this floor?"

RAY STOPPED FOR a minute and realised he'd totally misread her question. That explained her strained intonation and annoyed expression while he'd been talking.

"Sorry. Yes. I reckon we'll be okay here. We are the heart of the investment vehicle. Without us, the strategies don't operate and you have to assume we've been bought because of the success we've had here, right?"

"I hope. You guys create great returns here, don't you?"

"Sure do, Erin."

For the first time since she'd sat down in his office to talk, Erin sat back in her chair. Her bosom, which had been getting larger over the years since he'd known her, seemed to fill up the entire expanse of her blouse as she inhaled deeply just so she could let out an enormous sigh of relief.

"So I don't need to worry then?"

"Not at all. Nott will be a safe pair of hands. Life will carry on just fine."

She smiled, stood up, and offered to make him a coffee. As Erin left, Ray reminded himself what a great arse that woman had trailing in her wake. Then he remembered he was a father-to-be and got back to reading his emails.

After Erin returned with his drink, Ray asked her to close his door on the way out. He swung his chair round to face the window behind his desk and put a call through to Peter on his mobile.

"Tell me about the swaptions desk again."

# 51

**PENNY**

Sunday morning, Penny awoke early, not feeling right. She looked at the clock and saw it was ten past five, got out of bed and went to the bathroom. There was blood in her pee and she knew there was nothing good about that fact.

She figured she'd give it a while and see what happened. Penny had read three pregnancy books in the last two weeks and she'd even managed to get Ray to look at one of them. She couldn't recall any of them mentioning any bleeding but, then again, she wasn't in any pain and another hour wouldn't make much difference either way, she thought.

Penny spent her time sitting up in bed, desperately trying to ignore what her body was telling her. By seven, there was still some blood seeping out of her and what felt like a menstrual cramp had started to take over her stomach.

She nudged Ray awake, who grumpily turned round and stared at her; grumpy just because he had been asleep.

"I think we need to go to the hospital."

"What's happened?"

"I've been bleeding and I'm scared for the baby."

"Jesus."

Ray sprang out of bed and whipped his trousers on. Then he went round to Penny's side, sat down and gave her a big hug.

"We'll get through this, Penny Pitstop."

PENNY COULDN'T BRING herself to say anything and just clung to him for as long as she could before he bounded back to his side of the room to grab a shirt. She put on a hoodie and some sweatpants and mooched downstairs, sitting on the edge of her chair in the living room until Ray was ready.

The nearest A&Es were Watford and Barnet, both a good twenty minutes away. Ray's mother had died in Watford General so he took Penny to Barnet.

When they arrived, Penny went straight to the counter and less than five minutes later, she was sitting on a bed being interviewed by a triage nurse, who then called a doctor over to give her an internal exam.

He told her what she already knew but dare not vocalise. She had miscarried. The nurse gave her some sanitary pads and a couple of painkillers and that was that.

Penny didn't say a word all the way home and Ray had the decency not to talk either. When they were back at home, they both crumpled on the sofa. She started to sob and Ray held her in his arms. Penny felt a small crumb of comfort from the warmth of his body but that was all.

There was only the aching pain of loss and a fierce sense of grief. Nothing more. Silence. Then Penny cried some more and eventually she fell asleep on Ray's shoulder.

An hour later she awoke to find herself sprawled on top of him as Ray had managed to lie down on the sofa without waking her. For a second, she wondered what the hell was going on and then she recalled why they were in the living room so early and what had happened during the night.

"There was nothing I could do."

"I KNOW, PENNY. It wasn't your fault. No one's blaming you. The doctor said these things happen."

"I know. Doesn't make it hurt any less though, does it?"

"No. Not at all."

"I'm hurting now, Ray."

"Shall I get you some painkillers?"

"This is the other kind of hurt. Meds won't sort this out."

"Oh. No. Sorry. I didn't understand."

Ray gave her another squeeze and she squeezed him back slightly, but Penny didn't feel like offering him any comfort or response. She wanted to sink into the feeling of loss and despair which engulfed her.

"Would you like a cup of tea?" he asked after a while.

"Yes, why not."

She rolled onto the sofa to let Ray escape to the kitchen and he returned shortly afterwards bearing a steaming mug of brown liquid.

"Thanks."

"De nada."

As she sipped her drink, Ray sat down beside her again, only this time it was his turn to sob. Penny couldn't stand it. She couldn't cope with the thought that some of the air space would be given over to his sadness. She was the one feeling the pain. She was the one who had lost her baby. It was her day today.

"Stop crying. You can cry tomorrow. Today it's my turn."

Ray looked at her through his red eyes and smeared his tears off his cheeks with the backs of his hands. He didn't cry again for the rest of the day—at least as far as Penny noticed.

He put his hand on her knee to try to give her some comfort—and probably obtain some for himself—but Penny wasn't interested. All she could experience was that sadness, that all-consuming scream of agony, which felt like a knife twisting in her side.

Once she'd finished the tea, she shuffled into the kitchen and left the mug in the sink for Ray to put in the dishwasher. Then she came back to the sofa and curled up in a tight ball, trying to become nothing in the room.

By the evening, she'd managed to eat a slice of toast and had consumed several more mugs of tea. Ray stayed with her but hadn't offered much conversation during the afternoon. He knew there were no words.

They put on the TV for an hour or so before they went to bed and when they were lying under the duvet, finally, they hugged again before Penny rolled over onto her other side, switched off her bedside light, and went to sleep.

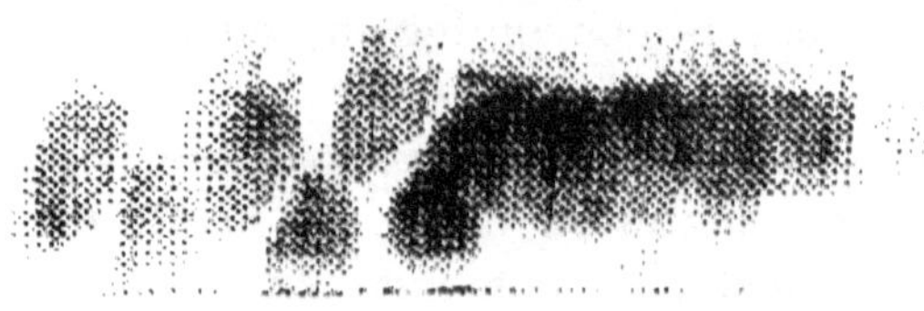

# 52

**RAY**

Pintzer Financial was located in the middle of Canary Wharf, which meant Ray had to go into Bank station on the Northern Line from Edgware and then hop onto the DLR to reach his office. He wasn't used to the new financial district and when Peter Abbott first told him Nott was in the Wharf, Ray thought long and hard about accepting the role.

Ray's image of the Wharf predated Nott's arrival in the area and he recalled the odd foray down there when there was nowhere to go for lunch and no shops. The place was a like a fucking graveyard. But not now. There were two shopping malls and more restaurants than you could shake a stick at.

The building itself was a classic post-modern reference to New York or Chicago skyscrapers—only much shorter and a lot more glass. Nott's building was on the corner of the main square and overlooked West Ham Docks, one of the two waterways that split the redeveloped Canary Wharf from all the other pieces of real-estate nearby.

Ray's induction was short and only lasted the whole of his first day, Monday. As he was sat in a room staring blankly at a set of slides covering staff expectations and the Nott Way, Ray thought about the Friday just before the weekend and his leaving drinks at Freiberg.

HE HAD INVITED anyone he knew from all the parts of its mighty empire as this truly was the last time he would work there—as trader, pension fund manager or hedge fund risk taker. Ray had also popped an invite to Ollie over the Caldwell but he never showed. Typical, Ollie must have been tied up somewhere.

The venue was a local wine bar and, more out of politeness than anything else, Ray had told Erin she was more than welcome. He knew he'd see her on the Monday anyway because he'd already arranged for her to be hired as his assistant before his knees had even got warm under his desk.

He had put his credit card behind the bar and everyone was taking full advantage of it, including Erin, who was getting much the worse for wear by the time Ray bumped into her halfway through the evening.

"Y'know something?"

"What, Erin?"

"Thanks for bringing me over to Pintzer. I'd die if I stayed in Nott."

"We're a team, Erin. I wouldn't have it any other way."

"You're very kin' to say so. You're a lovely man."

She leant forwards on her cocktail stool and slammed an arm round the back of Ray's neck to stop herself falling off. Then she planted an enormous kiss on his cheek. Leaning forward, as she was, Ray couldn't help but look down and see her cleavage revealing itself to him, popping out of her blouse. She'd undone a button or two because the temperature was very warm inside the bar. Her breasts were trying to escape from her bra and Ray had to remind himself, lest he forget, that he and Penny had lost their baby only two weeks before.

Three hours later and the leaving do was done. Everyone had left apart from Erin, who seemed stuck to the same barstool where Ray had left her after copping a look at her tits.

"Let's get you home."

"Ooh, Ray."

HE HELPED HER off the stool and she clung to him as they walked outside and he hailed a taxi.

"First, let's aim for Islington and after the drop, I'll be going on to Edgware," he informed the driver.

On the way, Ray managed to extract Erin's address from her and within half an hour, the cab had stopped outside her flat on the Hackney side of town. She'd nodded off and Ray realised the only way to get her inside, given her state, was to walk her in himself.

"I'm going to be a while getting her sorted."

"I can wait, boss."

Ray considered his options and knew, deep down, that Erin was going to be a handful and that paying for the cabbie to sit outside was a waste of money.

"Yeah, but I think we'd better call it quits."

The cabbie eyed Erin in his rear-view mirror then repositioned it for driving.

"Know what you mean, boss."

Ray paid up and got Erin out the taxi. He put her arm around his neck and one of his arms under her armpit so's he could take her weight and lead her up to the entrance.

Somehow Erin found her keys in her handbag relatively quickly but her drunken co-ordination was too poor to be able to fit the key in the lock. Ray took over for her.

"Will you help me get sorted, please, Ray?"

He had known this was inevitable before he'd left the taxi—it was the main reason he'd sent the cab away.

"Sure thing, Erin. No worries."

THEY GOT INSIDE her flat and she stumbled out of her hallway and into a bedroom. Ray took her handbag off her shoulder and placed it on a dressing table. Then he led her to the bed and she flopped on top of it. Because his arm was around her waist and her arm had returned around his neck, Ray was brought down onto the bed by Erin's momentum. She chuckled.

"Gotcha."

Those breasts jiggled up and down with her mirth and, briefly, Ray was mesmerised by them.

"Help me get into bed, will you?"

Ray thought he'd done enough, getting her from the Wharf to her flat.

"No, help me out of my clothes. I can't focus on the buttons to undo them. And I don't want my clothes to get creased, now, do I?"

While saying this, Erin had released her grip on Ray and was floundering as she stabbed at her buttons to no great effect.

He shrugged and undid her blouse buttons, all the while keeping his eyes glued on those breasts. They weren't jiggling anymore as Erin had stopped laughing. Instead, they were rising and falling in time with her breathing.

"And my skirt too please. This zip won't budge."

Ray looked at where her fingers were scrabbling about on one of her hips and pulled the side zip down. He could see the orange lace of her pants peeping out over the skirt's waistband. They matched her bra, he thought, and his eyes returned to Erin's nipples. Even under the material of her underwear, Ray didn't think he had seen areolas as big as that before in his life.

Without thinking, he rested his hand on Erin's round stomach. She giggled again.

"Like what you see?"

Ray's head auto-responded by nodding. She took his hand and placed it on one of her breasts so he could touch her, at least through some orange lace. Ray squeezed once and checked himself. This was not the kind of situation he wanted to be in right now. This was not the time nor the place.

Erin's eyes closed and her breathing changed down a notch like she had fallen asleep. Ray decided against a second squeeze but he really wanted to touch that nipple unimpeded by any lace. He tried to move his hand under the bra but the underwire was too firm. Even though Ray was certain she was out of it, Erin grabbed his hand and shoved it down her pants until he felt the top of her bush.

"If you're going to fuck me, make it quick, dear. I don't have all day."

Then she started snoring and whatever had been going on inside her head; the moment was past. And no matter what temptation or interest Ray might have had, the opportunity was gone.

Ray walked out the flat, closing the door on the way out. When he got to the street, he called for a taxi and went home. Penny was asleep and he knew he was pretty far gone. On Saturday morning, his hangover proved he was right.

And by the time he saw Erin on Monday afternoon once their respective inductions were over, the feel of Erin's pubes had left his memory and she didn't appear to acknowledge she'd even asked him for a fuck.

RAY BROODED OVER the Erin incident for quite some time. Even though he hadn't done anything wrong—almost despite himself—he still felt bad, still felt guilty. And that general sense of upset hung over him for days.

His mood darkened, layered by Erin's areolas and Penny's miscarriage. This did not improve with time and Ray felt himself getting increasingly tetchy. There was nothing anyone could do to make him feel better—and he knew it.

At night, Ray slumped on the sofa after dinner and stared at the TV until he was ready to go to sleep. Penny sat on the chair reading. They repeated this day in, day out for weeks, which turned into two months. Ray wasn't happy about the situation but he couldn't think how he wanted things to be different.

Bottom line was he wanted Penny to still be pregnant but she wasn't and, nowadays, they were hardly touching, so the chance was slim for another of her eggs to get fertilised any time soon.

"Want a drink?"

"What?"

"Drink?"

"No thanks."

"Sure?"

"I said no, didn't I?"

"All right, Ray. I'm only asking."

"Sure thing. Stop asking me questions you know the answer to."

"Let it go, Ray. I only asked."

"If I'd wanted a drink, I'd 've got off my arse and fucked off to the kitchen to get one."

"Ray..."

He could hear the intonation in Penny's voice getting terse and annoyed, but he couldn't help himself. Like Penny was annoying him on purpose. Ray hadn't considered the possibility that his instant anger at being asked about a drink was connected to his sense of loss at the child that never was. But any cod psychologist could have told him this. If he had then added into the mix his guilt about the situation he'd found himself in with Erin, the reason for his response was obvious and almost inevitable. Even though his memory of the details of the night were hazy, he recalled enough to know there was a sexual opportunity missed.

Penny came back with a glass of water for herself, glared at him and settled back into her novel.

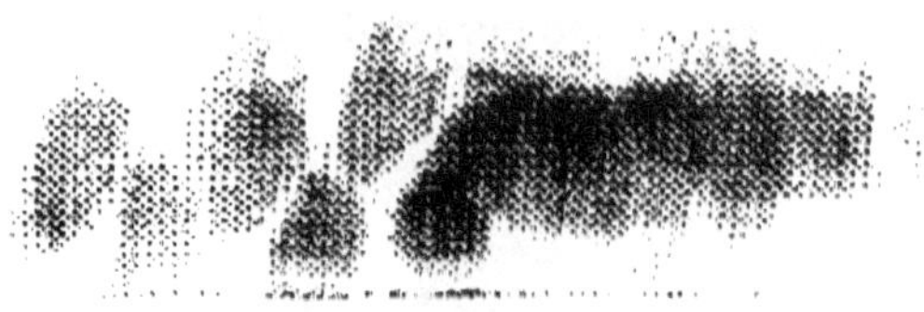

# 53

**PENNY**

Towards the end of the month, Penny sat in her office and tried to make sense of her world. The inherent darkness at the heart of her being had not shifted. She'd read about mourning but this was the first time she'd experienced grief since the family cat died when she was eleven.

She had taken two days personal time before she returned to work; Penny couldn't face walking straight back into the office, but she also knew hiding at home wasn't the solution either.

Penny sat at her desk and hatched out a plan to keep herself busy so she wouldn't have to think too much. The best way to keep concentrating was to not be hanging around Edgware where it happened. Instead, she knew she needed to get over to the States as much as possible for the next few months.

She pinged Nina to let her know; Penny intended to take the fight back to the Americans. The next big US deal was hers for the taking. Nina responded positively, because revenue was revenue, Penny reckoned.

A decision made, Penny felt no pleasure with her conclusion. She still thought about the nagging hangdog of sadness pervading her world and didn't particularly care about anything or anyone else.

So by the time she got home, Penny's resolve was total. She informed Ray after they had eaten.

"I'm going to pick up the slack in our US business."

She was sat in the armchair and Ray was on the sofa with the remote control in his hand.

"What?"

"You heard me. We need to prop up the East Coast and I'm the partner best placed to do it."

"I don't understand. Was this mandated by Nina or have you volunteered?"

"It doesn't matter. I'm letting you know what's happening. I'm not asking for your permission."

"I'm not trying to give it to you, but I am trying to understand where this came from."

"Doesn't matter. This is what'll happen."

"Penny, it does matter. We might not have talked much about it after the weekend when it happened, but we lost a baby last month and I thought we'd try again fairly soon. But if you're going to be in the US then that's off the menu."

"And who told you we'd be trying again?"

"No one told me, but I thought that's what we said we were going to do."

"Ray, that was what we were trying to do but it didn't work out. Our baby died when it was only a bundle of cells. My body rejected it and destroyed those cells."

"I know that."

"Good. And I am now telling you that, at this point, I do not want to try for a child again. I just can't bear the thought of going through that happiness and sadness again. I just can't cope with it."

RAY'S RESPONSE WAS absolute silence as this news sank in. As Penny stared at him from over her book, she could see him processing the implications of her words. She wasn't wanting to hurt or upset him, but she wasn't that bothered if she did. The important thing was to get the message across and for it to stick.

"Can we at least talk about this?"

"We are talking about this. I'm telling you what I've decided. It's not your choice. It's my body, it will be my pregnancy and it was my miscarriage. Period."

"And are you saying no to children forever, for a few months, what?"

"I don't know. I just don't know, Ray. But I am definitely saying no for now and the next month or two."

Silence again as Ray considered her words.

"I thought we wanted to become a family?"

"We did. I did, but I can't go through another miscarriage, Ray. And I can't face the possibility of setting myself up to go through another one either. Not right now."

His eyes reddened and a tear rolled down his cheek, which he rubbed away as soon as it had formed. Penny watched him but did and said nothing. It was time for some tough love.

"Sometimes I don't understand you."

Penny shrugged. There was nothing more to say. She had told him what was going to happen and that was that. She didn't really care what he thought. It was what it was. Maybe in a year or two she'd feel differently—or maybe tomorrow—but the loss was still too great today.

Ray brooded on what she'd said for the rest of the night and went to bed before her. When Penny opened the bedroom door, he was asleep and had left her bedside light on. Two days later, Nina gave her a new deal to work on and she headed over to New York, leaving Ray to suck in his upset and giving Penny something to do other than obsess over her failed womb.

PENNY STAYED IN chi-chi Hotel Bristol as ever and let the recent past ebb away from the forefront of her consciousness. It only slipped back in the evenings after all the corporate schmoozing was over. Then she'd take her book to a restaurant, eat, and hit the Vodka Bar afterwards until she was ready for bed.

Having a book enabled her to fend off the travelling salesmen and other turds who tried to hit on her while she was sipping her cosmo. On the fourth night of this particular trip, she'd been to a local Italian and was pounding through to the last couple of chapters of her current read back in the Vodka Bar. Then she heard a vaguely familiar voice;

"Fancy meeting you here."

She looked up and saw a face which, yes, she did recognise but she couldn't quite place. Her expression reflected her lack of recognition.

"Christmas Party? We danced. Your fella got all gorilla on me?"

PENNY'S EYES DILATED as she pictured the scene. Enrique. He was right; the last and only time she'd seen him, he'd had his hand on her arse and Ray had lost the plot. What a fucking dick.

"Yes, there was quite a scene and your boss bitched you out."

Enrique's eyes headed to the floor and his cheeks reddened ever so slightly.

"Yeah... happy days."

Penny smiled and took a sip of her cosmo.

"So what are you doing here?"

"Having a drink and watching the world go by."

"And daytime?"

"Business. I have clients over here. You?"

"Same. Our US desks usually handle the locals, but I was over anyway and thought I'd press some flesh."

He reached out to shake Penny's hand.

"Enrique Rodriguez, pleased to meet you."

"Penny Kurtz. Charmed, I'm sure."

Enrique looked around the bar, conspicuously turning his head one way, then the other, all the while still holding the pose with Penny's handshake.

"If you don't mind me asking, is your fella around?"

Penny laughed.

"No, you're safe. He's back in Blighty."

Enrique let go of her hand and Penny returned it to the side of her cocktail glass, which was nearly empty.

"Would you like a drink, in that case?"

"Sure thing. Another cosmo would be lovely."

Enrique caught the attention of the barman, who sent a waiter over, giving Enrique just enough time to sit down at Penny's table. He ordered a martini for himself as well as the cosmo.

"What kind of business are you doing over here with your American clients?"

"I'm a lawyer. Specialise in cross-border M&A."

"Good times aplenty, I'd guess."

"We aren't doing too badly. I'm at a boutique firm so you always have to hustle."

"Same in investment management. There's always another reason for a client to move their portfolios. Gotta keep 'em sweet the whole time."

"I'll drink to that."

They clinked their glasses and sipped away, chatting for fifteen, twenty minutes without a break. No embarrassed silences. Penny was glad to lose herself in meaningless talk; Enrique was quite a charmer. She knew it was all a front, but he hid it well. The wry smiles, the occasional touches of her lower arm; designed to keep her at her ease and to invade her personal space. Normalise Enrique being close to her.

Penny didn't mind that; she hadn't flirted with someone for years and when Enrique pushed the conversation into more personal territories, she let him transgress without chastising him.

THEY LEFT THE cocktails behind and moved onto a bottle of Pinot Noir. By the time they'd emptied two bowls of nuts and Japanese nibbles, another bottle had been opened and Penny found herself laughing for the first time in a century.

"Night cap?"

"No thanks, but if you want something, don't stop on my account."

"A gentleman never drinks alone," he said with intended pomposity, made all the more amusing by his soft Spanish accent.

"Well, a lady must get her beauty sleep."

"May I see you home?"

"Sure, a girl might get lost in the Big Apple."

They headed to the elevator and waited, still flirting a little. Penny was a little tired on her feet and decided to lean on Enrique to save energy. The elevator doors opened and they stepped inside. Penny pressed the number for her floor and up they went. They both leaned back against the same side of the elevator until it screeched to a halt, jolting them, and the doors opened again.

"Let's get out of here before the whole town blows."

They giggled and Enrique followed Penny to her room; down a corridor and on the left-hand side. She swiped the key and the door opened. She was having fun.

"Fancy a minibar nightcap?"

"Only if you're having one. Remember; a gentleman never drinks alone."

"I'm sure I'll find something to satisfy me."

They walked in and Enrique closed the door.

"Nice room. You got a double aspect!"

Two of the walls were floor-to-ceiling glass with an incredible view of the Manhattan skyline. Webber Paine chose a boutique hotel so the upgrades would be worth it.

"I'm glad you like what you see. Here."

Penny passed Enrique a miniature bottle of vodka and a half bottle of tonic. She held a tiny bottle of gin and two glasses.

They both sat on the bed even though the room's sofa offered a much better view of the night-time's skyline.

WHEN THE DRINKS were finished, Penny took both glasses and leaned over to put them on the bedside table. As she turned away from him, Enrique reached out and placed his hand on her back, firmly but with a gentleness that came with practice. Penny did nothing to stop him, instead remaining motionless so he could carry on.

Enrique rubbed her back and leaned over to kiss the nape of Penny's neck. Now, he was near enough, he reached round and put a hand on her stomach and raised it up her torso until his palm was covering a breast. After the tingles started inside her, Penny turned round and kissed him on the mouth, while placing a hand on his thigh.

Meantime, he undid the buttons of her blouse and massaged one nipple, then the other. She felt his fingers stroke near the base of her spine and a hand slipped beneath her skirt and squeezed her bum.

"Get your hand off my arse, you beast!"

They laughed.

"Sorry, ma'am."

Penny grabbed his hand and pulled it out of her skirt. She unzipped it and took his hand again and led it under her stockings, under her knickers and onto her crotch.

"That's better," she giggled and they carried on until Penny had finished with him and Enrique returned to his own room around two. He tried to find her in the bar the following night, but Penny had already left the hotel to take the red-eye home.

KAWAMURA WAS STILL predatory, seeking some financial vehicle, in which to invest. But before the end of the month, head office had been visited by the Japanese regulator, the Financial Services Agency, and words had been spoken. The FSA official had been remarkably candid with Mr Kawamura; exposure to derivative instruments was way too high across the group with little or no group-wide risk oversight. Now the FSA had even a glimpse into the real balance sheet holding the conglomerate together, it had no choice but to warn a meaningful plan to increase regulatory capital needed to be put in place and the derivatives book needed to be unwound.

What did that mean? Between the commercial bank, the investment bank and the investment management businesses across the planet, Kawamura owned too many poor-quality derivatives and they had to sell them. On top of that, they had to stuff a lot more money into the corporate mattress for a rainy day; the amount of cash Kawamura held had to be sufficient to cover any potential seismic losses that might befall it. Regulatory capital was the cash you kept in case the shit hit the fan and your government decided not to bail you out like Lehman Brothers instead of saving you like Bear Stearns.

So Kawamura was on the lookout for a bank with a stash of cash and not too big a derivatives book, which it would need to flip almost immediately. The search began in Tokyo and expanded internationally until a short list of potential targets was generated before the end of the month. Most were mid-sized US entities which had caught the brunt of the shit-storm of the past four years. Top of the list? Pintzer Financial, a fundamentally sound bank with a small derivatives desk. It could be shut down without any heartache or sold off to anyone who'd take it off their hands.

Penny sat in the video conferencing suite and nodded at Mr Kawamura at regular intervals. This was going to be a huge deal and there was no way it could be shelved like the last time. The other advantage, from Penny's perspective, was the complete absence of any goofy US investment bankers on the call. Kawamura only had trusted advisors—from Japan, the UK and Germany. This was a deal that would go through. It would take quite some wrestling to the ground, but they all knew they could do it and Kawamura knew he couldn't afford for them to fail. Financial incentives were in place to focus everyone's minds on the problem at hand; twenty per cent of fees bonus on deal closure. Of course, such a sweetener came at a price; all fees were discounted by ten per cent, but they'd still come out on top before the end of the year.

# PART TWENTY-TWO
## NOVEMBER 2009

# 54

**RAY**

Rumours about Pintzer first surfaced in March but Ray paid no attention to them, because every firm was the target for an acquisition on a regular basis. Regulators around the world scrutinised financial institutions until the banks could hardly move. After the summer the rumour mill was in full swing, but everything fell silent after September and Ray reckoned the gossip moved on to some other house.

This head-in-the-sand approach lasted the whole of October, but the plan soured the following month, when Ray noticed several Japanese visitors turned up every day for a week. You didn't need a maths degree like Ray to make two and two add up to four.

He put a call through to Peter Abbott as soon as he recognised the strangers' intentions. They met up that evening and Peter gave him the simple news.

"I'll do my level best to help you find your next role, but I have to tell you Pintzer's derivatives desk is poison right now."

"Poison?"

"Yes, word on the street is that it'll get shut down as soon as the ink is dry on the Pintzer acquisition."

"Shut down?"

Ray couldn't believe his ears. Peter's words carved gashes in his side.

"So what do you suggest I do?"

"Look, there are loads of trading roles. I'm sure I can find one for you... only you might have to lower your expectations in the short term."

"Take a pay cut, you mean?"

"Something like that."

Ray had enough money squirrelled away to cope with a diminished base salary, if he thought he'd be able to make up the shortfall in commission, so that didn't faze him. The problem was Ray's ego, not his wallet. He had built himself up from an ordinary floor trader, through the ranks and into investment management and hedge funds. Ray had jumped into the world of swaptions because he figured he belonged in the trading elite—and he wasn't wrong. But he hadn't considered the possibility that this rarefied club might be made redundant and their investment positions wound down until they no longer existed.

"Do you think there's a swaps desk that'd have me?"

"Maybe. I can put the word out if you'd like me to."

"Yes please. How worried should I be?"

"Right now, you shouldn't be too concerned, but when the deal goes through some point soon, the clock is ticking on your job. I mean the alarm will be almost ready to go off. Boom."

"Put the word on the street; I want out. I'm open to any sensible offer, provided I can make decent commission along the way."

"That's what I like to hear; fighting talk. Go slay 'em, tiger!"

Two weeks later, Ray handed in his notice and was frogmarched out the door with a cardboard box containing his personal possessions. Before he gave his letter in, he spoke with Erin and told her to stay put and do nothing until he'd got his feet under his new desk at Saturnbanc, then he would send for her. When you are back on a dealing floor, you have no need of a personal assistant and Ray never saw those heaving breasts and plump arse again.

"DEAR BOY!"

Ollie was already in the restaurant by the time Ray arrived.

"You're here first!"

"Sometimes I am a capable professional and loyal friend."

He smiled and hugged Ollie as he stood up to greet him.

"Sure, but you usually are ensconced in your club until the last minute."

"Some things are more important than mere sexual gratification, dear boy."

"And am I one of them?"

"For tonight, yes. I have a favour to ask of you."

"Menus and then talk."

They read and chatted until the waiter took their order and delivered their first bottle of wine, a cheeky Merlot.

"You mentioned a favour?"

"Yes, dear boy."

"How can I help?"

"I have a business opportunity for you."

"Do tell."

"It's an interest rates play."

"How so?"

Ollie talked Ray through a scheme he was putting together in an obscure unregulated arm of the financial services galaxy; the UK's interest rate benchmark, known as Libor. This was an interest rate which represented the charges made by one bank when it lent money to another bank on wholesale terms. Big deal. But the same value was used as a basis for calculating lots of other interest related contracts—mortgages, business contracts, anything where interest was chargeable. Again, big whoop.

The value was calculated on a daily basis using proposed prices submitted by a clutch of banks involved in interbank lending. Traders would say on what terms they'd lend certain amounts of money to each other at eleven in the morning. Strange but true. The highest and lowest values were ignored, the average of the rest was taken and the results published and used all across the planet.

OLLIE HAD A friend—didn't he always?—who worked in one of the contributing banks. They submitted values, but no one checked to see if the numbers connected to actual loans. It was a fiction. Pure fiction. With the right quotes provided, the resulting benchmark could be pushed in any direction. You'd make a killing knowing which direction Libor was heading daily before the new rate was published.

"I have one or two friends submitting quotes so we can move the market. The only problem I have is that to make any money, I need someone who can trade interest rates to turn the quotes into cash."

"And I'm sitting on a swaps desk."

While swaptions described an option to swap interest rates, the swaps contracts themselves were what they said on the tin; trades in the interest rates themselves. Just what Ollie needed; a direct way to tap into the movements of the interest rate benchmark.

Money they made from their group efforts would be split between them. Ray would not get his usual fifty per cent cut as Ollie had several other people whose beaks needed to be whetted. This was the big one; if they kept it going for a year or two, they'd make tens of millions. Each. The trick was not to get greedy; regularly shaving a small amount of extra Libor profit was better than ripping the arse out of it in one day.

The submission of false quotes might not be regulated but fraud was still fraud. Even though they hadn't mentioned this legal point at dinner, Ray understood this, which was why he wasn't the least surprised when Ollie told him to use his Caldwell for communication on this deal. Not his mobile, not his landline and not email. The Caldwells had a secure messaging system embedded in them and offered private chat rooms to boot. The perfect place for people to meet and discuss trading strategies in confidence.

OLLIE'S FRIENDS HAD already submitted rejigged rate quotes and nothing had happened apart from their learning how to finesse the rate in their favour. Ray agreed to help and came up with some winning strategies and how to execute them.

"Thank you, dear boy. For this deal, you eat what you kill beyond our initial agreement. Any investment you make is proprietary outside the plays we put together as a group, but let's slowly boil this frog, eh?"

Ray understood; if they were careful, individuals would make side bets on their own using a variety of interest rate related options contracts. Ollie was signalling he was intending to make some big money outside the group. Ray saw no reason to avoid scooping up the cash too.

"Let's celebrate."

Ollie whisked them out of the Mayfair restaurant and into a cab. Ten minutes later, they pulled up outside a venue off Soho Square in the heart of what used to be London's red-light district. Since the '90s, the streets had been reclaimed for the tourists, but an occasional billow of steam blew through if you knew the right places to look. Ollie made it his business to follow those wisps of air.

Ray didn't spot the name of the basement dive before Ollie hustled them inside past the bouncer in an ill-fitting dinner jacket. Within a minute of their arrival, the maître d' arranged a table to be set up near the front of the stage and, just after they'd placed their order for two martinis, semi-naked girls appeared and the show began.

WITH ONLY TWO poles built into the performance space, there were always three girls thrusting their groins or slapping their arses within thirty inches of Ray and Ollie. Every so often, Ollie would stand up and plant a ten or twenty note into the G-string of a girl as she thrust by, but Ray stayed in his seat, watching.

After a while, the stage calmed down until there was only one girl earning a living on a pole and the others mingled in the audience, encouraging patrons to buy them a watery drink or have a lap dance. Often, a man would follow a girl to a room near the main stage for a private dance, stay with her for ten or fifteen minutes and return alone.

"This is the life, dear boy."

Ray nodded but wasn't too sure he agreed with Ollie. In a lap dancing establishment, the rule was "look, don't touch" and that took a lot of the fun out of a dangling tit.

"Sure is. Everything okay with you and Karen at home though?"

"Why yes. We have an open attitude to these things. Besides, nowadays, we both go to my other club."

There was a twinkle in the corner of Ollie's eyes Ray hadn't seen before.

"It's good you've found a common interest!"

They both laughed and clinked their martini glasses. Once the chuckles had died down, Ollie turned to him.

"Trouble is, we still don't have an heir to the Olesworth fortune."

It had been so long since he'd heard Ollie's family name, he took a second to recognise it.

"Have you been trying?"

"Not really. Karen doesn't sound that interested in the whole baby thing. Terrific child bearing hips though and a womb you'd die for."

The martinis were making Ollie less than coherent, but Ray got the gist.

"WHEN THEIR BIOLOGICAL alarm clocks go off, believe me you'll be told."

"Really?"

"Like there's no tomorrow."

"Sounds like the voice of experience."

"Yes, only we..."

Ray's words slipped into silence. He hadn't talked to anyone about their loss before and if he told Ollie, Karen would find out and she would then close the loop with Penny.

"Yes?"

"Promise not to tell Karen?"

"I promise, dear boy."

"We had a miscarriage at the beginning of the year and we haven't got back on the horse, if you see what I mean."

"Oh, dear boy. Let me buy you a private dance."

This was not the response Ray was hoping for or expecting, but at least he discovered the level of intimacy that a three-hundred-pound-plus-tip private dance bought.

Back home at five, Ray leaned back on his pillows, not able to sleep but dog tired. The house sounded so quiet without Penny, but night was becoming morning and he needed some kip before he eked his way through to the end of Friday. That night, Ray clambered into bed as soon as he got in and woke around midday. He lay in bed as the sun started its descent in the sky.

Penny's absence still hovered over him, just as it had done every day she'd been in the US that week. Ray couldn't resolve his dissatisfaction with her not being around with the experience of cold civility he aimed at her when they were at home together. It made no sense.

The one idea he clung to, throughout that afternoon as he lazed in bed; their bad patch would sort itself out and then they'd get back on track. The miscarriage from January was almost a dim memory for him. His initial abject sadness had faded fast and he had come to terms with the loss, but he didn't believe the same could be said for Penny.

They hadn't talked about it since they came back from the A&E and Penny had cried on his shoulder. Ray had not described his emotions from that day; she was only concerned with her own pain then and there had been no opportunity for him to express himself since, as she shut the miscarriage out of their lives.

Ray resented the fact Penny hadn't let him talk about his own sadness at any point. He didn't see why his pain was worth any less than hers. The child was as much his as it was hers. And this thought, now expressed, gnawed at him. It had been bubbling under the surface for months, but saying it to himself made it real. More real than he had expected.

Penny was forging a new business life in the States and he was left holding his dick in the UK, waiting for her to come back into his life. It wasn't right and it wasn't fair. He deserved better than this.

Ray stayed in bed the whole afternoon, only coming downstairs long enough to order a pizza for delivery. Then into bed to masturbate himself into unconsciousness using the memory of the lap dancer's head bobbing up and down between his legs as she sucked him off.

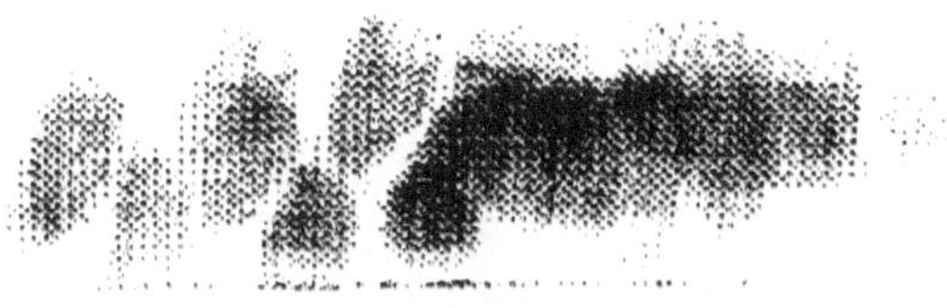

# 55

**PENNY**

In New York, the acquisition of Pintzer Financial was taking shape. The heads of agreement had been signed and the sprawling due diligence phase was coming to a close. Everyone had known this would take longer than scheduled, because they always do and in part because Pintzer had its own set of tangled relationships and derivatives portfolios needing to be separated and analysed.

For Penny, this was the quiet time. The heavy lifting was to get all the principles embedded in the initial agreement and then once all the skeletons had been found, she would kick up a gear to deliver the final contract in an appropriate state to enable her to recommend her client to sign it. That was still a few months off.

To prepare for the deal, Pintzer had made some informal enquiries to find interested parties in taking over its derivatives portfolios and derivatives desks worldwide—or even piecemeal. No one was giving it a second glance; too many regulators focused on capital adequacy and the banks' balance sheets for a firm to want to take on more unspecified risk. Worse still for Pintzer, no one wanted to appear to increase any derivative exposure in case their regulator started an investigation. Times were tough, all right.

Penny was less invested in the outcome than she should have been —and she knew it. They were talking about the bit of the business which contained Ray's swaps trading. She knew without a buyer, Ray'd be unemployed.

SO WHAT STOPPED her from telling him? Penny had known for months now and Ray was none the wiser. She felt conflicted. It was one thing to tell Ray the bare bones of some deal going on in another industry sector, but she tried to avoid discussing financial services deals with him. Why? Because she didn't trust him not to trade off the knowledge she was giving him. And, if he was found out, her actions would come round to slap her in the face. Besides, this year she didn't tell him because they were hardly talking to each other, even before she went back to her US beat. They were falling apart anyway.

If they were to have any hope of getting back closer together, Penny knew she must come clean with him. She resolved to do it when she came home. The truth might be a basis for a fresh start. She wouldn't give up on her New York and Boston escapades but Penny'd tell him why she was doing it and why she needed to escape from their Edgware lives. And the miscarriage.

Perhaps they should make a break from the past. A new place. A new country. When you had money like they did, New York is a great place to live. Or Boston if you wanted a trickle of Englishness seeping through the walls.

With these thoughts whirling round her head, she returned to London with something closer to a skip in her step. World weariness and the essential black cloud of grief hung over her even now. But she had found a new purpose and some way of keeping Ray and herself together.

PENNY LANDED ON Saturday morning and, being the red-eye, she spent the rest of the day as zombie flesh fighting to remain conscious until she slunk into bed around ten. The following day, she felt fine, knowing she'd crash by the afternoon. As they were both awake, Penny struck while the iron was hot.

"Ray, I've been working on a financial services transaction these past few months."

"What? Yes. Sure."

He looked up from the business pages of his broadsheet.

"Well, I need to tell you what it's about."

"Oh?"

"Yeah. I'm representing a client who's going to buy Pintzer."

"What?"

"Buy Pintzer."

"How long have you had your arms around this deal?"

"A few months, but..."

"No fucking way. No fucking..."

"I know."

"You know, do you? I've been spending these last few months dicking about in a company that's about to get bought. I mean, we all heard the rumours but I didn't pay no never mind."

"There's more."

"More? What more is there?"

"The new owners will close down your unit."

"What the motherfucking..."

"It's why I'm telling you. It's why I'm telling you now."

"Well you're too fucking late, you bitch. If you'd bothered to be here instead of plotting to chuck me out of my job, you'd 've known I quit Pintzer last week. Because even a schmuck like me'd worked out Pintzer was being scooped up by a Jap bank. My wife has known for months and withheld that information from me. Fucking hell!"

Ray punched the arm of the sofa. He was livid and she understood why. She wondered how she'd thought he'd take it calmly. Not a realistic prospect, come to think of it. Penny let him stew because no good would come from any conversation at this point. Ten minutes later, the steam stopped coming out of his ears and his snorting breaths had abated.

"I ONLY FOUND out they were closing down the swaptions desk this week. Until then, it looked like one bank buying yet another bank," she whispered.

Ray stared at her, shaking his head.

"You should have told me, Penny."

"Yeah, but it wasn't right."

"Is there anything else I should know about this transaction of yours?"

"No, Ray. That's all. It's due to close at year end and they'll shut the derivatives desks down by the end of January second."

"Nice."

"Them's the breaks. You said you quit. Where'd you go?"

"Saturnbanc."

"Haven't heard of it, sorry."

"Wouldn't expect you to. It's a pimple on the arse of the City, but it has a swaps desk and I'm back being a trader."

"Ouch. How are you with that?"

"Not great, but it's a job. When word got out that Pintzer was a dead bank walking, everyone who's been trying to leave has been treated as if we have the plague. So Saturnbanc was the only option."

"Jeez."

"Them's the breaks, like you said. The one good thing is Saturn is a big swaps player, so it has a seat at the Libor table."

"Right."

"And I've got a play worked out with Ollie that'll help me not need to work in the City any more. At least in a while."

Ray explained the outline of the interest rate gambit and described how he would devise strategies to make some real money out of the benchmark.

"I'm not comfortable with this, Ray."

"I have no choice, Penny. The wheels are set in motion and, besides, I'm tired of taking these shitty finance jobs that lead nowhere. I want to get out."

"Do it if you must, but don't talk to me about it. I don't want to know."

"Okay."

"Just make sure it's all done and dusted before the end of March. Then we can both go off to some Caribbean island for a proper holiday and put everything behind us."

Penny was thinking they'd reignite their passion together—like they'd done before in Paris—if only they could escape the sheer agony of their day-to-day lives. Also, it would give her time to let the pain of loss heal a little more.

"By the end of March. I promise."

PENNY RETURNED TO New York to continue closing the Pintzer deal. They were near but the US headquarters still had issues to address and Mr Kawamura wanted end-December as a drop-dead date. She landed Thursday lunchtime, taxied straight over to the Kawamura offices and reached the hotel by eight. A quick shower and down to the bar with a book by nine for a light bite and a drink. Penny looked round to see if she could spot Enrique, but he wasn't there. She realised she hadn't been into the Vodka Bar since that night with him. Subconsciously, she'd avoided the location. Funny old thing, the brain.

A cosmo on the table and a Greek salad on the way, she vanished inside her prize-winning fiction. A couple of pages later and out of the corner of her peripheral vision, Penny sensed someone standing near her. Maybe the waiter? She looked up.

"You are considerably overdressed compared to the last time I saw you."

Enrique grinned, took her hand and kissed it. The charmer.

"Sit down, Enrique. I've a salad on order. When I've finished eating it, we are going up to my room and I will fuck you into the New Year."

Enrique's grin extended further.

"Drink?"

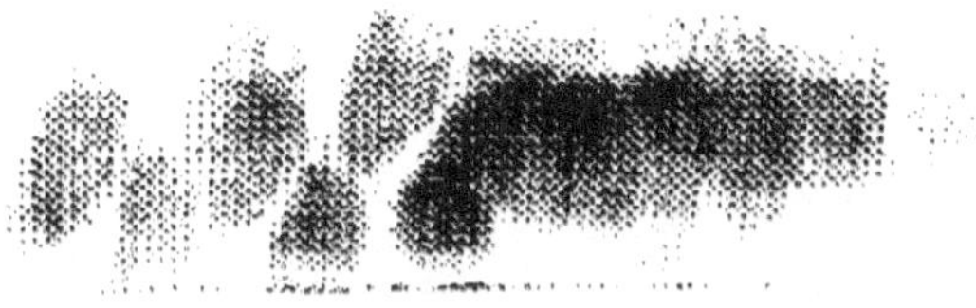

# 56

**RAY**

Knowing how Penny had betrayed him, Ray spent more time at Ollie's strip club than was healthy for him. You are a too-frequent patron when the girls know your name and you can recognise their arses better than their faces.

Penny spent almost all her time in the US ahead of the deal closure. Ray popped into the club on his way home most weekdays and at weekends too, now and again. He justified and fuelled this habit with the money he was making from Libor rigged trades. Twice a week, he'd buy a private room with some Eastern European teenager and occasionally, he'd pay double to fuck her instead. To stop himself feeling too dirty, he snorted white powder at the club, supplied by the bouncer on the door.

"Happy Christmas, one and all!" he thought as he left a fifty-pound tip on a scrunched-up G-string owned by the latest piece of jet trash he'd fucked after a private dance.

# Part Twenty-Three

# April 2, 2010: Good Friday

# 57

**PENNY**

Despite their fine words at the end of last year, Penny didn't feel as though anything was getting better between herself and Ray. Although she had stopped the constant runs to the States, Ray was out most evenings until the small hours. If she was awake when he came in, she sniffed booze on his breath and a sickly-sweet smell, which couldn't be his aftershave. His behaviour was out of control and she knew she no longer loved him.

Penny could blame the miscarriage if she wanted, but it was deeper than that. She had got to the point where she couldn't trust him. Drink, drugs, sex. She had no moral high ground as she was two for three herself, but insider trading was more than that. With Libor, Ray was cheating everyone; with drugs and sex, he was only cheating on her. Wasn't good, but she could forgive him that because she'd need and want him to forgive her for similar crimes against their marriage.

Ray was downstairs, having hopped out of bed that Bank Holiday morning to rustle up something for breakfast.

"One of my world-famous fry-ups."

He had thrown on a dressing gown and stomped to the kitchen, full of a gusto she hadn't seen in him for months, years.

Penny stayed in bed and heard Ray whistling to himself. That man had a loud whistle, she thought to herself, realising he'd never whistled before. She starfish stretched and, twisted her back one way then the other, turning her shoulders in the opposite direction to her hips. Left then right.

Suitably relaxed, she let a hand rest on her lower belly and the other on a breast. She felt for lumps like she'd read in a magazine. Then she fingered herself and imagined Enrique inside her. Ray's whistling interrupted her reverie and she licked her first finger to taste herself.

Penny slid out of bed, wrapped a dressing gown around her body and mooched downstairs into the kitchen. He looked up and winked at her as he carried on whistling and stirring the frying pan, which contained sausage, tomatoes and some hash browns from the freezer.

"Ray, listen. Are you still involved in Libor trading?"

Ray stopped stirring and stared at her, a wooden spatula in one hand.

"Yes I am. The money's too good and everyone needs me to keep going."

"Did you see the paper this week?"

"What?"

"The Serious Fraud Office has started investigating Libor submissions."

"Don't be ridiculous."

"I'm not. It was on the front page of the financial press."

"I only read the Companies section."

"You need to stop."

"I can't, Penny."

"If you don't stop, I'm leaving you."

RAY LAUGHED, A snort of derisive snot shooting out of his nostrils, and turned back to the hob and carried on his stirring. He wiped his nose on the arm of his dressing gown. Penny took two steps toward him to make sure he paid attention to her.

"I need you to stop, Ray. If you carry on, I'll divorce you. I can't live with you like this anymore."

He picked up the frying pan and swung it round until it smacked Penny on the side of the head. Not expecting anything as crazy as that, she lost her balance, twisted and fell down. She hit the corner of the kitchen table before she landed. A red trickle escaped from her forehead before she hit the ground, spraying droplets across the table and over Ray's face. As her head smashed onto the tiled floor, a pool of blood erupted from her skull and her right leg twitched for twenty seconds, then stopped.

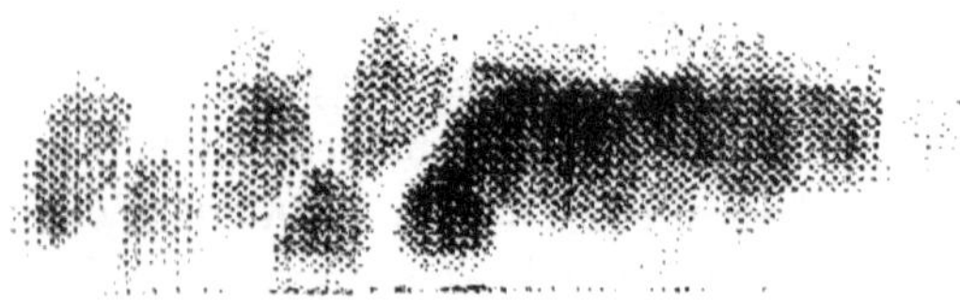

# 58

**RAY**

He stood there for a second, holding a now-empty frying pan with Penny lying at his feet. Ray ran to the phone to call for an ambulance but, just before he dialled the three-digit number, he hung up.

How could he explain it was only an accident? He hadn't meant to hit her. He hadn't meant for her to smash her head on the way down. And if the police poked their noses in their business, what else would they find? Libor loomed over his mind. He couldn't let that happen. He wouldn't allow that happen.

Ray ran upstairs and grabbed a sheet from a cupboard and sped back down the stairs. He rolled her body onto the sheet and wrapped it up. A red stain appeared as soon as the bedding touched her flesh. He threw up but had enough presence of mind to do it in the kitchen sink and not over Penny.

First thing was to hide her until he could figure out what to do. But where? He opened the backdoor and grabbed a key from the cutlery drawer. Into the garden and unlocked the Anderson shelter. Then back to roll about on the tiled floor until he managed to get her corpse over his shoulder—the closest he could get to a fireman's lift.

Ray knew dragging the body would be nothing but heartache and pain.

BY THE TIME he'd dropped her body on the ground, the sheet had unravelled and Ray caught sight of a tit and her bush where Penny's dressing gown had flapped open. Carefully he covered her up. A tear welled in his left eye and he slumped down inside the shelter, next to his dead wife and bawled his eyes out, stuffing a hand over his mouth so no one would hear.

Then he closed the door of the Anderson, locked it and returned indoors. What a fucking mess. There was blood all over the tiles, on the table, on the walls. He spotted sausage, tomatoes and hash brown on the walls and floor too.

Ray found the cleaning liquids under the kitchen sink and bleached every surface he could see—after he'd scooped up all the fluid and food he could find.

By lunchtime, the house reeked of ammonia but it was clean. Real clean. Not a trace of anything untoward. Not even in the grout between the floor tiles. Ray had been thorough.

Then he took off his dressing gown and left it to soak in a bucket of diluted bleach. Ray knew he'd throw it away later but right now it counted as evidence. He went through kitchen cupboards until he found some black bin bags and a large roll of gaffer tape. He went back to the Anderson shelter and wrapped the plastic around the body using the tape to keep everything secure. No liquids inside the bags would escape; he didn't need her seeping out. Then he sat on the sofa and tried to hatch a strategy.

# Part Twenty-Four

## April 3, 2010:
## Saturday

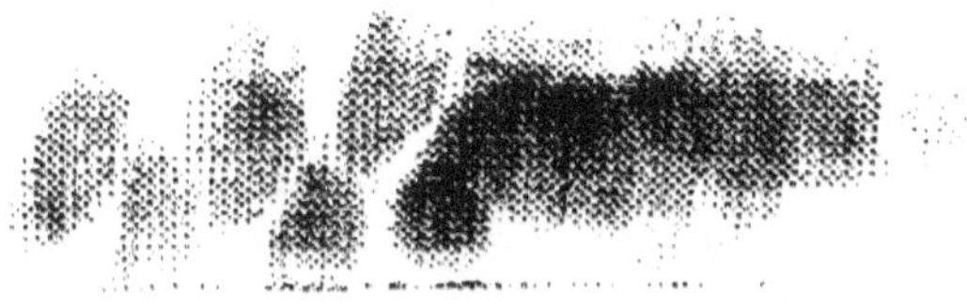

# 59

RAY STAYED AWAKE most of the night, trying to decide the best course of action. The one thing he was glad about was he'd used up all his coke two nights before. Cocaine was not the answer.

He needed a solution fast. Soon the body would start to decompose and the neighbours would complain about the smell. He'd surfed enough on Good Friday to know this was an inevitable consequence of Penny dying. The other thing; whatever he came up with, he must do alone. No call to Ollie or anyone.

Ray considered many options, including taking the body in the boot of his car and leaving it on the other side of London. Before he took that too seriously, he realised the police would have no trouble identifying her and they'd be round quick-as-a-flash interviewing him and up to no good.

Then he remembered seeing a reality TV show where a serial killer got rid of bodies by dumping them in his bath and adding acid. But he'd need industrial quantities of sulphuric and be forced to watch Penny's corpse dissolving in front of his eyes.

Finally, Ray came up with the idea of hiding her in plain sight. The ground was soft, clay mixed with rainwater right now. And they had talked about getting a patio or deck for the garden and this was the weekend when more DIY kit was bought than any other time in the British year. So that's what Ray decided.

HE MEASURED THE width of the grass and then estimated how far the decking should extend before the Anderson shelter's curve got in the way. Armed with an envelope and a bunch of pencil scratchings, Ray drove round to the nearest superstore in Watford and grabbed all he needed. A sports car wasn't the best mode of transport for a large amount of wood but he hired a trailer for the weekend to take it all back to Edgware with him.

By the time he'd got everything offloaded into the garden, it was eleven. With a pile of wooden mess surrounding him, Ray dug a hole. Big enough to bury Penny's body. Around twelve, he unlocked the Anderson shelter, picked up the corpse, dumped it in the ground and covered it unceremoniously with soil. Then he stomped on her grave to flatten the disturbed earth to prepare for the building of the decking.

First, he laid down a membrane to stop weeds growing up through the boards—or worms burrowing out of her body heading towards the surface in heavy rain. Next, he dumped a load of concrete slabs down to hold the plastic covering in place and to raise the height of the wood so it wouldn't sit on the soil itself. Then more membrane over the slabs to protect them from the wood and to hide them from view.

Ray looked at his watch and saw it was gone three. Then he stared at the ground and realised he hadn't checked to see if Penny was actually dead. In his haste, he might have buried her alive. He sat down on the grassy slope of the Anderson shelter and cried again, hand in mouth to smother the noise of his pain.

Then it was time to measure wood, cut and place it on the slabs, making sure it sloped ever so gently away from the house. The French windows had a step down to the garden anyway, so he used that as the height to aim for.

THE FRAME WAS completed by six with a series of beams sloping from the building wall and shorter pieces running parallel to the house screwed to each joist. Then the last thing was to take the boards and lay them on the joists, screwing them to the frame along the way. He estimated the gaps between the boards because there was no point being more accurate.

When he finished, he grabbed the sun loungers and two tables he'd also bought that morning and placed them on the deck. All looked normal. The decking held his weight and Ray took another quick peek in the Anderson shelter, but nothing seemed out of the ordinary. There was no blood on the floor thanks to the bin bags from the previous day.

Ray packed up the unused wood, screws and membrane and dumped the lot in the shed at the bottom of the garden. He'd tidy up some other time. Before walking through the house, he took off his shoes, T-shirt, shorts and socks. He was totally filthy and felt completely dirty. Ray found another rubbish bag in the kitchen and threw everything in, tied it up and put it by the back door to throw in the bin later.

Standing in his underwear, he traipsed up the stairs and hit the shower. Ray switched on the water and stood under it for an age, letting the liquid wash over him, cleansing him of the dirt from the garden. Once the brown colour had gone down the plug hole and he knew the soil was no longer on his skin, he squatted down, holding his head in his hands and sobbed.

Ray cried for himself and the situation he was in. He cried for Penny, the woman he had lusted after, loved, then not loved at all. And whose body he had buried a few hours earlier. He cried for the world because he was a howl of pain and self-loathing. Then he cried because he was sad.

He stood up and scrubbed himself clean, a white soapy lather covering his legs, torso, arms and head. Then he rinsed off, got out and dried himself. Ray sat on the bed and lay back, his towel dropping off away from his hips. Naked on top of the duvet, his nose was close to Penny's pillow and he inhaled her vanilla perfume. He didn't have the energy to cry again.

Ray closed his eyes for the first time in about twenty-four hours and hit a wall of sleep.

# Part Twenty-Five

## April 4, 2010:
## Easter Sunday

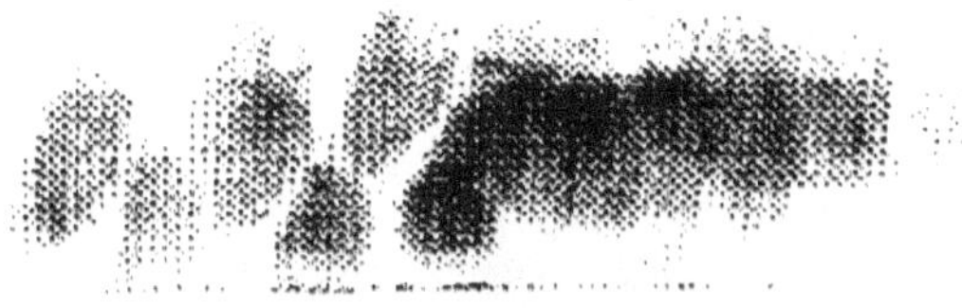

# 60

RAY WOKE UP a little after ten and his stomach rumbled. He twisted around to work out what had happened because he appeared to be naked under and over the duvet at the same time. A few seconds of mad twirling and turning round enabled him to discover that he was lying on top of one half of the duvet and, in the middle of the night, he had grabbed the other half to wrap over himself.

Clothes on, downstairs and out the house to buy a newspaper and then Ray made one of his famous fry-ups. He had bought two papers today, the broadsheet as usual and a scurrilous rag of a tabloid where the news played second fiddle to a nice pair of tits and a thong.

He lazed over the kitchen table with the proper paper and flicked through the red top until he'd checked out all the pictures and laughed at a couple of the shock-horror stories.

Ray poured a gin and tonic in a long glass and walked onto his decking with its sun loungers and small table between them. He wiped down their surfaces to get rid of the leaves and dirt, which had accumulated from the garden. Then he lay down and enjoyed the nothingness of his day.

Apart from the occasional hoot of a wood pigeon, Ray heard only the odd rumble of a car or lorry going by. Although the incident had happened only two days ago, it was a lifetime before. He missed her, but he was also very pleased she was gone. She'd fucked some guy in New York for years but colluding to rip his job away from him and then threatening to divorce him was the last straw.

CLAUDIA'S VOICE FLOATED over the hedge.

"Anyone there?"

He stood up and mounted the Anderson shelter. Claudia waved at him and Jacob stoked the barbecue.

"Hi, Claudia."

"Hi. How's it going?"

"Fine under the circumstances."

She looked at him trying to understand what he was on about.

"Eh? Do you wanna pop over for a barbie in a little while?"

"Sure, but Penny's not here."

"Oh, work?"

"No, she's gone."

"Gone? You mean, gone... for good?"

Ray nodded and shrugged his shoulders.

"Jesus Christ!"

"Yep."

"I'll be over in a sec."

Claudia vanished from sight as she ran into their house. Ten or fifteen minutes later, she knocked on the side return door. Ray opened it and there she was with a bottle of red in one hand and her keys in the other.

"I told Jacob I'd be here as much time as you needed. All day if you want."

Then she looked down and tapped the deck with her heel.

"Hey, this is new."

Claudia popped her things down on the table, turned towards Ray and put her arms around him, stroking the back of his neck. He let her for a while, but, as she carried on, he felt awkward so he hugged her too. Her rose water perfume engulfed him and he had a fleeting flashback to their summer together three years ago.

As the hug continued, Ray noticed her back and realised she wasn't wearing a bra. The only time he'd known her do that was when she was sleeping with him. She wrapped that bra around her breasts as soon as they'd stopped fucking and she'd gone back to Jacob. Thinking about it, Claudia had changed before coming over. Now she had on a cropped T and knee-length pleated skirt; before she'd worn jeans and a checked shirt.

CLAUDIA SET NEXT to him on the sofa, two glasses of wine on the floor. He remembered the first time they'd sat in the same position and, if his memory wasn't playing tricks on him, she was wearing the self-same skirt when he first kissed her.

Ray had rehearsed his story while he was laying the decking and tried it out on her.

"We had a big argument on Friday and then she stormed out."

"Aw. What were you arguing about?"

"Things hadn't been good between us for a year at least. She's spent so much time in the States we've had no space as a couple."

"You suffered from that problem three years ago." Claudia smiled and squeezed his knee.

"Well, I told her I'd had enough and we argued some more and then she stormed out. That was Friday and she hasn't been back."

"You poor thing."

"She just walked out."

"Did she say where she was going?"

"No. I assumed she'd go over to her friend Karen."

"But, not there?"

"Nope."

"I'm so sorry, Ray."

She leaned in to give him another hug. Her nipples were visible through her T-shirt and, like before in 2007, her skirt was riding up her leg. Ray imagined he saw all the way up to her knickers. Instead, he took the hug and owned it, squeezing her but making certain he kept his arms around her back. He couldn't be dealing with a wrong situation here. He knew his head wasn't clear enough to be sure if this was wish fulfilment or if Claudia was coming on to him.

"Do you want to tell me what really happened?" she whispered, her mouth so close to his ear, Ray could sense her warm breath on his lobe.

HE TENSED, WONDERING how she could know, possibly have guessed. Unless she saw him moving the body. Or even burying it. But how?

"You guys had learned to follow separate lives under this one roof. Was there more going on than you've said?"

Ray relaxed and took a hand off the back of Claudia's neck.

"Yeah, well... Truth is she's been having an affair."

"Poor baby."

"And I didn't want to say because I'm kinda embarrassed and I don't want to bad-mouth her or anything."

"Do you know the guy?"

"No, but he lives in the States. That's why she spent so much time there."

"You poor, poor baby. I totally understand. I really do. Why do you think Jacob and I are still together?"

"Huh?"

"When you and I got together that summer, he wasn't interested in me because he was sleeping with his secretary while he was on that speaking tour. Talk about a fucking cliché."

"But you're over all that now?"

"You're joking, right? He's still with her, but I'm not going to leave him until the children have gone to university. And he knows it."

"Jeez. We're two peas in the same pod."

Ray's hand had dropped from Claudia's back and was resting on the outside of her thigh—the one where her skirt had ridden up.

RAY HEARD A siren and he froze.

"Hey, watch it."

Claudia grabbed his hand, the nails had dug into her flesh.

"My you're jumpy. Chances are Penny's not coming back. Right?"

Ray took a second to get a grip and saw he was alone in the living room with her and, no, the police weren't bashing his door down. The paranoia wasn't good and he vowed not to touch any more coke. It must still be in his bloodstream from the beginning of the week. He stroked Claudia's thigh to make up for his aggressive nails.

"Sorry, I'm tense. It's been a strange couple of days."

"Well, I'm here now. You've got nothing to worry about."

Ray realised that was his problem. While he still couldn't figure if Claudia wanted him or was just being mighty neighbourly, Ray didn't know whether to trust her, trust his instincts or trust anything or anyone again. He stroked her thigh and noticed she didn't stop him. Perhaps that meant she was game. Perhaps she was giving him some leeway because he was so strung out at this moment.

"Thanks. I don't want you to go. You won't go, will you?"

Claudia laughed.

"I'll only leave you when you're ready for me to go. Not all women are like Penny."

You're breathing for a start, he thought.

"Sure. Thanks."

His hand stroked up and down her thigh until he leaned further forward and squeezed her butt. Then he stopped, realising he had overstepped the mark and looked at her eyes to see what damage he'd done. There was a warmth shining back.

Claudia grabbed his wrist and slid his palm away from her arse and under her skirt, round the front. Ray felt the heat from her crotch on his fingers and knew it would be all right.

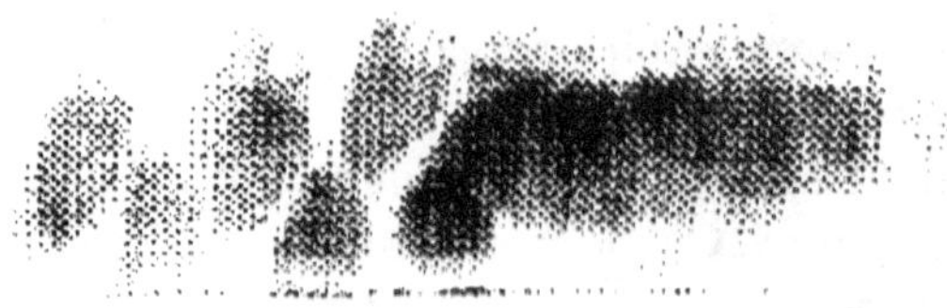

# 61

RAY AND CLAUDIA lay in bed next to each other. He'd had problems getting it up, but under the circumstances he thought it'd gone pretty well. She had been understanding and he'd gone down on her so she'd not missed out on anything. And she had manually finished him off. Not as dexterous as an Eastern European hooker, but more than adequate for a suburban housewife, living in a sham of a marriage, with a tongue that wrapped itself all the way round his shaft. Or so he imagined.

"What're we going to do?"

"Well, I don't know about you, but I'm ready to sleep pretty soon."

"No, silly. What're we going to do about us?"

"Carry on as though nothing has happened—at least as far as the outside world is concerned. Penny might be gone, but it's a blessing to have you back in my life."

Ray put one hand on a breast and licked Claudia's body from nipple to bush.

"Besides, if you stay until morning, I'll make you one of my world-famous fry-ups."

"Jacob can handle the kids for one breakfast, but I need to be back by ten."

"That's agreed then. And we'll have some time to fool around before breakfast."

"Especially if we wake up early enough," she giggled.

They settled down to sleep fifteen or twenty minutes later, after another bout of kissing, licking and fucking. Ray had forgotten how much he liked the scent of her rose water body.

AFTER THE LIGHTS were out, he vowed to throw out Penny's mobile tomorrow and wished he'd had the brains to bury her handbag along with her earthly remains. In a month, he'd quit Saturnbanc and extricate himself from financial services. Penny was right about the Libor arrests. They were not to be ignored. It was only a matter of time before the police came knocking. He'd need to be gone before they did so. With the money he'd stashed over the years, he would have enough to live on without having to worry too much. Claudia might come with him. Or not. He could always buy pussy wherever he ended up.

No, if he ran away and vanished in a puff of smoke that would only prove his guilt. The police with their sniffer dogs would trundle through the house and would dig up Penny with their white tents and line tape.

He needed to tough it out. Spend time with Claudia and hope his extramarital affair cemented the impression the woman had left him.

As he went to sleep, he found himself haunted by the image of Penny's head spraying blood across the kitchen. He tasted iron as he licked his lips while her haemoglobin splashed over his face and her body spluttered to the ground. The taste got inside him. Red liquid death. He was alone. A judder like the coldest shiver in the world.

"Penny!" he screamed and shut his eyes tight.

Claudia wrapped an arm around him so close he could feel a tit pressed against his back and her bush on his arse.

"It'll be all right, darling."

"No it won't," he sobbed. Deep down, nothing would be right again.

# THANK YOU FOR READING!

**Get a free novella**

Building a relationship with my readers is the very best thing about writing. I send weekly newsletters with details of new releases, special offers and other bits of news relating to the Lagotti Family and Alex Cohen series, as well as information about my stand-alone novels.

And if you sign up to the mailing list I'll send you a copy of the Lagotti Family prequel, The Stickup. Just go to www.leopoldborstinski.com/newsletter-signup-book and we'll take it from there.

**Enjoy this book? You can make a difference**

Reviews are the most powerful tools in my arsenal when it comes to getting attention for my books. Much as I'd like to, I don't have the financial muscle of a New York publisher. I can't take out full page ads or put posters on the subway.

(Not yet, anyway).

But I do have something much more powerful and effective than that, and it's something that those publishers would kill to get their hands on.

**A committed and loyal bunch of readers.**

Honest reviews of my books help bring them to the attention of other readers.

If you've enjoyed this book I shall be very grateful if you would spend just five minutes leaving a review (it can be as short as you like) on the book's page. You can jump right to the page by clicking www.books2read.com/pitstop.

Thank you very much.

Leo

# SNEAK PREVIEW

In private eye thriller, The Case…


I'd been in Vegas for a couple of days paid break to take photos for Eliza Rothstein, a jealous broad obsessed with the belief that her husband, Aaron, was shtupping a call girl from out of town. I told her not to worry and I'd check things out. Two hundred dollars a day plus expenses. Rothstein was rich and I knew I could get away with it. The thought I was taking Aaron's dough to break up his marriage didn't cross my mind. Besides, I knew Aaron wasn't shtupping a call girl.

He was shtupping Rachel, Eliza's closest friend, but I wanted a holiday and Aaron had taken Rachel to play the wheels in Vegas. So I came along for the ride. Aaron had set up a cozy apartment on the upper east side for the two of them, overlooking the park. If I hadn't wanted a holiday so bad, I'd have rented a place on the west side and used a telephoto lens. The case would have been that simple. Aaron was shrewd in business - he owned enough water utilities to drown the nation - but he let his dick do the walking whenever a blonde with big blue eyes and breasts to match came into his line of vision. And anyway, Rachel and Aaron were the worst kept secret in Manhattan. But Eliza was so dumb, she didn't understand why the guy who collected her trash was called Giuseppe. So I took the greenbacks and headed west.

Vegas is the only town where hookers and Frank Sinatra both feel at home, only they're surrounded by a million wannabes, hoping the next spin of the wheel will give them the big break. I didn't mind visiting it for a few days, but after a couple of weeks I missed the sun so bad my ulcer started playing up.

Aaron's money meant he could afford to stay at the Tropicana, the swankiest joint in Vegas. I was on expenses so I took a room on the fifteenth floor. By the time I arrived at reception, Aaron and Rachel were already tucked up for the night, so I wandered around the casino for some relaxation. I knew I wasn't going to bump into them because Aaron hadn't flown over here for the wheels, if you see what I mean. He was after some silky sheet action rather than blackjack and watered down Budweiser.

Anyway, I checked out the poker tables and watched a drunk lose his shirt at the wheel. Jeez, I could tell he was a loser from the moment I saw him. The lush was playing with his chips like a kid plays with his food. His first time at the wheel. Even the green baize felt his virginity every time he put the fifty buck chips on it. Pathetic. The kind of guy that gives a casino a bad name. And that's saying something.

After a couple of hours, I'd drunk enough vodka to knock out the ghosts and stumbled back to my room, number 1526. As soon as I put my head to the pillow, I was out until morning. By the time my eyes opened, the maid had already tried to clean my room. Fumbling for my watch, I saw it was half ten. I slouched out of bed and bumped into the shower. The water woke me up; I shaved and headed straight for reception.

To grab your copy, go to www.books2read.com/thecase.

# OTHER BOOKS BY THE AUTHOR

# ABOUT THE AUTHOR

Leopold Borstinski is an independent author whose past careers have included financial journalism, business management of financial software companies, consulting and product sales and marketing, as well as teaching.

There is nothing he likes better so he does as much nothing as he possibly can. He has travelled extensively in Europe and the US and has visited Asia on several occasions. Leopold holds a Philosophy degree and tries not to drop it too often.

He lives near London and is married with one wife, one child and no pets.

Find out more at LeopoldBorstinski.com.